Advance Praise for Andrew W.M. Beierle and
First Person Plural

"Deftly written and intricately imagined, Andrew Beierle has created twin brothers so original and compelling in *First Person Plural* that this extraordinary novel is destined to leave a profound and indelible impression on its reader. An auspicious achievement by a remarkably talented author."

—Jameson Currier, author of *Where the Rainbow Ends*

"This is an utterly original story about two talented, drop-dead handsome men that share a, well, eccentricity. It's tender, comic, bittersweet, and well-written, with lovable characters, heartbreak, and redemption—in other words, with all the right ingredients."

—Jan DeBlieu, author of *Wind* and *Year of the Comet*

"Upon reading the premise of this novel, I expected the easy route, a comedy, but what I got instead amazed and moved me, a daring novel filled with insights not only into the bizarre aspects of human anatomy but into the equally bizarre anatomy of human love. Andrew Beierle has given us a love story between two men bound by something stronger than love, flesh. *First Person Plural* reads like a memoir, as if it has been poured out of the heart of a man who has suffered first-hand the indignities and miracles described in this novel. How Mr. Beierle submerged himself so deeply I have no idea. This book will stagger you; but better yet it will remind you of something too easily forgotten: that human existence is by its very nature heroic."

—Lee Durkee, author of *Rides of the Midway*

"Beierle's imagination and empathy have no limits. In *First Person Plural* he charts new emotional territory, bravely escorting us deep into the tangled relationships and complicated desires of his two unforgettable protagonists, whose tragedy is that they are both inseparable and profoundly divided. Welding great compassion to psychological acuity, Beierle forces us to confront the unthinkable."

—Paula Peterson, winner of the Katharine Bakeless Nason Prize
for nonfiction for *Penitent with Roses*

Please turn the page for more outstanding praise for Andrew W.M. Beierle and *First Person Plural*!

More Advance Praise for Andrew W.M. Beierle and *First Person Plural*

"In this story of two men born with different heads and different hearts but the same body, Andrew Beierle explores one of the most perplexing dilemmas we humans face: how much does a man owe to himself, as he searches for his own identity, and how much to those closest to him, in this case the other half of his own body? The fact that one of these joined twins is gay and the other straight leads, almost inevitably, to loneliness, confusion, and finally angry confrontation. Although we as readers may find ourselves wishing that each of these two men could have his own life—and his own love— we ultimately come to understand, as they do, that they cannot change what destiny has handed them. Their only choice is to find a way to live in harmony with each other. I salute both the courage and the insight that Beierle has brought to this engrossing and sensitively written story."

—Robert Taylor, author of *All We Have Is Now*

"A metaphorical tale of differentness, an extended exploration of the complexities of identity—the possibilities, limitations and internal contradictions that exist in us all—*First Person Plural* is striking and original, and that rarity in fiction, a novel of ideas."

—Katherine V. Forrest, author of *Daughters of an Emerald Dusk*

"What a remarkable book! The protagonist of Andrew Beierle's new novel is one of the most unique and unforgettable characters in fiction. Deftly written, funny, wise, and poignant, *First Person Plural* is an excitingly original addition to contemporary literature."

—Jeff Mann, author of *Loving Mountains, Loving Men*

First Person Plural

ANDREW W.M. BEIERLE

KENSINGTON BOOKS

KENSINGTON BOOKS are published by

Kensington Publishing Corp.
850 Third Avenue
New York, NY 10022

ISBN-13: 978-0-7394-8814-0

Printed in the United States of America

To Susan Lowell Butler—
Wisdom, friendship, courage

Acknowledgments

My sister, Maggie Harlan, is the rarest of siblings, a "twin of my heart," without whom I would be incomplete. I cherish her presence in my life.

Some forty-four years ago, Virginia Keshel MacArthur lit in me the literary fire that burns within me still. I am thrilled to be able to thank her, at long last, for my love of books and language. Bryce Voter Lambert taught me to "Love words. Be precise."

My editor, John Scognamiglio, has once again demonstrated his deft and nuanced literary sensibility, his insight into character, and his sensitivity to authors, as well as his genuine friendship and compassion.

I benefited greatly from working with Alice McDermott, Randall Kenan, Claire Messud, and Christopher Tilghman at the Sewanee, Bread Loaf, Napa Valley, and *Kenyon Review* writer's workshops, respectively.

I owe a particular debt of gratitude to my advance readers, Jameson Currier, Jeff Mann, Paula Peterson, Libby Sachs, and Frances Schenkkan. I also am grateful for the personal and professional support of Gonzalo Barr, Hal Campbell, Jan DeBlieu, Lee Durkee, Charles Flowers, Katherine V. Forrest, Richard Hermes, Elizabeth McCracken, Lucas Miré, Ann Pancake, Max Pierce, Robert Taylor, and Alec Young, and the loving support of Susan Carini, Karen Carnabucci, Grady Chance, Richard L. Eldredge, Janet Firestone, Emil C. Hines, Katherine Hinds, Billy Howard, Jeff Long, Don Luckett, Martha Matzke, Krista Reese, Victor Rogers, David Rothley, Page Starzinger, John W. Stephenson, and John Trumbo. A special thank-you goes to Richard Tyler Jordan.

And last but not least, I want to "salute" the sisters of Delta Schmelta, Sewanee Chapter: Allison Amend, Sheri Joseph, Dika Lam, Margo Rabb, and Lara J. K. Wilson. High five.

Chapter 1

My twin brother, Porter, and I have been inseparable since birth. That's not merely an observation. It's a diagnosis. We are *conjoined* twins. The technical term for our particular physiognomy is *dicephalus*, which for all its Latinate camouflage is most frequently translated as "two-headed," a term both Porter and I find distasteful, if accurate. We live cheek-by-jowl in what most people would consider one body: we have two heads, attached to two necks, and a single torso with separate spines fused at the pelvis. Within our single rib cage are three lungs, two gall bladders, two stomachs, and two hearts. An important distinction: two very *different* hearts.

We are a little broader at the shoulders than the average man, but otherwise, from the neck down, we look pretty normal. Porter is to my left and controls the left side of our body, including the movement of our left arm and leg. I control the right. Tickle us on the left side and Porter laughs; prick us with a pin on the right and I flinch. We alternated childhood vaccinations, although Porter frequently insisted it was my turn to get the shot when it was actually his, and I have endured more than my share of pain.

We are a relatively rare breed. Although *dicephali* account for roughly ten percent of all conjoined twins at birth, their survival rate is significantly lower than those of less extreme configurations. And because of the almost unfathomable horror we strike in parents and medical professionals alike, mercy killings of *dicephali* were not uncommon as late as the 1960s, just a decade before Porter and I were born. The medical texts contain reports of fewer than a half dozen sets of conjoined twins like us who survived into adulthood. In other times and other places, when the world was less enlightened and life less valued, we might have been forsaken by our mother and father, left in the woods for wolves to devour or deposited on the steps of an orphanage or insane asylum. No one could blame them. To do otherwise under certain circumstances—say, in a small central European village in the Dark Ages or in Spain during the Inquisition—was to invite further heartbreak. They might have been shunned for producing such a monstrosity, an abomination, a "crime against nature." Or they might have been forced to leave their village, might even have been stoned on the way out or been pelted with spoiled vegetables and human waste.

But times have changed. Our parents are educated and financially secure, and we have led, if not a sheltered life, then one as close to normal as possible. Although most people are uncomfortable in our presence, at least initially, and our childhood was not free of taunts and hurtful comments from strangers, intentional or not, the *zeitgeist* of political correctness has spared us the pain and humiliation we otherwise might have suffered at the hands of the cruel and the curious.

Still, it has not been easy. From the beginning, our parents faced a series of difficult and increasingly complex ethical and logistical questions, including the advisability of euthanasia for both of us, the morality of sacrificial separation of either Porter or me from our body, and the pros and cons of institutionalization. In each instance, they chose the option they believed the most merciful and life affirming for us, even though it might be the most difficult, costly, and emotionally demanding one for them.

There is simply not enough meat between us to make two men. Had our parents chosen to sacrifice one of us, the procedure would have been complicated, the physical devastation traumatic, the long-term outlook for the surviving twin bleak. Instead of being strong and athletic, swift and graceful, as we are together, the one who remained would be hobbled, immobile, confined to a wheelchair. Instead of being healthy—robust—he would be shrunken, shriveled, particularly prone to infection and illness, or worse. But together . . . together we thrived.

Porter and I are about as well adjusted as we could possibly be, given our circumstances. I can't imagine any parents doing a better job. Beyond Mom and Dad, however, I don't think any of our relatives ever wholeheartedly embraced us. People think kids don't notice things—little things—about the way they are treated, but they do. At least *I* did. I could tell that hugs from either of my grandmothers were more reserved, more tentative, than those we received from our mother. Even when we were well past the age at which we wore diapers, it was as if we were always soiled and they were afraid of getting close enough to smell our shit. Other relatives were even worse. Our aunts and uncles offered smiles that were ambiguous at best, vaguely threatening at worst: quick flashes of teeth that just as easily could have been some primal warning for us to stay away. When we arrived at their homes for holiday celebrations or birthday parties, no one ever picked us up or hugged us. They were always too busy taking our mother's and father's coats, or they were occupied with carrying things—cocktails, or a stack of newspapers they suddenly noticed on the floor, or one of their own children. I don't think there was ever a time we showed up at Aunt Susan's for Thanksgiving that she didn't spend the first fifteen minutes after our arrival walking around the house carrying the turkey in a big roasting pan like a hostess on *The Price Is Right*, smiling, chattering away with my mother—her sister—acknowledging Porter and me with a nod, but *always* carrying around that big old bird so she had an excuse not to touch us. And our cousins—our poor cousins! They had to be cajoled into playing with us, constantly being nudged toward us and then inching away, just to be shooed toward us again, back and forth, as if we were on the deck of a ship rolling through heavy seas.

Early on, Mom and Dad determined that Porter and I should be a part *of* the world, not apart *from* it. They decided, in the language of educators, to "mainstream" us: to introduce us to the world and to prepare us to live in it; to protect us as much as possible from life's inherent cruelties but not to pretend they did not exist.

With Porter's consent—and mine—our parents made the very deliberate decision to allow *Time* magazine to write about us extensively at the ages of six, ten, and sixteen, and to permit PBS to broadcast a two-hour documentary on the occasion of our twenty-first birthday in 1996, the year in which we carried the Olympic flame on one leg of its journey to Atlanta, our hometown. This public relations campaign was the brainchild of my mother, a professor of marketing at the Druid Hills University School of Business, who thought a gradual, limited, and carefully controlled introduction to the world at large would make our inevitable emergence into public life easier. My father, who holds an endowed chair in cognitive psychology at Druid Hills, agreed, and for the most part they were right. Millions of people were introduced to us at arm's length. The squeamish could turn the page or change the channel; the remainder became aware of our existence and acclimated to our appearance. In the process, we became celebrities of a sort. Having watched us grow up in print and on television, people think they know us, and that has engendered respect, even admiration.

Our parents structured our private lives with extraordinary care, fending off curiosity seekers and the more lurid media, nurturing self-esteem, encouraging individuality. We did not become the property of the public, as the Dionne quintuplets had a half century earlier, nor did we suffer the fate of the most famous pair of *dicephali*, the Italian brothers Giovanni and Giacomo Tocci, whose parents grew rich exhibiting them in Europe and America in the late nineteenth century. At their peak they earned a thousand dollars a week, a princely sum for the time, though they frequently were forced to share the limelight with lesser acts, such as Jo-Jo the Russian dog-faced boy, a boxing kangaroo, and Mademoiselle Vallette and her dancing goats. In 1897, at the age of twenty, they used their earnings to retire to a villa near Venice, where they lived in isolation for more than forty years. Their seclusion was disturbed only once, in 1904, when each brother married a different woman, an event that aroused interest in them anew and prompted a Frenchman, Dr. A. P. de Liptay, to publish a book that speculated about their peculiar intimacies titled *La Vie Sexuelle des Monstres*, "The Sex Life of Monsters."

As infants and toddlers, Porter and I were given separate toys, usually the same items but in different colors. As we grew up, we were taught that some things belonged to each of us individually and some we had to share, usually big-ticket items like our bicycle (there was really no point in buying two, since we could ride only one at a time). We played regularly with a small group of kids from our Ansley Park neighborhood whose parents, like ours, were well heeled and well educated and taught their children not to fear Porter and me, to treat us as individuals, and never—never under any circumstances—to ask us why we had two heads.

Personally, I am fascinated by the question of why. Conjoined twins are always monozygotic, the product of one egg and one sperm, so there was a time when Porter and I were one, truly one—undivided. There was no me, no him, only us, but a singular us, an I, not a we. Our singularity lasted no more than two weeks, since the division of identical twins typically takes place during the first fourteen days of a pregnancy, when the tiny fertilized egg is little more than a collection of cells, a microscopic dollop of genetic caviar. In our case, the process of division also came to an end during this time. The parts that were there continued to develop normally, but the die was cast: we were destined to have two heads, like a double-struck penny.

My mother refuses to talk about her pregnancy—not just to me but to anyone—or at least to talk about it in a way that reflects on the fact that it was different from anyone else's pregnancy or that her "issue" was in any way unusual. So I have never been able to ask her the questions I have always wanted to ask: What happened during those first two weeks? Was there ever a time she felt as if something unusual were taking place? Did she notice the moment when one began the journey toward two—or the moment when the process stopped?

Of course, I know the answers to those questions: "I don't know." "No, no, no." No woman knows—really knows— she is pregnant during those first two weeks. But I've always felt that given the circumstances, she *ought* to have known, that it should have been revealed to her, that there should have been some sign, that suddenly everywhere she looked she should have seen the number two or noticed things in pairs. Later, when we stopped dividing, she should have taken particular notice of the letter Y, split at the top, joined at the bottom; should have driven past the YMCA on Highland Avenue and observed that the neon Y was burned out or was the only letter illuminated. But apparently she didn't.

Just as I am fascinated by the process that brought Porter and me into being, other people are intrigued by us. Unless they are medical professionals accustomed to dealing with conjoined twins and the other horrors of which nature is capable, they probably have never seen anything as strange as us. Alas, their inability to grasp the complexities inherent in the situation, their lack of insight, is appalling. They repeatedly ask the same unimaginative, unanswerable questions. "How did you learn to walk?" is a favorite. ("Do you remember how *you* learned to walk?" I respond.) The more audacious among them muster the courage to ask about our excretory functions. Only a discussion of sex would be more titillating, but *that* seems too personal a subject to broach. The meek or less imaginative settle for, "When did you first realize you were *special*?" God, I hate that word.

The fact is, I can't recall the exact moment at which I understood that Porter and I were different from other children, or rather that they were different from us, which is how I first saw it. My memory of such things is clouded, if it is a memory at all and not a subsequent fabrication, some family folklore, but I have often heard the story of how my mother first addressed the subject. I was a precocious child and learned to read early—nearly a year before Porter. I was reading a book in which a young blond boy, a farmer's child with rosy cheeks and bib overalls, was described as "tow-headed," and I asked Mom why the drawing of the boy showed only one head. I suppose I thought it was a typographical error, that the author meant "two-headed." My mother likes to say that after explaining to me that "tow-headed" meant blond—Porter and I were tow-headed as well as two-headed—she worried that on top of everything else I was dyslexic.

For some time as a child, I believed Porter and I were normal, that being half of a pair was the natural order of things. I'm not sure how I rationalized the fact that all the adults around me had only one head. I know for a while I thought Porter and I might continue to divide, that as we grew up we also would grow apart. When I realized such a metamorphosis was unlikely, a terrible new fear took its place. I was afraid one of our heads, finally recognized by our body as superfluous, might dry up and flake off like a scab. As far as I know, I never verbalized that apprehension, but my parents sensed it might have occurred to us and years later told us that, like African American parents who bought their daughters only dark-skinned Barbie dolls, they briefly flirted with the idea of enhancing our self-esteem by having our toys custom-made for us. A two-headed G.I. Joe was fleetingly considered, but the potential trauma of having the supplementary head fall off was too great a risk, and they abandoned the concept altogether.

Mom told me I went absolutely nuts the first time I saw a cartoon about Noah's ark, and thereafter I insisted on collecting anything that depicted the beasts of the world boarding the big, windowless boat two by two: storybooks, puzzles, pajamas, LEGO sets. I squealed with delight every time a Doublemint gum commercial aired, driving everyone to distraction by singing the jingle endlessly, and every time I saw two people kiss on TV, I turned my head and kissed Porter, who usually started to cry and eventually responded by hitting me. My mother has since told me she never knew what to make of all this, but I'm convinced I converted all those things into a positive self-image, which has helped me survive despite the gradual realizations that existence is a solitary thing in our world; that although the animals boarded the ark in pairs, they were actually separate, a male and a female of the species; and that while lovers may look a lot like Porter and me when they kiss, they inevitably part.

Chapter 2

Porter and I have been blessed as well as cursed. On the one hand, we are what we are: a freak of nature, an oddity, a monster. On the other, we have the faces of angels—and a heavenly body. A writer for *Vanity Fair* who was perhaps a little too enamored of her own prose suggested Porter and I were so beautiful that we were, literally, cursed by the gods—conjoined as punishment for such a hubristic affront. If you ask me, she'd been reading a little too much Edith Hamilton.

As children, we were positively cherubic. I've seen the pictures: two boys, sweetly sleeping, Porter's head lolled just a bit to the right, mine a bit to the left, so we looked as if we were two normal twins cradled together. The casual observer could not imagine the horror and heartbreak swaddled in that blanket. Dad always cropped in close when taking our picture, so our faces usually filled the frame or extended beyond it (many were out of focus because the focal length was insufficient) and our body was rarely seen. I've always meant to ask him if he did that on purpose or if, like a lot of fathers, he was just a lousy photographer.

As we matured, it became clear we would be "lookers," extraordinarily handsome young men. I think it would have been easier on everyone if we had been ugly or even just plain; if we had been sickly, deformed, repulsive. Instead, it was frequently hard to tell whether the gasps of strangers were expressions of horror at the sight of a two-headed boy or anguish at the tragedy of our flawed beauty.

You may have seen pictures of the Brewer twins, those shrewd, blond California surfers who have made a career of being a matched set of hunks, who have amassed fame and fortune by pandering to the romantic fantasies of impressionable teenaged girls. Well, the Brewer boys have nothing on us. Oh, they're pretty enough, in a bland, boyish sort of way. Dreamy, you might even say. But if there weren't two of them, they might have gone unnoticed. It is their *twinness* that is the essence of the attraction; the fact that there are two of them is what makes them a novelty. I'd gladly go head-to-head with them in a beauty contest. We are the Brewer twins squared.

Of the two of us, Porter has always been the more physical. He's taken a proprietary interest in our shared personal real estate that I haven't; he inhabits it to a greater degree than I do. I'm convinced he thinks this body is his and I'm simply along for the ride. My mother told me that when we were learning to walk, Porter brought sheer brute force to the process, an indomitable will. At times, she said, it almost seemed as if he were bullying me: he'd redden and grimace as we attempted to learn to crawl, to stand up, or to walk. He'd thrash the air with his fist and occasionally thump me on my side of our chest. Mom says he was trying to motivate me; I suspect he was trying to scare me away.

Porter has always been interested in expanding the limits of our functionality, increasing our size and speed, enhancing our appearance. When we were teenagers, he forced me to embark on a rigorous physical-fitness program with him, including cross-country running and weight training. To this day, he is an implacable taskmaster in the gym, forcing me to join him in shouting out our rep count on the bench press, accusing me of slacking off on my biceps curls, taking precise measurements of our corresponding muscles to make sure he isn't going to be forced to live inside a lopsided body.

The result of all this effort is a lean, hard physique. We are a classic mesomorph, with a torso such as you might see on certain Renaissance statues, so elongated it seems it might fold over on itself midway. Our chest and back are somewhat broader than average, but were it not for the fact that we have two heads, it might simply look as if we were overly dedicated to the butterfly stroke or obsessed with doing cable flies. Our legs seem to go on forever, but while Porter is pleased with our thighs, he frequently complains our calves are too small, and I have done more calf raises than I care to count.

At birth, the only true anomaly below our necks was our third nipple, a withered and misshapen protuberance in the center of our otherwise smooth chest that, at least for my mother, seemed to be a talisman of our freakishness. She arranged to have it surgically removed when we were fifteen years old, because, I suppose, it was manageable; it was something she could do to make us more normal. Personally, I thought it was sort of cool. It reminded me of the third eye of a martian on an episode of *The Twilight Zone*, which he kept covered by a soda jerk's hat, and Porter frequently would pull up our shirt to gross out friends who had become inured to the fact that we had two heads.

Porter has always been the better athlete by far, and during pickup games or in gym class we always were selected by his name. When we played Little League Baseball, we alternated turns at bat and switched gloves in the outfield every other inning. Porter always batted first and played the odd-numbered innings, insuring he would be in control of five of the nine innings; our team rarely improved its standing during the even-numbered innings.

Porter played quarterback for three years at Lovett, the private prep school we attended; was co-captain of the football team his junior year and captain his senior year; and was the star pitcher for the baseball team. Initially, there was some opposition to his participation in school sports, mostly from competing teams that thought having two heads, especially two sets of eyes, would give him an unfair advantage. Administrators at Lovett weren't opposed to having Porter play—attendance at games was way up—and in fact they were willing to go to court to guarantee him a place on the teams, but that proved unnecessary. About the same time Porter was trying out for football his sophomore year, a girl was suing to become the quarterback of a team at a public high school in south Georgia, and once the courts ruled in her favor, none of our opponents were willing to go to the effort and expense of trying to prevent him from taking the field.

Now that Porter's athletic career is behind him, I'll admit those who thought he had an advantage probably were right. His throwing arm gave his passes and pitches speed and distance, but my eyes may have contributed to his uncanny accuracy by providing enhanced depth perception, if only subconsciously. He also could discern, by subtle shifts in my stance or increased tension in my leg or my half of our back, that I had seen someone trying to steal home or had detected an oncoming tackle.

Personally, I could not have cared less about sports, but they were important to Porter. He was not merely gripped by the competitive spirit, but he wanted to win, to be the best despite what others might consider a significant disability. More than that, he wanted to be part of a winning team, particularly if his contributions were seen as essential to its victory. What he was trying to do—what I saw but suspect he did not—was to earn the acceptance of his teammates, indeed of the whole school, through his athletic achievements; to cash in his game-winning Hail Mary passes and his no-hitters for the love and respect of his classmates. He had to be a hero so he could become just a regular guy.

My mother and father rarely missed one of Porter's games. They were among the most active members of the Lovett Parents Association and co-chaired the hospitality committee our senior year, although each of them had a different motivation. It seems to me my father was using Porter's athletic prowess to compensate for the fact that he had always been kind of a geek. I'm certain he had never set foot in an athletic facility during his years as an undergraduate at Brown, unless it was for a required physical education class. But now he had the opportunity to live vicariously through Porter's exploits—and to become chummy with the other jocks' dads (many of whom also were over-educated couch potatoes), who also were trying to appropriate their sons' accomplishments on the gridiron or the court or the baseball diamond. They would watch home videos of recent games while smoking cigars and drinking scotch, reliving crucial field goals or slam dunks or home runs, more often than not without any of their sons actually present to share in the recycled glory.

Although my mother had little real appreciation of the value of Porter's athletic accomplishments, she was astute enough to recognize there was significant social capital to be mined from his resulting popularity, and she did her best to extract it. Her motivation was a bit more complex than my father's and I presume had something to do with her need to redeem herself in the eyes of the world for having given birth to a freak. (Mothers seem to get a disproportionate amount of blame in such cases, since they serve as the vessels in which the monstrosity took form, while the fathers merely contributed half the raw material.)

Like my father, my mother had been academically gifted, even precocious, as a child. Unlike him, she possessed all of the most desirable attributes of her gender. Where he was something of an ugly duckling, she was a swan whose intellectual attributes did not come at the expense of grace or comeliness. Reduced to its most basic elements, their fairy tale romance might be titled "The Debutante and the Egghead" (although what drew her to him remains a mystery to me). I suspect their families imagined them the perfect prospective parents genetically: my mother's beauty would leaven my father's lack of a more pleasant countenance, while her intellect would only enhance his own. But when their double-yolked progeny hatched, the most judgmental clucking was aimed in her direction, and she had to work harder than my father to counter it. Thus was born Super Mom: accomplished academic, devoted spouse, proud and attentive mother. But even she had her limits, and I think that, astute business professional that she is, she chose to advance the cause of the son with the most "marketable" attributes, and that of course was Porter.

My own interests and accomplishments garnered little attention from either one of them beyond a perfunctory "That's nice, dear," from my mother when I read her a poem I had written or performed a scene from a play I was rehearsing at school. One can't really blame them, I suppose. Rare is the parent who prefers a son who recites iambic pentameter to one who wins an Olympic pentathlon. It was not about *me*, I told myself; it was about the choices I had made. Though in the end, I still thought it was my fault.

Naturally, they both denied they favored Porter over me or paid more attention to him.

"That's nonsense, Owen," my mother chided when I asked her about it. "Your father and I go to every one of your little plays. It's just that you have only one a semester, two at most, and none in the summer, while Porter plays in one sport or another every week, all year long."

I didn't buy it. It seemed to me that what they were doing by concentrating their attention on Porter and ignoring me was trying to make me disappear, in their minds as well as in their friends' minds. If the conversation was always about Porter, if the subject of their sentences was always singular, they could fool themselves into thinking I did not even exist.

Chapter 3

Sometime between the ages of six and eight, children begin to develop as individuals, to exhibit distinct character traits and preferences. In twins, the process often is more pronounced, as each twin struggles to create a persona different from that of his or her genetic double. Sometimes the differences are real; sometimes they are manufactured. For example, as kids neither Porter nor I liked the taste of milk, but because he insisted on drinking his only with the addition of Nestlé Quik, I took mine plain. It occurred to me only years later that I could have insisted on Hershey's Syrup as a less radical—and more palatable—alternative.

Porter and I naturally had more trouble than other twins differentiating ourselves from one another. The problem was that people always saw us as a unit, or at best as parts of a unit, and only rarely as individuals, so for much of our lives we have been not Owen and Porter but *Owenandporter* or *Porterandowen*, even among members of our family. Indeed, it is difficult to tell with absolute certainty where Porter ends and I begin. (Imagine one of those M. C. Escher drawings of a staircase that seems to double back on itself. It has no beginning and no end. Sometimes it seems you are looking down on the stairs, but when you blink it appears you are beneath the stairs looking up at them.) The most significant difference anyone could discern was that, of necessity, Porter was left-handed and I was right-handed.

In elementary school, we developed the habit of alternating the days on which each of us had control over what we wanted to do. The odd number of days in a week made the process perfectly equitable, since it meant over the course of two weeks each of us had control of every day of the week in turn, including, as we got older, the all-important Friday and Saturday nights. Almost from the beginning, however, it seemed to me that Porter tried to get more than his fair share of our time—and that my parents were usually more sympathetic to him. When we couldn't agree on what to do with ourselves, Mom and Dad generally sided with Porter because his preferences were always more active, more outgoing, seemingly more well adjusted than mine. He wanted to be around other boys, to feel included, to disappear among them. I preferred to stay inside, reading, writing, drawing, thinking. My parents interpreted this as withdrawal, depression, failure to adjust. When I complained, they insisted the fresh air and exercise would benefit me as well as Porter.

"It's just not healthy for you to sit around the house all day moping," my mother said one golden October afternoon when I repeatedly rebuffed Porter's suggestion that we join a soccer game in the pocket park across the street. "It's a beautiful day outside, and all of Porter's friends are there."

"I'm not moping," I said. "I'm reading."

"Well, *I'm* bored," Porter said. "You're always reading. You can read tonight when we're in bed."

"He's right, Owen," my father intoned. His voice had the weight of authority, but I held out the hope that he was simply rubber-stamping my mother's decision and that with a little whining I might prevail.

"Da-a-ad," I mewled.

"Owen," my mother said sharply. Dad retreated. End of argument.

When Porter wanted to join a Little League Baseball team and I didn't, my parents sat me down and had a heart-to-heart with me. Did I think it was fair to deny Porter the opportunity to do something he wanted so badly, Mom asked, especially when I had so little to offer of a compelling nature to replace it with? It didn't seem to matter to them that baseball required daily practice and would force me to cede to Porter much of the time that was rightfully mine. Little did I know that this one small step would lead to Porter's successful athletic career and consume so much of my time as an adolescent. If I had, I might have fought it a little harder.

Porter and I have had our own bedrooms since we were nine or ten, when we began developing different interests. By giving us our own rooms, our parents fostered the idea that we were individuals with separate tastes and a right to privacy. More importantly, it demonstrated our individuality to other people. We tended to do different things in our respective rooms: to study in mine (where Dad built us a desk wide enough for two), to eat pizza and watch movies in Porter's. So we developed a sense of who was in control, on whom attention was focused, based on whose room we were in. We each had our own telephone extension and, once we turned sixteen, our own private line and separate telephone numbers. We had our own computers, placed next to each other on our desk (Porter had a PC; I preferred Macs), but shared a video game console, since most often we would play together, sometimes competing against each other, sometimes joining forces to beat the game. To this day, our body reacts differently depending upon whose room we are sleeping in. Porter sleeps on our stomach when we are in his room, I sleep on our back in mine, and I don't think either of us sleeps as well in the other's room as we do in our own, although Porter is able to fall asleep more quickly in either place.

After the onset of puberty, things became more complicated. As an adolescent, Porter was proud of the body he had worked so hard to perfect and liked showing it off in muscle shirts; I favored colorful, loose-fitting Hawaiian prints. He enjoyed playing and viewing team sports; I preferred watching diving and gymnastic competitions, in which individual athletes were recognized for their unique abilities. And, we soon discovered, Porter liked girls; I did not.

There are few secrets—and no sexual secrets—when you share a body with another human being. Any privacy Porter and I have is artificial: carefully manufactured, rigorously structured, and at best both limited and temporary. But even within the confines of our enforced intimacy and despite the well-documented psychic connection between twins, it was ultimately no less difficult for me to broach the subject of my most intimate feelings to Porter than it would have been between any siblings.

As I've explained, Porter reacts to stimuli on the left side of our body; I feel things on the right. The exception to this rule is our penis, which apparently is the very nexus of our commonality and which provides both of us with sexual pleasure (though we each arrive there by different routes). We probably were not quite twelve when we first ejaculated, a purely physical thing divorced from any particular sensory input other than a sort of serendipitous friction against our bedclothes. We looked at each other (if we turn our heads inward about forty-five degrees, we can see each other in semi-profile, like a pair of one-eyed jacks), astonished not only by the sensation but also because we both realized we were feeling exactly the same thing at the same time—a self-contained yet simultaneous orgasm.

Thereafter, despite the usual teen angst over the propriety of masturbation, it was an indulgence we shared several times a day, frequently fighting to be the one to control it until Porter discovered it was more pleasurable for me to do all the work. During those first two or three years, when Porter and I enjoyed sex together in its purest form, spontaneously, driven only by the imperative of the experience itself and not yet by the desire for another person, I felt closer to him than at any time in my life. Sex unified us in a way nothing else had before or since. I was able to give and receive pleasure simultaneously, exactly the same pleasure at precisely the same time. I could prolong our bliss or hasten its conclusion, all the while knowing Porter was feeling what I was feeling, our hearts pounding in unison, our chest rising and falling, and then, in the moment of our release, when our climax eclipsed all other sensations, the feeling that we were one again, truly one person, if only for a single blinding instant.

Several years later, when Porter introduced *Playboy* into the equation, it became an entirely different experience. The shared sense of our awakening sexuality, which until then had united us, suddenly and irrevocably divided us. When it became clear to me that Porter's interest in sex was diverging from mine, when our private jerk-off sessions became a *ménage a trois* with Miss October, I felt disenfranchised and lost interest in sex. Porter was confused. *I* was confused. At times we lost our erection, and Porter wanted to know what the *hell* was going on. He knew it was my fault; I wondered what was wrong with me.

Each time we masturbated, the gulf between us widened. I didn't want to be different, but when I finally understood that Porter and I diverged in an elemental way, I was bereft. There's no other word for it. Porter was lost to me. His focus had shifted to a point outside our shared world, and I was left behind. I had nothing to replace him with; I did not yet consciously desire men, but I knew I didn't want to be with a woman. I was empty, lost, scared, confused.

At first, I couldn't talk to him about it. I stopped jerking him off, and I disengaged as much as possible. That really pissed him off. He said it felt different, not as good, when we both weren't into it. In fact, the quantity of our ejaculate declined by very nearly half, and we have since discovered that I actually control sperm production and release in our right testicle.

And then, at fifteen, I discovered the power and the beauty of men. That's oversimplifying it, I suppose. What happened is that I had my first inkling of the full range of emotions men could elicit from me: desire, love, tenderness, jealousy, anger, yearning. For the first time, I understood Porter's passion for women, for sex outside the self.

I have long been fascinated by the concept of a person of one gender claiming to be "trapped" in a body of the other gender. Most people can't see past the immediate sexual aspects of the situation and view such a claim as the rationalization of a maladjusted gay person. I disagree. For me, the most important part of such a point of view is the acknowledgment of a difference between body and soul, between the physical and the spiritual. I don't think people who are happy with their bodies—attractive people—bother to make a distinction between body and spirit, between flesh and the self; if anything, they tend to confuse the two. But it's an important difference to me because I, too, feel "trapped" in my body. I am an individual, a discrete entity, and a very private person, trapped in a body that also happens to contain someone else—someone with a decidedly different point of view about life.

Porter has never been big on self-analysis; he utterly lacks a sense of his own freakish nature. He is not even remotely curious about how we came into being, about what might have caused or contributed to our condition. He has no interest in reading about people like us in history, about how they were treated or mistreated, abandoned or exploited. But even saying that does not fully convey his attitude. It's not merely that he is incurious; he fails to understand what there is to be curious *about*. He is either the most well-adjusted freak on the face of the earth or is so far in denial that nothing anyone could say could rouse him from his state of blissful ignorance. It might be detrimental—perhaps even dangerous— to do so. When he thinks about his place in the world, he tends to lay claim to those things he shares with society at large, or at least with that segment of society in which we find ourselves and which is, or has been, dominant. He thinks of himself as white, as male, as educated, and as upper middle class, and in those respects he perceives himself as superior to non-whites, to women, and to people on the lower rungs of the socioeconomic ladder. I see that as something of a straight attribute, a quality of straight men in particular. Because straight men are part of the "normal" world, because they are the way they're *supposed* to be, many of the more subtle and complex aspects of life are invisible to them. Oh, their lives have their ups and downs. They're happy or un-happy. They succeed; they fail. They want things and either get them or not. But they don't have a sense of being different, of always questioning themselves, their existence, their wants and needs.

Gay people are not as lucky. They are constantly aware of the fact that they're different, that even given the advances they've made in the last thirty years, some people don't like them. Some people hate them. And some people would kill them just for being who they are.

But being gay has helped me differentiate myself from Porter, helped me to understand that while physically I may be half of a two-headed man, spiritually I am something quite different. I am my own man. I love Porter and I love the part of me I share with him, but I cherish the part of me that is mine alone.

Sometimes an oddity can provide us with insight into our-selves and our condition—the human condition—in ways something normal cannot. The unexpected illuminates the ordinary.

Chapter 4

"Hey, what's goin' on?" Porter asked one rainy Saturday afternoon at a Lovett wrestling match as I cheered for my favorite competitor, a compact but muscular boy named Wayne Parks, whose winter-white arms and legs, glistening with sweat, flashed like lightning against his competitor's navy blue singlet.

"What?" I said, barely acknowledging him. I was focused entirely on Wayne, afraid to miss even a second of his match, praying for his victory yet secretly hoping for his defeat, wanting to see him vanquished and vulnerable. At that moment, I was getting my wish. Wayne's opponent had pinned him to the mat, his knees on Wayne's shoulders, the bulge in his sweat-soaked singlet an inch from Wayne's face.

"You're hard!"

"What do you mean *I'm* hard?" I asked, but I knew he was right. My underarm went damp with panic.

"It's not me!" he said.

"Well, it's not me, either."

"Yeah, right. You're a little perv!"

"I am not!"

"Are too! God, don't even talk to me!"

I could feel him trying to figure this out. He turned his head away from me and didn't respond when I spoke his name. I swear I could feel him pulling away, as if our separation, arrested *in utero* some sixteen years before, had begun anew.

The erection was as much a surprise to me as it was to Porter. I hadn't consciously been lusting after Wayne Parks. I hadn't been imagining myself having sex with him. I wasn't even thinking of how he might look naked. It wasn't my fault Wayne's opponent had pinned him in a way that put his genitals an inch from Wayne's perfect mouth, the contours of which I had memorized while watching him absentmindedly suck and chew and tug on the eraser of a number-two pencil in math class. Nor was I to blame for the way the two of them had grunted each time they came close to pinning their opponent or every time they escaped from a near-pin, the one on top issuing a guttural bark, the one on the bottom a muffled whimper. And I certainly couldn't be held accountable for the fact that most of the boys on the squad had yet to begin using deodorant, at least not with any regularity, and that the sharp tang of their still largely hairless armpits wafted through the air like some exotic, aromatic cheese on the verge of going bad—all of which conspired to pull the adolescent hair-trigger of desire in me.

In the car on the way home, my mother sensed something was wrong between Porter and me and asked about it.

"Owen ruined the damn meet," Porter said.

"Language, Porter," Dad said, glancing into the rearview mirror.

"What did he do?" my mother asked, looking directly at Porter. She always took his side and now accepted his assertion without question.

It was difficult for me to deal with such unadulterated favoritism. I spent a great deal of time as a child telling myself stories about why my parents liked Porter better than me, and I came up with some wildly different scenarios. My most optimistic hypothesis actually cast me in a favorable light: that Mom and Dad considered Porter the underdog, the runt of the litter—from birth, I was clearly smarter and more responsive than he—and that their favoritism towards him was a way of building up his ego, of reassuring and encouraging him. But that fantasy was short-lived. More often, I believed it was because I *was* different, flawed, lacking in some fundamental way that was clear only to them. On the rare occasions I confronted them about it (always when Porter was asleep; I wasn't going to give him the added advantage of knowing how I felt), Mom and Dad insisted it was a mere figment of my imagination. "Of course we love you both equally," Mom would protest. "How could we not?" The growing realization that I was gay, however mysterious and frightening that was, at least did one thing: it gave a name to something that until then had been without one; it gave me a place to stand, a position from which to defend myself.

Porter glanced sideways at me, then turned his face to the rain-streaked window. The only sound in the car was the squeak and thump of the windshield wipers.

"Porter?" Mom said. "Owen? *Boys?*"

"It's nothin,' Mom," Porter said. "He . . . he just talked the whole time. Never shut up." And then he punched me in the thigh. I wasn't sure if he did it to hurt me or to seal a conspiratorial pact.

"Owen, I'm surprised," she said, turning further in her seat to fix me with her stare. "You're usually so considerate."

"Yes, ma'am," was all I could manage. What else could I do? I had gotten off easy. Porter had the power to make my life miserable, but for some reason he didn't use it. It was not necessarily a generous or altruistic decision. I just don't think he really understood the situation, at least not well enough to explain it to our parents with any credibility. Sure, he could have said something like "Owen's a sissy," or "Owen's a fag," but then he would have been chastised for calling me names. Perhaps more significant is the fact that kids don't like talking to their parents about sex of any type—and vice versa. Our parents had never gone much past their two-by-two explanation of the fundamentals of reproduction during my Noah's ark phase. So how in the world was Porter going to explain to them that I had gotten an erection while watching Wayne Parks be humiliated by his opponent, not to mention that he was absolutely certain that I and I alone was responsible for it?

The notions of blame, complicity, and justice have always been more complicated for us. Occasionally we had both been punished for something only one of us had done. Our parents had no choice—at some point, punishment had to be meted out. Spanking was an imperfect option, since more than likely the innocent party also would feel at least some of the pain (as we do up front, we share a number of nerve endings behind). At the other end of the punishment scale, it was impossible to take privileges away from one of us without that affecting the other. Since we had but one penis between us, it was going to be difficult to sort out exactly who was responsible for any given episode of arousal. So Porter couldn't "out" me to our parents and escape unscathed himself, at least not until he was older and developed a significantly more sophisticated rationale. And there was always the possibility, however dim, however sublimated, that Porter was asking some pretty serious questions of his own subconscious. Should he somehow find the guts—and the words—to broach the subject, Mom likely would be horrified. Later, when she was not around, our father, scientist that he is, probably would have explained the psychology and physiology of desire and the particular peculiarities Porter and I faced.

Porter didn't even bring up the subject with me for several days, although I felt him listening to our body more intently, trying to feel what I felt when I saw Wayne Parks in the hall or at a meet. For a while, we even stopped masturbating. Eventually, driven by his own need for sexual release, we talked about it. I told him as much as I understood at that age, that I was more interested in boys than in girls, sexually and ... just as people. I didn't know why or what it might mean to us in the future, but that was how I felt.

"Jesus, O," he said, "you really think you're like ... *gay*?"

"I don't know, Porter. Not for sure. All I know is that those pictures in *Playboy* don't do the same thing for me they do for you. I mean, I can tell you're excited, but I don't feel anything—nothing at all."

"Well, that's a big clue right there. But Christ, O, do you even know what gay guys do in bed? I mean *really*?"

At the time, I *didn't* know exactly what gay sex entailed. I suspected it might involve some kissing and mutual mastur-bation, and I made the mistake of telling Porter it might be similar to what I did to him when we jerked off.

"Are you suggesting *I'm* gay because I let you jerk us off? That's sick, O!"

We started fighting again over who controlled our cock and agreed we would take turns beating off, alternating be-tween straight and gay stimuli—today his purloined copy of *Playboy*; tomorrow my scrupulously assembled, vaguely ho-moerotic advertising spreads from *Interview* and *Rolling Stone*. But Porter being Porter, he frequently claimed it was his turn when it was actually mine, a perverse twist on the way he once tried to worm his way out of getting vaccinated as a kid.

For a while after I came out to Porter, my personal hy-giene suffered. He was reluctant to touch my half of our body, to wash under my arm in the shower as he had done for years or afterward to apply deodorant. He didn't want to help me clip my nails or floss my teeth. But I have to give him credit—eventually he came to understand the situation was non-negotiable. There were many adjustments, many conces-sions, to come—on both sides—but ultimately the fact of my gayness, its inevitability, was not challenged.

Initially, there *were* limits to Porter's accommodation of

my homosexuality. He agreed not to reveal my secret to Mom and Dad as long as I agreed not to speak to anyone else about it—not to my best friend, not to my favorite teacher. I suppose he may have worried that any reasonably detailed and specific discussion about me being gay might ultimately include him. His deepest fear was guilt by association. Having a gay brother was bad enough under normal circumstances; having a gay twin was even worse. But sharing a body with your gay brother—more specifically, sharing a penis— would appear to irrefutably tar him with the same brush.

"I've got a lot more to lose than you do," he told me. "A *lot* more."

It was true. Porter was without a doubt the more popular one. Outgoing and utterly unselfconscious, he always had more friends than I did. I tend to be reserved. Aloof and bookish. Some people call me self-absorbed (and, occasionally, morose). When we were growing up, a knock on our screen door in summer was, nine times out of ten, followed by the question "Can Porter come out to play?" I was tolerated among his circle of friends only because they had no choice. As a teenager, I became a convenient scapegoat. I frequently was blamed by Porter's pals for such things as his reluctance to stay out past curfew, to carouse, to drink, or to smoke pot.

"You wouldn't rat out your own brother, now would you, Owen?" our red-headed, tough-guy, next-door neighbor, Craig Johns, would ask. "Besides, if he takes a hit, you're going to be just as high as him, and you'll both be in deep shit if you squeal."

Although Porter could accept that I was gay, he worried he would lose friends if it ever came out. That seemed to be his personal litmus test: would something I said or did embarrass him? He insisted I remain virtually silent when he was hanging out with his teammates and jock buddies. "You don't know squat about sports," he told me (despite the fact

that I was out there on the gridiron and the baseball diamond with him), "and I don't want you making some stupid,
faggy remark."

At the same time, he'd defend me if any of his buddies so
much as implied that I was a little different, a little "off." I
was his brother, after all, quite literally his own flesh and
blood; an assault on me was at least in some respects an assault on him. For my part, I fully acknowledged that our
quality of life was significantly better because Porter was a
popular athlete, and I did what I could to make sure his status as such remained unchallenged.

Although I didn't understand the dynamics at the time, I
can see now that it was only natural for Porter's friends to
pick on me. The nature of our confederation would seem to
require it. They had succumbed to the "good twin-bad twin"
myth, a common psychological stereotype that shows up
most often as an overused soap-opera device: if we were one
thing divided into two, we could not share the same characteristics. If Porter were the athlete, I had to be the dork. Since
Porter was the extrovert, I had to be shy. (My own friends
thought similar things in reverse: I was the better student, so
Porter *had* to be stupid; since I was the neat freak, he had to
be the slob.) I'm sure if Porter's friends ever thought it
through, it probably would seem "logical" that we couldn't
both be straight, couldn't both be *normal*. If Porter was
"okay," I was "not okay."

Fortunately Porter never was troubled by a straight man's
greatest fear—that I might show wood in the locker room—
because we were never allowed to dress with the other boys
at school but were required to use the coach's private changing room and shower for gym classes. Later, after Porter became a star athlete, similar accommodations were made for
us at rival schools during away games. This was presented to
us as a courtesy, though Mom saw through it immediately,
considered it blatant discrimination, and contemplated legal
action, although she ultimately declined to pursue it, decid-

ing to conserve her resources, emotional and financial, for bigger battles. I've heard that a group of parents was behind the move, though I'm not exactly sure I understood their motivation. Apparently it was okay for their sons to sit next to a freak in class or even play on the same team, but to actually see us *naked*? That was something else entirely. I don't know if they thought we had two dicks or that our single penis would be so massive as to intimidate their sons or arouse in them an unhealthy curiosity, but they weren't about to allow their boys to see what we were packing. I was initially relieved by the decision—I was only thirteen and more self-conscious than normal about my body and my privates—but later I regretted I had missed out on the visual delights of a teenage boys' locker room.

My passion for Wayne Parks remained unspoken and unrequited. I watched from a distance as he continued to develop as an athlete, ironically living in the shadow of my brother, whose dominance in two major sports eclipsed Wayne's not-insignificant accomplishments on the wrestling team. Wayne was part of the high school jock-hero clique to which my brother belonged, and so I frequently found myself in his presence, even though Porter tended to avoid him, whether out of kindness or cruelty I have never known.

Chapter 5

Porter has always been something of a lady's man. Girls adore him. Everyone appears to adore him, but girls especially. When our high school classmates passed around those insidious "slam books," in which everyone recorded their feelings about each other, Porter always collected raves while I was ignored or put down. To make matters worse, we usually shared a page and his name always appeared first: "Porter/Owen Jamison," the heading said. The comments, too, were linked. "Hot/Not" was the most common. "Whew!/Who?" and "Wow!/Ow!" showed up with some frequency. But my favorite—it was so clever it almost didn't hurt—was "Naughty/Haughty."

How, I wondered, could two guys whose physical attributes were identical elicit such disparate reactions? The answer, it seemed to me, was that Porter exuded some sort of pheromone that drew people to him, while I beamed out something like one of those invisible electronic fences people installed to keep their dogs out of the living room. That's what it felt like to me, and try as I might, I couldn't find the switch to turn it off. Of course, I also wondered if it was because somehow people intuitively knew I was gay.

I'm probably portraying myself as more of a pariah than was actually the case. I did have friends of my own, and there were a couple of girls whose hopeless crushes on me had turned, eventually, into a genuine, if passionless, sort of friendship. I was literary editor of our high school newspaper and was active in the drama club (Porter wore a full black mask and skullcap when I was on stage to minimize his visibility). In our senior class cabaret, Porter and I did a skit based on *The Odd Couple*, and the big joke was that we cast ourselves against type: I portrayed the sloppy, boorish Oscar Madison character while Porter played the fussbudget, Felix Unger. I was well known, I may even have been admired in certain quarters, but I wasn't popular. I wasn't loved. None of this really mattered to me. I didn't require the company of other people and enjoyed spending as much time as possible alone, or as alone as I would ever be. And, naturally, I wasn't interested in dating, at least not dating girls—and at the time there was no other option.

What first drew girls to Porter was his face, his impossibly gorgeous face. He was without a doubt the most handsome boy in school. Such a face was a gift, such a gift that the fact there were two of them may have seemed more generous than grotesque. (Like the British Princes William and Harry, Porter and I were sometimes called "the heir and the spare.") What drew girls to Porter, as opposed to me, remained a mystery. Perhaps it was the goofy, bewildered look he put on around them, an expression of befuddled vulnerability I saw reflected in the eyes of these sixteen- and seventeen-year-old girls that brought out the first traces of the mothering instinct in them: a big, guileless smile, followed by downcast eyes and, yes, a blush (I could feel his cheek warm against mine). It was the kind of look that made some of the most beautiful girls in the school take his face in their hands while they talked, turn it ever so slightly away from mine, and lean in and kiss him—not on the mouth, perhaps, but at the very least on his cheek, and for him that was good enough. It was a start—and it was more than most of the one-headed boys at school could elicit from the top-tier girls. During those frequent pantomimes of puppy love, I felt embarrassed, self-conscious, and somewhat superfluous. And so I remained distant, silent, frozen, as motionless as a deer alerted to a hunter's presence by the snap of a twig. I willed myself to be invisible.

Relating to girls physically did cause some difficulties. Something as simple as a hug must be carefully coordinated when you control only one arm. When Porter hugged one of his girlfriends, I had to wrap my arm around her, too, at the same time as Porter, applying equal pressure or perhaps a bit less so she knew it was Porter who was hugging her, not me. If we were successful, it would seem like a perfectly normal hug; it wouldn't even occur to her that I was doing anything.

In our freshman and sophomore years at Lovett, a succession of girls doted on Porter. He received so many pale, scented envelopes, passed to him in the hall between classes and stored in our locker, that it was as if we had hung a potpourri ball from one of the coat hooks. None of these relationships was serious, none formalized by so much as a single actual date, which would have required Porter to meet the girl's parents, something all involved knew would have been the kiss of death ("You're dating *who*?"). But group dating—in which six or eight or ten boys and girls, often only loosely paired off, went out together—recently had become popular, and parents approved of it because it seemed less serious, less intense than the old-fashioned style of one-on-one dating. For Porter and his friends, it was a way to define themselves and their turf, to set themselves apart from the other kids at school. *These women, the* best *women, are ours.* From this group there emerged a series of girls who would set their sights on Porter, who would offer themselves to him in small but unmistakable ways. A certain girl would suddenly turn up wherever Porter was: at our locker, at his lunch table, at pep rallies. Initially, Porter was unresponsive to their overtures. Oh, he was as crazed by testosterone as any boy of sixteen or seventeen—to that I could attest—but he was naturally self-conscious about having two heads and seriously doubted any girl would find him attractive. It was I who encouraged him to pursue the girls who were so clearly interested in him. I wanted at least one of us to be happy, and it seemed more probable he would be the one to succeed, since his romantic preference was at least sanctioned by the world at large. But my actions weren't entirely altruistic. I was simply being practical: at that age, most gay boys simply aren't dating other boys. They are still struggling with the shame and uncertainty of their feelings. I didn't really even know any other gay boys at the time. And so I figured, why not let Porter have some fun?

To avoid parental sanction, the girl of the moment would catch up with Porter at a school dance or at a party after yet another Lovett football victory made possible by Porter's miraculous passing arm. They would spend the evening together, usually in the company of one or two other couples, breaking away only at the end of the evening to make out briefly and to plan their next surreptitious assignation.

If any of these girls were squeamish about dating a two-headed boy, they hid it pretty well. Some acknowledged my presence; most didn't. (Some never even bothered to get my name right, referring to me as Owing or Odin. I could tell Porter wasn't really interested in them if he didn't bother to correct them.) But I observed some, perhaps subconscious, accommodations. For example, Porter's dates usually preferred to have conversations with him while walking hand-in-hand rather than standing face-to-face; that placed them at his side, allowing his head to obscure mine most of the time. I did my best to enhance this illusion by mirroring the position and movements of his head as precisely as I could, thus remaining out of their line of sight.

These innocent liaisons usually lasted three or four months, roughly about the length of a sports season—one girl for the football season, another in spring for baseball, a third for summer—and generally ended when Porter wanted to advance to a more intense level of intimacy. Despite his looks, initially he never got much past first base. Perhaps because his dates were largely group events, he was rarely alone with a girl long enough to do so. And most Lovett girls weren't the type to allow a guy, any guy, to paw them beneath the bleachers at a pep rally. Beyond that, I'm not sure if it was anything more than a young girl's natural reticence to give in to her boyfriend's biological imperatives. But Porter and I both knew his batting average probably would have been better were it not for me, and his frustration slowly turned to resentment. These girls drove a wedge between us. At the end of a particularly frustrating night, when circumstances had conspired to allow his hand to slide beneath a blouse and he had fumbled with the clasp of a bra one-handed while my arm swung at my side like so much dead meat (my rules of engagement forbade me from helping), he refused to allow me to touch our cock when he masturbated, preferring instead to take things into his own hand. In a way, I think he felt like only half a man, and I could feel his growing need to exert more than fifty percent control over our shared body as a way of proving exactly who was in charge.

Porter had his first real girlfriend in our senior year. Her name was Christi Oakes—Christine, really, but she altered it so she'd have a better chance of making the cheerleading squad, an invitation to which apparently required your first name to end in an "i" (replacing the dot with a heart was optional). One of the perks of being co-captain of the football team and the most successful quarterback in more than a decade was dating a cheerleader. It was a given, two heads or not. Porter's best friend and co-captain, Gary Burns, already was dating the captain of the cheerleaders, Kari (formerly Karen) Mayport, but Porter pretty much had his pick of the remaining seven girls on the squad.

Christi was different from the other girls—quiet, shy, and, by comparison, positively demure. She was so soft-spoken it seemed impossible she would ever raise her voice, let alone shout, as she was required to do as a cheerleader. (To this day, I'm not sure she wasn't just mouthing the cheers.) And I never—ever—saw her chew gum. Christi was not as pretty as her counterparts, which is to say only that she didn't draw attention to herself with flashy clothes or heavy makeup. But I thought she was more beautiful than any of them, in a serene and virginal way that seemed incredibly old-fashioned to me. She wore her honey-blond hair long and loose, tied back with a ribbon when she cheered, never artificially highlighted or styled to draw attention to herself.

Christi Oakes came from old Atlanta money, Coca-Cola money, which is about as close to a pedigree as one gets in Atlanta, a city known more for commerce than culture. Her great-grandfather was a contemporary of Asa Candler, founder of The Coca-Cola Company, and got rich by investing heavily in Coke stock. The Oakeses lived in a sprawling 1930s art deco mansion off Andrews Drive in Buckhead, next door, in fact, to one of the scions of the Candler fortune, if a house separated by a couple of football fields of meticulously landscaped lawn could be considered next door to anything. The homes in our Ansley Park neighborhood, once considered the most desirable enclave of in-town living, seemed small and shabby by comparison.

As a cheerleader, Christi attended all the same parties and pep rallies as Porter and his jock buddies, but she remained somewhat aloof. Invariably, she was the one who offered to help the parents who had volunteered to host a party in their backyard or around their pool or, if an event were being held at school, who assisted the faculty and administrators who were serving as chaperones. In fact, the night I first noticed her interest in Porter, she was serving punch at the Lovett Homecoming Dance.

Mom and Dad refused to let us get our driver's licenses until we were eighteen (they figured—rightly, it turns out—that we might encounter some resistance from the DMV and wanted to get all their legal ducks in a row), so out of necessity, Porter and Christi always doubled with Gary and Kari. I, of course, was the proverbial fifth wheel. Kari and Christi initially talked about finding dates for me, which I suppose was actually quite thoughtful, but Porter, knowing my story, understood that this would make me even more uncomfortable and dissuaded them.

When we were in the car on the way to a party or dance, or when we were at the movies, Christi always sat to our left, next to Porter. He'd put his arm around her, and she would sometimes rest her head on his shoulder. Occasionally, he would turn his head to the left and kiss her lightly on the forehead or lips. On their dates, I would isolate myself by wearing headphones and listening to my Walkman. Sometimes I brought a book and one of those clip-on reading lamps.

But as Porter and Christi's level of intimacy deepened, things got more complicated. Lying flat on our backs, Porter and I are nominally concave, turned in toward each other ever so slightly, perhaps just a few degrees. This curvature, which is now barely noticeable, was at one time more pronounced and was largely corrected through the use of a specially designed back brace into which Porter and I were harnessed daily between the ages of two and five. We can now make both shoulders touch the floor with minimal effort, but we are still oriented inward, toward each other. It is easier for Porter, on the left, to look at someone standing slightly right of center; the reverse is true for me. We also soon discovered that it was more comfortable for Porter to make out with a girl if she were seated on the right, next to me, and he leaned toward her, past me, to kiss her, rather than twisting his head around to the left, which was awkward at best and, over the long haul, quite uncomfortable. So when things were about to get hot and heavy, Christi would get out of the backseat of Gary's dad's Mercedes, walk around the car, and get in next to me. I, grudgingly, put my arm around her. This configuration enabled Porter to turn slightly to the right and kiss her full on the mouth. It also put his arm in position to be able to meander up and down her legs, across her chest, and, ultimately, beneath her blouse or sweater.

Despite years of close proximity, even listening to Porter eat sometimes offended my sensibilities. He nearly sent me over the edge when he chewed his goddamn Life Savers instead of sucking them. These shared intimacies were worse. Much, much worse. I could hear every whispered endearment, feel every sigh, smell their commingled exhalations. Sometimes he knocked my earphones askew and forced my mouth into her hair or onto her left ear. I suspect Christi was sometimes uncomfortable as well, embarrassed by my presence. I frequently sensed a reluctance on her part to speak, to either encourage or discourage Porter's current course of attack, to declare her feelings, or to offer suggestions. I sometimes could sense her beginning to say something, then catch herself, bite her lip, sigh.

I developed a set of rules governing my behavior when I was out on a date with Porter and Christi designed to give all of us some sense of privacy, normalcy, and fairness. There was, of course, my use of the Walkman and my Itty Bitty Book Light to keep me occupied. I also sometimes brought along a handheld computer game, not an obnoxiously loud one like a Game Boy, but something like a Merriam-Webster electronic dictionary, which offered the option of playing games like hangman and anagrams. I accepted the fact that I was never consulted about where we should go or what we should do, and I learned never to make my preference for movies known, even if Porter and Christi were hopelessly deadlocked (I invariably would have sided with her).

This charade of invisibility became even more important later, when Porter began dating Christi without Gary and Kari after we finally got our driver's licenses. When we arrived at a restaurant, Porter always emphasized to the maître d' that he wanted a table for two, and on those occasions when we were still provided with three place settings, he had the one to his right removed. (Even when I didn't actually eat dinner, the waiter sometimes asked me if I'd like to have dessert or coffee.)

Porter's relationship with Christi Oakes lasted, against all odds, into our freshman year at Druid Hills, and I honestly think Porter believed he would marry her. He was in love with her and, hard as it was for me to understand—she was, after all, this gorgeous cheerleader who probably had to fight guys off—I think she was equally in love with him. Midway through our senior year at Lovett, Porter had given Christi a sapphire ring set with two diamond chips—not an engagement ring, per se, but a symbol of their exclusivity. And when they were crowned king and queen at the senior prom (to which I grudgingly took a date so as to seem less of an appendage), it seemed like a fairy tale come true. When the end came—suddenly, unexpectedly—it was because her parents (her father, really) disapproved of Porter—of us.

It happened during Christmas break of our freshman year. Christi had just gotten home from her first semester at Auburn, and when Porter and I went to pick her up, we were met at the door by her father. Mr. Oakes was typical of the parents of other kids at Lovett: a vice president in the accounting department at Coca-Cola, well educated, seemingly liberal. He was a large man, a former quarterback at the University of Georgia, and it struck me as odd that he had ended up being, more or less, an accountant. But he seemed like a decent guy, and he had always been nice to us. During our senior year, he had been president of the Lovett Parents' Association, a group that sponsored car washes and bake sales to underwrite the cost of sports uniforms and band trips to Europe, though I suspected most of the money they raised came from their own checkbooks. He had attended all the games at which Christi cheered, and he always seemed to enjoy talking sports with Porter. Mrs. Oakes, too, appeared to have embraced Porter and had given him and Christi her blessing. She even liked me, and the first time we were invited to dinner at the Oakes's home, Thanksgiving of our junior year at

Lovett, I was quickly disabused of my habit of forgoing meals during Porter's dates. "Nonsense," Mrs. Oakes said when I had protested that I wasn't hungry and instructed her maid to set another place at the table.

At first, nothing seemed amiss. Mr. Oakes smiled and put his arm around our shoulders, approaching from Porter's side so his hand ultimately rested atop my shoulder. He squeezed my deltoid and patted it three times reassuringly, oblivious to the fact that Porter could feel this only as a faint echo across our shoulder blades. He steered us into the living room, an expansive space painted pale yellow with white trim, like lemon meringue pie, and decorated in a style most accurately described as French country, with the occasional Oriental accent. A life-size oil painting of Christi, done when she was maybe thirteen or fourteen, hung over the mantel, and family photos in silver or gilt frames sat on end tables next to marble eggs and Chinese bowls filled with potpourri.

Christi already was seated in a big, overstuffed chair, and there was no room for Porter and me to sit down next to her. Instead, we sat down in a love seat facing Mr. Oakes. I could tell Christi had been crying, but I don't think Porter noticed at first. After some small talk about Porter's stellar athletic career at Lovett, Mr. Oakes paused. I could tell something was up because Christi started sniffling.

"Now, Porter, you know I've always liked you. You're a terrific athlete—a fine young man. You've really overcome . . . You've done quite well for yourself. And I've heard nice things about your brother, too." (This made me squirm. Clearly, he didn't get it if he was including me in the equation.)

"Thank you, sir," Porter said tentatively. I noticed he was clenching and unclenching his fist, something he had always done prior to a big game.

"But I've got to tell you, I just don't think there's any future in your seeing Christi."

"Sir?" His hand froze in clench mode.

"There's no *point*. It's not going to go anywhere. You're both at different colleges now. You're meeting lots of new people. You shouldn't be tied down to each other. It's not fair . . . for either of you."

"Christi? Is this what you want?" Porter said imploringly.

"Porter . . ." she said, and I knew the cause was lost. Sentences that begin with your name usually end badly. The person speaking to you wants you to think they're using your name as a term of endearment, but it's actually an admonition. There's a world of difference between "I love you, Porter" and "Porter, I love you," which is inevitably followed by the word "but." "Porter, I love you, but it's not going to work." "Porter, I love you, but I've found someone new. He's a quarterback, like you"—this is supposed to make you feel better by allowing you to think that they are not rejecting you entirely, that there are things about you they still admire, memories they will always cherish, that you are still *okay*—"*but with only one head.*"

Mr. Oakes stood up and paced the room. He selected a cigar from a humidor, mouthed it like the connoisseur he was, and lit it.

"You kids . . . you think you know all about love," he said, gesticulating toward us with his cigar, which he held as if he were throwing a dart. "How many high-school romances end in marriages—*successful* marriages? Probably fewer than one in a hundred. It's all about hormones. You don't know anything about the complexities of love or the difficulties of long-term relationships."

Porter was at a loss for words. Christi just looked at him, a tissue clutched in her right hand, waiting for him to present an impassioned defense of their relationship. But nothing came.

"Sir, I think you're wrong there," I said, surprising everyone, including myself.

"Owen," Porter said. "Shut up."

Both Christi and Mr. Oakes stared at me as if I were a ventriloquist's dummy suddenly come to life, but I persisted.

"If there is anyone who knows the difficulties involved in maintaining a long-term relationship, it's Porter."

"Owen, this is none of your business," Porter said in a sort of stage whisper.

I pressed on, heedless.

"Unlike most boys, he doesn't think only of himself. He understands the importance of compromise, which is probably the cornerstone of any successful relationship. But most importantly, he loves your daughter and would be good to her."

Christi burst into tears at this point.

"Owen, *shut up!*" Porter thumped me on the chest with the fist he'd been clenching and unclenching, like when we were kids learning to walk.

"I'm sorry, Mr. Oakes. It's really none of his . . ."

"No, no, no, Porter. I'm afraid it just goes to prove my point. I have no doubt that you're more mature than most boys your age or that you're better able to deal with the problems and complexities of life. But you boys *are* different. You've done remarkably well for yourselves. Truly, it's amazing. And I have no doubt that you love my daughter. But it's just not right. Boys, you've got two heads. You need to stick with your own kind."

"Meaning what?" Porter said, angry now, angry enough, I hoped, to forget about my contribution to the conversation, which I could see had been ill-advised.

"Well, Porter, surely you must know other people like you."

"There is no one else on the *planet* like me."

"Well, not *exactly* like you, certainly, but similar, perhaps."

"You mean freaks! You think I should marry another freak? Another conjoined twin?"

"Well, it certainly would make more sense. You'd be killing two . . ."

"*Daddy!*" Christi shrieked. I think she was truly horrified.

"I don't mean anything by it, honey. I *don't*, Porter." He sort of shrugged his shoulders and extended his hands, palms up, as if to say, "What can I do?" "I genuinely like and respect you. And believe me when I say I have nothing against a person with two heads. . . ."

"You just don't want your daughter to marry one!" Porter said.

There are few times when Porter makes a move that completely surprises me, but this was one of them. He stood up so quickly that the process of pulling me up with him nearly popped my shoulder out of its socket. I actually had to catch my breath.

"I'm leaving," he said. "Goodbye, Christi."

Porter moved toward the door; I remained rooted to the floor. He stumbled, pulling me, awkwardly, off center. I simply could not believe he was giving up without a fight. It was so unlike him. Christi, too, seemed surprised. She had not moved, though her fingernails seemed to dig more deeply into the fabric arms of the chair, but on her face I could read shock, disappointment, betrayal. It was as if her father had given her a drug that paralyzed her from the neck down but allowed her face to remain expressive. Even Mr. Oakes seemed to have been caught off guard. He initially must have thought Porter's impetuous leap from the love seat had been an attack; his right arm jerked upward toward his face momentarily, then relaxed. I saw in his eyes the moment he realized he had won, but in an odd way it was a look of defeat, as well, as if perhaps he knew at that moment the value of the thing he had destroyed.

In the car on the way home, Porter was furious, but the brunt of his anger, which should have been directed at Mr. Oakes, was deflected entirely toward me for having spoken up on his behalf.

"This is all your fault, Owen. You should have kept your damn mouth shut," he said.

"I was just trying to help."

"I don't need your help, and you can see how *helpful* it was, anyway."

"Do you honestly think it would have turned out differently if I hadn't said anything?" I asked, exasperated.

"This had nothing to do with you."

Of course, it had *everything* to do with me, with the presence of my head on Porter's shoulders. Could he really not see that?

Until that moment, I don't think either of us had truly experienced discrimination, or if we had, it had been so subtle (or so insidious) we had not been aware of it. Our parents had the financial and intellectual wherewithal to shelter us from taunts and name calling by surrounding us with polite, intelligent adults and their well-bred children. We attended private schools, were shipped off to summer camps for smart and privileged kids, and vacationed in Europe and the Far East when Mom and Dad lectured abroad. Nothing had prepared us for this.

Just as no one expects a fat person to be quick-witted or an ugly person to be charming, few people had significant expectations for Porter and me. The simple fact of our survival was our greatest achievement. So, for most of our lives, our shortcomings had been overlooked and our smallest successes had been acknowledged as impressive milestones. Everything from learning to walk to dressing ourselves and tying our shoes received not merely the acknowledgment and encouragement that's expected from parents and relatives, but the awe accorded something as remarkable as the parting of the Red Sea. It was as if we had grown up in a house rigged with *APPLAUSE* signs.

Porter's accomplishments on the playing fields of Lovett— the highest pass-completion percentage in state football history and three no-hitters in his brief prep career—would have been notable had they been achieved by a boy with only *one* head. But the fact that he was a Siamese twin, and a *dicephalus* at that—one of the most extreme forms—made him the object of wonder. So we had been lulled into a false sense that, without exception, people admired us. But our self-confidence and self-esteem were, unwittingly, dependent upon a fragile bubble of goodwill from the world at large.

There is a limit, however, to how accepting people are, how far they will open their hearts to those who are not like them. They are more than willing to be congenial as long as nothing significant is at stake. But sooner or later, everyone circles the wagons, separates themselves, their family, their *kind*, from those who are different and might threaten them. Mr. Oakes had drawn the line that day, and our protective bubble had burst as quickly as if he had applied the hot red tip of his cigar to a balloon. Porter honestly believed it was because his athletic glory days were behind him. Lovett was not a powerhouse among prep teams, and despite his "big fish" status, Porter had not been recruited to play college ball. Druid Hills, which we attended because of the courtesy scholarships that were a handsome addition to our parents' compensation packages, was an NCAA Division III school and didn't even *have* a football team. But I believe it went much deeper than that. Mr. Oakes would have been more than willing to accept Porter as a son-in-law despite his fading gridiron fame if he had had only one head. A fabled, game-winning pass has been the basis for more than one Southern marriage, and Porter had title to a legendary prep football career. I suppose Mr. Oakes let Christi's relationship with Porter continue in high school because he could not imagine his daughter would "go all the way" with someone of Porter's freakish anatomy. "Heavy petting," as it was called in Mr. Oakes's day, was acceptable because, after all, it was Porter's hand that was doing the work. But actual intercourse—with a *shared* penis? Out of the question. Not only did the act itself seem grotesque, unnatural, but the possibility of producing a two-headed offspring, which you have to admit was probably on everyone's mind, was unthinkable. *Lie with monsters, beget monsters.*

Because he was powerless to exact revenge on Mr. Oakes, Porter took out his anger on me. It's hard to give someone the cold shoulder when you occupy the same body, but Porter did his best. He couldn't exactly not speak to me. Although much of our communication is nonverbal, intuitive, we have to speak to each other to get through the course of a day. But there is speaking and there is *talking*. We didn't *talk* for three or four days. Most of his communication came in the form of demands: "I want a drink" or "I want to watch the game." He became completely self-absorbed, even denying me the right to "my" days. He got drunk, I got sick.

I do think there is a part of us that Porter and I share, other than our penis, a well of emotion we both draw from or make deposits to. We don't feel exactly the same thing at the same time very often, but it is hard for me to be *completely* happy when he is depressed. I realized what he was doing, even if he didn't: he was trying to push all of his pain over to me, to my side of our body. He thought that by blaming me, by rejecting me, he could somehow exorcise himself of the demon of unrequited love.

"Look Porter," I said to him two weeks after the incident with Mr. Oakes. "I'm sorry things didn't work out with Christi, and I'm sorry if anything I said that night contributed to it."

We were in bed after having spent a joyless day on the slopes at Aspen, where we had come for our usual post-Christmas family vacation.

"I know it wasn't your fault, O," he said moodily. "Mr. Oakes is an asshole. He was never going to let things get serious with me and Christi. That's why he sent her to Auburn—I know that now. I'm sorry I've been such a shit to you."

I wanted to tell him everything was going to be all right,

to remind him he had dated plenty of other girls in high school and would again, but at the moment I wasn't convinced of that myself. The episode with Mr. Oakes was a reminder that our parents could no longer insulate us from the petty cruelties of the world at large. We were moving into uncharted territory, *terra incognita*, the place on the ancient maps marked "Here be monsters." Nonetheless, that night I tried to comfort myself—and Porter—with the knowledge that a lot of kids our age were going through the same things we were: moving away from home for the first time, having their hearts broken, trying to figure out who they were and what their place in the world would be.

"It'll be okay, Porter. We'll get through this together, the way we always do."

"Right, bro," he said. "Sure thing."

I knew he wasn't buying it. He was in pain, and nothing I could say would fix it. I couldn't know it that night, but it would take him more than a year to get over Christi and another year to truly understand what had happened and to allow himself to be vulnerable again.

I could think of nothing else to say, so I lay there in silence. Eventually, I lifted my foot slightly, crossed it over Porter's ankle, and interlocked my big toe with his. It was something we had done as kids when we were sad or afraid—when both of us had been punished for something only one of us had done, or when we were worried about something that was going to happen the next day, a medical procedure or a big test at school. It was our way of letting each other know we were in this together, that we would be there for each other. It was the closest we ever came to holding hands.

Chapter 6

Despite our significant personal differences, Porter and I share one over-riding common interest: our music. I think it has been the key to our survival. At the very least, an innate sense of rhythm has informed our every move. From the time we learned to crawl, we have had to be more aware than the average person of the importance of rhythm, of syncopation—a sense of left-right, one-two, bouncing back and forth between us almost audibly. Doctors have told us our hearts beat in a precise counterpoint to one another. I *lub* while he *dubs*. Our parents picked up on this and began piano lessons for us early. Each of us was responsible for executing one half of a musical composition, and creating harmonious sound enhanced our coordination and rewarded our cooperation. We weren't musical prodigies by any means, but we were quick studies and genuinely enjoyed both the process and the result. And ultimately we learned to love applause as well, because it was a response to something we had done, which was different from the kind of attention we previously had received for simply existing.

When we were ten, Porter took the first step toward writing music, improvising little melodies on the keyboard when we had finished practicing for the day. Sometimes he'd hand off an improvisation to me, and I'd carry it along for a while—until I stumbled—then hand it back to him. As his compositions became more complex, I began writing words to accompany them. I'd been writing poetry for as long as I could remember, and at first I simply adapted some of my poems to fit his music. A lot of our adolescent stuff was crap, especially the lyrics, which I can see now were either overly sentimental or utterly bleak, but they improved as I got older and actually experienced something of life.

We got our first guitar, an acoustic, at twelve and an electric at fourteen, and began performing in our garage soon after. We called our band Janus and played at birthday parties and the occasional dance in the Lovett gym, but our musical career didn't really get off the ground until we were out of high school and Porter had put his hopes of an athletic career behind him. At first, we didn't think music would actually provide an income for us. We did it because we loved it, without any expectation there would be rewards beyond the joy of the music itself. But by the time we were in our sophomore year at Druid Hills, we had been playing local venues for nearly a year, with some success. The clubs were small— Eddie's Attic in Decatur, the Little Five Points Pub in Atlanta—but our audiences were loyal and increasingly enthusiastic. We got our big break in 1995, when we met the Indigo Girls—Emily Saliers and Amy Ray—when they played a spring-break gig at Druid Hills. After their concert, we introduced ourselves and invited them to hear us at the Little Five Points Pub. Three months later, they asked us to open for them at the Variety Playhouse. Soon thereafter, we recorded and independently produced our first CD, *Double Play,* at a small studio in Athens, birthplace of the B-52s and REM, selling them mainly at local stores like Wuxtry Records and Wax n Fax or out of our van after performances.

At first, our parents were a little leery of our pursuit of a musical career. Both of them come from relatively well-to-do northern families, and although they are generally socially and politically liberal, they inherited at least a vestige of the stuffiness of their moneyed New England forebearers. I'm sure they intended our childhood music lessons to set us on the path to becoming classical pianists or cellists, and they must have been sorely disappointed when we turned our attention to the pop and rock arenas. I'm sure they thought it a little exhibitionistic, a bit too much like putting ourselves on display in a freak show. (Mom nearly had a heart attack when she saw a poster for one of our earliest gigs that proclaimed, "Come for the freaks, stay for the music," a marketing concept we quickly abandoned in deference to her.) But in reality, it was an obvious choice—one might even call it inevitable. Music was the one point at which Porter's and my talents and interests intersected. I never would have survived Porter's career as a professional athlete (if that were even an option), and he would not have suffered my career as a professor of English with anything approaching grace or equanimity. And when it became clear that a recording career could provide us with a more-than-ample income, allowing Mom and Dad to use their personal resources for their own retirement, both of them unequivocally threw their support behind it.

When we began playing musical gigs with some regularity, we developed something of a cult following—emphasis on the word "cult"—complete with groupies. At least in the beginning, when our reputation as freaks still eclipsed our fame as musicians, we attracted a strange, dark coterie: punks and ravers and Goth girls, mostly, with black lipstick and black fingernail polish, pierced tongues and eyebrows, and, when they got close enough, a vinegary smell to their jet-black hair. It was unexpected and a bit scary. Our music was really pretty mainstream—largely acoustic and lyric-driven, a lot of ballads, some folk and rock tunes, occasionally a little dark in a David Baerwald sort of way, but nothing that would attract the interest of devil worshippers or vivisectionists—and yet our early audiences were mostly leather-clad, inked, and pierced S and M types, though of the straight variety as far as I could tell. These were not the type of girls you could bring home to mother, but if nothing else, they got Porter laid.

In the years since Porter graduated from Lovett and left his athletic career behind, it had not been easy for him to get dates. We can't exactly walk into a bar and hit on people like in some sick *Saturday Night Live* sketch: "Siamese Wild and Crazy Guys." The fact is, most strangers avoid us if they can. When Bruce Weber photographed us for *Vanity Fair* after he saw us run in the Olympic torch relay in 1996, the person in charge of making sure our noses weren't shiny and our hair was sensuously disarrayed almost fainted when first confronted with our presence and had to race to the men's room, where he hurled for about fifteen minutes before he was able to resume his responsibilities.

It's different with people we know, of course, and at Lovett we had the advantage of having grown up with most of the kids with whom we went to school. They were used to us, they knew us as individuals, and they didn't really think of us as freaks. Porter also had the advantage of being captain of the football team, which automatically conferred on him an elite status. None of that applied at Druid Hills, where we had to build new friendships from scratch.

In the time since Porter's relationship with Christi ended in the fall of our freshman year, he had mustered the courage to ask out exactly two girls, but both of those dates were uncomfortable for everyone involved and were not repeated. I'm not sure why either girl initially agreed to the date. One was actually a classmate of mine and we had struck up a friendship of sorts. Porter had quietly developed something of a crush on her and asked her out, much to my surprise. I think she agreed to go as much to spare my feelings as Porter's, but nonetheless the date more or less ended our friendship. The other girl, upon returning to our booth at the Buckhead Diner after a visit to the ladies' room, looked across the table at us, angled her head a few degrees to the left, and thanked *me* for a lovely evening—at which point Porter made me pick up the check.

"I'm never going to get laid, let alone married," he confided to me late one night in bed. "Christi was my shot, my one chance at happiness. She's the only girl who will ever love me."

"That's not true," I assured him, though in fact I feared he was right. Although Christi Oakes began to date Porter solely because he was co-captain of the football team at Lovett, I believe there was something special about her, something that made her love him for more than just his athletic prowess and the accompanying status, made her connect with him on a deeper level. Beneath her beauty and her popularity, there was a kind of goodness, almost saintliness, about her. She could have stood in the spotlight at the *Miss America Pageant* and honestly said she wanted to help all of the hungry, orphaned children of the world, and people would have believed her. I would not be surprised to hear that she had married a doctor or a minister and moved to Africa to become a missionary. It would be hard to find anyone remotely like her.

One night, we were doing tequila shots between sets at the Little Five Points Pub with three anemic, black-clad girls and one long-haired guy with a red bandana he had fashioned into a skullcap by tightly tying the corners together. I found myself curiously drawn to him and to men like him: lean to the point of malnutrition, with long hair and the kind of sparse mustache and beard Jesus wore. One of his hands thrummed the table rhythmically, his long, pale fingers undulating in succession like the legs of an impatient arachnid. There was some talk about just how much liquor Porter and I could hold—whether we might be able to handle twice as much as a normal guy, or maybe only one point five times as much, or the same amount. Suddenly, I felt a hand on the fly of our jeans, a claw, really, or so it seemed, that belonged to the girl sitting next to me. Like a scorpion, it skittered down the inside of my leg and back up Porter's inseam before coming to rest atop our crotch. I tried to ignore it, and Porter, engaged in conversation with the raccoon-eyed girl next to him, was oblivious to it—or possibly thought it was me, scratching ourself. Finally, I picked up the hand and removed it. *You're barking up the wrong tree, Morticia,* I wanted to say. At that point, Porter must have figured things out. He leaned forward, caught the girl's eye, and nodded. Without speaking, she stood up, ordered a double shot at the bar, downed it, and turned to glare at me as if she were trying to scare me off. I think it had dawned on her that Porter and I were not the same person, that he could be interested in her while I was not, that she could have him but not me. I could almost see the gears turning behind the black saucers of her eyes. For the next half hour or so, until we got up to do our last set, she hung over Porter's shoulder, drinking with him now and again, running her right hand through his hair. She disappeared mid-set and I was happy to be rid of her, but afterward, when we had broken down our equipment and were packing up our van, she appeared in the parking lot and slouched up against the car next to ours, snapping her gum and twirling a strand of her acrid black hair around one finger.

"You boys want to have a little fun?" she asked, coyly tracing the outline of her lips with the split ends of that lock of hair.

"What did you have in mind?" I said. "Pin the tail on the donkey?"

She smiled. "Something like that."

I laughed. "Maybe another time."

"Whoa, whoa, whoa, Owen. Not so fast." Porter shoved the amp deeper into the van, wiped his hand on our jeans, and turned toward her. "You were saying?"

"I'm having a little party at my place," she said, giving an address on Euclid Avenue. "Interested?"

I knew the answer.

"Come on, O. Let's do it."

I was dog tired and had done a few too many shooters, but Porter was clearly interested, suddenly alert, nearly rabid. I could almost feel him sniffing the air for her scent. It would be pointless to resist. "Okay. An hour. *One* hour."

"Gotcha. An hour."

The bitch gave me an evil smile that made me regret my quick capitulation. We locked the van and made our way to her place, a grungy little apartment within walking distance of the club, where we were greeted by one of the other pallid girls we had been drinking with—her roommate, it turns out—and the bandana guy, who was the roommate's boyfriend. I could tell Porter was surprised and a bit dismayed by his presence, but now that Bandana Man had taken off his leather jacket, I was thrilled by his wiry little body, his sinewy arms stained blue and green with tattoos. His appeal was only somewhat diminished by his two missing front teeth, a detail I had failed to notice in the bar. At least I'd have something to distract me while Porter played footsies with the evil one.

The girl's name was Jade, or so she said. I suspected that it was part of her Goth persona, that her real name was probably something unforgivably drab like Velma or Louise, and that she had tried on several pseudonyms, including Elvira and Vixana, which were too exotic for her to live up to, before ultimately settling on Jade. She probably had been lonely and unpopular in high school (as it turned out, in Macon), and I could see that beneath her exaggerated makeup and severe hairstyle, she most likely was extraordinarily plain. But I guessed she had been smarter than most of her classmates and creative enough to find her way to Atlanta and gravitate toward a community of misfits like herself in the notoriously bohemian neighborhood of Little Five Points, adopting a new, gemlike, vaguely Oriental moniker.

Vixana—that's how I thought of her; she *should* have chosen Vixana instead of Jade—poured both of us glasses of red wine from a green screw-top bottle, and we sat down on a dark and sort of dampish sofa that smelled of dog, with Jade next to Porter. She pulled her left leg up onto the couch, leaned into him, and ran her right hand through his hair, which of late he wore considerably longer than I wore mine.

The Cure was blasting from the stereo, making conversation all but impossible. Bandana Man produced a bottle of off-brand tequila from the kitchen, clutching five clinking shot glasses with the fingers and thumb of his right hand, and his girlfriend brought out a plastic bag and a small tray covered with the dusty residue of a thousand joints and began rolling. When she had finished two numbers, she handed one to me and one to Porter, which I saw as a sweet and thoughtful gesture, if somewhat redundant, since our shared circulatory system guarantees that if Porter smokes dope, I eventually get high even if the joint never passes my lips. We lit the joints and passed them around, Porter's traveling clockwise, mine counterclockwise.

It was some powerful shit. It must have been laced with something—crystal, maybe. Whatever it was, it hit with such force that it alarmed me. I got paranoid. Bandana Man suddenly looked evil, the skin drawn tight around his eyes and mouth when he sucked on a joint. He reminded me of one of those skeleton warriors in a cheesy 1960s stop-motion animation film by Ray Harryhausen, *Jason and the Argonauts* or something. I was afraid we had made a terrible mistake. Several times I tried to get up off the couch to leave, but Porter wouldn't budge.

"Where are you going, man?" he said. "Relax. This is good shit. Just sit back and enjoy it."

At one point, Bandana Man got up, rummaged around in a battered leather fanny pack, and produced a small white tablet, which he handed to Porter.

"Chill pill," he said. "Take it."

Porter complied unquestioningly, swallowing it with a mouthful of the rotgut tequila Bandana Man had passed to him. I was feeling helpless and vulnerable, but Porter seemed unfazed. I hoped he knew what he was doing. Sure enough, the pill soon took the rough edge off my buzz, smoothed it out. We settled back into the damp couch, and I began thinking we might actually be sinking into the space between the seat cushion and the back of the sofa, as if it were swallowing us. The loud music seemed to fade, and I became aware of Vixana's crablike hand scuttling across the stiff material of our jeans again.

"Fuck, this is so twisted," I heard Bandana Man say as Vixana undid our belt buckle and unzipped our jeans.

I grabbed hold of her hand as she reached inside our boxers and pulled out our semi-tumescent penis.

"O! Dude! What are you doing, man? Let her have it!" Porter said to me in a half-whisper.

"It's gross, Porter. She's a . . ." I wanted to say, "She's a skank," but I couldn't bring myself to do so. As repulsed as I was, I didn't want to hurt her feelings. I let go of her hand, defeated and too wasted to care.

Porter and I had never actually had sex before. None of the girls he had dated had done anything more than massage us through the fabric of our jeans, stroking our penis like it was some small, scared animal, a hamster that had crawled up our leg and gotten tangled in our shorts, thrashing about to free itself. But Vixana had it in her mouth before I even realized what was happening. I have to admit it felt good, unlike anything Porter and I had ever been able to achieve during a j.o. session, hot and wet and *alive*, her tongue moving out of the way on the downstroke, then caressing us like velvet sandpaper on the upstroke. We came almost immediately, in unexpectedly large, violent spasms, Porter groaning out the words, "Fuck yeah," even as I tried in vain to resist the feeling, clenching my teeth, not wanting to surrender, not wanting to spew my come into Vixana's mouth, wishing, if anything, that I was shooting my stuff down Bandana Man's throat—and that thought is what allowed me to relax, to un-clench. "Oh Christ," I said. "Jesus fucking Christ!"

With my eyes closed, I sank further down into the couch, embarrassed, ashamed. I heard desultory clapping on the other side of the room, heard Bandana Man say, "Way to go, Jade! One for the books. Truly, truly fucked up." I opened my eyes just a slit as she stood up and wiped her mouth, like a vampire after feeding on the blood of innocents. Our cock was still convulsing rhythmically, like the aftershocks of an earthquake, leaking, with each spasm, ever-smaller amounts of our viscous come.

"Fuck, that was awesome," Porter said. "O? You feel that? Fuckin' awesome!"

It's hard to describe *what* I was feeling at that moment, but it was not fucking awesome. It was more like fucking nasty. I could not believe we had shot our seed into that black-lipped maw.

"Get out of the way, Jade. Step aside," Bandana Man said. "I want to see it. Is it . . . does *it* have two heads?"

I had the sudden urge to get up, head to the bathroom, and wash off Vixana's slimy saliva. I managed only to stuff ourself back in our jeans, wiping my hand on the couch and wondering how many other guys previously might have done the same. My skin crawled. I hated Bandana Man at that moment, hated this sleazy bitch, hated Porter for getting us into this situation and myself for allowing it to happen. I could not believe our first sexual encounter had unfolded in such a tawdry fashion.

I've since come to recognize and anticipate a blue period after an orgasm, when I feel low and dirty, depressed and ashamed, and I also know that feeling passes, especially if I am with someone I care about. But at that moment, all I

wanted to do was zip up and leave, to get as far away as possible from that nasty apartment and its creepy inhabitants,
who now seemed like so many extras on the set of *The Texas
Chain Saw Massacre*. But Porter was blissfully immobilized,
and Bandana Man had gone to the kitchen and emerged with
a six-pack of Rolling Rock longnecks, which he distributed,
grinning and shaking his head, chuckling to himself like a
madman.

"Craziest fuckin' thing I've ever seen," he said, "two guys
getting off on one blow job. I wouldn't have thought it was
possible—but man, she rocked both your worlds at the same
time. Far fucking out."

Porter tapped my arm twice with the neck of his bottle.

"O, little help?"

I unscrewed the cap while he held the bottle.

"Yours?"

I had set my beer down on the utility-cable-spool coffee
table, not wanting to stay long enough to drink it, but I
sighed, picked it up, and let him help me open it.

"O? You okay?"

"I'm beat, man. Let's get the fuck home."

"Hang on. One more beer. It's not polite to blow and
go . . . so to speak."

But Vixana had other ideas. She settled herself next to
Porter again. What kind of people were these—performing
sex acts in front of each other? I wondered if it were an
everyday occurrence or if it was only because Porter and I
were a curiosity. Another joint appeared at my hand, and I
gave up any hope of getting out of there anytime soon. I took
a hit, and then another, before passing it to Porter. At some
point, Porter swallowed another "chill pill."

When I came to, Porter and I were naked in Jade's bed,
and there, too, was she, Vixana Regina, in all her glory. Her
flesh was a pale blue-white in the wan morning light, her ass
waxen and dimpled like cottage cheese. It was the first time I

had seen a woman so up close and personal, and I averted my eyes. *Oh my god,* was all I could think, over and over. *How fucking disgusting is this?*

"Porter," I hissed, not wanting to rouse Vixana. "Porter, wake up!"

I reached across our chest and shook his shoulder until he stirred.

"Wha-a? Fuck, man, I feel like shit."

I waited for him to discover our circumstances.

"Whoa! Christ! Damn!" he said, jerking us into an up-right position.

"Shhh. Quiet! Listen, we've got to get out of here—now!"

"Oh man, this is bad."

"It will be worse if she wakes up. Hopefully, she's as wasted as we are."

"You're right, man. As bad as it is to wake up next to a scrawny, naked bitch, waking up with a two-headed guy has got to be worse!"

Like Porter, I felt like shit—flushed, nauseated, with a nearly blinding headache. On top of which I felt vulnerable and a bit confused. I remembered the gig the night before, talking to Vixana in the parking lot, following her home. I remembered smoking a little weed and drinking a little wine. I recalled, with some disgust, getting blown. And then . . . nothing. I remembered falling down at some point. Getting up. A voice in my ear.

I freaked. What had happened in that bed? I had no recol-lection but hoped Porter might; somehow, his tolerance of drugs was marginally higher than mine. Had we fucked her? Had we used a condom? Or had she merely blown us again? I worried about pregnancy . . . disease . . . scandal.

I was certain that if Vixana woke up, there would be hell to pay. She'd probably lose it, freak out, go apeshit. In the clear light of day, she might allege rape to counter the shame and disgust she felt at having slept with a freak. But with luck, if we were gone, she might consider it nothing more than a bad dream.

Porter and I got out of bed carefully, picked up our clothes, cautiously opened the bedroom door (the hinges always squeak in dumps like that). I looked out into the living room. The coast was clear. From the other bedroom, we heard the sounds of Bandana Man banging the roommate. They were still going at it?

On the street, we were momentarily disoriented. Porter thought the van was to the right; I knew it was to the left. When we got back to our apartment, all I wanted to do was shower. I was afraid I might puke, which invariably would set Porter off. That's the way it happened when we were kids. Before we got into the shower, Porter took our penis in his hand and rubbed it between thumb and forefinger, then brought his hand to his nose and inhaled.

"What the fuck are you doing?" I asked.

He grabbed hold of my upper lip, his index finger just below my nostrils.

"Inhale!"

"What?"

"Smell that. Does it smell like pussy to you?"

I grabbed him by the wrist and pushed his hand away.

"You sick fuck! I don't know what pussy smells like and I don't care. Why should I?"

"I'm trying to figure out if we fucked her."

"Oh my god, that's so gross."

"We should probably know. We should probably try to figure it out, just in case there are consequences."

"Jesus, Porter."

He sniffed his fingers again. "Unless you put one on us, I don't think we used a rubber. But I don't smell pussy, so I think we're okay."

"You know this never would have happened if you had listened to me."

"Hell man, we got laid. Or at least blown. I don't remember much about it, but I do remember that. It was awesome."

"Yeah, well, just remember when we have to go to the VD clinic for a shot, you're gonna take it in your side of our ass."

I grabbed a pump bottle of antibacterial hand soap from the sink and brought it into the shower with us. I lathered and rinsed ourself repeatedly, until Porter stopped me.

"O—dude!—you keep washing our thing like that, we're not going to have anything left. I'm sure we're okay. I mean, it didn't look like she had such terrible oral hygiene or anything."

We didn't have another gig scheduled at the pub for two months, and when that one rolled around I wanted to cancel it. But neither Vixana nor Bandana Man showed up, and in the months that followed there were no surprise appearances by process servers informing us of a paternity suit. We had dodged a bullet.

But Vixana was only the first of Porter's sexual conquests. Despite the murky circumstances of our deflowering, the experience gave Porter the confidence to put the make on other groupies, and in the following months I lost track of the number of women with whom he had sex. They didn't seem real to me. Thrill seekers and sluts, I called them. They seemed to have been recruited from the green room of a *Best of Jerry Springer* taping or a Jenny Jones episode called "The Family That Lays Together Stays Together." But Porter didn't seem to care.

"They're nasty, for sure," he said. "But where would we be without them?"

"Correction: Where would *you* be without them?"

"Home alone is where. Wankin' to porno."

On breaks during our sophomore and junior years at Druid Hills, we did some small, regional road trips, just Porter and me and a couple of guys to help with the driving and the setups. Birmingham–New Orleans–Nashville. Boston–New York–Washington. Florida. Texas. We were saving the West Coast until we got bigger. On the road after every show, there was usually a party in the roadies' motel room, and there was always at least one chick who would come on to us. They were usually high or drunk. They giggled and told us how good looking we were, how much they loved our music. They flirted with both of us. Maybe at that point they were so out of it they thought they were just *seeing* double. Porter would suggest to the girl that they go back to our room, and she would either suck us or allow herself to get fucked. Ninety percent of the time they'd prefer to do it doggie style; even drunk, I think it was too much for them to be face-to-face with us. Several of them did ask to have their pictures taken with us, though, usually with disposable cameras they had in their purses. None of them ever stayed.

In light of the Vixana incident, I always made sure we used condoms when we fucked, although we never used one when we got blown. I was concerned about sexually transmitted diseases and researched the likelihood of oral-genital transmission from female to male, which seemed infinitesimal, so I stopped making a stink about it.

During these encounters, I generally tried to distance myself from what was going on. I usually occupied myself by reciting the states and state capitals silently, first alphabetically by state—Alabama, Alaska, Arizona—then again by city—Albany, Annapolis, Atlanta—forward and backward. (If Porter was particularly horny, we very rarely got past *Montpeeeeeeelier*!) If there was time, I'd begin on the periodic table of elements, alphabetically and then by atomic number. While Porter was shouting out obscenities as he approached climax, I sometimes lost myself and screamed aloud, "Potassium, calcium, scandium, titanium, vanadium!" This was, granted, an acquired skill and one I spent hours perfecting in my spare time. But it was well worth it, as it truly insulated me from the matter at hand. Unfortunately, it sometimes worked too well and we risked losing our erection due to my complete lack of interest, at which time Porter usually shouted to me, "Forget the fucking chemistry lesson, bro, and help me out here!"

Chapter 7

Porter has always been the more physical of the two of us—and the more sexually precocious. It came as no surprise to me that he was the first to lose his virginity. (As far as I was concerned, I was still a virgin.) But as Porter gained ever more sexual experience, I grew restive; I wondered what *my* romantic fate would be. I was twenty-one years old and, exclusive of my inevitable and somewhat reluctant participation in Porter's amorous adventures, my sex life to date had been entirely masturbatory, facilitated by gay skin magazines, anthologies of gay "friction," and the occasional pornographic video.

When I was in my early teens and pornography was the only outlet for most boys—straight or gay—it was a promise of pleasures yet to come, the paradise we would find in the sexual Shangri-la of adulthood. Like other boys our age, Porter and I looked at *Playboy*, or in my case *Playgirl*, as a divinely inspired Sears catalog of sex, assuming the "products" featured within their pages would become available to us once we were old enough to purchase them and had the wherewithal to do so. Porter began ordering from that catalog much earlier than I was able to. Although he did not actually have sex until we were in college, he got an inkling of what life had to offer in high school as a jock-hero, when girls like Christi Oakes were presented to him, gift-wrapped, on a regular basis, like selections from the Fruit-of-the-Month

Club. The products and services in which I was interested were far more rare and came at a much higher price—when you could find them.

I suppose I was something of a reluctant romantic. I had been satisfied simply to spend time in the company of men I secretly adored, to admire them furtively, to take pleasure in their mere existence. I'd had adolescent crushes on movie stars like Brad Pitt, as well as vivid sexual fantasies involving more unsavory characters such as Bandana Man. But knowing my desires were different—some would say unnatural—I felt that was all I was entitled to. So I was more than willing to accept love as a one-way street; in fact, I *wallowed* in the concept of unrequited love, pining away for a succession of handsome, athletic boys and young men in high school and during my first three years at Druid Hills. I'd carried a torch, futilely, for Wayne Parks for the remainder of our time at Lovett and developed crushes on classmates at Druid Hills— Garrick, a blond soccer player from Chicago who was majoring in philosophy; J.D., a theology major from Boston; Dennis, a diminutive bioengineering major from the little town of Punxsutawney, Pennsylvania, made famous by its groundhog. I was satisfied just to spend time in their company, more interested in gaining their trust and friendship than in actually having sex, with all the technical difficulties and emotional entanglements that would involve (not the least of which would be getting Porter to agree to actually let me have sex with another man). And, of course, I lived in fear of the rejection I knew was inevitable should I ever confess my feelings to any of my unsuspecting paramours. They were all straight, as far as I could tell, but even if they weren't, a freak like me would never stand a chance with them. I considered myself lucky even to have them as friends, and I would rather have their friendship, however exasperating, than their enmity.

But there ultimately came a time when I decided my sanity depended on figuring out how to meet eligible gay men. Gay bars were out of the question: Porter absolutely refused to be seen in one. He didn't want anyone to think *he* was gay. I didn't press the point because, frankly, I wasn't keen on bars myself. Most strangers are reluctant to initiate a conversation with either of us in even the most basic social settings; it would take an *extraordinary* man to approach me in a situation in which even a simple exchange of pleasantries is tantamount to flirtation. I can only imagine what might happen in a gay bar: I'd catch the eye of an attractive man across a crowded room and he'd cock his head, stop talking to the person next to him, smile for just a fraction of a second . . . and then he'd notice Porter. The smile would change, become sort of enigmatic, quizzical. And then—shock, horror, disbelief.

So I decided to meet people outside of bars, in situations in which being gay was the common element but in which sex wasn't the ultimate goal. During my freshman year, I had signed up to help prepare food at Project Open Hand, which provides meals for homebound AIDS patients and other shut-ins. Later, I volunteered at AID Atlanta, the city's main AIDS service agency, and I worked with the Atlanta Pride Committee helping organize the annual gay pride march up Peachtree Street to Piedmont Park.

Initially, Porter grumbled about doing volunteer work. He said he just didn't see the point of giving up that much time to help other people. (I didn't let on that I had ulterior motives.) I suppose he had a right to have his say. After all, he'd have to lend a hand to whatever we were doing: stuffing envelopes or assembling safe-sex kits at AID Atlanta; packing lunches at Project Open Hand. But I reminded him that over the years I had done plenty of things he enjoyed but in which I had little or no interest—playing football, for example, or going out on dates with girls.

This was really the first time I had taken the initiative to get out into the world myself, to do something I wanted to do that Porter would have never done on his own. Neither of us had ever done volunteer work of any type (I imagine most people thought we should be the recipients of charity, not the providers), nor had we ever been in a social setting in which the participants were predominantly gay.

I never know quite what to expect from people the first time we meet. Porter and I had long ago agreed never to apologize to anyone for our appearance or to warn people what to expect when they met us for the first time. Invariably, people are startled, if not shocked into speechlessness. It is impossible to predict how any given person will respond, whether they will be able to muster enough composure to deal with whatever it is that needs to be dealt with, or whether they will have to excuse themselves, leave the room to gather their wits, to laugh, to cry, to alert their co-workers to the presence of a two-headed man at the ticket counter or check-in desk, to pick up the phone and make a breathless, hysterical call to a friend. I suspect that after meeting us, some people laugh or cry uncontrollably once we're out of earshot. I imagine some even lose bladder control.

Not surprisingly, I found the people at both AID Atlanta and Project Open Hand to be more mature and considerate than most, more willing to accept Porter and me, more eager to embrace us—literally. Both organizations originated in response to the AIDS crisis, and the people who volunteered for them were, by definition, compassionate, committed individuals who wanted to reach out to others in need. So it seemed natural they would be more willing to accept us. Nor was I alone among the volunteers who viewed these activities as a social outlet. People said as much to me. They didn't like bars, couldn't stand cigarette smoke, abhorred loud music, but wanted to meet other gay men. One guy called it "compassionate cruising."

I met some wonderful people through my volunteer work, including some guys I was definitely interested in, but I never mustered the courage to actually ask anyone out on a date, nor did anyone ever seriously approach me. The difficulty I had finding dates contrasted sharply with the ease with which Porter scored with women, something that had always baffled me. I found it hard to believe women were easier to bed than gay men; from everything I had read or heard, the reverse was true. Nor did I think the women who chose to sleep with Porter were desperate. In fact, they were quite attractive. I finally decided it was simply a numbers game: Porter had a shot with nine out of ten women he encountered; my odds were considerably worse, maybe one out of ten at best. Add to that the fact that the venues we played did not attract a significant number of gay men, and my dismal batting average was more understandable.

Occasionally, though, someone at AID Atlanta or Project Open Hand would ask me (and, necessarily, Porter) to their home for cocktails or dinner. One such invitation came from John Weiss and Mark Sandler, a pair of schoolteachers who owned a renovated bungalow in Virginia-Highland, an in-town neighborhood that had benefited from an influx of yuppies and gay men in the 1980s. Mark was forty-five but appeared to be in his late thirties: handsome, if short, with a compact, athletic build and black hair. John was ten years older, stocky, with wiry salt-and-pepper hair. They had been together for more than twenty years.

Porter has *never* enjoyed spending time with my friends. It wouldn't matter if they were gay or straight; we're just too different. (Though in all fairness, I have never been particularly thrilled with his choice of companions, either, and generally found myself bored in their company, except for those rare friends of his upon whom I developed crushes—feelings I naturally worked hard to hide from Porter.) The idea of spending an evening with John and Mark in particular did not appeal to Porter.

"Could they *be* more boring?" Porter asked. "I mean, a pair of gay schoolteachers. They're like an old married couple. The least you could do if you're going to force me to spend time with your gay friends is to get to know some more interesting people."

"Like who? The head-banging morons you hang out with whose only thought is where their next line of coke is going to come from?"

This was an extreme example. In fact, Porter and I had a good number of friends in common, mostly musicians and people associated with the industry, some of whom happened to be gay, although that was not a significant factor in our friendship. But each of us also had friends the other could not relate to or found boring or did not like, and clearly John and Mark fell into that category for Porter. Although he complained about it before we went—and would continue to lament the loss of an evening once we got home—there was little Porter could do to prevent me from spending time with whomever I chose, as long as it was on one of "my" days. That was a core principle of our relationship.

"My advice to you, Porter, is just to forget they are gay. If you can't connect with them as people, just think of them as teachers and give them the same respect we gave to our instructors at Lovett. I know that doesn't sound very exciting, but I think you might be pleasantly surprised if you just give them a chance to be themselves."

Both John and Mark had come out in the 1970s, when gay sex was in its heyday and almost every social situation offered up a sexual smorgasbord, and they were able to offer me firsthand insights into the way gay life had been then, as well as what I could expect today.

"You're a handsome man, Owen," Mark said as we sat in their living room sipping after-dinner drinks. "You, too, of course, Porter. And you're smart and funny and more well-adjusted than most guys we know. I know the right man will come along for you someday."

"But we won't lie to you," John added. "It's tough to find a good man, even without the obvious challenges you're up against."

Mark sighed. "The truth is," he said, "there is nothing in nature as unforgiving as the homosexual male. Judgments are made in instants. Nanoseconds. 'Yes/no.' As simple as that. 'In a heartbeat/not on your life.' Rarely is there a middle ground. A middle ground would take time. Contemplation. No, decisions must be made. Constantly."

To hear John and Mark tell it, it was as if all gay men were quality-control inspectors on some cosmic assembly line, winnowing out defective widgets from the thousands that rolled past them on the frayed rubber belt, but in the inverse, selecting maybe one out of a hundred men as acceptable and letting the others roll into oblivion. The process takes place during every second of every waking hour of every day of their adult lives, and it is all based on appearance: the quality of skin, hair, bone, and the overall effect of the way in which they are assembled. It depressed me to hear such things.

"Porter, you date, don't you?" Mark asked. "Owen's said you don't have any trouble with the ladies."

"Though I didn't call them ladies," I said.

"Thanks a lot, bro," Porter said. "But they're not exactly ladies, I'll admit."

"He did date a lovely girl in high school," I added.

"You know," John said, "it may be easier for Porter to get dates because a woman is looking for something in a man that she doesn't have herself, even if in this day and age that can be boiled down to a teaspoonful of his ejaculate."

"In the gay world, it's not the case of opposites attracting, but of likes," Mark said. "Instead of men being attracted to women, like to unlike, north magnetic pole to south, it's man to man, like to like, north to north. So many gay couples I see look disconcertingly alike—similar height, weight, coloring, hairstyle, even general facial features. It's less exaggerated today, but at one time it was actually so desirable to look like the men you found sexually attractive that the word 'clone' came to represent the gay physical ideal."

"Remember that couple in the early nineties, Bob Paris and Rod Jackson?" John said to Mark.

"The bodybuilders?" Mark said. "The ones who did that hot coffee-table book?"

"Yeah, they posed for nude photographs, and the similarity of their bodies was striking. Even though one of them was blond and one dark-haired, in most other respects they seemed identical to one another. And there, I suppose, lay the attraction. It was as if they were making love to themselves—the pinnacle of narcissism."

"Whatever happened to them?" I asked.

"Divorced. Messy, messy, very public," John said. "How could it not be?"

The whole idea that guys seek out other men who could be their twins was painfully ironic, since I am inextricably linked to a person who is genetically identical to me, inseparable, and yet unlike me in the most elemental way. I suppose if Porter were gay, we might have a perfect, if incestuous, homosexual union. I think a lot of people suspect that might actually be the case, and if they knew that I frequently jerked him off, their suspicions would be confirmed.

"Of course, not all gay men are attracted to the same thing," John added. "Hard as it is to believe, not every gay man is attracted to nineteen-year-old blond surfers. Some gay men actually *like* bellies and prefer bald to blond. A few actually choose brain over brawn, as my husband would attest."

But who in the world, I wondered, would ever find *me* attractive? Where on the hierarchy of desirable attributes does one find two-headed? Might I suggest at the very bottom? Below every other possible human attribute or disability. Two-dicked might go over spectacularly well. Oh yes, that would be an advantage. No matter how odd it might sound at first or how ungainly it might be, a gay man would find a way to capitalize on it. But two *heads*? (And on top of that, but one dick between them.) No, two heads are decidedly not better than one.

John and Mark told me that at the very least, having sex might have been easier for me twenty or thirty years ago, before the AIDS epidemic. Specifically, they said I would have benefited from the practice of "tearoom" sex: anonymous encounters in bathrooms and at the rest areas of interstate highways accomplished through that uniquely gay invention, the glory hole, created by cutting through the partitions between stalls. Some men were drawn to this type of sex by the danger, John said, others by the anonymity. For me it would have been entirely a matter of logistics. Sitting in a restroom stall, I would have been able to disguise or withhold the fact that I was two-headed. The sexual act would be reduced to its basic elements: a cock, a mouth. My partner would never have to know the penis he was sucking served the psyches of two men, or conversely that the creature who was servicing him was capable of fellatio and oration simultaneously—that is, if Porter were given to public speaking.

Chapter 8

In the summer between our junior and senior years at Druid Hills, Porter and I ran in the torch relay for the Centennial Olympic Games in Atlanta, each of us carrying the flame for half the allotted distance. We were featured in an "Olympic Minute," and Janus performed onstage during the closing ceremonies. The response was overwhelming. Our phone rang off the hook with offers of club dates, national television appearances, and auditions for several major record labels. *People* magazine photographed us for 1997's "Fifty Most Beautiful People" issue, scheduled to appear the following May. (I insisted to the reporter who interviewed us that we be counted as two of the fifty, not one, and she assured me that would be the case, as it had been with Mary Kate and Ashley Olsen before us.) It quickly became obvious that we were going to have to hire an agent—and possibly a business manager—if we wanted to keep our sanity while at the same time cash in on our newfound popularity.

When we returned to campus in the fall, I sensed a change in the way people reacted to us. Previously, strangers had always given us our space. From time to time, I'd seen people cross the street or cut diagonally across the Quad to avoid us—discreetly, of course, but quite deliberately. What other explanation was there for their repeated sidelong glances as they angled away from us? But our increased visibility at the Olympics had given people permission to look at us. I suppose they reasoned that if we were willing to put ourselves on display in such a public way, we had to expect them to stare. But it also made people *want* to be seen with us; we were now truly famous, not merely freaks but celebrities.

We were still buzzing with the excitement of the Olympics when we began our senior year, and it took considerable effort to refocus on our studies. But as hard as it was for me to adjust to the mundane realities of school, it was nearly impossible for Porter, who was majoring in music and had lost interest in pretty much everything else. He preferred being in the studio working out the kinks in his latest composition, and if it were up to him he never would have gone to class.

Porter has never been much of a scholar. One Halloween years ago I suggested we trick-or-treat as Jekyll and Hyde, but when we began assembling the material for our costumes, it became clear to me Porter thought I had meant Heckle and Jeckle, the wise-guy crows we'd seen on Saturday morning cartoons. ("What'll we use for the beaks?" he asked.) If it were up to him, we would have quit school, despite the fact that we were within striking distance of graduation, moved to L.A., and worked on our music full time. To an extent, I empathized with him; I was majoring in English, with a minor in film studies, and was less interested in writing papers than poetry, which I then turned into lyrics. Our parents were adamant about us finishing college, however, and forbade us from making any significant career moves until the spring. Porter objected, but I had always placed a premium on doing the right thing—gaining the respect and approval of my teachers and other adults, my parents in particular—and earning my degree from Druid Hills seemed like the ultimate form of respectability.

At a meeting with our faculty adviser at the beginning of the semester, I was shocked to discover that Porter was missing two of his mandatory liberal arts requirements, which he had somehow overlooked. It seemed entirely likely he wouldn't graduate with me in May, and I knew if he didn't finish by then, he never would. If that were the case, I would never hear the end of it.

For as long as I can remember, I have been made to feel responsible for Porter's success in school, although "success" seems like an overstatement—with Porter, it was more like a struggle for simple survival. I always outperformed him on standardized achievement tests by a considerable margin, although no one precisely knew why. Our parents found this irksome, if not downright troubling; our teachers called it "curious" and "pedagogically interesting." What baffled everyone was not merely the *existence* of a disparity between two genetically identical individuals reared in precisely the same environment, but its scope. Was it biological? Had Porter somehow been compromised in the process of separation? Had I gotten more of what had once been our common brain? Or was it more personal, emotional? Had my early successes demotivated Porter?

Regardless, not only my mother and father but also my teachers seemed to be pointing the finger at me. Their fears seemed somewhat atavistic, shrouded in ignorance, cloaked in the unfathomable mystery of double birth. I knew better. The answer was obvious: Porter was lazy, pure and simple. He didn't *want* to study, didn't *want* to read, and so he didn't. When it came time for us to do homework, he would lose interest quickly and turn to doodling, fire up a handheld computer game, or put on a pair of headphones and listen to music. If anything, *he* hobbled *me* with all his interruptions and distractions. When I was done with my homework, he'd grab my paper or my workbook and copy my answers onto his own. My protestations that Porter had cheated fell on deaf ears.

"Now, Owen," my father cautioned me on one of those occasions, "you know you have a responsibility to help your brother keep up in class."

I knew no such thing.

"Porter takes responsibility for your body by exercising

for both of you," Dad continued. "It's only fair that you take responsibility for his intellectual development."

Of course, that was not exactly true. Porter did *not* exercise for both of us. What he did was to force me to exercise *with* him, but I matched him bench press for bench press, leg lift for leg lift. (I'd long ago given up complaining about Porter's obsession with perfecting our body. Both Mom and Dad were convinced it was a good thing, that it helped socialize us, and that in the end it might help us overcome as-yet-unforeseen medical problems that could arise due to our "condition.")

In contrast, I was being asked to carry Porter scholastically with very little assistance from him. When the time came for a heart-to-heart with our parents or our guidance counselors, *I* was always the one who found myself on the hot seat—if not actually as the cause of the problem, then as the one person who might be able to do something about it.

So that fall, when we went to see an assistant dean about the coursework that would be necessary to fulfill Porter's graduation requirements, I found myself on familiar ground. Although I was ambivalent about the effort it would take to get him up to speed—attending Porter's added classes as well as my own would put a considerable burden on me—I nonetheless agreed to do so, and I used our lifelong habit of alternating days to force him out of the studio and into the library.

Two months into the semester, on one of "my"days, we were studying at the Woodward Library, where I was researching a paper titled "Identity and Role Reversal in *The Prince and the Pauper*," using archival materials from the special collections department that were on closed reserve. (My interest in Mark Twain had begun with the misadventures of a pair of conjoined twins in *Pudd'nhead Wilson*, and Twain was the subject of my senior honors thesis.) Porter, characteristically, was using the time to scribble down some musical notation. We were seated at a large table in one of the common areas of the library—a carrel didn't provide enough surface space for both of us to work simultaneously—and Porter was irritating people near us by humming and tapping out the beat to a new song with his pencil. As distracting as this habit was to others, it was actually an important part of our creative process, and I often found myself making up words to go with the tunes Porter hummed, without either of us exchanging a word. I had long since grown accustomed to it, but the library was not the place for it, and it embarrassed me when he got so loud he annoyed other people.

Then, suddenly, Porter fell quiet. I was more conscious of the silence than I had been of the noise; it was as if someone had turned off a droning television set in an adjacent room. I looked up from my work and saw we were no longer alone. A young woman had sat down across from us and was spreading out her things on the highly polished surface of the blond wood table: three fat textbooks, a notepad, purse, pens. Out of the corner of my eye, I could see Porter staring straight at her, his pencil quivering between thumb and forefinger like a metronome on methamphetamines.

For her part, she appeared to be completely self-absorbed as she neatly laid out her belongings, seemingly unaware of our presence. For a moment, I wondered why she had chosen to join us, but the library was busier than usual for a Friday night and there appeared to be few other places to sit. Despite our recent skyrocketing popularity—or perhaps because of it—I remained suspicious of strangers and usually considered anyone who chose to be around us suspect, a voyeur at best, at worst a frat boy completing his initiation. So I was a bit wary, even though there was nothing in particular about her other than her choice of seats that set off my perimeter alarm. She was pretty in an unspectacular way, conservatively dressed, with straight, medium-length dark brown hair; a fair, faintly freckled complexion; and blue eyes. She reminded me of Brooke Adams, a minor actress I

had always thought of as second runner-up in an Ali Mac-
Graw look-alike contest. I smiled at her, tightly, and returned
to my book.

Porter was less judgmental, less cautious with strangers,
and perhaps that's why he had more friends. He rarely
stopped to consider people's motives but generally accepted
everyone at face value, especially pretty young women. And
so, predictably, he chose to introduce himself.

He cleared his throat. "I'm Porter Jamison," he said.
"And this is my brother, Owen."

The young woman looked at him and smiled—somewhat
stiffly, I thought.

"I know," she said.

"Have we met before?"

"No, but I know who you are. The two of you. You
know . . . I've read about you in the *Constitution*. Although I
didn't know . . . which was which."

She seemed embarrassed, looking down for an instant as
if she had lost her place in a speech, then back up at Porter.
Her smile, while seemingly genuine, appeared self-conscious,
as if she were wondering what the people around us might be
thinking.

"Well, I'm Porter," he repeated, extending his arm across
the table, pulling me forward with him.

"Faith Colquitt. Pleased to meet you." She offered a small
porcelain hand, a charm bracelet dangling loosely from her
slender wrist. An old-fashioned girl. It was, well . . . *charming*.
Porter's heart skipped a beat—I felt it—and his cheek burned
next to mine.

"Nice to meet you, Faith Colquitt," he said, swallowing
hard. I remained silent until he kicked me under the table.

"Likewise," I said, with another forced smile. I felt bad
even before Porter kicked me. I hadn't meant to be rude or
hurt the girl's feelings. It wasn't *her* I objected to, not her
specifically, but I knew she would distract Porter for the re-

mainder of the evening, and I wouldn't make much progress on my paper.

"Don't mind him," Porter said. "He can be a jerk."

"I'm sorry," I said. "I'm just kind of distracted. I've got a big paper due, and . . ."

"I understand. Don't let me bother you," Faith said. She smiled and picked up one of her books, turned its cover toward us, and frowned. "Big test Monday."

A physiology textbook. *Ah ha!* I thought. *Professional curiosity.*

"Are you pre-med?" Porter asked.

"Nursing."

"Cool," he said.

It sounded like a moronic thing to say—what could possibly be "cool" about nursing?—but she seemed oblivious to its transparency.

"And you? What are you majoring in?"

"Music," he said.

"Music?" She seemed surprised, as if she expected someone in our condition to be enrolled in vocational education.

"Owen's majoring in English."

She didn't comment on my choice of majors. I could have been majoring in Swahili or animal husbandry for all she cared.

"Composition or performance?"

"A little bit of both. I play guitar. Well, *we* do. Owen strums while I finger the chords. I write the music, and he takes care of the lyrics."

I'll admit to being pleased that he kept trying to introduce me into the conversation—he was not always so thoughtful—but she looked at Porter as if she were seeing him and him alone, as if *I* were invisible. After her apparent initial discomfort, her gaze never faltered, never disengaged from his. It was quite remarkable.

"That's right, of course. You've got a band . . ."

"Right. Janus. We've just signed a contract to produce our first *real* CD, although we do have a self-produced one out already."

"Do you sing or just play?"

Clearly, she meant did *he* sing, not did *we* sing.

"We both sing. We swap lead and harmony depending on the song."

"I'd like to hear you sometime."

"We're playing at Eddie's Attic next weekend," I said. I wasn't going to be totally ignored—and I knew I wasn't going to get anything done until Porter concluded his conversation with her. "One of our increasingly rare local gigs."

"Come," Porter said. "Come hear us."

"I'd like that."

Faith had never been to Eddie's, so Porter gave her directions. I thought we were making progress and I'd soon be able to return to my work, but each time their conversation appeared to wane, Porter found a new topic to explore. We ultimately learned that she was a senior in the nursing school, lived in Truman Hall, was from a small town in south Georgia where her family grew cotton, had four sisters (three of whom had preceded her into the nursing field) and a "baby brother" (apparently a computer whiz at MIT), and was a big fan of a little-known folk singer named Cheryl Wheeler. From time to time, people around us would clear their throats or make that clucking noise with their tongues that indicated their patience was being tried. Porter couldn't maintain a whisper for long (it was partly my fault; he tried to lean across the table but I held back in the hope of discouraging further conversation), and after he was shushed several times, he asked Faith out for coffee, right then and there, without so much as *hinting* to me about his intentions. Much to my amazement, she agreed, and Porter started packing up his stuff, over my muted objections. For Porter's sake, I didn't protest too much. I already had done enough to make Faith feel awkward and uncomfortable, and I was sure everyone else in the library was eager for us to leave. But I was pissed.

"You can study just as well at Starbucks as you can here," Porter said to me in the voice we used when speaking to each other—low, flat, soft, though not quite a whisper—as I returned the reserve materials I had been using for my paper.

"You know perfectly well I can't. Not for this particular paper. We're going to have to come back tomorrow, on *your* time, for me to finish up."

"All right, all right. Just humor me. I like this girl."

What's not to like? I thought. *She's breathing, and she hasn't yet run screaming from the room.*

Chapter 9

"Do you believe in love at first sight?" Porter asked me later that night in bed.

"What?"

He turned his head toward mine so his words warmed my cheek. "Love at first sight. Do you believe in it?"

"You're in *love* with that girl?"

"Her name is Faith."

"And you're in love with her?"

"I think so," he said, returning his gaze to the ceiling.

"Porter," I sighed. I was still irritated with him for having interrupted my research and was in no mood for some grandiose romantic discussion, especially one so premature.

"No, I mean it," he said.

"You're in love with her?"

"Yeah. And I think she likes me. There's a connection there—I know it."

I suppose I should have expected as much; the chemistry between the two of them *was* undeniable. After a nearly silent walk from the library to the Starbucks on the periphery of campus, occasionally punctuated by somewhat lame comments about the crisp autumnal weather or some arcane architectural detail of the Quadrangle, they had warmed up to each other and talked nonstop over coffee—the sort of innocuous, rambling, breathless conversation that characterizes first dates: family, hobbies, travel, hopes for the future. Porter talked at length about his glory days at Lovett, Faith about her siblings, especially her exceptionally gifted younger brother. I sipped a decaf latte, ignored them as best I could, and tried to read. But soon I could feel the caffeine from Porter's Café Americano coursing through my veins, and could feel something else, too—a sense of excitement or engagement I hadn't observed since Christi Oakes had broken up with him three years earlier. I tried to tune out their conversation, but occasionally I was distracted by Faith's laugh, and once I saw her stroke Porter's hand with the tips of her fingers, lightly, almost absentmindedly, but with surprising intimacy, and felt another jolt in our shared circulatory system. After nearly an hour, I yawned and looked at my watch.

"I'm keeping you," she said, returning the same tight-lipped smile I had twice bestowed on her earlier that evening.

"Not *me*," Porter said deliberately. "I'm fine."

"But your brother," she said.

Porter knew his limits with me, and he grudgingly admitted that perhaps we *had* better go. He kept his thoughts mostly to himself after we walked her back to her dorm, save for an occasional, "Oh my god, oh my god, oh my god," that bubbled up from deep inside him. Now, in bed, *now* he wanted to talk. He should not have had that second Americano.

"You're just horny," I said. "We can take care of that." I reached under the covers and laid my hand on our penis.

"Stop," he said.

"What?"

"That." He reached down and pushed my hand away.

"That's a first," I said. "*You*—not wanting to get off."

"Leave it alone, Owen."

"It's 'my' day, Porter. I get to do what I want." I grabbed hold of our penis.

He turned to look at the clock on his bedside table.

"It's 12:36, Owen. It's Saturday, 'my' day now, and I say we don't." He pushed my hand away again.

"Jesus! I've never known you to turn down a hand job. You can think about her while I do it."

"I don't want to. I don't want to think about her that way. Not while you jerk us off."

"Fine. You do it."

"I told you, I don't want to. I don't want to . . . defile her."

"You don't want to 'defile' her?"

"My thoughts of her."

"Who is she, the Virgin Mary?"

"Shut the fuck up, Owen."

"How is a hand job going to defile her?"

"It will if you do it."

"What? Why?"

"You'll be thinking of guys. I don't want to come while I'm thinking of her and you're thinking of guys."

"Jesus Christ, Porter. That's the most convoluted fucking logic I think I've ever heard!"

"Just leave it alone, Owen."

Porter cupped his hand protectively over our penis to prevent me from getting at it. He didn't say another word, and we both lay there in silence, angry, I suppose, for different reasons. It took a long time for his breathing to become regular. I suppose he was thinking about Faith. And yet, he didn't get an erection. What was going on in that head of his? Porter was such a horndog that I found it difficult to believe he could be thinking about a woman and yet remain unaroused. He *must* be in love. But then, he had been in love with Christi and that had never stopped him from wanking. In fact, I think it had increased the frequency of our masturbatory sessions. He needed it, especially after a long makeout session in the backseat of Gary's dad's car. We'd get home, make small talk with Mom or Dad downstairs for a few minutes, then head upstairs to our room. He wouldn't even let me brush my teeth before we stripped down and jumped into bed. "Do me, Owen. Do me, man," he'd say, and he'd close his eyes and, I suppose, think about Christi, lose himself in his sexual fantasies, pretending it was her hand on his cock while I brought him off. "Oh fuck, man. Oh yeah. I love you, Christi," he'd say, arching back into his pillow, his arm crooked back over his head, his hand sometimes running through his hair. Of course, I knew he didn't really believe she was there, because when it was over, he'd always say, "Thanks, O. Thanks, man."

This was, as far as I could remember, the first time he had ever declined the offer of a hand job *and* refused to do it himself. It worried me. And it made me mad. Not only was he denying himself the pleasure of our regular nightly wank, he was denying me the pleasure as well. And why? Because my "dirty" thoughts about men would defile his newfound girlfriend. Defile her! As if I were somehow going to pin her down and come on her face. This did not bode well. If I was not even going to be allowed to think about men while Porter jerked off, if he felt so strongly about it that he would deny himself an orgasm, what would he think when it came time for me to have sex with another man?

I felt betrayed. After all, I had sacrificed my time in the library so Porter could make small talk with Faith at Starbucks. That should be worth something, shouldn't it? Some gratitude? Some understanding? One of the reasons I had acquiesced so quickly to the impromptu trip to Starbucks was that I knew how rare it was for a respectable girl—a girl with real potential—to show interest in Porter, and I knew how lonely he had been since he had broken up with Christi Oakes. Oh, he'd had plenty of sexual encounters recently, but all of them had been one-night stands, most of them on the road and none with girls he could bring home to Mom. Obviously, this Faith was different. Like Christi, she was a "good" girl, eminently presentable. Mom would start making wedding plans as soon as she met her.

Our mother had something of a hair trigger when it came

to the question of romance for her boys, so it was under-standable that her interest in Porter's amorous prospects—and, presumably, mine—went far beyond that of any typical mother. In the beginning, she was mainly concerned that our feelings not be hurt, that we didn't get our hopes up or be-come the victims of some elaborate hoax perpetrated by cruel classmates. But later, if she were excessively curious about the girls Porter dated in high school and the progress of their relationships, it was because a steady girlfriend, an engagement, a wedding, all were badges of normalcy she had dreamed of since we were born but had thought were out of reach. Yes, it was annoying when Porter had to provide a play-by-play of the evening's events at the end of a date in high school, as most teenagers did, but ironically I think my mother would have preferred it if Porter had been even more romantically audacious, had pushed the envelope further, had come closer to sealing the deal. (I'm certain precisely the op-posite kind of debriefing occurred weekly in the living rooms of Christi Oakes and the other girls Porter dated, whose par-ents had more than the usual reasons to emphasize caution, restraint . . . and chastity.) Like all of Mom's exaggerated be-haviors, it was tolerable because we knew she had our best interests at heart. But it was for this same reason I found it so difficult to broach the subject of my homosexuality with her. Even more than it would most mothers, it would break her heart.

Porter was breathing regularly now; his hand had fallen away from our penis. I willed myself to go to sleep without thinking of anything that might arouse me.

The first thing Porter did the next morning was to call Faith. While I reviewed my notes from the night before, they talked breathlessly for forty-five minutes before agreeing to meet for lunch at Murphy's in Virginia-Highland. When he got off the phone, I reminded him that he owed me time in the library for my paper.

"Yeah, yeah, yeah, I know," he said. "We'll get there."

Porter had offered to pick up Faith at her dorm, but she said she needed to do some errands and preferred to meet him at the restaurant. Murphy's had recently become unbearably trendy on weekends, attracting droves of people who ten years ago would have been considered card-carrying yuppies, but although it was crowded, Porter and I were seated immediately, a phenomenon to which we have grown accustomed. No maitre d' in his right mind is going to want to have a two-headed customer in the foyer. The question "Would you like to wait at the bar?" was completely foreign to us. We were always deferred to, always treated politely, always seated promptly, even if our table *was* usually in the furthest reaches of the restaurant, away from the flow of traffic, and definitely—*definitely*—never on the flight path to the restrooms. To make our lives easier, we tended to go to a small group of restaurants repeatedly: Murphy's for American food, the King & I for Thai, Camille's for Italian, Tiburon Grille for fancy dinners. The owners and managers had gotten to know us, and had figured out where best to seat us and how to calm the nerves of panicked servers who found us at their tables.

Faith arrived about fifteen minutes later and was shown to our table in a far corner of the glassed-in addition to the main building. I wondered what she had said to the maitre d' when she arrived.

"Porter," she said as she extended a hand, smiling. "Good afternoon, Owen."

I pulled us up to our feet to greet her; Porter never was particularly attentive to such details.

"Hello, Faith. You look pretty today," I said. I had decided I was going to be nice to her, that she was sweet and nonthreatening and that I wasn't going to be rude or sarcastic. But I also had set a deadline for getting to the library—three p.m.—and I intended to stick to it.

"Yeah," Porter said. "You look great."

"Thanks, so do you." She smiled at him.

She was more attractive than the night before or had spent more time pulling herself together for their first "official" date: she wore a little more makeup, though still not much, and it looked as if she had had her hair done. Maybe that was the errand she'd had to do; I had thought it was only an excuse to prevent the embarrassment of having us show up at her dorm. Porter had taken greater care with his appearance, too. He'd let me select our clothes—a forest-green pullover, khaki slacks, loafers—and spent, for him, an extraordinary amount of time fussing with his hair. ("I need a haircut," he said. "Don't I need a haircut?") Faith was conservatively dressed, a skirt and sweater in autumnal tones, sensible shoes, the charm bracelet, a slender gold necklace with a single red stone embedded in the crosshairs of a crucifix. An impression was forming in my mind that she was poor—not dirt poor, in all likelihood reasonably middle-class, but poor by comparison to many of the other girls at Druid Hills, who were far more stylish, more glamorous, than she. She also was more modest. I couldn't imagine her ever baring her belly beneath a clingy, cut-off top, as many girls did, their navel rings flashing gaudily.

The hands of our waiter, a tall, handsome, boyish young man I had not seen there before, seemed palsied as he set down our glasses of water.

"My name is Richard and I'll be your server today. Would you like to hear our specials?"

This was the true test of a waiter's mettle: whether he could recite the daily specials from memory while recovering from the shock of seeing Porter and me for the first time. Richard was sweating. I didn't think it would go well. Faith had picked up her menu and was perusing it.

"Faith?" I said. "I think Porter and I know what we want."

"I'm going to have the chicken quesadilla," she said, smiling at Richard and handing him the menu. "And a Diet Coke."

I usually ordered the quesadilla myself, but in the car on the way to the restaurant Porter had begged me to order a sandwich or salad, something that wouldn't require his help to cut it. He ordered the hamburger; I got a grilled chicken Caesar.

"And we'll need another set of silverware, Richard, please," I said. We had been seated at a table with only two place settings, one on either side of the table.

"Um, sure. Of course."

The worst was over. I was sure there'd be a slight delay in the arrival of my utensils and our drinks while Richard had a meltdown in the kitchen, and there was a fifty-fifty chance he'd forget at least part of our order, but Porter and Faith could relax and lose themselves in conversation now.

"Owen, you're going to have to help me here," Faith said.

"With what?"

"Etiquette."

"The small one is the salad fork," I said.

"I knew it! I knew it! I knew you were gonna screw this up," Porter said.

"It was a joke, Porter. Lighten up."

"Perhaps a better word would be protocol," Faith said. She was smiling now, and I could tell she thought my joke was hilarious but hadn't been sure whether or not it was okay to laugh. I think she was reevaluating me. Last night I had barely said a word. I kept my nose in a book at Starbucks. I seemed a little whiny. I set limits. But now she could see I was more than just a growth on Porter's shoulder. The quiet one, the nerd, had a sense of humor. This was something a lot of Porter's friends didn't really get. Throughout our childhood and adolescence, our friends generally related to either Porter or to me almost exclusively. I had my friends, he had his. As nice as she was, Christi Oakes very rarely addressed me directly, as Faith was now doing. I don't know if it was a defense mechanism, immaturity, or just an inability to deal with the facts at hand.

"Okay, what do you want to know?" I could feel Porter relax a little.

"Well, for starters, are you okay with this? With me? I mean, have you done this before?"

"Do you mean has Porter dated other girls?"

"Owen!"

"Well, it's what she's asking!" I leaned forward a bit and lowered my voice, as if pretending Porter wouldn't be able to hear what I was about to say. "Porter's dated a few girls, one seriously, but that ended three years ago, in our freshman year."

I could tell Porter was uncomfortable and embarrassed. Our drinks had arrived, and he sipped his Coke and tried to pretend he wasn't listening. But it seemed to me that this type of information would be better coming from me.

"And what about you?" she asked, also in a mock whisper.

"I don't date. I'm . . ."

"He's shy," Porter interjected. I felt him go rigid.

"Shy?" Faith said.

"Yes . . . I'm shy."

"Okay . . . So how does this work? How would you like me to relate to you when I'm out on a date with Porter? I can see that you've learned how to keep yourself occupied. But would you like me to ignore you completely?"

"No, not exactly. I don't know. In the past, that's pretty much the way it was, but I have a feeling you're different."

"Different?"

"Yeah. I might actually have something to say to you. And I might be interested in what you have to say back. It wasn't that way with Porter's other girlfriend."

"I thought you liked Christi," Porter said.

"I did, Porter. I just didn't have anything to say to her." I looked at Faith and mouthed the word "cheerleader," but Porter knew exactly what I was saying.

"Owen!" he said.

"So she was pretty?"

"If you like that sort of thing."

"Which, I take it, you don't?"

"I'm not overly impressed with it."

"I see," she said.

I think she *did* see, that together with the information Porter had provided about his athletic prowess the night before, the fact that he had dated a cheerleader was very possibly changing the way Faith viewed him. I still wasn't sure what her motivation had been last night or what her intentions were today, but if her initial impulse had been largely charitable, I suspected that was no longer entirely the case. So far, Faith had revealed almost nothing of her romantic history, but it was safe to assume she had never been the object of affection of anyone as handsome as Porter. If she was able to get past the fact of my presence, an obstacle she had so far circumnavigated effortlessly, she may have thought this was an opportunity to land herself an attractive boyfriend no one else wanted. But learning about Porter's popularity and his ability to date one of the most attractive girls in high school may have given her pause to reconsider.

Meanwhile, I was reevaluating her, as well. I have to say that so far, I liked her. She was intelligent, self-confident, and apparently guileless; I didn't detect any ulterior motives or suspicious behavior. Call it luck or call it love at first sight, this girl had somehow formed an immediate bond with Porter.

Our meals arrived. Poor sweet Richard apologized profusely when he mistakenly set down Porter's hamburger in front of me and gave him my Caesar salad. It was the kind of thing that happens in restaurants every day—and which happens to Porter and me with some frequency—but Richard was so earnest, and so nervous, I thought he was going to break down and cry.

"It's my first day," he said, by way of explanation. I wondered if it would be his last.

Faith questioned Porter on the details of some of the top-
ics they had discussed the night before: high school, hobbies,
our extensive international travels with our parents. Although Porter's and my personal histories were more or less
identical, at least logistically, Faith would occasionally ask
me if I had experienced something in the same way Porter
had; whether, for example, I liked the same foods Porter did
or enjoyed the same places when we went on vacation. She
did so just frequently enough to acknowledge my presence,
to keep me from feeling bored, but without ever letting
Porter feel overlooked.

At two-thirty, as we sat over coffee and the remains of a
slice of Murphy's famous peanut butter-chocolate chip ice
cream pie, which Porter and Faith had shared (and which I
would have to help burn off at the gym), I reminded Porter of
my intention to get to the library by three to finish the research for my paper. He grumbled a bit, until Faith came to
my defense.

"It's all right, Porter. I totally understand," she said, daubing delicately at her mouth with a napkin. "We promised
Owen last night that he could finish his paper today in exchange for the time we spent at Starbucks last night."

"I know, I know," he said. "It's just that, well, I'm having
such a good time being with you . . ."

"A promise made is a promise kept, Porter," she said, and
stood up, brushing crumbs from her skirt.

"Can we do this again sometime?" he asked.

"I'd like that, yes."

"Great! When?"

"Next weekend, maybe? I don't usually make plans during the week. I'm busy with classes, and this semester I'm
doing a practicum at the rehab center, so I don't have much
time. Let's talk about it during the week."

"Remember, we're playing at Eddie's on Saturday."

"That sounds good. Saturday, then."

It was a gorgeous autumn afternoon, and the shops along

Highland Avenue were crowded, the sidewalks overflowing. We walked her to her car, a well-kept but equally well-used ten-year-old Honda Civic with one of those Christian "fish" appliqués on the trunk lid. I know Porter was hoping for a kiss—I could feel him yearning toward her—but he was too self-conscious to initiate one. Faith took his hand in both of hers, and smoothed and patted it.

"I had a nice time," she said. "Thank you."

We watched until the car disappeared from view.

"Damn," Porter said. "Was that a brush-off—or what?"

"No, I don't think so. Why?"

"That patting-my-hand business and saying she had a 'nice' time. Nice? *Nice?* Is that all? I had a *great* time. She had a 'nice' time?"

"Porter, you're reading way too much into this. It's a first date. What were you expecting? Wedding bells?"

"No, not exactly. But . . . I don't know. I feel so lonely all of a sudden."

"Well, you've always got me."

"Yeah, right."

We headed toward our car, which we'd parked on a side street three blocks away. Porter's foot scuffed at the leaves on the sidewalk.

"You almost blew it back there, you know," he said.

"Where? When?"

"When she asked if you dated."

"Why? What did I say?"

"You almost told her you were gay."

"I didn't say . . ."

"Because I interrupted you."

"So?"

"Christ, Owen, you can't tell a girl that, not on the first date, anyhow. Not if you expect her ever to go out with me again."

"Oh, I *see.*"

"Do you? Do you really?"

"Yes, I do. You're ashamed of me. You're embarrassed that I'm gay."

"It's not that, O. It's just that . . ."

"It's just that you don't want her to think that you're gay, or at the very least bisexual."

"I just don't want her to think I'm . . . defective, at least not any more defective than I already am."

I should have been used to this by now—Porter's insensitivity, his egocentric view that this was all about him, his wants, his needs. It was the way it had always been with him. But it still hurt me. I didn't say anything. I knew it was a losing battle.

"Look," he said finally, as we got to the car. "Don't blow this for me, bro. Not this one. *Please*."

"Well, she's going to find out sooner or later. I mean, if you get serious."

"But not now, O. Not yet. Please. Just keep your mouth shut."

I felt a familiar twinge in the pit of my stomach, an emptiness, a dread. It was something I hadn't felt in several years, something I had nearly forgotten about. Porter was pulling away again, separating himself from me, focusing on someone outside of us.

It's impossible for me to describe in all its depth and complexity the bond Porter and I share. Singletons cannot even begin to comprehend it. Twins may talk about their psychic link, of remaining connected across great distances or experiencing sympathy pains when their twin has been injured, and I don't doubt those feelings are real, however inexplicable, but they don't come close to what Porter and I feel. We are one—indivisible. The food we eat nourishes both ourselves and each other, as does the air we breathe. I feel him not only next to me, but inside me. With me and *within* me. My blood is his blood, my bone his bone.

But there's no denying that despite our closeness and identical genetic makeup, Porter and I are distinct individuals. I can *feel* him turn away from me—it is palpable. It's almost as if he and I are traveling through life in a space capsule, confined to cramped quarters, sharing the same life support systems—air and food and water—and then suddenly he discovers an airlock, a switch he can hit that separates us, that seals him in his own pressurized compartment. I can feel the sucking of the vacuum as he leaves me, the rush of blood from my chest. It leaves me breathless, and although I have never experienced any sensation on the left side of our body, I suddenly feel somehow numb there. That is *my* version of twin phantom pain. And of all the things that divide us—Porter's obsession with sports, his moronic friends, his ridiculously short attention span—it is his interest in women that drives the greatest wedge between us.

There had been nothing like this in the three years since Porter and Christi had broken up. Oh, recently Porter had had his sexual escapades, and I had tolerated them, as repulsive as they were to me. He was always horny and always talked about girls, but there had been nothing serious, nothing real, since Christi Oakes, and I have to admit I liked it that way. Life was less complicated, less demanding, more predictable, when Porter wasn't involved with a girl. And my sexuality was much less of an issue. But now I could feel him pulling away, shutting me out, judging me. Like we were fifteen again.

Chapter 10

Eddie's Attic is a small venue located, as its name implies, on the upper floor of an unobtrusive building on a side street in Decatur, a leafy, collegiate suburb of Atlanta. We had committed to a gig there prior to our recent post-Olympic fame, and the place was jammed with new fans. Fortunately, we had reserved a ticket for Faith, and when she arrived she took a seat at a small table near the tiny platform that served as a stage, looking somewhat self-conscious among our typically rowdy fans as we completed setting up our equipment. She seemed to relax as soon as she caught our eye, however, waving demurely and then lowering her head to sip delicately at her soda through a straw.

We hadn't seen her in the intervening week, but Porter had spoken to her on the phone at least once a day. I tried to rein him in, to keep his emotions in check. I discouraged him from showing up at her dorm unannounced, as he suggested we do several times. He slept poorly, and as a result so did I. We hadn't masturbated in a week, and I was about to explode.

We sat down with her for only a minute before we had to do a sound check, but Porter's demeanor changed instantly and dramatically—mercifully, for the better. He'd been anxious all week, unable to focus or concentrate, his foot tapping constantly as I tried to sit quietly and study. He was dead certain Faith would not show up at Eddie's.

"I should have offered to pick her up," he said as we drove to the club that night. "I should have made it seem more like a date."

"You *did* offer. Twice, as I recall. And she declined. Remember?"

"Did I? I don't know," he said.

Now, having seen Faith, he was like an addict who had just gotten a fix: still wired, ecstatic, but more relaxed than he had been all week. I breathed a sigh of relief.

It was an unusual night for us, not our best performance. Porter seemed distracted much of the time, flubbing a chord here and there, and blanking on a lyric now and again. But when we did our big ballad, he sang it to Faith, as if she were the only person in the room—and it brought down the house. Our regulars gave us a standing ovation.

After that night, Porter and Faith were virtually inseparable. I marveled at how quickly things fell into place for them and how smoothly it had all gone, although it took some time for me to adjust to having her around. Porter and I were an odd couple, but we *were* a couple. We were balanced. With Faith around, I frequently was lonely. It's strange to think that adding another person to the equation would result in increased loneliness—the math doesn't seem to really work—but that's what happened. Porter used to rely on my opinions a lot; now he didn't. I felt left out of their conversations. Sometimes, I could barely get a word in edgewise. And Porter seemed to think he should be able to control a greater percentage of our time. Until now, we had always divided things pretty much down the middle when it came to paying attention to our particular wants or needs: how much time would be spent exercising or playing sports versus how much time would be spent in a more contemplative way. And then along comes Faith, making demands on Porter's time—and mine. My life suddenly was divided into three parts: his, mine, and theirs.

Granted, there were some benefits to Porter's relationship

with Faith. A lot of the annoying small talk and petty observations Porter previously directed toward me were now
aimed at Faith. I could disengage and use the time to think,
to read, to write poetry and lyrics. And some of the things
Faith wanted to do—going to Callaway Gardens or the Atlanta History Center—I had wanted to do for years but had
been unable to persuade Porter to do with me. When it came
to selecting movies, Faith's tastes were closer to mine than
Porter's and we frequently outvoted him. I probably saw
three times as many movies with subtitles once they started
dating. Previously, his usual response had been, "I'm *not*
going to one of those movies where you have to read."

As an added bonus, Porter's grades improved. Faith took
her studies seriously, and in order to spend as much time
with her as possible, Porter took to meeting her at the library.
After the first couple of times, when he grew bored watching
her study—once she got down to it, she was relentless and refused to be distracted by his flirtatious antics—he actually
immersed himself in his own work.

By the time the holidays rolled around, Porter decided it
would be appropriate to bring Faith to the big party my folks
held every year in mid-December, attended largely by fellow
faculty members and star graduate students. Mom was delighted at the prospect. Although she would acknowledge it in
only the most roundabout way, she had been devastated
when Porter's relationship with Christi Oakes had ended
three years earlier, and I suspect she would have been less
than thrilled with the types of girls Porter was meeting backstage and on the road, had she made their acquaintance.

In the weeks preceding the big event, Mom must have
called us fifty times to glean information about Faith's religious background and preferences in food and music. When
she began asking questions about Faith's hobbies and dress
size ("How should I know *that*, Mom?" Porter whined), I
knew she would embarrass Porter, and probably Faith, by
presenting her with extravagant and probably much too per-

sonal Christmas gifts on the night of the party. I put an end to that.

"One gift, Mom, and nothing expensive. A token. Something small."

"Oh really?" she said. "What do you suggest, Owen?"

I could sense the irritation in her voice. I felt the need to cite an authority—Amy Vanderbilt or Dear Abby.

"I don't know, Mom. A book, a sweater—nothing more personal than that, and not cashmere, for God's sake. She wears a charm bracelet. Get her a charm."

"She wears a charm bracelet? Really?"

I could tell she was thrilled. I suspected she had an inkling the kind of girls who hung around backstage were more likely to wear handcuffs than charm bracelets.

"Yes."

"What kind of charm?"

"I don't know . . ."

"Gold or silver?"

"Gold, I think. Yeah, gold."

"That's not too *personal*?"

In the end, she bought Faith a sweater and *several* charms, and Faith seemed only mildly embarrassed at her largesse. She had brought a token gift—a pair of votive candle holders from Pier 1 that looked somewhat Scandinavian in design, like irregular ice cubes. Porter actually got to spend very little time with Faith at the party; Mom swept her away almost as soon as we walked in the door and introduced her to family and friends as if she were the reincarnation of the Blessed Virgin Mary herself. When we left, Mom loaded Faith down with several plastic containers of homemade Christmas cookies—almond crescents dusted with confectionary sugar, butter cookies spangled with red and green crystals. The next day, after Porter said goodbye to Faith, who was heading home for Christmas break, we went back to our parents' house for brunch—and a postmortem.

"Delightful girl," Mom said, kissing Porter at the door.

"Simply delightful. Is it too much to hope she has a sister at home who might be interested in Owen?"

"She's got four, Mom," he said. "And a brother. But we haven't actually met them, and as far as I know, none of them has expressed an interest in O."

"That's too bad. Left to his own devices, I don't think your brother is ever going to meet anyone."

"Mom," I said.

"I see no evidence to the contrary." She sniffed and turned on her heels without so much as an air kiss for me.

Such digs had gotten more frequent lately—and more tart. Porter's success at finding an eminently presentable girlfriend apparently meant less to Mom than my own failure to do so, which surprised me. She had always been a "glass half full" kind of person. ("Your baby has two heads."/"But they're healthy." *"Your baby has two heads!"*/"But aren't they adorable?") She had never let the shock and tacit disapproval of relatives or friends affect her attitude or disposition—not that I could see, anyway—had always protected Porter and me from their stares and whispers. Even her lifelong favoritism toward Porter seemed more soft-edged, less threatening than her recent almost-cruel interest in my lack of romantic possibilities.

"O—dude," Porter said. "She is like so on to you."

"Shut up, Porter. She is not."

I honestly didn't believe Mom thought I was gay. I suspected *that* revelation would result in an emotional Vesuvius none of us could ignore. No, I think it had something to do with the need for balance, for an even-numbered head count. She may have feared that an unattached Owen might somehow threaten the stability of the Porter-Faith pair bond, as if I were some rogue atom that might disturb their delicately balanced chemical composition. When I was feeling good about myself, I thought Mom looked at me as a threat because I obviously was smarter and more accomplished than Porter. How could Faith resist my charms? And that may have very well been the case, because in the end it always came down to *protecting* Porter, the favorite son—even if it was only me they were protecting him from.

I won't deny that I have had more than a few fantasies about coming out to my parents—especially to my mother—and that frequently the scenarios weren't pretty. But each time an opportunity presented itself—like now—I lost my nerve, even though I knew from a psychology class that oftentimes the anticipation of pain is more stressful than the pain itself.

Porter mooned over Faith throughout our annual ten-day ski trip to Aspen, combined this year with a couple of hastily arranged performances in Boulder. Skiing was one of the few athletic activities we both enjoyed, but on this trip I practically had to coerce him onto the slopes. And at the end of the day, instead of hanging out around the fireplace at the ski lodge, he wanted to head back to Mom and Dad's timeshare, even on the last four days, when our folks joined us. He called Faith on his cell phone so frequently and for so long each time that its battery barely made it through a day without a recharge, and once, when it died midway through a conversation, he borrowed mine, for what I warned him would be the first and last time.

"Jesus, Porter, it's not like you've broken up with her or something," I told him as I reluctantly parted with my phone. "You're just on vacation. You'll see her again in a couple of weeks."

"More like three. Classes don't start until the twenty-fifth."

"Okay, three. You'll live. Besides, she's at home with her family. Don't you think it's sort of rude for her to spend all of her time on the phone with you? Give her some space."

I tried to understand what he was going through. This had been the longest he had been separated from Faith since they had met, and she was now back home in south Georgia, on her own turf, away from Porter. I could tell from some of the things he said that he was worried she might suddenly come to her senses without him around, as if we had cast some magic spell over her, enchanted her, and now that she was no longer under our direct influence, the spell would be broken and she would suddenly realize what monsters we were.

It was still unclear to me exactly how much, if anything, Faith had told her family about Porter—or whether they even knew he existed. From everything she had said, they were apparently a close-knit family. Faith's dorm room was filled with small framed pictures of her sisters that must have spanned fifteen years, the five of them lined up in descending order of birth, each one smaller than the last, like a set of Russian nesting dolls or a scene from an all-girl version of *The Sound of Music.* There were pictures of her brother, too, usually alone, but none of her parents that I could see. I found it hard to imagine that with five girls at home for the holidays, there wouldn't be talk of boyfriends. I figured if she had said anything at all, she had been coy about it, vague, evasive about details. If she truly loved Porter, and I was more certain of that fact every day, she must have found it hard not to be able to talk about him freely. And even beyond her genuine affection for him, there was the matter of our "celebrity," which had grown at an alarming rate since our appearance at the Olympics. Here was this girl from a little hick town in south Georgia and she was dating one half of a rising rock band, yet she couldn't tell a soul about it because we were freaks. There is a corrosive aspect to such secret-keeping. It leads to second-guessing and self-doubt. *How am I going to spend the rest of my life with a person I can't introduce to my parents? What will happen, God forbid, if they ever do find out who I am dating? Is it even remotely possible they will accept him, overlook his obvious differences, and see into his heart, as I have?*

For some time, Porter had been advancing the idea of visiting Faith's family. He was pushing for full disclosure. In a way, I think it was a form of self-preservation. He was falling more deeply in love with Faith with every passing day, but at the same time, there was a part of him that was holding back. He knew there was the very real possibility that once her family met him, or even learned who he was, they would put an end to his relationship with her, much as Mr. Oakes had burst Porter and Christi's romantic bubble some three years earlier. I think he was arguing for a confrontation sooner rather than later because it might hurt less that way. He'd be devastated, of course, but less so now than after investing a year or more in the relationship. Circumstances had made him a practical romantic.

Faith seemed to take an opposing stance. Each time Porter pressed for a meeting with her family, she resisted, countering with excuses and rationalizations. They were vague at first, seemingly unrelated to the matter at hand. It was harvest time and her family would be busy taking in the crops. And then: It had been a bad year for cotton, and her father was scrambling to figure out how to keep the wolf from their door. (That happened every year, she said consolingly; it had nothing to do with Porter.) Her family suffered a litany of personal tragedies that fall that would have tried the patience of Job. Her grandmother had fallen and broken a hip. An aunt suspected breast cancer. The family dog contracted rabies and had to be put down. I never suggested it to Porter, but I thought it prudent to track the health of her closest relatives, so that, for example, no more than four grandparents could die and be used as excuses.

But I could understand her position. For one thing, they had been dating only since October; even under normal circumstances, an introduction to the parents seemed premature. And she had a lot more to lose than Porter. While he risked having his heart broken, she stood to lose her entire family, or most of it. (Surely there would be *one* sympathetic person among her siblings, someone who would understand.) Porter was gambling on a relationship of three or four months; she stood to lose the relationships of a lifetime. For him, who had been marginalized all of his life, a breakup would mean disappointment, sadness, but otherwise would not change his life. She would be forever marked by the revelation that she dated a freak. Her family would look askance at every midget and amputee that crossed their paths from that day forward. The circus would be ruined for them.

Porter managed to survive the holiday separation with my help. When we returned from Colorado, I told him the remaining two weeks of break would be a good time to get a jump start on his classes for spring semester. If he was going to graduate, he'd have to make up two classes he had failed previously in addition to taking his regular course load. We also used the time to hire an agent and a business manager, and put them to work on a plan that would minimize our concert appearances until after our graduation in May but keep us busy come summer.

When Faith returned to Atlanta during the third week of January, Porter finally relaxed. When we picked her up for the first time, she was wearing the sweater Mom had given her for Christmas, which Porter interpreted as a very good sign. I thought it less so. We were having a cold snap that was severe by Atlanta standards, and I didn't know how many other sweaters Faith might have owned, coming as she did from the more temperate southern part of the state.

Spring semester passed in a blur. I'd never seen Porter work so hard at his studies. With careful planning, we found two classes that would count toward both of our degrees and enrolled in them, minimizing the amount of time each of us would have to spend attending the other's classes. I helped him with the coursework for the classes we shared and did everything short of actually cheating on exams to help him get through, including more or less writing an entire paper for him, which I suppose *bordered* on cheating. It was a lot of work. We spent far more time in classes and at the library than in the studio, and we cut back our performance schedule considerably, despite a dramatic increase in demand. But in late April, as we finalized our plans for graduation and waited nervously for test scores and grades on senior theses, we learned that Porter would indeed be joining Faith and me on the Quadrangle as a full-fledged member of the Druid Hills University Class of 1997. For graduation, our parents gave us a little yellow Porsche Boxster, with two monogrammed sets of keys.

Faith accepted a nursing position at University Hospital and made plans to enroll in the master's of nursing program the next year. She was fairly sure that what she ultimately wanted to do was teach. Porter and I had been signed by our agent to the most grueling concert tour we had yet undertaken, with play dates in thirty-six cities across the country, including several breakout dates in Los Angeles, San Francisco, and Seattle, before heading into a studio in Atlanta to record our second CD, *Inseparable*.

It was a long and difficult summer, made more so by frequent, exhausting flights back to Atlanta from various cities so Porter could spend time with Faith. But their relationship thrived, thanks to the attention we paid it, and in October, on the first anniversary of the day they met, Porter brought Faith to Winn Park, across the street from the huge, genteel-shabby Dutch colonial in which we had grown up on Westminster Drive. Surrounded by gracious faux-antebellum homes, their intricately manicured and terraced lawns drawn up around them like hoop skirts, Winn Park is meant to appear wild and untamed, untouched by the hand of man, and so, like some Scottish heath, it is rough-hewn, dotted with hillocks and glens that make it perfect for a game of hide-and-seek. Lawyers and corporate executives walk their golden retrievers and chocolate labs there late on summer evenings, and their privileged children play soccer on a three-inch-deep carpet of oak leaves in the fall. At its western end, in a small grotto with an Oriental aesthetic, a delicate waterfall drips and babbles down a rocky wall and feeds a serpentine creek that forms the backbone of the park. It is there

Porter proposed to Faith, near a small brass plaque, oxidized to a green patina, inscribed with a sentimental bit of poesy:

> *A garden is enchantment,*
> *That knows not fear nor wrath,*
> *Where birds sing sweet at eventide,*
> *And God walks down the path.*

She accepted. How could she not?

Chapter 11

Sometimes I feel as if Porter and I live in two different time zones on opposite sides of the planet. When it is day for him, it is night for me. Even given the impossibility of changing our circumstances at birth, things would have been so much easier, so much more fulfilling for both of us, if we had been more alike, had shared more interests, had more friends in common. As it was, we each had to sacrifice half of our life to the other. This became increasingly true as we matured emotionally, becoming two different sexual beings. And it became even more so for me after Porter met Faith and began creating a life with her.

The longer Porter and Faith dated and the more complex their relationship became, the more alienated I felt. They now had things that were "theirs," things in which I didn't share: their song, their favorite restaurant. Even the grotto in Winn Park, where Porter and I had played as children, was special to them because Porter had asked Faith to marry him there. I had to fight to maintain my sense of self, to not disappear entirely within their relationship, but at the same time I found myself sometimes wishing I *could* disappear—not just become invisible, but be gone, cease to exist. Increasingly, I felt superfluous, hopelessly irrelevant.

Ironically, Porter's relationship with Faith resulted in a dramatic decline in the amount of sex he was having, since he stopped seeing other women as soon as he began dating her and she made it clear she intended to remain a virgin until their wedding night. He no longer invited groupies back to our motel rooms on road trips, even though there were now more opportunities than ever before—and of considerably higher caliber. Especially in Atlanta, he pointedly ignored the girls who flirted with him during our local gigs, in particular those with whom he'd previously had sex. (Fortunately, we never saw Jade, a.k.a. Vixana, again. Perhaps she had awakened the morning after having sex with Porter and entered a convent.) He even went so far as to delete all the pornography on his computer and to distribute his erotic magazines and videos among the roadies, something I think he regretted almost immediately but which he could not undo without considerable embarrassment.

Even considering Faith's upbringing by Southern Baptists in a rural farming community, I thought her views on premarital sex somewhat anachronistic in the waning days of the twentieth century. I felt certain the total number of virgins in our graduating class at Druid Hills could easily fit into a telephone booth with room to spare, though come to think of it, with the proliferation of cell phones, telephone booths had themselves become pretty scarce.

"Do you think it's me?" Porter asked one night after we had dropped off Faith at the apartment she now shared with two other nurses in Decatur, a couple of miles from University Hospital.

"Do I think it's you *what*?"

"Do you think Faith is too freaked out by me—by us—to have sex?"

I didn't know what to tell him. Faith didn't seem squeamish about our situation when we were alone, nor did she appear self-conscious in public. She would always hold Porter's hand when we walked through Piedmont Park or went shopping at Lenox Square, and if she ever noticed people staring, it didn't seem to faze her. After several months, Porter had achieved roughly the same level of intimacy with

Faith as he had with Christi Oakes, and I became reacquainted with the minor physical accommodations and loss of privacy that required: me putting my arm around Faith's shoulder when they made out, Porter leaning across me to kiss her. At least she wore her hair shorter than Christi had, so it ended up in my mouth far less frequently. Faith allowed Porter to massage her breasts over her sweaters and blouses but not beneath them. And there was no touching of any kind below the waist.

"Maybe that's not it at all, Porter. She had a very strict upbringing. I'm sure that's got a lot to do with it. She's just an old-fashioned girl, one of the last women on the face of the earth who actually value their virginity. You ought to feel good about that. I doubt there are many men who get to marry a virgin these days."

Privately, though, I blamed myself for Faith's apparent lack of interest in raising the sexual stakes with Porter. There was no question she was in love with him; she was always attentive and affectionate when we were with her. It *must* be that she was freaked out by me—that I was the cause of her unease. I'm not suggesting she didn't accept the fact that the man she was dating could wear two hats; Lord knows she had to get past that pretty quickly. What I am saying is that she might have been embarrassed to be intimate with Porter in front of someone else—namely me.

This abrupt decline in sexual activity on Porter's part served only to underscore my own lack of sexual experience, in much the same way the sudden silence in your bedroom when you shut off the TV allows you to focus obsessively on the irritating drip of the faucet in the adjacent bathroom. You never fall asleep unless you get out of bed and tighten it.

Coming to terms with my homosexuality had been relatively easy; it was possessed of its own sense of inevitability. Communicating it first to Porter and then outward in concentric circles of diminishing intimacy was more complicated. But doing the thing that makes gay guys *gay*—actually having sex with another man—*that* was to prove to be somewhat more of a challenge.

Despite Porter's numerous erotic escapades prior to meeting Faith, I was still insecure about my ability to so much as talk to another gay man, let alone initiate a sexual relationship. Gay bars had never been even a remote possibility, and with our increasingly demanding concert schedule, to say nothing of the amount of time we spent in the studio, I'd long ago had to give up my volunteer work at AID Atlanta and Project Open Hand, not that either had proven particularly fertile ground for romance. And I ultimately decided it would be impossible to take advantage of the glory holes my friends John and Mark had told me now existed only in the porn shops on Cheshire Bridge Road, a sleazy stretch of strip malls, strip clubs, and gay leather bars. Despite the relative anonymity the glory holes offered, we would still have to enter the shop and make our way to the video booths in which they were located. If our mere appearance did not set off a stampede for the exits, our fame would guarantee the least anonymous blow job since Monica Lewinsky delivered pizza to the Oval Office. We simply couldn't risk the impact on our career, or on Porter's relationship with Faith, if word of our visit leaked to the media—even the gay media—as it seemed inevitable it would, or if, God forbid, the bookstore was raided while we were there. I wasn't about to become another Pee-wee Herman.

For some time, my sex life had revolved around gay Internet porn sites. So ubiquitous was pornography in cyberspace that I began to think of the World Wide Web as an electronic iceberg, the visible part being legitimate sites and the vast submerged portion, the unseen nine-tenths, comprising sexual Web sites of every conceivable variety (straight, gay, lesbian, bisexual, transgendered) and fetishizing every imaginable part of the human body (feet, armpits, nipples, toes). I purchased passwords from two adult identity-verification services, one gay, one somewhat more mainstream but with a strong gay component. Porter agreed to pay for the password on the latter system so he could visit straight porn Web sites. I don't know if gay porn did anything for him, but I will admit to surreptitiously watching some of his straight videos out of the corner of my eye, except on those rare occasions when he selected something from the girl-on-girl category, at which time I usually engaged myself in a game of electronic hangman.

I may be the only gay man on the face of the earth in whom pornography engenders an existential crisis. I look at pictures of sculpturally perfect men, their penises erect or lying casually on smooth thighs like reptiles sunning themselves on sandstone outcrops, and I don't know what I want more—to *have* them or to *be* them. Both options are equally out of reach, of course, but I can't help yearning for them. That is, after all, what pornography is all about: offering possibilities equally alluring and unattainable. The fact is, it's difficult for me even to get aroused by such images anymore. These men and boys are gods to me, far beyond the coarse grasp of desire. I worship them but feel unclean in their presence, unworthy of their attention. Intimidated by their perfection, I feel like an Untouchable.

In search of less intimidating potential partners, I ventured into online chat rooms and began talking to other gay men, who had not a clue that I had two heads. (I once saw a cartoon in the *New Yorker* with a canine at a keyboard musing to itself, "On the Internet, nobody knows you're a dog.") I suppose I sounded like quite a catch from the description I concocted for my online profile: "Gay white male, 23, 6' 2", 190, blond/blue, very good looking"—all of which was true. I cheated a bit by listing both my interests and Porter's: music, reading, foreign films, weightlifting, football, baseball. I said I was "versatile" and even hinted I might be bisexual. Once I entered a chat room, a flurry of instant messages ensued. I frequently had four or five conversations going on at once and sometimes found myself in the embarrassing position of having to explain to one cyber suitor why I had answered his most recent question with an apparent *non sequitur*—a response intended for one of my other chat buddies.

It was incredibly liberating to be able to "talk" to other men about sex, about what I wanted to do to them and what I wanted done to me. From time to time I ventured into chat rooms with names like "M4M Unusual," knowing I was the most unusual person there. I talked to a few guys who were amputees or paraplegics or who were looking for those types. I thought if I could find someone "unusual" enough to identify with me, I could come out to them about my condition. I didn't find anyone like that, although some of the "hobbies and interests" listed in profiles of men in that room made the idea of having sex with a two-headed man seem almost normal.

It was pointless from the very beginning, of course. I knew I would never actually meet any of the men with whom I was talking. My conversations came to a screeching halt when the man I was talking to asked to see a picture. I thought about faking it—sending a picture of some guy I had snagged off the Internet—but that seemed dishonest and ultimately self-defeating, since it *guaranteed* I could never meet the man to whom I had sent it. It seemed almost as bad to send a Bruce Weber photo of us that a friend had reworked in Photoshop so Porter was no longer in the picture. I tried that a couple of times, but the photo was so clearly the work of a professional photographer and I looked so good in it that some of the guys I sent it to accused me of lying. When they asked me to prove I wasn't by meeting them for coffee, I couldn't.

I never dared dream I might actually be able to find someone who would be willing to have sex with a two-headed man, at least not in Atlanta. It might have been easier in San Francisco or New York, where larger populations of fetishists supported a more diverse—and more jaded—erotic community. And then, to my surprise, I became aware of the possibility that something might actually happen with one of our roadies. His name was Casey—or rather his initials were K.C. and people slurred that into Casey. I really didn't know what his story was, but I was attracted to him from the first moment I saw him. Casey was young—the first time we had a conversation of any length, he told me he was barely eighteen—and charming in a goofy redneck sort of way, all shucks and golly whenever I said anything nice to him. And he was short, maybe only five-six or five-seven, with a lithe, tight little body he showed off by wearing form-fitting T-shirts with horizontal stripes—sometimes red and white, sometimes blue and white—that reminded me of pictures I'd seen of French sailors in the nineteenth century. He wore his curly blond hair just long enough to be full and sort of loose, although not long enough to look in any way girlish. But what I found most attractive about him was the way he smelled, an intoxicating combination of soap and sweat and milk. I was happy simply to stand next to him and breathe— just breathe.

Initially, Casey had hung around after our performances at the Little Five Points Pub or Eddie's Attic and offered to help us break down our equipment and load it into our van. It appeared we had our first male groupie. After a year or so, we realized he was more reliable than most of the other guys we'd occasionally hired, and we formalized the relationship. Soon he was accompanying us on road trips, and I found myself genuinely growing fond of him, even beyond any sort of physical attraction. Casey was one of those rare people who seemed to have no trouble accepting Porter and me at face value right from the very beginning. He looked us straight in the eye when he introduced himself and had the presence of mind to ask us to repeat our names so he could remember which of us was which. Most people we meet, at least those we meet unexpectedly, are so flabbergasted they don't even realize we *have* names. Maybe he was unfazed by our condition because he wasn't very bright (I frequently watched him repeatedly mouth instructions I had given him, as he tried to absorb them) and had retained a childlike innocence. Or maybe he had been taught to be respectful toward anyone he thought was his better. For whatever reason, I felt comfortable around him in a way I did with few other people.

After getting to know him and spending time on the road together, I occasionally suspected he might actually be flirting with me, because of little things he did. When he lit a joint for me, the fingers of his left hand sometimes would brush my cheek in what seemed a deliberate way, and frequently after we'd finished adjusting a piece of sound equipment he'd let a hand or arm remain in contact with my body for a length of time that seemed meaningful. I really wasn't used to being touched, and those innocuous yet unexpected contacts were electrifying. Initially, I wrote off my feelings as wishful thinking, but as I observed him more closely, I realized he never touched Porter's side of our body in the same way he touched mine, never offered to shotgun a joint with Porter but always was more than willing to place his lips close to mine and force the hot, hallucinatory smoke into my mouth like a kiss. When we were on the road, he frequently offered to buy me coffee or a Coke when we stopped for a break but never volunteered to pay for Porter's beverages. And if Porter and I slept later than the roadies (granted, an extremely rare occurrence), Casey would get the maid to unlock the door and would awaken us by shaking my shoulder and whispering my name into my ear.

It was after a gig in Asheville that something finally happened. We had two rooms at the Best Western, one for Porter and me, the second for Casey and our other regular roadie, Vic, a Latino boy I privately had nicknamed "Kiwi" because his zero-crop buzz-cut hair, when it began to grow in over his olive-toned scalp, reminded me of that fruit. Kiwi had gotten lucky that night, something of a rarity since he had become involved with a girl he had met in Charleston, and because the motel was fully booked, Casey would either have to play possum while Kiwi and his conquest had sex or sleep in the van. But it was cold as hell, so I offered to let Casey use the second bed in our room. He seemed somewhat embarrassed by the idea, but it was really the only reasonable option.

While Porter made his nightly call to Faith, Casey brought in his small backpack, and he and I started in on the first of several joints Porter and I usually smoked to wind down after a performance. When Porter got off the phone, we followed up with a couple of beers and sat around bullshitting for an hour or so. Eventually, we shucked our jeans, and the three of us drifted off to sleep wearing just our briefs.

I was awakened in the middle of the night by Kiwi and company in the adjacent room, the sounds of their lovemaking traveling easily through the motel's paper-thin walls. And then I became aware of another sound, a squishy, sucking noise like a boot being pulled out of mud rapidly and repetitively. Casey was masturbating not more than two feet from me. I suppose the sounds of Kiwi's amorous adventures had awakened him, too, and turned him on. I was hard within seconds, and I moved my hand beneath the covers to adjust myself in Porter's and my briefs. Casey noticed the motion and stopped jerking off, embarrassed at being caught.

"God, Owen, I'm sorry," he said.

"It's okay," I whispered. "Don't pay any attention to me."

"Oh Jesus, I couldn't . . ."

"Go on, Casey," I said, and then I added, daringly, "Please?"

For a moment he said nothing, but then he released a sigh that was part relief and, I hoped, part recognition, perhaps even affirmation. And then, god bless him, he drew back the covers and allowed me to watch him finish what he had started, a grin on his boyish face. I ached to bring myself off with him, but that would have required waking Porter, and to be honest I preferred having this moment to myself. When Casey got out of bed to use the bathroom, he hesitated by the side of my bed, then bent down and kissed me on the cheek.

"Good night, Owen," he said.

That was the beginning of our six-month romance. I hesitate to call it a relationship because it didn't have the complexity that word implies. It did not last long enough for us to talk about the future or make long-term plans, nor did it include the usual sentimentality and professions of love that typically characterize romantic relationships. But it definitely was more than sex; I believe we genuinely cared about each other. Looking back, I suppose I would characterize it as a "friendship with benefits."

One of its more unusual benefits was that it made real my homosexuality, which until that time had been entirely theoretical—both to me and to Porter. Sex with Casey confirmed for me what had been only hypothetical until that point: that I enjoyed intimacy with men in a way I did not with women—Porter's women. And it introduced Porter to the realities of sex with men.

At first, Porter was shocked when I told him Casey and I wanted to be intimate with one another. We had kept our feelings a secret from him for several weeks by discussing them (and, to a very limited extent, acting on them) only on the road and only when he was asleep. Porter told me he never would have guessed Casey was gay, because he was so different from the gay men we had met so far—the young urban professionals we had encountered at AID Atlanta and Project Open Hand. Apparently, to Porter, a pronounced Southern drawl and an address in a trailer court south of town, both of which Casey possessed, disqualified him from membership in the gay brotherhood.

Porter got fairly drunk the first time Casey and I openly had sex. I think it was awkward for him because he knew Casey as a person—he wasn't some pickup we had never seen before and likely would never see again, like the girls Porter had met on tour. Initially, all Porter allowed Casey to do was to blow me—and reluctantly, at that. We often had ejaculated into the mouths of Porter's female partners (he had actually developed something of a fetish about having women swallow his sperm), so I thought about telling him he should just try to relax and enjoy it. But then I put myself in his place, and I knew that would be asking too much. After all, I had not *enjoyed* it when he had allowed a succession of skanky bitches to blow him before he met Faith. I found them grotesque and disgusting, and had begun packing a bottle of liquid antibacterial soap with which to rid our genitals of their black lipstick and spittle.

With Casey, Porter's primary guiding principle appeared to be keeping the business at hand as far away from his face as possible. While he ultimately had few complaints about me *getting* a blow job, he was less than comfortable with the idea of me giving one. Aside from the proximity to another man's cock that would be required of him, he just couldn't bear the thought of some guy's sperm being resident in our body, no matter how small the quantity and despite the fact that by the time it got anywhere close to the shared real estate in our gut it would be—what?—some undifferentiated protein or something.

"I don't want that shit in me, O. No way, no how," he protested.

Anal sex was out of the question, at least initially, even as the active partner and with a condom. And he told me in no uncertain terms that I—*we*—would never, under *any* circumstances, be the passive partner.

Although he was never overtly rude, Porter disengaged during sex to an even greater degree than I did, but not as subtly, often continuing to drink beer and smoke joints while Casey and I made love (to the best of our ability under the circumstances), doing his best to ignore what was going on and ultimately acknowledging our orgasm with as much enthusiasm as might accompany a similar, less glamorous bodily function—a necessary evil, satisfying only in its completion.

When Casey wasn't around, Porter spoke of him disparagingly. He implied that it was either "curious" or "convenient" that my first sexual partner was someone who was on our payroll. (I didn't know whether that was meant more as an insult to Casey or to me.) And he suggested that I ought to set my sights higher when it came to finding my next sex partner.

I can't entirely blame Porter's attitude for the eventual and, I suppose, inevitable end of my affair with Casey. It may be that it just ran its course the way many such things do. Fortunately, there was no dramatic breakup, no exchange of "words." Casey simply stopped showing up for work (a situation Porter used as an opportunity to give me an "I told you so" lecture about mixing business with pleasure) and didn't return my phone calls. Eventually, I heard through Kiwi that he had moved to Boulder, Colorado.

Although I was disappointed when my affair with Casey ended, I honestly can't say I was surprised. He was young and it was the first gay romantic experience for both of us. It was as difficult to know what had motivated his interest in me as it was to understand why he ultimately disappeared from my life. I imagine we both had a lot of feelings we didn't know what to do with, and there was probably some measure of truth to Porter's observation about the social and cultural gulf that separated us. It was going to take an extraordinary man to be able to deal with the complexities of a relationship with me (with *us*), and for all his innate charm and good intentions, I doubted Casey was up to the challenge. I thought about him often in the months that followed, and I was disappointed that in a world of cell phones, e-mail, and instant messaging, he chose not to keep in touch, even at some remove.

But the affair with Casey opened my eyes to the fact that sex with another man—and even a certain level of emotional attachment—was not impossible for me, that there were men who were willing, even eager, to sleep with me. And while they were not exactly coming out of the woodwork, they were more plentiful than I might ever have imagined.

It did not hurt that Porter and I were rapidly becoming minor rock celebrities. The fact that we were more than competent musicians, combined with our unique physical attributes, had opened many doors for us that remained closed to other performers of equal skill and made us logical candidates for instant celebrity. A number of unauthorized fan sites sprang up on the Internet, largely amateurish and occasionally offensive (like the one that Photoshopped Porter's and my faces onto an image of Sonny and Cher next to the lyrics of "I Got You Babe") but nonetheless providing an undeniable level of visibility. Given the voyeuristic quality of most fan sites, it was not surprising that many of them included speculation about Porter's and my sex lives. The information posted about us, though vague, was largely accurate. For example, it appeared to be widely known that we did, in fact, *have* sex. Grainy, red-eyed pictures of us in motel rooms (pre-Faith), taken with the disposable cameras our groupies carried in their purses, began to show up on the Internet. Nothing salacious—at worst, Porter and I shirtless, swilling drinks from go-cups with one or two women of dubious character, oddly enough their faces often at least partially obscured by black boxes of the type designed to protect the privacy of the innocent or the dead, as if they should be ashamed of being seen in a compromising situation with us. I also found the shirtlessness kind of creepy. I always suspected people urged us to take off our shirt (Porter recently had taken to ripping off our shirt at the end of our performances) so they could determine definitively that our condition was genuine and not some sleight of hand or elaborate trick, like that perpetrated by the brothers Mark and Michael Polish, who quite convincingly pretended to be conjoined twins in their film *Twin Falls Idaho*.

Of late there seemed to be a consensus that, for whatever reason, we had stopped inviting women back to our motel rooms while on tour, with more than one Web master suggesting that "we" now had a girlfriend. There also was quite a bit of speculation about our anatomy "down there," and the consensus seemed to be that we *had* to have two penises, that it would be impossible for two men to survive if they had to share a single sex organ. That would be too great a cosmic joke to play on a couple of poor suckers who already were at a significant disadvantage physically. And more than one site hypothesized about the possibility that either Porter or I were gay, but the lack of specificity in their claims made me think they were the result of mindless, prurient speculation. Our pictures did begin showing up on a number of sites devoted to fan worship of attractive male celebrities, often in sections devoted to twins (the Brewers, the Carlsons) or other famous siblings (the Baldwin brothers). The Bruce Weber *Vanity Fair* images were particularly popular. Although these sites were not overtly gay, they had a gay sensibility to them and frequently were listed among "male-interest" sites in adult Web site directories.

The kind of men I ultimately had sex with were, more or less, gay analogs to the "Vixanas" who had been Porter's earliest sexual conquests: freaks in the long-haired hippie and rockabilly sense of the word, who hung out near the stage during performances and somehow made their way backstage afterward. Their intentions weren't always clear. Sometimes they were, in fact, just some completely innocent good ol' boys who had enjoyed our music and wanted to hang out with us or show us around their town in a "neighborly" way. But occasionally one or more of them would insinuate themselves into our van or motel room and get friendly with us once we all had gotten high. If you ask me, there really wasn't much of a gay sensibility about it at all, more like an easygoing, hedonistic mindset: "It's late, we're high, we're horny. Let's do something about it."

Our sexual encounters were almost entirely passive and oral, without Porter and I reciprocating in any way. It seemed entirely safe from an HIV standpoint, and in any event it was more or less all Porter was willing to tolerate at this point.

He was somewhat freaked out at the thought of word getting around that "we" were gay, and he always made it clear he was merely along for the ride, sometimes going so far as to bring out his wallet and flash a picture of Faith. As to the possibility of rumors spreading on some underground grapevine that we had engaged in gay sex, I figured the guys involved had so little credibility that their claims to have slept with a two-headed man would be met with the same winks and knowing smiles that might greet similar assertions regarding a rural late-night abduction by aliens.

Chapter 12

Once Faith agreed to marry Porter, an entire universe of additional decisions emerged. How would she convey the news to her family—and when? Should she present the engagement as a *fait accompli* or break it to them gently, over time, beginning with the news that she was dating someone a bit unusual? Not surprisingly, Porter favored the former: full disclosure, including a date for the wedding, without so much as a hint beforehand about our condition. Faith professed uncertainty, a sure sign she was leaning toward the latter.

"What do they know so far?" Porter asked as we discussed the situation with Faith over dinner at Tiburon Grille, a steak-and-seafood restaurant in the Highlands where the subdued lighting and dark-paneled walls offered us more privacy than most places—or at least the illusion of privacy.

"My parents? Almost nothing," she said. "My older sisters know I've been dating someone for six months."

"Six months? But we've been dating for more than a year," Porter said.

"I know that. I meant they've *known* for six months."

Under the circumstances, I'm surprised she told them anything at all. Even a single innocent question from one of her sisters would inevitably result in a complex web of lies. Because of our growing fame, she couldn't even tell them what we did for a living without risking exposure: *What's the name of their band? Janus? That's unusual. Wait, aren't they . . . ?*

"So you didn't tell them about me until six months ago?"

"Uh-uh." She sounded as noncommittal as possible, as if she were confirming that, yes, she had in fact voted but was not about to say for whom.

"Oh, I see." He held his salad fork at eye level, rotating it in his hand like a miniature radar antenna, inspecting it for spots.

"My younger sister, Elizabeth, I haven't said anything to, of course, but my brother, Chase . . . well, he knows more or less everything."

"Everything?" I said.

"We're very close. Of all of my family, I think he's the one most likely to understand."

"Why's that?" Porter asked, placing the fork back on the table.

"Well, he's super smart, the smartest of all of us, the only one who ever really escaped south Georgia entirely, who's gotten away from my mom and dad." She paused as if she had unintentionally revealed a secret. "Don't get me wrong, I love them. They're great. But they're kind of . . . *country*. Down-home and old-fashioned. Not at all like your parents."

Faith explained that Chase Colquitt had been the smartest kid in the Brooks County school system and had skipped the second, seventh, and tenth grades, graduating when he was not quite sixteen and getting a full scholarship to MIT while turning down similar offers from Princeton and Brown.

"Fortunately, he'd always been tall for his age and fit in better with kids a year or two older than him," she said. "It was as if his body and mind were in sync, just two or three years ahead of where they should have been."

But Chase's periodic leapfrogging to more advanced classes left him isolated and friendless among his new classmates, as if, like an Army brat, he had just transferred in from some distant city. This had only strengthened the bond between him and Faith, the sister to whom he was closest in age.

"He's been exposed to a lot of amazing people in Boston—at MIT and Harvard, places like that—so he's got more perspective, a broader view of life. He has a lot of interesting friends, though I suppose most of them are computer geeks like him. When he stops in at the farm on the way to spring break in Florida, he brings, like, *Asian* people with him—Japanese and Vietnamese, mostly. And an Indian guy once whose name sounded like some maharajah or a Hindu god, but we just called him Sammy. My family's always been pretty liberal when it comes to things like race, even back in the fifties and sixties. Both my grandfathers were ministers and were active in civil rights. Granddaddy Colquitt even marched on Washington in 1963 with Martin Luther King, although he didn't actually know him or anything—personally, you know. He just went up there with some folks from the local churches, both white and black. We were always taught tolerance and respect for black folks and poor folks, and we must have helped build six or seven Habitat for Humanity houses in the summers when I was growing up. And then, of course, there's Greta's husband."

"What's wrong with him?" Porter asked.

"Nothing's *wrong* with him, Porter. It's just that he's black."

"Oh, okay. That's cool," Porter said.

"Well, yes, it is. I mean, Dooley's a great guy. We're used to having all sorts of people in our home, so no one batted an eye when Chase showed up at the house with a mini United Nations in tow. Mom and Dad made sure his friends always felt welcome. Actually, I think he's only ever brought one white friend home with him, some preppy guy named Kyle. I remember him because that was so unusual for Chase—a white kid from Harvard. A couple summers ago, they backpacked through Australia and Indonesia. They even spent some time in Bali, which I think is just about the most romantic thing you could possibly do."

"Romantic?" I said.

"You know what I mean, in the larger sense of the word. The romance of travel. Adventure, exotic places."

"So where did Chase get the money for a trip to the South Pacific?" Porter asked. "Your folks don't seem like the type to bankroll something like that."

"I think Kyle paid for it. I'm pretty sure he's got money. He showed up at the farm in a BMW convertible."

Our dinners arrived. I'd ordered the salmon, which I could flake apart with my fork, but Porter had ordered a steak, and as usual we took the time to cut it into bite-size pieces right away, Porter stabilizing it with his fork, me wielding the knife.

"Anyway, I just figured he'd be sympathetic to our situation," Faith said.

"Kyle?" Porter asked.

"No, silly. Chase."

"And I take it he is?" I said.

"Oh, yes. Chase is very open-minded. I sent him your CD, and he says he loves your music. He's curious about the two of you, and he's really looking forward to meeting you. I wish he could be here when we tell my folks, but other than spring break, he doesn't get home that often. He's always got about a dozen projects going on at school, though I suppose that's really just an excuse. I just think he's sort of outgrown the farm and the family."

"Okay, so we've got Chase in our corner," Porter said. He held up his hand and folded his thumb into his palm. "That's one down and . . . what? Four, five, six to go?"

"More than six, Porter. I've got a huge extended family. My dad has three brothers and two sisters, and Mom's got three sisters. I've got sixteen cousins. But I really don't think any of them will be a problem. Even if anyone had misgivings, they'd probably be too polite to say anything."

"But it's just your mom and dad who have veto power, right?" Porter asked.

Faith reached across the table and took his hand. A woman seated at the next table turned her head to watch.

"Porter, I love you and I'm going to marry you. Nothing my family says—nothing anybody says—is going to change that. I'm sure that when my family gets to know you, they'll see what a wonderful person you are and they'll feel exactly the same way about you that I do."

That seemed to reassure him, and he dug into his steak.

Over the course of the next few weeks, we decided it would be too much of a shock to show up at the Colquitt farm without laying some groundwork, so Faith undertook a series of conversations with her older sisters in which she broke the news to them gradually. I got the impression she let the story unfold with all the skill of Scheherazade, offering ever-more-tantalizing details night after night, but always leaving some questions unanswered: She was getting serious about her beau. (The Colquitts were the type of people who still called boyfriends beaus.) Yes, he was good-looking. Very, very handsome, as a matter of fact. And a musician. No, not a violinist or pianist; a singer-songwriter. No, not C and W. He was in a band. Yes, it could be called a rock band, but not hard rock. No, she hadn't fallen in with the wrong crowd in Atlanta. He was a sweet, all-American boy, a former football star. No, you're right, Druid Hills doesn't have a football team. This was back in high school. A private high school in Atlanta. Lovett. Well, yes, his family does have money, sort of. His parents teach at Druid Hills—they're very distinguished—and they have a lovely home in Ansley Park, practically across the street from the High Museum of Art. His brother's in the band with him. They're close. Very close. And so on.

From what I could tell, the response had not been overwhelmingly negative. That, at least, was a start. Faith's sisters knew she was a sensible girl, not impetuous when it came to matters of the heart. She had been serious about only one other boy, in high school, like Porter a football player, who had gone on to some fame on the gridiron at the University of Alabama and now worked in his father's Ford dealership in Valdosta. She had turned down his marriage proposal her sophomore year at Druid Hills—deferred it, she explained, until after both of them had graduated. But he fell in love with someone else. Her sisters told her that Porter's athletic background would go a long way toward making their father happy, but the fact that we were Catholic would trouble their mother, who considered anyone outside the Baptist church somewhat suspect. Our family's Atlanta roots and relative wealth also would be debits rather than credits. Folks in south Georgia don't cotton much to Atlantans. The business about having two heads—well, we'd just have to wait and see about that.

Two of Faith's sisters, Gloria and Vivian, drove up to Atlanta one weekend to hear us play at the Variety Playhouse. They handled the situation as well as could be expected. It helped that, like Faith, they were both nurses—Gloria in the emergency room and Viv in the ICU. There was little that could shock either of them. They asked a lot of questions without being hostile or intimidating, and I would guess they have a good bedside manner, compassionate but direct. I got the impression we passed muster. When we said goodbye, they each took our hands, mine and Porter's, in both of theirs in turn, and I could imagine them grasping a patient's wrist, firmly but gently, taking his pulse with just enough pressure to feel his blood flow beneath their sensitive fingers without cutting it off.

Faith spent hours on the phone with Gloria and Vivian over the next several weeks. She reported that her sisters had, in fact, liked Porter and approved of him. They also had talked things over with their husbands, Peyton and Tradd, and broached the subject with their eldest sister, Greta.

"She'll like you once she meets you," Faith told Porter.

"That's all it takes. Gloria and Viv loved you, although I think, Owen, that Viv took more of an interest in you. She kept asking about you. Called you 'the quiet one.' I told her you were just shy."

On a weekend in early November, Faith headed down to the farm to break the news to her parents. She said she planned to be firm about her intentions: she would tell them that she and Porter *were* going to get married; whether or not her parents chose to embrace him as a son-in-law would be up to them.

Chapter 13

The three of us drove the four hours to Faith's home in Brooks County on the first Saturday in December. It would be a long day. Porter and I planned to return home alone that evening, so Faith could attend early morning church services with her family the next day and drive back to Atlanta with her mother and all four of her sisters, who made an annual trip to the city on the first weekend after Thanksgiving to Christmas shop at Lenox Square.

It was cool, damp, and overcast as we left Atlanta in our little yellow Boxster. The Bradford pears still clung to most of their foliage, deep green but faded and bruised red and purple, while most of the other trees were nearly bare. The sky gradually brightened as we traveled south, and the air grew drier. The Colquitt family property was called Weathertop Farm, a name Faith said went back to pre-Civil War days, although its origin and meaning had long ago been lost. The land had provided sustenance to the family for more than a hundred and fifty years, though clearly it had made no one rich. An unpaved, rutted, one-lane driveway sliced through two fallow fields spotted with the desiccated stubble of some unknown crop, presumably cotton. The main house was bigger than I expected, three stories, modestly Victorian in its silhouette, with gables and turrets but largely without the typically ornate decorations of that era. It fell somewhere on a continuum between the severity of

Grant Wood's *American Gothic* farmhouse and the fetid gingerbread of *The Addams Family* mansion. To the right of it, across a stretch of gravel where the driveway seemed to simply expire from sheer exhaustion at the top of a rise, was a low-slung brick ranch house of a type popular in the South in the 1950s and 1960s with a flat-topped carport and an angular, asphalt-shingled roof. Next to the big house, the name COLQUITT was painted in white on a weathered gray rock; a neat, hand-lettered sign next to the ranch house read: PEYTON COFFEY CUTLER, DVM, LARGE ANIMAL VETERINARIAN.

"Peyton operates the vet business right out of the little house," Faith said as we crunched to a stop on the gravel driveway. "My dad and his brothers built it themselves, and we lived in it until I was ten, when my Gram Colquitt died and we moved into the big house."

Faith had prepared her parents for our appearance by sending them a copy of the *Vanity Fair* article with the Bruce Weber portraits, which were the most "normal" photos ever taken of us; in most of them, we looked like two guys who might have been standing next to one another with our arms around each others' shoulders. No doubt they would be impressed. I was almost certain her folks had never even seen an issue of *Vanity Fair* previously. She also sent copies of pictures of the three of us taken by my dad the previous Christmas that were more realistic; in four out of the five, at least one of us had "red eye."

It's hard to tell how people are going to react to us the first time we meet. Finding themselves in close proximity to us, strangers often become acutely attentive or overly solicitous, the former out of morbid curiosity or misdirected charity, the latter because they are trying to prove to themselves or others how liberal or politically correct they are. They engage us in polite conversation, repeatedly addressing a question first to me and then to Porter in an almost pedagogical way. Sometimes the queries take on an almost singsong quality, as if we were children—or mentally disabled.

Mrs. Colquitt chose the fussbudget approach, the hall-marks of which are a high-pitched mania and an inability to keep one's hands at rest. Barely had our car rolled to a stop than she burst out of the front door of the house, wearing a red-and-green apron emblazoned with a huge felt candy cane and drying her hands on a pumpkin-colored dishtowel. Faith's father appeared next, smoking a pipe and wearing dun-colored chinos and a red plaid flannel shirt.

"Faith!" her mother said as she approached, arms out, towel flung over her left shoulder.

"Hi, Momma."

They hugged.

Mr. Colquitt approached at a stately pace, preceded by the not unpleasant aroma of cherry pipe tobacco.

"Momma, Daddy, this is the young man I told you about, Porter Jamison," she said, indicating us with a flourish of her arm. "And his brother, Owen."

"Nice to meet you, Porter," Mrs. Colquitt said. "Owen." The towel was back in her hands, and she returned to her Lady Macbeth impression.

"Boys," Mr. Colquitt said, apparently choosing not to dif-ferentiate between the two of us. He put out his hand.

Ordinarily, I do the handshaking when we meet new peo-ple, since I'm on the right and left-handed handshakes are ungainly. In this instance, though, I thought it was important that Mr. Colquitt shake Porter's hand first, so I held back and whispered Porter's name to prompt him to take the initiative. There was an awkward moment as Mr. Colquitt took Porter's hand in his own and held it there, the back of Porter's hand against Mr. Colquitt's palm, unsure of whether to shake it, squeeze it, or simply drop it after a decent inter-val. He finally pumped it quickly, twice, withdrew his hand, and put it into his pants pocket so he would not have to shake mine. Once was quite enough, thank you.

Inside, the Colquitt house was scented with the aromas of roasting fowl, freshly baked bread, and cinnamon. The furnishings were spare and spindly: a rocking chair with a thin orange corduroy bolster tied to its seat; straight, high-backed chairs with cane bottoms. I counted three patchwork quilts draped over furniture or hung on walls in the living room alone and two braided rugs on the wide-planked hardwood floors. A picture of Jesus hung over the upright piano above a small plaster-of-paris sculpture of a pair of praying hands. In the dining room, a long table was already laid out; there were eleven place settings.

"The girls are all coming with their husbands," Mrs. Colquitt said, indicating the table. "I understand you've already met Gloria and Vivian."

It sounded faintly accusatory, as if we had been engaged in a conspiracy. I looked at Faith.

"Yes, Momma, Gloria and Viv did come up to Atlanta to hear the boys play."

"Well, isn't that nice?" Mrs. Colquitt said. "The grandchildren won't be coming today. I thought . . ."

"Momma, is there anything I can help you with in the kitchen?"

"No, dear, everything's under control. I've got Elizabeth watching the pots. She's becoming quite the cook."

There was a knock and the front door opened. Gloria and her husband, over from next door, must have seen us pull up. Gloria kissed Faith on both cheeks.

"Hello, Porter, Owen," she said, holding out her hand for us to shake. "This is my husband, Peyton."

Peyton Coffey Cutler was nothing if not easy on the eye: square-jawed, his handsome face a bit weathered and crinkly around the eyes when he smiled. He took my hand in his, a hand I imagined cradling a foal's head as it emerged, and shook it. Somewhere in the back of my mind the Marlboro song played—or was it the theme from *Bonanza*?

Faith's other sisters and their spouses—Greta and Dooley, Viv and Tradd, neither of the men as spectacular as Peyton

Coffey Cutler, DVM—were not far behind. Mrs. Colquitt disappeared into the kitchen, releasing Elizabeth from her chores and sending her out to meet her sister's intended. She curtsied when she was introduced but kept her distance, standing across the room with her hands behind her back. It was impossible to tell if she was frightened or just shy.

Mrs. Colquitt emerged from the kitchen with steaming cider in old-fashioned cut-glass cups on a tarnished silver tray, each garnished with a thin orange slice, and for some reason I thought of my Aunt Susan on Thanksgivings past, navigating a crowded living room with the big brown bird on a platter. To my delight, Peyton Cutler was the least freaked-out of the husbands and seemed quite comfortable talking to us. It was a pleasure simply to be in his company. I presumed his conversational ease was due to the fact that he had delivered any number of two-headed calves in his years as a veterinarian.

Dinner went smoothly save for the moment Mrs. Colquitt realized that eleven place settings would not be enough. When arranging the table, she had counted asses, not mouths, and needed twelve. I made eye contact with Dooley a couple of times, briefly, and wondered what he thought of the situation. He probably welcomed the idea that he was no longer the oddest member of the extended Colquitt clan. Afterward, the dining room table was cleared and a Monopoly board set up at one end, cards laid out at the other for a game of hearts. Elizabeth worked a thousand-piece puzzle of Claude Monet's "Rouen Cathedral: Full Sunlight" on a card table, which seemed to me a nearly impossible task, with its number- less almost-identical pieces of beige.

The sisters and husbands gradually dwindled in number as the afternoon wore on. Peyton was beeped to an equine emergency, and he and Gloria were the first to leave. By the time Mrs. Colquitt moved a floor lamp next to Elizabeth's puzzle table to prevent eyestrain, I was more than ready to go home myself. I knew, however, that we were going to be forced to endure a man-to-man with Mr. Colquitt. That had been the whole point of the trip.

"Libby, honey, I do believe you've worked that puzzle long enough for one day," Mrs. Colquitt said. "Don't you have schoolwork to do?"

"No, ma'am, it's done."

"Well then, why don't you go up to your room and set out your church clothes for tomorrow? Maybe press that red corduroy jumper? Your pa and I would like to talk to the boys privately."

Elizabeth turned away from her puzzle and looked at her mother imploringly. I could see she had set aside a handful of darker-colored pieces and had been making some progress fitting them together.

"Upstairs, young lady," Mr. Colquitt said.

"We can work on the puzzle together later," Faith added. "When Porter and Owen have gone home. I'll bet we even finish it."

The way Elizabeth stared at us as she slowly ascended the staircase, I couldn't tell if she was truly upset about not being able to continue to work on the puzzle or if she knew she would be missing a juicy conversation.

Mr. Colquitt filled and tamped his pipe. He indicated with a nod of his head that we should sit in a high-backed love seat, upholstered with faded rose velvet, one of the quilts laid carefully over an arm. Faith sat with us, on Porter's side. Mr. Colquitt took his place in a battered green recliner; Mrs. Colquitt dragged in a cane-bottomed chair from the dining room so she could sit next to him, even though there were several more-comfortable, upholstered chairs scattered about the room. I thought back to an October night some five years ago, when the setting was more lavish but the topic of conversation all too similar.

"Son, it don't matter none to us that you look different

from 'most everybody else," Mr. Colquitt began. "You were born that way and didn't have no say in it."

"It's the Lord's plan," Mrs. Colquitt said, patting her husband's weathered brown hand. "Who are we to question it?"

"What matters to us is what kind of person you are on the inside."

"Amen to that," Mrs. Colquitt said.

"Now, Faith says you have many fine qualities, and I believe she is as good a judge of her fellow man as you'll find anywhere. It's a testament to your character that you've come as far as you have, that you haven't let your . . . *condition* . . . ruin your life. It hasn't soured you, made you bitter. And it didn't make you wild crazy reckless, neither. Faith's told me you were an athlete in high school, and a pretty fair one at that. I respect that. My own boy, Chase, was never much for sports."

"But the good Lord has given him other gifts, for which we are thankful," Mrs. Colquitt added.

"Yes, he's been blessed in other ways," Mr. Colquitt said, though it seemed to me the statement lacked conviction. "What concerns us, son, is your choice of careers, your livelihood. The Colquitts have been tending the land here in south Georgia since before the war. We are plain, hardworking folk, and we've always prided ourselves on being independent, self-sufficient. Even in the lean times, we've never accepted a dime of charity or government assistance. Faith's sisters have all married well—good, hardworking men—all except Elizabeth, of course, who's only thirteen. Peyton's a veterinarian, as you know; Greta's husband, Dooley, is in insurance; Vivian's Tradd is in real estate—owns half the county himself, I sometimes think. Good boys, all of them. Brooks County boys. Solid citizens. Active in the church and schools. But this music business you're in. It seems a bit . . . dubious. Uncertain, see? Questionable."

"Questionable, sir?" Porter asked.

"In many ways," Mrs. Colquitt said. She shook her head. "In so many ways."

At this point, I saw Faith take Porter's hand in hers, perhaps as a way of reassuring him, perhaps to prevent him from getting up and walking out.

"There's the money, the income, of course. It's not regular, I'm sure. Has its ups and downs, am I right? I know you're young and you probably dream big, but dreams don't put food on the table and clothes on your kids' backs."

"Sir? If I may?" Porter said, tentatively.

"Yes?" He looked perturbed, as if he might have thought Porter was being "uppity."

"I understand what you're saying, but Janus—that's the name we perform under—it's not just some garage band. We've got a CD out on a major label. We've got an agent and a business manager. We're flying out to L.A. next week to do our first music video. We've got club dates, nationwide, for the next year, solid."

"But what does that translate into, really?"

"In terms of cash?"

"In terms of security for my daughter."

"Daddy, please," Faith said.

"It's okay, honey," Porter said. He told Mr. Colquitt approximately what we had cleared in the last year.

"Well, that's respectable. More than respectable," Mr. Colquitt said, clearing his throat. "But how long can that last?"

"To be honest, sir, I can't say. But we're only just starting out. We're doing better—a lot better—than most new bands. Maybe, and I hesitate to say this, but maybe our success is due in part to the special nature of our act—and there's no telling how far that will take us. Rather than being a detriment to us, it's opened a lot of doors that wouldn't be open to us otherwise. I honestly think we could be big. Really big."

Mr. and Mrs. Colquitt digested this for a few moments. I think both of them had been a little surprised at just how lucrative our career had been so far, especially compared to what I imagine was a somewhat variable and uncertain farm income. Mrs. Colquitt, in particular, seemed to have disappeared inside herself in a way that made me think she was doing some calculating, tabulating, which turned out to be true.

"That's a lot of money for boys your age, but"—here she looked at her husband—"but there *are* two of you. And I imagine you are both planning families. Aren't you, Owen?"

"No, not right now," I said.

I nudged Porter with my knee, ever so slightly. *See,* I wanted to say to him, *this would be the perfect time to tell them that I'm never going to have to worry about sending my kids to college.* He placed his foot on top of mine and stepped down, hard, as if to say, *Shut up!*

"Nonetheless, I'm sure you will. Down the line," she said and cleared her throat, as if the thought of one of us procreating was bad enough, let alone two. "You'll both have children to support, with just this one job between you. And children are not inexpensive. Your current success aside, I'm not convinced music is something you can make a living at. Now, Faith says you met at Druid Hills, that your parents teach there, and that you both graduated with her last year. Perhaps that has given you something to fall back on. What did you study?"

I sighed, hoping as the air escaped that it wasn't audible.

"Music," Porter said.

"English," I said.

"Oh," said Mrs. Colquitt. "English."

I suppose that, knowing Porter was majoring in music, she had given up on him and hoped that I, at least, had majored in something useful, profitable, something that would see us through the lean times. I suspect they wanted at least one of their daughters to marry a doctor—Peyton Coffey Cutler's vet degree notwithstanding.

"Then you could teach?"

"No, ma'am, not with just my bachelor's degree. I have thought about going back for my master's, but . . . the band, you know. Right now, I don't think that's an option."

"There are other things, too," Mr. Colquitt said. "Other concerns, money aside."

"Such as?" Porter asked.

"Morality," Mrs. Colquitt said. "The music business is not well known for morality."

"Oh jeez, Mother."

"Faith, don't take the Lord's name in vain," her father said.

"I said 'Jeez,' not 'Jesus,' Dad."

"It's the same thing."

"What do you mean, 'morality'?" Porter asked.

"Sex. Drugs. Sins of the flesh. That world is rife with temptation," Mrs. Colquitt said.

Sins of the flesh? Oh my God! As if Mammon were not enough, now we were moving on to "sins of the flesh." And there I was, a sodomite! It's a good thing we hadn't named our band Baal, after all. I wanted to die. I wanted to pull my head inside our body the way a turtle does when he senses danger, leaving Porter to face the Spanish Inquisition on his own.

"Mother, Porter isn't like that. He doesn't do drugs."

"And I don't allow our road crew to do drugs, either," he lied.

"Do you drink, son?" Mr. Colquitt asked.

"Socially, sir. And never to excess."

Mrs. Colquitt shook her head and patted her husband's hand. Wrong answer.

"Mom, it's very nearly the twenty-first century."

"None of the other girls' husbands partake, Faith."

"That you know of," Faith said.

"Young lady!" her father said.

"I'll give it up," Porter said. I knew he was lying, and I wondered if Faith believed him or would hold him to it. She hadn't objected to our consumption of alcohol before, though she never drank herself. "If it's important to you, I'll give it up."

"That would be a start," Mrs. Colquitt said.

"Well, then, there's just one more thing," Mr. Colquitt said. He looked at his wife with an expression that implored her to take the ball and run with it, but it was clear she would have none of it. She looked straight ahead, directly at Faith. He cleared his throat, swallowed, shifted in his chair.

"There's the matter of . . . intimacy," he began, then fell silent.

"Intimacy?" Porter asked.

"In the marital bed," Mrs. Colquitt prompted.

"I don't believe this," Faith said. "Please don't do this."

"Faith, honey, it's okay," Porter said. "We can handle it. It doesn't embarrass us."

"How can I say this without being rude?" Mr. Colquitt asked. "Some people might think it is wrong for you boys to be intimate with a woman, since there are two of you. I understand that you are two individuals, that you are separate in your own ways. And I know that Faith is only in love with one of you and is going to give herself only to him. But that raises some questions of modesty and privacy that are pretty difficult to answer. It's embarrassing even to think about, so I'm not going to go into specifics. That really would be too personal. But I want to be sure that there is nothing . . . unusual . . . going on."

Oh my God! I wanted to stand up and shout, "I'm not interested in your daughter's body. I won't touch her breasts. I promise not even to look. Really!"

"I guarantee you there is not," Porter said.

"What I am getting at is this: What is going to happen when your brother takes a wife? What are you going to do then? I believe it would be against the laws of God if you were to be intimate with both of your wives at the same time. I wouldn't want Faith to engage in that type of activity. I'd want an understanding that your brother's wife would have the same right to privacy that I believe you are offering Faith."

"What we're worried about," Mrs. Colquitt said, "are physical and emotional entanglements outside your respective marriages. There might be temptations that few men could resist."

I wanted to jump into the conversation here, not to explain that I was gay, but perhaps to explain to the Colquitts some of the tricks I used to distance myself from the situation when Porter was having sex. And then it hit me. Letting the Colquitts know that Porter had made love to other women before meeting Faith would have been as disastrous as me coming out to them. I'm sure they thought he was a virgin, that no other woman had ever let such a freak touch them, and that their little girl was really an angel of mercy taking pity on a creature no one else would have. So I bit my tongue and hoped Porter would have the presence of mind not to mention his previous sexual liaisons, either.

"Sir . . . ma'am?" Porter began. I don't think he had sirred or ma'amed anyone in fifteen years. "I can tell you unequivocally that when my brother finds someone who loves him in the way Faith loves me, I will respect their privacy in the same way Owen respects mine. There is no way on earth I will ever be tempted to participate in or even to observe my brother when he is engaged in an intimate act, and I will certainly never, ever, covet the person he is with. Nothing could be further from my nature."

It was brilliant. Brilliant! I wanted to high-five him, to let out a war whoop, to rise from that love seat and do a little jig. Yes. *Yes!* He had given them the perfect answer.

The Colquitts looked at one another and smiled. They had clearly been impressed not only with Porter's words but also with the conviction with which he had delivered them.

"Well, son, those are some fine sentiments." Mr. Colquitt stood up. His wife joined him. "I'm sure we'll get to know each other better as time goes by, but I believe that we see eye-to-eye on most of the important issues."

It was clear the conversation was over and that it had been successful to a large extent. Mr. Colquitt tapped his pipe into an ashtray; Mrs. Colquitt twitched and fluttered in place like a caged bird.

"It was a pleasure to meet you, sir," Porter said, standing and extending his hand.

"Likewise, son," Mr. Colquitt said. He avoided shaking Porter's hand a second time by patting his shirt pocket, pulling out a pouch of tobacco, and going through the motions of refilling his pipe.

"You boys should probably start home, don't you think?" Mrs. Colquitt said. "You've got a long drive ahead of you."

"Yes, ma'am, we do," I said.

Faith's sister Elizabeth came down the stairs tentatively. I suspect she may have remained out of sight but within earshot upstairs.

"I'll walk you to your car, Porter," Faith said.

Outside, the light was fading fast, and there was no artificial illumination to brighten the gray, brown, and olive landscape.

"You remember how to get back to the main road and the highway?" Faith asked.

"I know the way," I said.

The Colquitts had followed us outside and stood on the porch, Elizabeth hugging her mother's waist.

"How do you think it went?" Porter whispered, glancing back toward the house.

"Fine. I don't think you could have asked for better," Faith said.

"He didn't say yes, exactly."

"He didn't say no, either. We'll work on him, Gloria, Viv, and I. I don't think there will be any problems."

We stood by the car. Faith put her arms around us. I heard the sound of the screen door opening on the front porch. She leaned in and kissed Porter. When I looked again, the porch was empty.

"Drive carefully, boys," Faith said. "I love you, Porter."

"And I love you. Can I call you tonight when we get home?"

"Don't. It'll be too late. I'll call you first thing in the morning, before we go to church."

Our headlights swept across the back of Peyton Coffey Cutler's vet sign as we turned the car around. Faith stood and waved as we drove away, then walked toward the ranch house, not the Victorian.

"Sweet Jesus," Porter said, once we were down the driveway. "That was so fucked."

"Porter, don't take the Lord's name in vain," I said.

"All that talk about morality. *Thou shalt not covet thy brother's wife!* What the hell are we going to do?"

"I don't think it went badly. I think they like you."

"Me? *Me?* They fucking love me. I'm not talking about me. I'm talking about you! If they knew what you had done with Casey or some of those guys on the road, I'd be dead meat. We can't ever let them know. None of them. Not even Faith."

"Porter, we're not going to be able to keep it from Faith."

"Sure we will."

That was a new development—the idea that Porter was actually going to try to keep Faith in the dark permanently. Until now, the talk had not been about *if*, only *when*. It frightened me that he was even considering not telling Faith, that he thought it might be possible, and that he had so little insight into what it would mean for me.

I eased up on the accelerator and steered the car over to the side of the road. I couldn't say what I needed to say and still concentrate on making our way down the darkened driveway. Except for the glow of the two houses in our rearview mirror—one vertical, one horizontal—there was not a light to be seen in any direction.

"No, Porter, we won't," I said. "I won't live my life like that. I'm not going to stay in the closet for the rest of my life. At some point, we're going to have to tell Faith. We may be able to keep it a secret from her family, sure, and I guess I could deal with that. But we're going to be living with Faith day in and day out, and I am not going to live a lie. I'm not going to worry about every word that comes out of my mouth. And someday I'm going to actually have another boyfriend, maybe even live with him. . . ."

"I guess I never really considered that."

"It never occurred to you that I was going to fall in love someday?"

"Well . . . until then, until we absolutely have to tell her, let's not."

"Look, I don't think it's going to be that bad. You saw how uncomfortable Faith was when her father started getting personal, asking about intimate details of our private lives. I'm sure she doesn't buy into that 'morality' stuff. And besides, I think she's mature and sophisticated enough to understand that I have my own life, my own needs, that I am going to go my own way. That's part of the deal. It's got to be. She's got to understand and accept that. Otherwise this isn't going to work. I've played along with you this far, but at some point, it's got to end. Exactly when did you plan on mentioning it to her?"

"Someday. Someday soon. But I don't want to tell her now, not before we get married. She might have second thoughts."

"Right. Like she won't have second thoughts after you're married?"

"But at least at that point we'll *be* married. It'll be a done deal. And that will make it a whole lot more difficult to end things. She'd have to give it a lot more thought."

"And it will also be a whole lot messier, legally, financially, and emotionally."

"Well, that may be true, but I'm willing to chance it."

"What's to stop me from telling her? From just blurting it out?"

"You wouldn't do that, Owen. I know you. That's not your style. You don't like to hurt people, and that would hurt Faith and it would hurt me. I know I'm asking a lot, and I know I could be making a big mistake, but you've gotta let me make it on my own. I know it seems like I am making this all about me, and in a way I am. But this is real for me. It's not a fantasy, a fairy tale. There's nö 'maybe' or 'if' about it, no question mark, the way there is in your life: 'Will I ever find a guy? Will I ever fall in love?' Who knows if that is ever going to happen for you. But I *have* found someone to love me. I can make a life for myself, have a family. I know you're not going to ruin that for me."

He was right, of course. I wouldn't say anything that would ruin his chances of finding happiness, even if it meant denying who I was a little longer. And so, even though I was certain we were heading for disaster, I agreed not to tell Faith I was gay, at least not until after the wedding.

We made our way down the long driveway in a bubble of light, our headlamps throwing the desiccated stubble of the Colquitts' harvest into high relief, our taillights, when we applied the brakes, making the dry stalks behind us flare up like embers. For some reason, I couldn't shake the feeling that little Libby Colquitt was upstairs in one of the turrets of the austere Victorian house, her face pressed against a window, her breath fogging the chilled glass, marking our progress through the mazelike roads that would take us back to the highway, her vantage point giving her a much better view of where we were going than Porter and I had ourselves from the warm and softly glowing passenger compartment of our little yellow sports car.

Chapter 14

As we do almost any time we appear in public, Porter and I caused quite a stir when we arrived at the Fulton County marriage license office with Faith some three months later. The room was full of hopeful young couples lined up two by two as if waiting to board the ark, without exception the prospective grooms standing to the right, their brides to the left, foreshadowing the positions they would occupy when they spoke their vows. But as we took our place at the end of the line, we initiated a strange chain reaction. The couple immediately ahead of us turned to see who had joined them in line, perhaps to welcome us as they had been greeted by those directly ahead of them minutes earlier, the brides smiling shyly, the grooms exchanging nervous jokes or sizing up their counterpart's future wife to see who had gotten the better deal. But upon seeing us, both partners involuntarily took two small steps to the side, parting, and at the same time creating space for Porter, Faith, and me to advance in line. The reaction was repeated by the next couple, and then the next, and we proceeded toward the clerk as if we were passing through an honor guard at a West Point wedding or were the stars in a carefully choreographed scene from an old Hollywood musical. Our guest-hosting gig on MTV's weekly top-ten countdown two weeks earlier, filmed at the same time as our debut music video, had received astronomical ratings, and it was impossible to tell if people were deferring to our celebrity or retreating at the spectacle of a two-headed man.

In any event, we quickly made our way to the front of the line, where we found ourselves face-to-face with a nattily dressed black woman in her late forties or early fifties. She was wearing a satiny black dress with large red polka dots and a broad red collar, the sort of outfit she might wear under her robes when she sang in the Ebenezer Baptist Church choir on Easter Sunday. Although Porter did all the talking, the clerk sometimes would lock eyes with me instead of him when she glanced up from our paperwork, poised to ask me a question until Porter cleared his throat. She looked at Faith as if Porter and I might have been holding her hostage.

We were not sure exactly what to expect. It was not so long ago that people like Porter and I were prohibited from getting married. Opposition to such unions ran deep. Conjoined twins were, after all, "an abomination." Throughout history, people have thought they were a punishment by God for wickedness on the part of the parents. Surely such creatures were something less than human and were not entitled to the rights and privileges of "normal" individuals. The unenlightened viewed marriages involving conjoined twins as suspect at best and very probably immoral because, of necessity, the unmarried twin shared the conjugal bed. As tame as that sounds today, fifty or sixty years ago, when open marriages, sex clubs, and swinging were unheard of, it would have been absolutely scandalous. My God, what if everyone's most puritanical fears proved true? What if the unmarried twin actually participated in the sex act? That was probably illegal in at least thirty-five states. And God forbid they should procreate! What beasts would issue forth from the loins of a conjoined twin?

In the 1930s and 1940s, Daisy and Violet Hilton, a pair of conjoined twins who came to the United States from Brighton, England, each attempted to get married on a number of occasions, with disappointing results. They were considerably less freakish than Porter and I, since they were two complete individuals nominally joined at the buttocks, each with two arms and two legs and her own private parts. Had they been born today, separation would have been accomplished with ease. They were pretty girls. I've seen pictures of them in which they resemble silent-film star Mary Pickford or a pair of hopeful British war brides, seated together, legs demurely crossed, in flouncy summer dresses, wearing white ankle socks. In 1934, Violet applied for a license to marry Maurice Lambert, the musical director of a vaudeville show in which the twins were appearing, and I can only imagine her disappointment when they were refused a marriage license in both New York City and Newark on the same day. ("Application is denied on the grounds that the bride is a Siamese twin," the edicts read.) Violet and Maurice eventually were turned down by nineteen other states, and their romance faded. A year later, however, Violet married a dancer named James Walker Moore at the Texas Centennial Exposition. The marriage lasted only a few months, and when it was annulled both parties insisted it had only been a publicity stunt. It may well have been, but I'm convinced Violet's first doomed attempt at marriage was heartfelt.

Daisy was even unluckier in love. Her marriage, to Buddy Sawyer, a master of ceremonies eight years her junior, lasted only ten days, and her soon-to-be-ex-husband made a comment that indicated the forced ménage à trois may have contributed to its failure. ("As far as being a bridegroom under such conditions is concerned, I suppose I am what you might call a hermit," he is reported to have said.) Apparently, neither twin got a second chance at love. Their stage career had been lucrative by the standards of the day, and when it ended they invested in a hotel in Pittsburgh, but after that venture failed they were reduced to operating a fruit stand in Florida. When they were in their early fifties, they moved to Charlotte, North Carolina, where they worked in a supermarket at adjoining produce scales. In 1969, when they were sixty years old, they failed to report to work for several days and were found dead on the floor of their apartment, apparently from complications of the flu.

Although the word "freak" has since been expunged from our politically correct vocabularies along with unacceptable epithets for blacks, Jews, and Asians, genuine acceptance of people in our circumstances has been slow in coming. And because Porter and I share the all-important piece of equipment that is at the heart of the marital process, our situation is even more complicated and troublesome than those of either the Hilton twins or the more famous Chang and Eng, who also had two distinct, if joined, bodies. I could see the precise moment when this occurred to the clerk in the marriage license office. A look of puzzlement clouded her face, and she asked Porter and me to step away from the counter so she could check us out (*"A little farther, please"*). Using both hands, she lifted a pair of glittering, cat's-eye glasses, which rested against her ample bosom, suspended from a slender gold chain punctuated regularly by small pearlescent beads. *Hmm . . . let's see. Two legs, one pair of pants, one fly.* She looked over the top of her glasses at the paperwork we had submitted, searching, I suppose, for some sort of explanation, some special authorization. As she absentmindedly fingered one of her chunky red costume-jewelry earrings, I thought she might break out in a smile and ask us to reveal the location of the hidden camera. Ultimately, she summoned some co-workers, and there appeared to be a consensus that perhaps I needed to sign the application as well. Her supervisor ultimately overruled that, saying it would amount to bigamy. He then invited us into his office, where he apologized for the confusion, beads of sweat forming on his crimson face, and expedited the remainder of the process. When we emerged from his office, I got the distinct impression that everyone in the outer room had been in a state of suspended animation, straining toward the supervisor's scuffed, frosted-glass door to eavesdrop on our conversation. As the doors closed behind us on the way out, I heard muffled shouts and screams and high-pitched nervous laughter.

I feel certain someone in the marriage license office placed a call to the *National Enquirer* in hopes of obtaining some sort of freak bounty, since events less curious than the pending marriage of a two-headed man have been reported in its pages, but we left before any hack journalists arrived. We would find ourselves basking in the media limelight soon enough, however, when Porter and Faith's wedding announcement appeared in the society column of the *Atlanta Journal-Constitution* (even though I had been carefully cropped out of the engagement picture). The news of Porter's engagement proved wildly appealing to the media, although I suppose no one should have been surprised. Our agent received requests from Oprah and Ricki Lake to be married on their programs; NBC offered a slot on the *Today Show; Primetime, Dateline*, and *20/20* wanted, at the very least, to cover the wedding. Against my mother's wishes, we turned them all down. A simple wedding at the First Baptist Church of Quitman was what Faith wanted and what we were determined she would have. Nonetheless, we ultimately did agree to several high-profile interviews, all of them held in the living room of my parents' Ansley Park home, since Atlanta was far more accessible to reporters than Quitman and since Faith's parents wisely were loath to get involved with the media circus. For a time, my mother attempted to stage-manage the media as she had done when we were younger, but I think it soon became clear to her that things had reached a level of momentum over which she had no control.

Suddenly, everyone was extraordinarily interested in our private lives. To the public, the fact that Porter was getting married meant, obviously, that he intended to have sex with Faith, if he had not already done so. They put two and two together and came up with one—one penis between us—and that just fascinated the hell out of them. Most of the really em-

barrassing questions were directed toward me, and sometimes they got downright kinky. The reporters could readily
accept the fact that Porter and Faith were going to have sex,
but almost all of them wanted to know what *I* intended to do
while they were being intimate. As the odd man out, I was
universally viewed as some kind of voyeur or pervert. Would
I watch? Would I join in? Wouldn't our shared penis actually
make me an equal partner in their intercourse? How would
we know who was having sex with whom?

Then, too, there was the issue of emotional entanglements,
the same question that had dogged Faith's parents. Although
at first I thought this line of inquiry absurd, upon reflection I
could understand it. The more scientific types in the world
believe love is more or less a complex chemical reaction between two people, a response to pheromones and the like. If
that's true, it would be easy to conclude that two genetically
identical people would have identical, or at the very least
similar, receptors; would be primed to respond in the same
way to the same physical stimuli; would "fall in love" with
the same person. Among conjoined twins, the danger of this
happening is heightened by the fact that both twins are present at every erotic encounter, whether or not they are the intended object of the affection. There was always the danger
that the unmarried twin would be jealous or lustful, would
have his or her passions aroused by a twin's amorous adventures, would sneak a longing look at a twin's partner, might
even touch something he or she had no right to touch. (I wondered what Daisy Hilton did while Violet made love to her
husband. It's not far-fetched to imagine her wearing ear plugs
or one of those satin sleeping masks you see in movies from
the 1930s.) Of course, there was also the possibility that the
third party, the non-twin, might fall in love with both of the
twins, who would look and taste and smell the same.
Amorous accidents might happen, too. A groggy husband,
on his way back from a nocturnal trip to the bathroom,

could get confused, especially if his wife and sister-in-law had turned over in bed while he was gone.

In a live, remote interview conducted from the sitting room of my parents' house, Katie Couric asked me if I was dating anyone and, only half-jokingly, inquired as to whether Faith had any unmarried sisters at home.

"I've got four," Faith said before realizing the question was meant more or less in jest, "all married save one, but she's only thirteen."

Angry and impatient with the media's unseemly interest in my sex life, I was tempted to demonstrate my ability to detach myself by reciting the state capitals and periodic table of elements for them on the spot. That would have shut them up. But it seemed, in this context, a little freakish, a sideshow stunt. Flabbergasted, I suggested to Porter privately that coming out publicly as a gay man might simplify things.

"It would make it a lot easier to explain, don't you think?" I asked him. "I mean, if our penis is in contact with a woman's body—specifically Faith's—you're the one who is having sex, and if it's in contact with a man's, I'm having sex."

"No way, O. Absolutely no way," Porter said, panicked. "You know we can't do that. Faith's family would throw a fit."

"Relax, Porter, I'm just kidding . . . sort of."

Chapter 15

Porter's pending nuptials inevitably raised the question of my own marital plans. At engagement parties, I had to put up with sympathetic pats on the back from friends and family, endure their winks and nudges, parry their vaguely prurient questions about my plans for the honeymoon night.

"Solitaire," I told the more persistent inquisitors, or "Practice C.P.E. Bach's *Klavierstucke* for one hand."

But in general, I simply smiled coyly, shook my head, waved dismissively. "Marriage isn't for me," I said, firmly if somewhat cryptically. "Owen Jamison won't be getting married any time soon."

Principal among my antagonists was my mother, whose emotional state since Porter's engagement had been so elevated, it could be described only as "manic-aggressive." In her eyes, I suddenly had become Atlanta's most eligible bachelor. Female MBA candidates from her classes and daughters of our affluent neighbors regularly appeared at the Ansley Park house on the nights Faith joined us for dinner—"to fill out the table."

"Very bright," Mom said of each and every one of them. "She could help manage your career, Owen. And I think she'd get along well with Faith. That's going to be important—the spouses getting along. Of course, Faith is such an angel, she could get along with anyone."

I couldn't believe Mom had spent this much time thinking

about what the future held for me, creating a fantasy universe in which Faith and my future wife could play house, a kind of *Hallmark Hall of Fame* script in which we all lived happily ever after—or a twisted *Brady Bunch* takeoff on a blended family. Of course, there was never any chemistry between me and the post-debs my mother invited to dinner. I think the young women were only being polite—or respectful of the power my mother wielded over their academic and professional careers—when they agreed to come.

Before things went too far, I decided I would have to tell Mom I was gay. Her enthusiasm for matchmaking was unflagging, and although it seemed unlikely any of my prospective brides would actually fall head over heels for me, I wanted to put an end to the charade before anything untoward happened.

From everything gay friends have told me about the coming-out process, I've concluded that fathers either accept you when you tell them you're gay or they don't. They embrace you or they turn their backs on you. There's no negotiation, no middle ground. I suspected that given Dad's analytical thinking and his training in psychology, there was little chance he would fall into the latter category. He might not be happy, but he wasn't going to get emotional about it. He might even find the situation of some academic interest: two genetically identical men nurtured in precisely the same way and yet with different sexual orientations. So I was not worried about Dad. It was telling Mom that troubled me.

Mothers, when confronted with the fact of a gay son, frequently fret and twitter. I've heard stories about mothers who, when faced with such news, instantaneously become obsessive-compulsive cleaners, polishing the silver at the pricey restaurant their son selected in the hope of preventing a scene; smoothing the nap of their coats; picking lint from their skirts; depilling their sweaters. They respond to the revelation that their sons are gay by entering a trance of tidiness from which they very often need to be physically shaken.

You'd think that would not be the case for a woman who had given birth to what most people would consider a monstrosity. You'd think such a woman would have both the strength of character and the resilience to understand and accept the fact that one of her sons was different. After all, when the nurse first handed my mother her two sons swaddled in one blanket (probably compensating for her horror with an overly solicitous smile), did my mother respond by rigorously inspecting the buttons on her night jacket, looking for loose threads? I hope not. I want to think she clutched us to her bosom and suckled us, that she not only loved us but loved *each* of us, separately, uniquely, from the first moment she saw us.

I can only imagine the strength it took to put us in our stroller and walk us around Ansley Park for the first time, bravely enduring encounters with strangers whose cooing and baby talk stuck in their throats when they realized the adorable twin boys they were admiring shared a body. I've often wondered what it must have been like pushing a two-headed toddler through the Piggly Wiggly in a grocery cart as dumbstruck shoppers parted before her like the Red Sea for Moses. What must she have felt the first time she heard the expression "Isn't it precious?" from some well-meaning but subconsciously horrified passerby?

So you'd think she'd be able to handle the news that I was gay with grace and understanding, wouldn't you?

I've talked to gay friends whose families actually shunned them when they came out. That's the word they used— "shunned"—as if they had violated the most sacred tenet of some arcane religious sect. Disinherited. Banished. Expunged from the ancestral Bible. Lopped off the family tree like a diseased branch off a century-old oak before the contagion could spread. I didn't think that would be a possibility here. After all, Mom couldn't exactly invite Porter to Thanksgiving dinner and not me.

On a Sunday in January, a week before our twenty-third

birthdays, I took Mom and Dad to brunch at the Ritz-Carlton in Buckhead, long my Mom's favorite. Porter told me he had "no interest whatsoever" in taking part in the discussion, which I knew meant he would more or less check out during the conversation. I was always the one to broach complex or difficult subjects with our parents—when we broke things as kids or when we had our first fender bender after having insisted on learning to drive. Porter would shut down, closing his eyes as if he were asleep, or he would fumble with one of our handheld computer games, struggling to achieve a score that was well below half of what we were able to attain when we worked together. This time, I asked him to just sit quietly and to refrain from any guttural comments. It was his idea to listen to the Discman I had given him for Christmas.

I broke the news over our lobster bisque. Mom had been wondering aloud about Faith's absence and prioritizing a list of four young women who were next in line for an invitation to dine. From the sound of it, I suspected she may have quietly transitioned to her B list.

"Mom," I said, "there's something you should know before you register me for the next eligible-bachelor auction at the Piedmont Driving Club."

"Always with the smart remarks, Owen," she said. "But if I didn't look after your interests, who would? I'll bet you thought your brother would never get married, either, but he is. And Faith is a charming girl, a lovely woman. There's no reason to think the same thing couldn't happen to you."

"There's one reason. One very good reason."

I'd caught her with her soup spoon in midair, leaning forward ever so slightly, her lips, barely parted, coincidentally the same shade of coral as the bisque.

"I'm gay, Mom. There's not going to be a girl in my future."

She carefully replaced her spoon on the table, setting it down precisely where it had lain before she'd picked it up, as if she were in a movie running backwards, rewinding, as if

with that gesture she could turn back time to before my announcement, if not to prevent it, then at least to be better
prepared for it. With both hands, she smoothed her hair back
from her face, up over the top of her head, and let them rest
there. She looked like a woman in a plastic surgeon's office,
tugging at her forehead to see what she might look like if she
had a face-lift.

"Gay?"

"Yes, Mom. Gay."

I can't tell you what went through my mother's mind
when I said those words, though I can be fairly certain from
the look on her face that my announcement had been completely unexpected, that she hadn't had a clue as to what I
had been planning to tell her when we first sat down. If she
had been a religious person, this would have been one of those
moments that would have gone into the testing-of-faith category—another trial, like the seven plagues of Egypt. A two-
headed child. A gay son. What's next? Locusts? Fortunately,
she is *not* a religious person. She has never sought comfort in
faith, and she frequently describes her sister's prayer vigils as
times when "Aunt Sue is talking to her imaginary friend."

No, her disappointment—and that is clearly what it was—
was more personal, more direct and immediate. It was a
chink in her carefully constructed armor, a fatal blow to her
plans for having her sons live as normal lives as possible,
given our circumstances. After twenty-three years, Porter
and I were accepted for who we were. This was an unwelcome deviation.

I guess what hurt me most was her initial response. After
a moment of abject befuddlement and a fiercely protective
glance at Porter, lost in his music, she looked at me, turned
her eyes downward, and—there it was!—brushed the flakes
of a *pain au chocolat* off the tablecloth.

"But . . . Porter? What about . . . ?"

"Porter's *fine*. He and Faith are very much in love. I'm
sure they'll be very happy, have kids, the whole nine yards."

"Thank God."

I knew her response had been involuntary, that she hadn't meant to hurt me, but nonetheless I was crushed. Her first thought had been of Porter. Was he "okay?" Had he somehow been tainted? In that moment, I felt utterly abandoned, alienated from my mother, from my family, even from the brother with whom I shared a body. I actually felt like a growth, a malignancy on Porter's body, and the thought occurred to me that she might be thinking, fleetingly, perhaps only subconsciously, that she should have excised me twenty-three years ago when she had the chance, when it might have been considered reasonable, even desirable, to do so. (Though I can also imagine she might have thought, "My God, what if I had killed the wrong one?")

"Maybe you're just confused. This whole thing with Porter, the wedding . . . It hurts, I'm sure. You feel left out. You're hurt, angry. Maybe that's what's made you think . . ."

"Mom, I don't *think* I'm gay. I know it. I've known it for years, long before Porter ever *met* Faith."

But she wasn't listening. As she pinched a browning sprig of baby's breath from our floral centerpiece with an expression composed equally of disgust and disinterest, she actually suggested I might have "chosen" to be gay simply to be different from Porter, in much the same way I had chosen to drink my milk plain as a kid.

"Mom, this isn't about Nestlé Quik!"

Dad, who had remained silent so far, weighed in with the psychological perspective, more for Mom's benefit, I think, than mine. He suggested it was possible I had confused my physical attachment to Porter, our closeness, with sexual feelings, and now that he was, at least symbolically, being taken away from me by Faith, I was seeking to replace him with another man. I don't think anybody bought that. Mom looked at Dad as if he had suggested that, after all, the world *was* flat. Thereafter, he kept his mouth shut.

No one except Porter continued to eat. Our waiter stopped

by the table to ask if everything was all right and then, realizing he had stumbled across a scene from *Hush . . . Hush, Sweet Charlotte* or *The Little Foxes*, backed away from the table saying, "The food . . . I meant the food."

"I simply can't believe you could do this to your brother!" Mom said, once the waiter was out of earshot. "My God, the embarrassment, Owen. Have you thought of that? And he's suffered through all of this without saying a word to anyone? And your fans, the people who buy your music—what will they say if they find out? People look up to you. You've triumphed over adversity. You're a role model. How do you think they are going to react if they find out you're gay? It could destroy you—both of you. At a time when your brother is about to embark on a whole new life, you're a threat to his very future."

I could see her resolve hardening on her face as clearly as the skin that had congealed on the cooling surface of her neglected lobster bisque. Porter was the victim, I the villain. She was going to fall back on the good twin-bad twin scenario, something she had fought since we had been born. She even accused me of grandstanding, of making a deliberate attempt to take the limelight away from Porter and Faith and their wedding.

"I'm ashamed of you, Owen," she said.

Ashamed. She was *ashamed* of me.

At that moment, my sense of separation was more intense than anything I had felt years before, when I first realized I was gay, because it came from outside me, from someone I loved and I thought loved me. I longed to be able to physically separate myself from my brother, to run away and not look back, maybe never to return. Porter knew something was up. He could feel my side of our body tense up, feel our bowels constrict. He took off the headphones but didn't say anything, just looked blankly first at Mom and then, obliquely, at me.

"It's okay, dear," she said to him. "You just listen to your music."

Porter shrugged his shoulder and complied.

We all have our own personal mythologies, stories we devise to explain the generally disagreeable circumstances in which we find ourselves. The children of paupers pretend they are the offspring of millionaires or movie stars—maybe even royalty—switched at birth or kidnapped at an early age by these creatures who *call* themselves their parents. My own personal mythology is somewhat more complicated. I sometimes wonder who came first: Porter or me? Would the undivided individual have been straight or gay? Who is the rightful heir and who the usurper? Which one the prince, which the pauper?

I don't have the answer. I don't know if there *is* an answer. But I believe I know what Mom's would be, and I believe she began composing it that very day as she brushed flakes of pastry from the tablecloth at the Ritz and pinched dead vegetation from our centerpiece. I believe she thinks that Porter, *in utero*, recognized there was something "wrong" with him, something defective, something he wanted no part of. That "thing" was me, or at least it was the gay part of me. People think that way, especially parents—disappointed parents. They need to find an answer to the question "Why? Why is my son gay?" An answer outside of themselves. So here we have Porter, the original son, the *good* son, Porter's "spirit," his life force, recognizing something alien within him and trying to get rid of it, to distance himself from it, to push it away from him, maybe even to kill it. And so we began to divide. Porter normal, whole, good, straight. Me abnormal, defective, alien, gay. Even if he wasn't able to kill me, he'd at least be able to separate himself from me.

But I was too strong for him, too determined, and I fought back. He tried to push me away, but I clung to him. He was able only to separate his head from me, his brain, his mind, and that was all, before I stopped him. So not only had I doomed him to a life of sexual perversity, I also was responsible for his freakish physique.

"Exactly what is it you intend to do about these feelings, Owen?" she asked, finally.

"Do?"

"Yes, dear, *do*. Do you intend to . . . *pursue* them? If you haven't already?"

My father looked at my mother as if she had just opened Pandora's box.

"Well, naturally, I'd like to meet someone . . . have a relationship," I said.

"A relationship?" she said, as if I had suggested I wanted to give birth. It seemed that implausible to her. "A *relationship*."

"Yes, Mom. With another man."

Her lower lip curled down at that, like a rose withering in time-lapse photography.

"I'm not an idiot, Owen. I understand it would be with another man."

"I'm sorry, Mom."

"And do you expect Porter to . . . *participate* in this 'relationship'?"

"To the extent that he has to, yes. Not in an emotional sense. But physically. We share . . ."

"Owen!" my father said. "That's quite enough. Neither your mother nor I need an anatomy lesson at this point. We're well aware of the way in which you boys are constructed."

My mother's complexion had turned doughy. It was as if instead of merely alluding to our penis, I had flopped it out onto the table next to the ornate sushi sampler we had ordered. A more alert maitre d' might have wrapped her in a warm blanket and dialed 911.

"I don't understand this, Owen," my mother said. "I don't see how this is possible."

"For what it's worth, Mom, I don't understand it, either. All I know is that it's true. It's how I feel. It's what I want."

"What you *want*?"

"It's more than that. It's what I need. It's who I am."

That was that. My mother pushed back her chair, dropped her linen napkin into her abandoned bisque, and left without another word. My father hurriedly stood, clutched at his wallet until I waved him off, and followed her, turning to look back at me apologetically. Our waiter winced at the bisque-stained napkin when he came to clear the table.

At this point, Porter finally removed his headphones. Despite the theatricality of our mother's departure, I actually think he waited until the song to which he was listening had finished.

"What's going on, O?" he asked with the nonchalance of a doomed airline passenger rousing himself from slumber to discover his jet plunging headlong toward the earth. I thought I saw the waiter roll his eyes at me conspiratorially.

"It did not go well," I said.

"Duh! As if . . ."

"Fuck you, Porter. Don't 'as if' me. As if what? As if you give a shit?"

I imagine Porter and I look somewhat ridiculous when we are having a heated discussion. We're so used to talking to one another that we don't generally bother even to turn our heads toward each other, so when we're angry we look as if we are barking at invisible antagonists in front of us.

"Whoa, whoa, whoa, man. Chill. I just meant, like, what were you expecting, bro?"

"What was I expecting? Well, *bro*, what I was expecting was maybe that you'd take off your goddamn headphones long enough to say a few words on my behalf, to stand up for me, to not make me face this completely on my own."

"Hey, man, I tried, but Mom told me to shut up and listen to my music."

"I don't believe the words 'shut up' were uttered."

"You know what I mean, O. She's tough to argue with."

"Like you tried."

Porter shook his head, his right ear grazing my left one. "You're too frigging intense, man. What did you want me to say? 'Yeah, Mom, Owen's gay, but don't worry, it's not contagious'?"

"Actually, Porter, that's exactly what I wanted you to say."

"You're kidding, right?"

"I don't mean use those exact words, but you could let her—and Dad—know that you're okay with things the way they are . . ."

"'Okay' might be too strong a word. I *tolerate* it."

"Well then, fine. Tell them you *tolerate* it, if that's the best you can do for now. But don't let them think I'm forcing you to participate in anything against your will. And it would be helpful, too, if you could somehow let them know that what I do isn't something dark and mysterious, that it's the same thing you do, or did before you met Faith, anyway. Except I do it with guys."

"Oh, so you want me to come clean with Mom about boffing all those groupies?"

"No, shithead, I don't want you to lay bare your sordid past. But if you could make her understand that, for example, the feelings I had for Casey weren't all that different from the feelings you had for Christi or any of the other girls you dated in high school, that might go a long way toward helping her understand that I am not some kind of pervert."

"Okay, bro, I'll do my best."

"Really? You'll say something to Mom and Dad?"

"Sure, bro. Like I said, I'll do my best."

But Porter did not have that little heart-to-heart chat with our parents. Somehow, he never quite mustered the right words, which ultimately didn't surprise me. On a few occasions he did give them a few mumbled reassurances, which I suppose is the best he could do.

In the weeks that followed, I think my mother reinterpreted my life history to "explain" why I was gay. For no apparent reason, or none that seemed obvious to me, she began to make generalized comments about how I was always this or always that: always the neat one, the smart one, the sensitive one. It wasn't necessarily in the context of explaining my gayness. They were just offhand comments, as much to herself as to me or anyone else, as if she were now almost constantly, incessantly, musing about why I had "turned out" the way I had, why I was different than Porter (about whom she made no such observations). Despite my father's rebuke of my indelicacy at brunch, she developed an insatiable curiosity about Porter's and my shared physicality. She asked questions no mother in her right mind would ask her twenty-three-year-old son—and no son in his right mind would answer.

Say what you will about the progress gay people have made in the past thirty years, homosexuality is still not considered normal and never will be—at least not in my lifetime. For heterosexuals, accepting it is, to varying degrees, still an accommodation, a conciliatory gesture for which they feel they should be congratulated and which should be gratefully acknowledged by the recipients of their emotional largesse. Granted, some people move beyond this and embrace their gay sons and daughters, their gay siblings, wholeheartedly and utterly without reservation. But there is that first step, that transition, be it a moment, a minute, or a month, during which they have to shift gears, relinquish familiar expectations, acknowledge new realities. In many ways, it's a grieving process, marked by some of the same steps that accompany the diagnosis of a terminal illness: denial, anger, bargaining, acceptance.

I think the way Mom ultimately resolved it was by think-ing of us, Porter and me, as bisexual. There was something chic and not quite so damning about that, something experi-mental and, hopefully, *transitory*.

I let it go at that.

Chapter 16

As we approached Porter and Faith's big day, it occurred to me that I have sometimes thought of my relationship with my brother as a variation of an arranged marriage. Porter and I were wed to one another in my mother's womb. We've had to learn to live with each other in circumstances of suffocating intimacy, under which virtually no normal couple could survive intact. Our relationship has been marked by competition as well as cooperation, by understanding and misunderstandings, for better or worse, till death do us part. I could only hope Faith and Porter's union would be as successful.

Porter and I have always taken great pains to define what is his and what is mine. We maintain separate checking accounts, pursue different investment strategies, and file our income taxes separately. We've created a corporate entity to manage the proceeds from our music careers as well as to handle copyright issues and, sometime in the future, possible licensing agreements. So prior to the wedding, I told Porter we needed to take special care drawing up documents to protect my share of our community property and my future income in the event of divorce. While we were at it, I suggested he consider a prenuptial agreement. Porter was so in love with Faith, he found it hard to imagine a time when they wouldn't be together or when he wouldn't want to provide her with anything she needed, so every time I brought up the idea of visiting our lawyer, he found some excuse for why he wasn't able to go. Finally, I had to take control of the situation and force the issue. As a result, he was far better prepared, legally, for his wedding, than if he had approached it on his own.

I finally met Faith's fabled brother, Chase, at the wedding rehearsal dinner in the basement of the First Baptist Church in Quitman. He was finishing his senior year at MIT and had come down from Cambridge for the wedding, which we had specifically scheduled to coincide with his spring break.

"I always had this sense that he was gaining on me," Faith said as she showed us pictures of Chase on the evening before he arrived. "He's four years younger than I am, but by the time I was a senior in high school, he was only a year behind me."

The photos showed a young man who was lean and gangly at eleven, even before a rush of hormones made him shoot up another foot seemingly overnight. By the time he and Faith posed for a picture on the night of their small rural high school's combined junior-senior prom, his powder blue tuxedo jacket the exact shade of her dress, he was a couple of inches taller than she, despite their age difference. In most family portraits—they had one taken annually at Olan Mills in Albany—he towered over his five sisters; in more recent pictures he eclipsed even his lanky father, standing a full six feet two. In other respects, too, he stood out as almost suspiciously different. His hair was pale—not colorless, exactly, but a sort of silvery blond, like corn silk—while the rest of the Colquitt family was dark haired. His skin was exceedingly fair, while his siblings tended toward tanned complexions and freckles, a coloration more suitable to the south Georgia sun. It was as if the Swedish milkman had surreptitiously entertained Mrs. Colquitt while her husband was in the henhouse feeding the chickens.

As different as he appeared physically, Chase was obviously the pride and joy of the Colquitt family, perhaps because he was the only boy among five girls, or because of his preternatural intelligence, or maybe because he was the only Colquitt offspring who appeared to have achieved escape velocity and was thus cherished all the more. From the moment he walked into that church basement, he was the center of attention. He was rarely so much as an arm's length from his mother as they circumnavigated the room, talking to members of the wedding party and renewing acquaintances with old friends and family. He seemed simultaneously effervescent and shy, smiling quickly and easily but also shrinking somehow from whomever he was talking to, seeking the protection of his mother's arm when he was accosted by well-wishers but shrugging it off when they were alone.

In that musty basement, lit by candles to eliminate the need for the harsh blue-white glare of the overhead fluorescent units, Chase seemed to glow, to exude a kind of light that was reflected back in his eyes, his hair, his smile. I wondered if anyone else saw this aura—it seemed impossible to overlook—and I wondered, too, if that light was accompanied by a palpable warmth, if his pink skin would be flushed, warm to the touch, and if, standing near him, I might be able to feel him, sense him, even with my eyes closed, radiating heat and light. So mesmerized was I by Chase's presence that I remained immobile when Porter made a move toward one of the long dining tables covered with red-and-white checked tablecloths as members of Mrs. Colquitt's eighth-grade Sunday school class brought out the first steaming plates of spaghetti and meatballs they had prepared with the help of their parents.

"Dude, pay attention! We're eating," Porter said, tugging me along with him.

As luck would have it, Chase sat directly across from us. Faith was occupied by talking to her mother, so I took the initiative.

"We haven't been introduced," I said. "I'm Owen."

"I figured," Chase said, smiling somewhat self-consciously.

I reached my arm across the table, but the distance was too great and a floral centerpiece—also created by the eighth graders, largely with red and white carnations—was in the way, so we couldn't quite reach to shake hands. He half stood and bridged the gap.

"Pleased to meet you," he said.

Throughout the meal, Chase and I talked about mundane, impersonal things—how much he hated the winters in Boston, the futility of attempting to make garlic toast out of Wonder Bread—so when he rose to toast the bride with iced tea (there was not a drop of alcohol in sight), I was unexpectedly moved when he said that he welcomed his brothers, plural, to the Colquitt family. "I've always wanted a brother," was what he said, "and now I have two." I think that startled everyone; there was a bit of a rustle around the table, and I thought I saw a troubled look pass over Faith's face. But I was touched by the gesture, especially since he had only just met us. And I saw a tear sparkle in Mom's eyes, although perhaps it was only the candlelight.

Maybe I was imagining it, projecting an intimacy that did not exist, but I had the feeling Chase understood how isolated I was feeling that night, what with Porter being the center of attention, and he was trying to make me feel as if I, too, were becoming part of the family. After dinner he attached himself to our little group—Faith, Porter, and me—as we moved among the guests. Perhaps Faith had coached him on this earlier, either to make me feel less alone or to give her and Porter the illusion of privacy that resulted when I was occupied. In any event, I found Chase by my side for most of the rest of the evening. He was quick to bring me a bottle of water when I needed one, and later that night he showed me and Porter a place behind the church where we could smoke a little dope with impunity, a particularly courageous act, since he may well have been excommunicated had we been discovered. He even had the presence of mind to provide us with breath mints afterwards.

Over the course of the evening, I grew accustomed to his attention and felt adrift on those occasions when he was called on to help with one thing or another or when he was pulled away to greet yet another relative he hadn't seen in a while. It was during one of those introductions, as I watched a young female relative hug him excitedly, that I realized I was developing a crush on him.

I was surprised. Chase was not gorgeous in the way my porno fantasy crushes were gorgeous, nor was he ruggedly handsome like Faith's brother-in-law Peyton, about whom I fantasized regularly. But he was adorable, especially when he took off his glasses from time to time to massage the bridge of his nose with his thumb and forefinger. His broad shoulders poked out from beneath his suit jacket as if he had left the hanger in when he put it on, and I found myself wondering what he might look like naked, whether he was wiry and muscular under his clothes or smooth and soft and covered with downy fuzz like a baby chick.

I practically bit off my tongue when I realized what I was thinking. This was Faith's brother! Porter's soon-to-be brother-in-law. *Family.* What on earth made me think it was a good idea to be harboring lewd thoughts about him? Where would that get me? My palm had gone moist, and I was crushing a blood-red paper napkin in my hand. I prayed, oh god I prayed, that my thoughts wouldn't trigger an erection. Wouldn't *that* be a pretty picture?

For the rest of the night, as we went through our paces in the church upstairs, and again the next day, through the long hours of socializing with Faith's family and friends at the Colquitt home, I disengaged, became moody and distracted. I tried to avoid Chase whenever possible. On those occasions when I found myself in his company, I was polite but didn't initiate a conversation or follow up at length on anything he said. I don't think he noticed the change in my disposition, or at least he didn't react to it. And why should he? The entire crisis was of my own making; it was taking place in my head and no one else's. If he was thinking about me at all, it was only in the context of the truly odd circumstances into which his sister was marrying.

Without Chase to distract me, I became bored and depressed. Everyone was exceedingly polite, but almost no one said anything to me once we were introduced and they ascertained that Porter, not I, was the groom-to-be. I was superfluous, and yet there I was, hovering on the periphery of their conversations with the happy couple. When I remembered that Porter's Discman was in the car, I told him I needed some air and we went outside to retrieve it. I listened to a Beth Nielsen Chapman CD while Faith and Porter made small talk with guests. The batteries soon went dead—those things *eat* batteries—but I continued to wear the headphones, and from time to time, especially when it seemed as if someone—Chase in particular—might actually attempt to talk to me, I nodded my head to an imaginary beat, occasionally even mouthing ghostly lyrics, until Mom suggested I was being rude and asked me to put it away.

The wedding itself went off without a hitch. It was a formal event, as traditional as they come. There was never any question about doing something as avant-garde as having Porter and Faith write their own vows; that would have been far too contemporary for this little south Georgia farming community church. Faith looked spectacular in what I later learned was her mother's wedding dress, although it was hard to tell whether it was ivory silk or had just yellowed slightly in the thirty-some years since it had last been worn. Her four sisters were her bridesmaids, and they wore sorbet-hued dresses—lemon, lime, mandarin orange, raspberry—with billowing skirts buoyed by clouds of crinoline that reminded me of an episode of *Designing Women* that spoofed Southern belles.

Porter selected as his groomsmen four of his fellow teammates from Lovett: two football players, one of whom had been recruited by the Philadelphia Eagles after he graduated from the University of Georgia; a baseball player; and a cross-country star. I think some people were surprised that Porter had chosen Gary Burns, his best friend from Lovett, to be his best man, and I'll admit to being a little hurt when he first told me. I did seem like the inevitable choice.

"Don't get me wrong, O. If our circumstances were different, I'd be happy to have you as my best man, but it just doesn't seem right," he had explained to me. "I mean, when my best man stands up to make a toast at the reception, I shouldn't be right there standing next to him. And during the service, when my best man hands me the ring . . . well, it doesn't seem right that you should be taking it out of the pocket of our tuxedo. You know what I mean? Having you as my best man, well, it would be kind of like not *having* a best man, you know? Kind of like being my own best man. I mean, I don't see it that way, but I think other people would. I don't think any of these people are having an easy time adjusting to this, and having you as my best man would only confuse things. You understand, don't you?"

"I suppose so," I said, although I think I could have argued just as persuasively that it made as much sense for him to have selected me. With no role to play in the ceremony, I felt very much beside the point, which I suppose was nothing new.

I'd had a major crush on Gary Burns when we were in high school, and I consoled myself by fantasizing about him as he stood next to me during the ceremony. He had gotten only better looking, sexier, as he had matured into manhood, and I imagined, if ever so briefly, how nice it would have been to have been able to realize my mother's now-dashed dream of a double-ring ceremony, Porter and Faith, Gary and me. I even let our hands brush as we stood there. Gary coughed nervously and took a half step to the right.

The wedding reception was actually more difficult for me than the ceremony. Perhaps "difficult" is not precisely the right word. "Tedious" might be a better choice. We were surrounded for much of the time by women: the pastel cloud of sisters, Faith's other female relatives, her girlfriends from childhood and adolescence, her fellow nursing school students, and her co-workers from the hospital. The fog of cloying perfumes gave me a headache, exacerbated by the high-pitched chatter and squeals. Although I was probably the only brother-in-law in history to have wedding-night jitters that surpassed those of the bridegroom himself, I actually began looking forward to the moment when we would shut the door to the honeymoon suite at the Valdosta Holiday Inn and leave the wedding party behind.

Chapter 17

"Owen?"

"Yes, Faith?"

"You're not asleep, then?"

"No, Faith."

It was the fourth night of Porter and Faith's honeymoon in Honolulu. Moonlight slanted into our suite through the sliding glass doors that opened onto the balcony overlooking Waikiki. The room, so full of tropical brilliance in daylight, was bright by the light of the moon but almost colorless—black, silver, deep icy blue.

"Sorry," she said. "You know what I mean."

I did. After sex, Porter fell asleep within minutes. He had always drifted off more quickly than I, his heartbeat slowing swiftly and smoothly, as if he controlled it with a rheostat. I usually remained awake for about half an hour, although something about Porter's slowed metabolism ultimately affected mine; his sleep was contagious. Growing up, I prized these slices of silence and solitude the way a greedy child in a large family covets the last piece of chocolate cake. They allowed me to reflect on the events of the day, to plan for tomorrow, to dream about my future. It was the only time I was truly alone. Now it was during these intervals that I had my most intimate conversations with my brother's wife. Although I wasn't entirely sure how I felt about giving up my nightly dialogues with myself, I rather enjoyed these conversations, and they brought Faith and me closer together. They also allowed us to relate to one another without Porter intervening and permitted us to talk about him "behind his back," as it were.

"What is it?" I asked.

Porter's rapid retreat into sleep after sex had always seemed a bit selfish. Loutish and insensitive. *Conan the Barbarian does not engage in post-coital conversation.* I felt bad for Faith, and the third time it happened I felt compelled to explain that it was purely physical, that Porter always had fallen asleep quickly after an orgasm, even one we had brought on ourselves. It was almost as reliable as a sleeping pill. I wondered now if she needed to be reassured again. Her face was turned toward me, her head and neck cradled in her husband's arm, her left hand cupped over his heart. It could have been a gesture of affection, or she simply could have been trying to ascertain that he was truly asleep by monitoring the rhythm of his heartbeat.

"Are you okay?" she asked.

I knew what she was driving at. Throughout the week there had been a lot of sex, and it had been both physically and emotionally demanding on all of us. Faith had been surprisingly sweet and solicitous to me afterward, and at times like these I was happy Porter was so predictably insensate.

"I'm fine. Thanks."

"Good. I was a little worried."

She turned her head and kissed her sleeping husband on the cheek, then looked at me, smiled, and brushed a stray lock of hair from my eyes. Although at first I was uncomfortable being the recipient of such small intimacies—they seemed to border on a mild form of infidelity—I quickly grew to accept them. To me, there was never anything sexual or even sensual about these moments; they were simply an acknowledgement on her part that I was *there*. It was far more than I had previously imagined would be possible, and I was deeply touched.

"Are *you* okay?" I asked.

"Yes, fine, thanks."

"Happy?"

"Very. It's sweet of you to ask." She paused. "Do you think Porter is happy?"

"I think he's ecstatic."

"Not a word he'd ever use himself."

"No, not Porter. But he is," I said.

"And you? Are you happy?"

"Me?"

"Yes, you."

"Does it matter?"

"Of course it does."

I wondered what to say.

"When Porter is happy, I'm happy. Beyond that, Faith, it doesn't matter, or shouldn't matter, to you. It's the way we lead our lives. We each pursue happiness in our own way. We're there for each other, but my happiness doesn't depend on his, or his on mine. Not entirely. It's possible for one of us to be happy and the other not."

She absorbed this; processed it. She stopped breathing for a few seconds, and I thought she was poised to ask a question. Then she exhaled.

"You're not . . . lonely?" she asked, finally. "Now? This week? You haven't been lonesome?"

"No, not lonesome. I'm . . . homesick. I miss my life. I've given up a certain amount of independence this week, but I'm not *lonesome*. I do need some time alone—if you know what I mean. But I enjoy your company, Faith. And I love Hawaii. I'm having fun. I'm okay with this."

"Good," she said. "I'm okay with it, too. I didn't know what it would be like, but you've been terrific. When Porter and I are being intimate, I hardly know you're there. But then when I do think about it, I know that you are, that you have to be, for things to really work. Thank you for that."

I was touched that Faith recognized my contribution to

their lovemaking; it was something Porter would never acknowledge. He didn't like to talk about having sex with
Faith, particularly about how I was to behave while they
were so engaged. On the two occasions I'd had to bring it up
privately that week, he quickly changed the subject. I think
he felt that to talk about it, to plan what I was to do or not
do, say or not say, would be to acknowledge my presence in
a way he wasn't comfortable with. Perhaps it seemed conspiratorial or maybe like an invasion of their privacy. Or perhaps he thought it unnecessary: he had an uncanny ability to
tune me out during his most intimate moments.

Sexually, Porter had never been much on technique. He
was what I would call an in-and-out man. In. In-and-out.
And out. I don't know how much of this can be attributed to
our unique physiognomy (intercourse was difficult without
at least some involvement on my part; to negate the need for
my participation, he often had chosen to be largely passive,
allowing the woman to do most of the work) and how much
to Porter's personality or to my perception that straight men
are sort of dull and unimaginative in bed. Perhaps it was just
that until now, the only women he'd had sex with had been
the groupies who had followed us back to our motel room
after concerts, women who were mere objects to him. When
the sex was over, they left. Porter rarely so much as suggested
that we get out of bed and walk them to the door.

I felt a responsibility to make him aware of what I thought
were some potential pitfalls in his approach to sex, lest he
treat Faith in the same perfunctory manner. I feared he was
interested only in his pleasure and that Faith would be left to
cope with a largely unsatisfactory sex life. Indeed, Porter's
lovemaking with Faith had so far been remarkably unin-
spired. He seemed reluctant to explore even something as
tame as doing it doggie style, which he had found quite en-
joyable with cycle sluts in cheap motel rooms on the road.
She, too, was conservative. She would not go down on him—
on us—although she allowed him to pleasure her orally,

something I found noxious and distasteful and for which I prepared by placing a couple of drops of Giorgio Armani's Aqua di Gio under each nostril—and after which I insisted Porter brush, floss, and use mouthwash.

"You know, Porter," I said to him a week before the wedding, "sex with Faith is going to be a lot different than you've experienced with women so far."

"Oh, is that right, Dr. Ruth? And exactly how would you know?"

"Well, I *don't* know, smart-ass, but I've got a feeling."

"What is it, your feminine intuition?"

"Fuck you. I'm trying to help here."

"Okay, okay, so what are you suggesting?"

I told him what was on my mind: that as far as I could tell, he thought of the sex act as vaginal intercourse, pure and simple, more mechanical than sensual; that foreplay had consisted of slipping some bimbo our room key and suggesting she bring some cocktails in go-cups; and that just because he had achieved orgasm, the party wasn't necessarily over.

"Sounds to me like you've been reading *Cosmopolitan*, bro," he said.

"You could do worse than listen to me. I'm not sure exactly what Faith's expecting on her wedding night, but you can be sure it's more than your usual five minutes of grunting and swearing and a pat on the ass afterward."

Porter and Faith's first couplings had been . . . well, sedate seems an appropriate description: a sort of reverse missionary position with Faith straddling our cock while Porter and I remained more or less motionless. The only difference between us was that Porter kept his eyes open, while I closed mine and turned my head to the right, feigning sleep. I felt like the ultimate fifth wheel.

I suspect Faith also was uncomfortable at first. A modest woman, she was not inclined to traipse around the hotel room undressed and did not expect her husband and brother-in-law to do so, either. One of her wedding gifts to Porter, who was accustomed to walking around our apartment naked, was a custom-made midnight-blue bathrobe, broader in the shoulders to accommodate both of us but bearing only his monogram over the left breast pocket. For the first couple of nights, Faith wore lingerie during sex—it was an old-fashioned style, a gauzy jacket and panties, more *I Dream of Jeannie* than Victoria's Secret—and I got the impression she did so to prevent *me* from seeing her breasts, a gesture that was sweet but, I wanted to assure her, unnecessary. Porter had always been a breast man, so he discouraged this practice, and I could sense his increased arousal the first time she drew her negligee up and over her head.

Despite my sexual orientation, my complete lack of interest in the feminine anatomy, and my deep personal embarrassment at having to be present during Porter and Faith's most intimate moments, I became an attentive if somewhat reluctant participant in their lovemaking. I devised my own rules of engagement, however. I never indicated that I was experiencing pleasure during the process. Certainly I never said anything to that effect. No "Yes," or "Omigod," or "Oh shit," which were all favorite expressions of Porter during intercourse. Initially, I denied even to myself that I was enjoying the sensations down there. The first time, in fact, I squeezed my eyes shut and clenched my teeth so hard that Faith stopped to ask if I was in pain—and my jaw was sore the next morning. Clearly, that was not the answer. I had tried so hard to become invisible that I had become intrusive. Initially, this sort of denial extended to discomfort, as well. If I got a cramp or if Faith's weight cut off circulation to my leg, I said nothing, just gritted my teeth and dealt with the pins and needles. It took a while for me to speak up about my pain. Sometimes Faith's hand strayed to my arm or my side of our chest, and while I never said anything, she soon realized Porter wasn't responding to her touch, that her hand had meandered into my territory, and she pulled back, the first few times with a startled apology, eventually with a simple smile.

But I didn't want Faith to feel as if she were making love to a paraplegic or a stroke victim with control over only half his body. I think that would have been kind of creepy. I wanted her to be able to wrap her arms around our back but to think of it as only Porter's back. I didn't get any emotional gratification from this, but I would be lying if I said I was unable to take away some sensual benefits from the physical relationship Faith and Porter shared. When she gave him a massage, for example, she included many areas that were, technically, mine: the right half of our back and chest, the small of our back, where Porter's nerve endings and mine were tangential and which was frequently sore, perhaps because we were a bit top heavy. She was generous in that way and I repaid her by making her more comfortable whenever I could. Of course, there were things I did and things I did not do: I supported her head and neck during sex while Porter's hand played over her body, but I did not stroke her hair and tried not to touch her, even accidentally, anywhere remotely intimate.

I also knew there were ways I could enhance Porter's pleasure, and I was happy to oblige. These things were mostly cock-centered, of course. Simply by shifting my pelvis an inch or two sometimes might enhance what we were feeling. Early on, he responded by saying things like "Oh yeah" and "That's it," but in private I discouraged him from making such remarks, at least as they applied to things I had done, although admittedly sometimes it was hard to tell who was responsible for the pleasure he felt, me or Faith.

Chapter 18

During Porter and Faith's honeymoon, I found myself thinking about Chase almost all the time, cautiously but repeatedly turning the conversation to a discussion of Faith's childhood so I could hear the inevitable stories about Chase as a boy (and so I could escape, at least for a few minutes, the flirtatious self-absorption of a pair of newlyweds.) Faith never asked why I was so interested in her brother, but she seemed genuinely pleased to talk about him.

"Chase was like my shadow," Faith told us over lunch on the veranda of our hotel overlooking Waikiki Beach. "He followed me everywhere—and I mean everywhere. I didn't really mind, most of the time, but when I started dating boys it got to be kind of awkward. When he was twelve or thirteen, he always wanted to tag along. The guys were pretty nice about it, to a point. They liked Chase. Everybody likes Chase. He was always happy and had all this energy. Plus, he could hold up his end of a conversation with adults. You kind of forgot he was so young. But, good Lord, sometimes it was hard to shake him. I remember once he got on his bike and followed me and my date down the driveway. That stopped when he got a little older. He matured very quickly. By the time he was sixteen, he was ready to go to college, a real adult. He and I would sit around for hours, drinking tea, talking about what he wanted to do with his life, which was to get as far away from Brooks County as quickly as possible."

Although I knew I was tempting fate, I found myself yearning for even the most impersonal contact with him. I had brought my laptop with me, so I sent him an e-mail asking if he'd create a Web site for Janus when we got back from Hawaii. It seemed a reasonable approach, an overture utterly opaque in its innocence. Web sites quickly were becoming as commonplace as e-mail addresses and cell phones, and Porter and I had been discussing the idea of creating one for some time, but we'd put off doing anything about it because neither of us had the technical expertise to even know what questions to ask.

The remainder of the honeymoon passed without a response. Every time we returned to the hotel room from the beach or a sightseeing tour, I booted up my iBook to check my mail. When I didn't hear from him, I panicked, thinking my cold-shoulder routine at the wedding had worked all too well: while trying to protect my own feelings, I must have hurt his. Or perhaps my plan had backfired in a different way. After the initial good chemistry between us, my sudden lack of interest had telegraphed not disdain, but my obviously suppressed desire. He had seen through my pitiful Web site pretext. My intentions were as clear as if I had sent him a valentine, and he was appalled. I must have reread my e-mail to him a dozen times, searching for clues I may have subconsciously embedded in the message. Was the salutation too casual or familiar? Had I inadvertently signed it "Love, Owen"? (No, just "Best wishes, Owen.") Disconsolate, I finally decided he probably just wanted to give Faith and Porter some privacy on their honeymoon and thought e-mailing me would be an intrusion. I left the laptop untouched for the last three days in Hawaii.

One morning about a week after we had returned to Atlanta, I asked Faith over breakfast if she had heard from him.

"Oh, yes," she said without even looking up from buttering her English muffin. "I get e-mail from him almost every day. He's just been accepted to graduate programs at MIT and Stanford, and he's trying to decide which one to accept."

"Oh, graduate school. That's great," I said, returning my spoon to my cereal bowl and pushing it away, no longer hungry. I knew I was being silly, but I felt somehow betrayed. How *dare* he go to graduate school? I suppose I had assumed, foolishly and without reason, that Chase would come to Atlanta and get a job after he graduated—and that I would have the opportunity to get to know him better. "Has he said anything about me?"

She looked at me, the butter knife frozen in mid-stroke, and I felt as if the air between us had somehow become charged. I could feel my face flush.

"I mean, has he mentioned my question about a Web site?"

"Not that I recall," she said, leaning forward slightly and taking a demure bite out of the crisp muffin. "Which Web site?"

"Mine. Ours. You know, for the band."

"I didn't know you had one."

"We don't," Porter said.

"That's why I wrote to him—to ask about building one for us," I explained.

"Can he do that?" she asked.

"I thought so. I thought that's what he was studying up there."

"Oh, not really. His specialty is virtual reality. He's working with a team of psychologists to develop virtual-reality therapy for things like fear of flying and post-traumatic stress syndrome in Vietnam and Gulf War veterans. He designs the graphics—the interface, I think he calls it. He said it's sort of like the holodeck on *Star Trek*, except much less sophisticated. But maybe he can do Web sites. Do you want me to ask him?"

"No, that's okay. It sounds like he's too busy to do a stupid Web site for a band. Virtual-reality therapy? That's cool. I had no idea. I'll just wait to hear from him, or I'll get in touch with him again. Is he coming home for the summer or staying up there?"

"I don't know. He hasn't said. It may depend on whether he plans to go back to MIT in the fall or move to California. But I do know he hates the summers in Georgia."

"Who doesn't?" Porter chimed in. "I've always said we need to move to L.A.—for our career."

"There's so much high-tech stuff in the Boston area that it should be easy for him to get a summer job," Faith said. "And he really loves Cape Cod. It's all he talks about. He says if he can't find a tech job or internship, he'll wait tables in some place called Peetown. Can you imagine that?" She squinched up her nose. "*Pee*town? Isn't that nasty? I didn't think you could actually name a town something like that."

"It's not 'pee' as in *pee*, Faith," I explained. "It stands for Provincetown. P-town. It's a resort." A notoriously gay resort, I thought. Interesting. It was the best indication I'd had that Chase might be gay, at least since Faith's mention of his "romantic" trip to Bali with Kyle. I had hoped, but never dared imagine, that he might be gay, and in the back of my mind . . . no, that was asking too much. *That* was asking for trouble. I had to tell myself, again, that he was family, that a relationship with him was out of the question. But then, Chang and Eng Bunker had married sisters, Sarah and Adelaide Yates, even though rural North Carolina in the early nineteenth century was not the most enlightened place. Friends and family thought the marriages were improper at best, possibly immoral. Conjoined twins—and Asian at that! I wondered what bothered people more. Some of the family's more aggressive neighbors apparently even broke windows in their home and threatened to burn their crops if the relationships continued. But at least they both were straight.

"So when do you think he'll know?" I asked.

"Know what, Owen? About graduate school?"

"Or if he'll be here for the summer."

"I don't know. Why don't you send him an e-mail and ask him yourself? I'm sure he wouldn't mind hearing from you."

"He wouldn't?"

"No, why should he? He told me he liked you."

"He likes me?"

"Well, I suppose he didn't say he liked *you*. He said he liked Porter and you." She finished her orange juice in three large gulps, carried her dishes to the sink, and prepared to leave for the hospital. "Or maybe he just meant he liked Porter, as a brother-in-law, you know? I don't know. Look, I've got to get to work."

"Okay."

"I'm sure he'd be happy to help you with your Web site, if he's got the time."

Chapter 19

I really wasn't prepared for the way marriage changed Porter's life—or mine. The transformation was remarkable for both its speed and its totality: he became domesticated almost overnight. Even though he had stopped seeing other women as soon as he and Faith had begun dating, Porter had still found time to drink and carouse, especially when we were on the road with the band. Once he was married, however, he consistently turned down offers from friends to so much as watch a football game or play an innocent game of cards. He no longer drank with the roadies after our gigs, and they made jokes about him being henpecked (although they employed a cruder term). But it was not at Faith's insistence that he had changed his ways; it seemed to be something he genuinely wanted to do.

I was delighted. With Porter opting for a quieter existence, my life became simpler and more sane. Instead of partying heavily after a show and then spending the next day recovering from our late-night exploits, Porter and I devoted a lot more time to our music and laid down six tracks for our third CD, *Till Death Do Us Part,* in the first three months after the honeymoon.

There was only one drawback: now that Faith was living with us, I was reduced to masturbating to my porn videos only when she was working the overnight shift at the hospital. I felt like a fifteen-year-old kid again, wanking desperately behind the locked bathroom door while Mom was out running errands. In addition, Porter had suddenly become very possessive of our penis. He and Faith had been having a lot of sex since they had been married, and it wasn't just because he was horny or because it was more available. No, Porter made it quite clear he wanted to get Faith pregnant as soon as possible. He wanted kids, he said, lots of them. Three at least, possibly four. And he wasn't going to be denied an opportunity to procreate just because it didn't happen to be "his" day. So they had sex daily—often more than once—even on those days that technically were mine. My own needs were of little interest to him. At the same time, it seemed pointless to resist him. I had no one with whom to be intimate myself, so what was the point of denying him something he wanted so badly?

Despite the number of times Porter had sex with Faith, however, I remained unsatisfied both physically and emotionally. Although we share a penis, the way we respond to sex is unique to each of us. We both experience the physical sensation of an orgasm, but depending on the object of our affection, our brains react differently. We hadn't ever had this measured (even though Dad thought it would have produced some interesting data), but I'm convinced that when Porter was having sex with Faith, I didn't experience the endorphin rush that normally was triggered by an orgasm, at least not to the degree Porter did, which is one of the reasons I think he fell asleep after having sex with her faster than I did. So, although Porter was having sex more regularly than at any time in our lives, I was hornier than ever.

"Oh Christ," Porter said one night as I popped an Eastern European twink porn tape into the VCR before we got into bed. "Do you have to do that?"

"I haven't gotten my rocks off in more than three weeks, Porter. You have sex with Faith every day, sometimes twice a day."

"It's not just for fun, Owen. We're trying to have a baby."

"I understand that, but that doesn't mean I'm not horny as hell."

"Well, what are you doing when we're having an orgasm? Can't you think about Brad Pitt or something?"

"It doesn't work that way," I said. "What do you think about when I'm having an orgasm?"

"None of your fucking business."

"Whatever. I still have my needs." I turned on the TV and pushed PLAY on the VCR remote. Two tanned, tousled teens materialized on the screen wearing red kerchiefs around their necks—and little else.

"It's not right, man, shooting my little guys into a hanky," Porter said. He thought of sperm as "guys" and eggs as "girls."

"Porter, that's ridiculous."

"Yeah, well, every one of those little guys should have a chance to be my kid."

"Porter, there are millions of sperm in every ounce of ejaculate. Maybe billions—I don't know. You only need one to make a kid. The rest go to waste."

"Well, it just seems like they should all have a shot. Who knows, maybe I've got the makings of a little quarterback in my nut right now. It'd be a shame to waste him. Maybe tomorrow we'll be making ballerina sperm. Or gay sperm."

"What? What the hell is gay sperm?"

"You know what I mean. Maybe tomorrow your nut will be turning out the juice. It's possible, especially if we whack off to gay porn tonight."

I hit the MUTE button on the remote. I couldn't properly respond to what Porter was saying if I had to listen to the connubial grunts of pretty Czech boys.

"Porter, being gay is not genetic. There's no such thing as gay sperm."

"You don't know that."

"Duh! Then how come you're straight and I'm gay and we both were fertilized by the same sperm?"

"Don't get all scientific on me. You know what I mean."

"All scientific? I should believe some cockamamie story about gay sperm instead of getting 'all scientific?' You think the sperm I produce is going to create a gay baby and the sperm you crank out is going to give birth to some big hulking quarterback? That's incredible, Porter. That's the most idiotic thing I have ever heard."

"I just don't want to get your sperm all excited."

Porter was not stupid. He had sat through the same advanced-placement biology classes I had at Lovett, the same sex education lectures in phys ed, the same mandatory, schoolwide AIDS- and STD-prevention programs, and yet here he was worrying that "my" sperm, the ejaculate from our right testicle, was somehow different from his and might result in a defective baby, a gay son. I'm not sure what his problem was. We were young, and we produced plenty of sperm; there seemed to be more than enough to go around. But Porter seemed worried. All of a sudden he didn't want to "waste" it by masturbating.

This infuriating ignorance on Porter's part frustrated me. Yet again I had run up against the limits of tolerance, encountered an until-now invisible line in the sand that marked the division between what was acceptable and what was not acceptable about me. Porter had come to terms with the fact that I was gay, had survived seeing me having sex with another man, but now all of a sudden we had reached another frontier, another obstacle: my homosexuality was a threat to his as-yet-unborn child. He apparently thought the fact that Faith had not yet gotten pregnant was somehow my fault, that I had wasted viable sperm jacking off to gay porn. (He actually suggested that on the nights after I had indulged myself, our sperm was less motivated—and thus less motile— because they suspected it might be another dry run and they wanted to save themselves for the real thing.) I shuddered to think of the burden I would have to bear worrying about

Porter's son's sexual orientation for the next sixteen or eighteen years, fretting about everything I said or did around the kid. I secretly prayed Faith would give birth to a daughter, though he would probably find a way to blame that on me as well.

I had to wonder why having a baby was so important to him. These days, before they become responsible for an entirely new life, most couples want to have an extended honeymoon—a time during which their intimacy deepens and they adjust to each other's habits and quirks. Two-career couples seem more than willing to delay child-rearing until well into their thirties. I think Faith may have preferred it that way, especially considering the unusually difficult circumstances into which she had married. In any event, she didn't appear to be the one who was pushing to have the baby. In fact, I never thought sex was her favorite aspect of marriage, and I sometimes got the impression that the act itself at times became somewhat odious. I even thought she secretly might be on the pill, possibly to prevent giving birth to a monster. Hell, for all either of us knew, she could have had her tubes tied before the wedding.

I hit the PAUSE button. I'd barely been able to keep track of the tangle of nubile boys on screen anyway.

"Why are you in such a hurry to have a baby, Porter? Wouldn't you like some time alone with Faith first?"

"I don't know, I just do. I want to get a family started."

"There's plenty of time for that."

"Is there?"

Was that it? Time? Porter has always . . . no, it's both of us, really—we're both worried we might die young. It's one of the things that happens to you when you're born different: the flawed nature of your body makes you wonder what might go wrong next. Parents of ordinary kids, once they count their fingers and toes, sort of push the question of death and injury to the back of their minds. They flash forward to images of Little League games, proms, and weddings. They always worry, never forget, I'm sure, but it's not the same for them. When we were born—and once our condition was revealed—Mom and Dad probably didn't ask "How are they?" That was too hopeful a question. No, I imagine the first words out of Dad's mouth, scientist that he is, were "What's the prognosis?" We didn't have a future. We had a prognosis.

"Sure there is, Porter. Plenty of time. We're both healthy. There's nothing wrong with either one of us. Hell, I've always thought we'd probably live longer than anybody else. The way I figure it, we've got two hearts, so maybe if one of us develops a bum ticker, the other one's heart could help out—you know, kick into higher gear."

Porter thought about that. It may have been the first time he ever considered my presence in his life an advantage.

"Well, it isn't really about that," he said. "It's just that I want to be around someone who doesn't think I'm a freak. A kid would be like that, at least for a while. A kid who doesn't know better, who's always had a dad with two heads. I don't really remember what it feels like not to think of myself as a freak, you know what I mean? But there had to be a time when I still didn't know I was different from everyone in the world. I just want to have some time with my kid, my *kids*, when they don't know any better, when I don't have to explain anything to them, don't have to feel self-conscious or worry about what they think. I know it will only last a little while—a couple of years, three or four maybe, if that long. At some point somebody is going to say something to them, and they're going to come home and ask Faith why their daddy is different. But I just want to have that time with them before that happens. I want them to love me for being me, their dad, without having to make excuses about the way I am. I think that would be great, don't you? I mean, I know Faith loves me. I know Mom and Dad love me . . . love us. But you've gotta think there's a part of them that wishes I was . . . that *we* were different, separate. That it would be easier to love us or that they would love us more if we were two people instead of one."

"We *are* two people."

"You know what I mean. I just have this feeling that there's a part of them that they hold back, the part that has to explain us to other people, that has to make excuses. I'm sure there were conversations in Faith's house when she had to explain to her mom and dad why she wanted to marry me. I'm sure there were tears—slammed doors. I mean, don't you think there's a part of her that's dead inside from all the times she's seen people look at me, at us—I mean her and me, not you and me—and wonder what the hell she's doing with me? And what about all the people at the wedding on her side who whispered things to each other as we stood there at the altar waiting for her to walk down the aisle? There was a sort of buzz coming from her side of the church, the ladies' hats bobbing side to side as they shook their heads. Our side of the church was quiet and polite because they knew us, they were used to us. Her friends and family were still getting adjusted to us. Didn't you notice that?"

"I can't say as I did. Maybe you were just nervous."

"I saw it all right. You did, too. You always notice those kinds of things. You're just being polite."

"I'm not, really."

"Well, I know there are going to be people who disapprove of me and Faith having kids, of bringing a kid into the world who will have to deal with the shame—the embarrassment—of having a dad with two heads. At some point we're going to have to have that awful talk about how their daddy is different from other people's daddies. I don't know how the hell I'm going to pull that one off."

The screen came alive again, and again I pressed PAUSE.

"And god forbid anything should happen to Faith,"

Porter continued. "I'm sure there will be people who will be ready to swoop down and take my kids away because it just isn't right for a two-headed man to be raising kids by himself, that it isn't natural, that I'll fill their heads with all sorts of wild, dark ideas. 'What kind of home can a man like that provide?' they'll ask."

I had never really heard Porter talk about his feelings like that before. I didn't know he had all of that locked up inside him. I'd always thought he was remarkably well adjusted, that nothing anyone had ever said had hurt him. I guess I had sort of assumed he never thought anything anyone had said had even been directed at him, but had always been aimed at me, the different one, the queer one; that the taunts that were hurled in our direction were the result of people suspecting I was gay; that I was the cause of his discomfort, the source of his disgrace and embarrassment. It seemed to me he felt that this was his body, that it was me who was the cause of our freakishness and he had nothing to do with it. And in a way I let him think that, maybe because I believed it myself.

But I could certainly understand his point. I could imagine the pleasure he'd take in looking into his son's or daughter's eyes and seeing only recognition, love, joy—not revulsion. If he were lucky, maybe it wouldn't have to end. Oh sure, Porter's son's classmates would probably tease him about his dad. Children are capable of unspeakable cruelty. We had been shielded from a lot of it by our parents, and they probably would be helpful in raising Porter's kids. Maybe they would have some ideas about how to insulate them from the slings and arrows of their playmates. But if Porter were a good dad, and I suspected he was going to try like hell to be one, his kids would always love him, two-headed or not. For them, he would always be normal—in their hearts.

Nonetheless, if Porter could understand the pain he felt for being different, I wondered why was it so hard for him to understand my sense of alienation about being gay, an outcast among outcasts, a stranger even to my own family, my own brother . . . my own body.

Before the onscreen orgy could begin again, I ejected the tape from the VCR and turned out the light.

"Good night, bro," Porter said. "Thanks."

"Yeah. Whatever."

Chapter 20

We continued to live in our old apartment for several months following the wedding, spending alternate nights with Faith in Porter's bedroom and alone in mine. I don't think any of us were particularly eager to venture into the real estate market, even though my parents had given Porter and Faith a substantial down payment on a house as a wedding present. But the apartment was obviously too small for the three of us—much of Faith's furniture and many of her other belongings were still at the apartment she had shared with friends before the wedding—and there were other issues.

"Sometimes when I'm sleeping alone in Porter's room, I feel like I'm staying in a hotel," Faith said at breakfast one morning. "I'd feel more comfortable in a place of my own—of *our* own. This was a great bachelor's pad for you guys, but I need a *home*. And I want a big kitchen, maybe with an herb garden just outside the door or at the very least one of those window-box greenhouses I could grow a few fresh herbs in. You don't understand how tiny and badly laid out your kitchen is."

Faith had hinted previously at the limitations of our kitchen, which was perfect for a couple of single guys whose principal cooking utensils were a microwave, a pair of scissors, and the *Yellow Pages*, but hopelessly inadequate for a serious cook. I really didn't need to be convinced. I definitely could see the wisdom in having larger quarters, especially once there was a baby on the way. A child, after all, would be messy and loud, and I would want to have somewhere to retreat to.

But unlike Faith, I was thinking not of one large home but two moderately sized ones. With my personal baby-free zone, I wouldn't have to worry about breakage, wouldn't constantly have to be wiping a kid's fingerprints off glass surfaces. And I'm sorry, but I've always thought a house with a child in diapers smelled a bit like an apartment with a litter box. I wouldn't get off scot-free, of course. Like most parents who took turns looking after a baby late at night, Porter and Faith were planning to divide up their responsibilities so that on "my" nights, Faith would care for the baby, and on Porter's he would. Knowing Porter as I did, I suspected he wouldn't really take to changing diapers and that I would have to take the lead with those kinds of things. And so I advocated for the purchase of two adjacent townhouses in one of the many new developments that were springing up around the city. Some people might think it extravagant to own two homes side by side, but from my point of view it was perfectly reasonable to expect two adult brothers to want to maintain separate residences, especially if one were married and planning a family and the other were gay and going out of his mind from lack of privacy. (Once they were married, Chang and Eng Bunker lived in two adjacent homes on their North Carolina farm, spending three days at a time with their respective wives in each one. The way I figured it, if two nineteenth-century farmers could afford it, the income from our music career was more than enough for each of us to maintain separate residences.)

We began looking at real estate in Decatur, which technically sat on the eastern edge of Atlanta but had long ago been swallowed up by urban sprawl and was considered "in town" by the masses of pathetic commuters who had to make their way in from the more distant suburbs daily. Atlanta was experiencing a construction boom at the time, and we actually found three new developments with available side-by-side townhouses. We eventually bought a pair on a quiet side street not far from our old hangout, Eddie's Attic. We could have found more affordable property further out, but Faith didn't want a long commute to her job at University Hospital.

As fate would have it, Chase did not spend the summer slinging hash in P-town, but got an internship with Mac-Brainiac, an Atlanta-based computer-consulting firm owned by the father of one of his MIT classmates. After suffering through a month in a nasty summer sublet with unreliable air conditioning and located adjacent to the interstate on the Georgia Tech campus, he moved into the second bedroom in Porter and Faith's townhouse, the room ultimately destined to become the nursery. In his spare time, he created a killer Web site for Janus, once I brought up the subject, although he never explained why he hadn't responded to the e-mail I had sent from Hawaii—and I didn't ask. When he wasn't at work, he spent a lot of time hanging out with us, and was helpful painting and moving furniture as Faith and Porter settled into their new home. He even volunteered to do some work around my place, although I insisted on paying him.

Had Chase not lifted a finger, the sight of him shirtless beneath a pair of white painter's overalls would have more than justified what little I paid him. One day, after he had finished painting my den, he asked if he could use my shower instead of messing up Porter and Faith's bathroom next door. Naturally, I agreed enthusiastically. Afterward, I hung around making conversation with him as he blow-dried his hair wearing only a towel. His physique was lean and boyish, virtually hairless, supple and nicely defined but not overdeveloped. When I looked at his nipples, brown against the creamy expanse of his chest, I thought of the toasted tips of frothy egg whites atop a lemon meringue pie. I hadn't dared mention my interest in Chase to Porter, but I wondered if he was beginning to figure it out. I could tell he was antsy because he flinched when Chase's towel slipped lower on his slender hips and threatened to come undone, and he kept reminding us that Faith was probably setting out dinner on the table next door at that very minute.

"You know she doesn't like to be kept waiting," he said, glancing at his watch.

"Yeah," I said. "She's always wondering how someone who wears two watches can always be late."

"You guys go ahead," Chase said. "I'll be there in a minute."

"That's okay, we'll wait," I said. "No problem."

Porter sighed. "We'll give you some privacy while you dress," he said, pulling me out of the bathroom with him.

The next day when I was collecting towels for the laundry, I realized I had left copies of *Out* and *Genre* on the bathroom reading rack, not anticipating Chase would use the facilities upstairs when there was a small half-bath downstairs for guests. The magazines were not in exactly the same order in which I had left them. I had hung the three most recent copies of each—the June, July, and August issues—chronologically on six descending rods, the three *Outs* on top, the *Genres* on the bottom. It looked as if Chase had picked up the August *Out* and June *Genre* and switched them when he put them back.

"Damn," I said.

"What?" Porter asked.

"I forgot these magazines were up here. Chase must have seen them when he used the bathroom yesterday."

"Porn? You left gay porn out where he could see it?"

"They're not porn, Porter. They're newsmagazines. A little beefcake here and there. No dick to speak of."

"Still, they're gay, right? Unmistakably gay?"

"Duh? Yeah."

"Shit. We're toast."

"Don't overreact, Porter. He's considerate enough that

he'll respect my privacy. He's not going to run and tell Faith."

"Well, for your sake I hope the hell not."

Faith never really spent much time at my place. She certainly had never been there unaccompanied. And she'd never used the upstairs bathroom—I was sure of that. The only time she'd even seen it was when we had done a walk-through of both units discussing color schemes, and then it had been completely empty. The rest of the house, while decorated more tastefully than any straight man could have pulled off, did not scream "fag," unless an oriental rug, in and of itself, was emblematic of being gay. But just to be on the safe side, I kept all my porn, even the relatively soft-core magazines like *Advocate Men* and *Freshmen*, locked away in my bedroom closet. I also never watched porn videos on the television downstairs, so none was ever lying around the living room or lodged in the VCR, just in case she walked in and turned the TV on. But while Faith set off all sorts of internal perimeter alarms for me, Chase did not, perhaps because I suspected—or hoped—that he was gay.

This incident strengthened my suspicions, if it did not confirm them outright. A straight man might have picked up one magazine and hurriedly returned it to its place when he realized what it was. He probably would have felt guilty about it and made absolutely sure he placed it back on the rack precisely as it had been, so I wouldn't think he had some deep, dark little secret. He might even have checked to see if he had left his fingerprints on it. But this casual mix-up suggested that Chase had looked at the magazines and didn't care who knew. It may even have been meant as a subtle hint to me.

Although I harbored no illusions that Chase could seriously be interested in me—that situation was fraught with complications—I had hoped at the very least that he was a kindred spirit. How great would it be to have someone else gay in the family? I wanted to talk to him about it, but it was almost impossible to find the right time to do so. Whenever he was around, Faith was never far away, and I obviously couldn't discuss it in front of her. Even on those rare occasions when we did find ourselves "alone," I hesitated to bring it up in front of Porter. It wouldn't be fair to Chase to put him on the spot like that. I'd just have to wait until Chase brought it up himself.

Over the course of the summer, Chase frequently accompanied us to the movies or to pops concerts at Chastain Park, where Porter and I had been offered a gig next season. Most of the time, Chase ended up sitting next to me instead of Faith, but that seemed natural enough, unpremeditated. After all, she was preoccupied with Porter, and while she could have split her time between her husband and her brother, that would have left me out in the cold altogether. Maybe he was just being polite in the same way he had been attentive to me on the weekend of Faith and Porter's wedding.

It was exquisitely disconcerting to sit next to him in a darkened theater, and I frequently spent half the movie inching my foot across a sticky landscape of spilled soda and errant popcorn kernels until my pant leg came into contact with his. That alone was enough for me. Most of the time, if you had asked me what the film had been about, I wouldn't have been able to tell you much beyond the bare essentials. Once, when we both wore shorts to the movies, I believe the hairs on my leg actually came in contact with the hairs on his, acting like the antennae of an insect. It was electric. He neither pulled away nor pressed closer; maybe he didn't even feel it. The connection was broken when I became aroused and Porter shifted in our seat to adjust the resulting erection, which just happened to be occupying his side of our shorts.

"What the hell is going on?" he whispered to me.

"I don't know. Spontaneous combustion?"

"Right." He leaned forward, ever so slightly, and looked around me toward Chase, who, mercifully, remained unaware of the situation. "Right."

The four of us spent a long weekend together in Asheville in late July, staying at the Grove Park Inn, touring the Biltmore Estate, and meandering for hours through a loud, drunken street festival the city puts on every year with rock and heavy metal bands that attract pot-smoking mullet connoisseurs from miles around. Porter and I blended right in to the carnival atmosphere. Several times I thought I saw Chase cruising some of the same hot redneck hippie boys I was interested in. (I still thought longingly of Bandana Man from time to time, even though that nasty little episode seemed a hundred years ago.) When a particularly hot shirtless boy with a Mohawk passed us, Chase's eyes met mine and he smiled. In the evening, I wanted to spend time with Chase, but Faith was radiant after a spa treatment and Porter was feeling quite amorous, so the three of us spent a romantic evening in our room while Chase amused himself at the festival downtown.

As the summer waned, Chase suddenly became distant, almost invisible. It was as if he were leading a secret life. He stopped going to movies and concerts with us; he missed meals; he was up and out of the house well ahead of everyone else. On the days I woke up in Porter and Faith's bedroom, I often could smell the coffee he had left brewing for us, though he was long gone. He returned late at night—sometimes not at all.

"Chase, I don't care what you do or where you spend the night," Faith said as he sat down for breakfast on a day he had apparently returned to the condo solely for a shower and change of clothes. "But the least you can do is call and let me know you won't be coming home."

"Jesus, Faith, I'm not a kid anymore," he said. His hair was wet from a hasty shower, his teal polo shirt damp and clinging to his torso, his glasses spotted with drops of water. "I don't have a curfew, do I?"

"No, you don't have a curfew, but that doesn't stop me from worrying about you."

"Well, I wish you wouldn't bring it up in front of Owen and Porter."

"Why not? This is their home, too—and you're a guest in it."

"It's not my home," I said. Then, attempting to lighten things up, I added, "If it were, I'd have to redecorate."

"You can call. You can do that much, can't you?" Faith repeated.

"Yeah, yeah, yeah. I'll let you know. Unless it's so late when I decide that you're already in bed. You wouldn't want me to wake you guys up just to tell you I won't be coming home, would you?"

"No, Chase. I suppose that would be like me waking up a patient at the hospital to give him a sleeping pill."

"Okay, then. We're good on that."

Like Faith, I wondered where Chase was going at night and what he was doing. Was he working late on some computer project with a friend and then crashing at his place, or was he meeting strangers in bars? Faith could offer little additional insight into the matter when I cautiously brought up the subject over dinner, with Chase's place at the table once again vacant.

"I don't know *where* he goes. He claims he's out with friends, but I didn't think he knew that many people in Atlanta." She paused, apparently searching for a rational explanation for Chase's behavior. "He says some friends of his from high school are students at Tech, but I don't know. I suppose it's entirely possible there are such friends and that they're spending the night in some computer lab hoping to become the next Bill Gates. I can't imagine what else he could be up to."

But then, just as suddenly as Chase's inexplicable absences began, his mysterious secret life came to an end after Labor Day weekend. The brief, uncommunicative appearances for showers and meals were replaced by an almost clockwork schedule of comings and goings, a cheerful presence at breakfasts and dinners, and a resumption of social activities with Porter, Faith, and me. The biggest surprise came over dinner one night, when Chase informed us he was declining both MIT's and Stanford's fellowship offers and enrolling at Georgia Tech instead.

"They've got a great virtual-reality program, one of the best in the country, right here in Atlanta," he said. "I met some of the guys this summer, and when they saw my work, they created a space for me in their master's program, just like that."

"You sound surprised," Faith said. "I don't see why. They're lucky to get you. But Georgia Tech? Over MIT and Stanford? That surprises me."

"I really like Atlanta, and I've had a lot of fun here this summer. Besides, the program at Tech is nothing to scoff at. They're doing some great work. They've got a really cool 'Virtual Vietnam' program up and running for veterans with post-traumatic stress disorder, and they're spinning off a for-profit company for virtual-reality treatment for all sorts of things. It's a chance for me to get in on the ground floor."

"Well, that's great," Faith said. "And it will be nice to have you here in Atlanta."

"Yeah, very cool," I said. I was thrilled. I didn't know why Chase had decided to stay in Atlanta, but I hoped it would give us the time we needed to get to know each other.

"There's only one problem," Chase said.

"What's that?" Faith asked.

"Well, because this all happened so late—and so fast—there won't be any space in university housing for me, at least until next semester. They've found some fellowship money and a teaching slot, but I won't be able to get into a dorm until January. If I could even find an apartment I could afford near campus this late, it would probably be pretty ratty—like the one I was in earlier this summer. So I was wondering if I might be able to just hang here until then . . . you know, in the guest room."

Faith looked at Porter, her brows arched. "Honey?"

"Yeah, sure, Chase," he said. "That'd be cool. For now."

"It'll just be a few months. One semester is all. Maybe less if something opens up. You never know."

"No, it's cool, man. Owen and I are going to be on the road a lot this fall—we've got something like eighteen, twenty concerts lined up—and it will be nice to have somebody here with Faith."

"And you're welcome to use my place when we're gone," I said, "if you need a little privacy."

Faith looked at me, her eyes narrowing slightly.

"You know . . . I mean, like, if the two of you get sick of each other."

"Oh, that would never happen, Owen," Chase said. "But thanks. That's nice to know."

Chapter 21

In early October we learned through a home pregnancy test that Faith was expecting. Porter was beside himself. Faith seemed ambivalent. Oh, she was clearly happy when she saw the two blue lines emerge on the testing stick, and I believe the tears she cried were tears of joy, but almost immediately I saw a cloud cross her face, and she seemed to retreat into herself.

I suppose Faith had gone through the same mental gymnastics as Porter when it came to thinking about having a baby, though perhaps she had reached a different conclusion. What was it going to mean to raise a child with a two-headed father? How was she going to explain it to the kid? I had a feeling that while Porter was optimistically anticipating the first couple years of life, when his child would love him unconditionally, Faith was focused more on the years that would follow, as her son or daughter gradually came to the realization that his or her father was a freak. More than likely, it would fall to her to explain it. The question probably would come out of the blue, perhaps the result of inquiries from curious playmates: "Why does your daddy have two heads?" There'd be no answer, of course, at least none a child of that age would fully understand. Faith would have difficulty describing Porter's and my unique relationship in all its subtlety and complexity—and there would be increasingly difficult follow-up questions. "Do I have *two* daddies?"

or "Which one is my *real* daddy?" No, she was probably not looking forward to that day.

When news of Faith's pregnancy reached our respective families, the response was the same from both quarters: a flurry of phone calls, followed by hurriedly arranged visits. Doctors' appointments were scheduled, specialists were lined up, tests were ordered. Her pregnancy was confirmed, and everything appeared normal. She decided, for the moment, to keep working at the hospital, though her plans to enroll in the master's of nursing degree program were put on hold.

Because we planned to turn Porter and Faith's guest room into a nursery, Chase moved into my den so we could begin the process of decorating and furnishing the room for the baby. It was a decision I encouraged as subtly as possible. I even offered to replace my sofa bed with a regular mattress and box spring, but Chase insisted his stay was only temporary and he'd soon be moving to on-campus housing at Georgia Tech. I told him that when Porter and I were away on tour, he could use my bed, if he wanted, but as far as I know he never did.

Our concert schedule that fall was grueling. Not only did we play major cities in the Northeast and Midwest—Boston, New York, Philadelphia, Washington, D.C., Chicago, St. Louis—we hit smaller venues such as Portland, Maine, and Providence, Rhode Island. We also made appearances on all three network morning shows and more talk shows—national and local—than I can remember. It was impossible for us to get home with any regularity or for much longer than forty-eight hours between gigs, and Porter was more stressed out than I had ever seen him. He talked to Faith on the phone three, four, sometimes five times a day. Every once in a while when I called my machine for messages, Chase picked up and we chatted briefly. It made my day. We finally got back home just in time for the holidays.

Whether for physical or psychological reasons, Faith had begun having difficulty sleeping while we were away and had taken to bringing a book to bed with her, usually an inconsequential chick-lit novel encased in Easter-candy colors of pink, yellow, or lavender.

"Good book?" I asked one night when her reading had gone on longer than usual. Porter was already sound asleep.

"Funny, sort of," she said, turning the cover toward me. It featured a humorous illustration of a ditsy female dog walker tangled up in a half-dozen rhinestone-studded leashes, with poodles and Pekineses and miniature schnauzers at her feet. The title was *Kay's Nine Loves*, a muddle of canine and feline allusion. "Not the best I've ever read, but it keeps my mind off things."

"Gotcha."

"Am I keeping you up? Would you like me to turn off the light? I probably could be asleep in minutes if I tried."

"No thanks, I'm fine."

She returned to her book, and I closed my eyes. It was a long time before I heard a page turn again.

"Owen?" she said eventually, "do you remember the conversation we had on our honeymoon?"

"Which one?"

"In bed one night. Porter was asleep already. I asked if you were lonely."

"Ah, *that* conversation. Yes?"

"You said you weren't lonely but that you were . . . 'homesick' is the way you put it, I think. Homesick for your life."

"Right," I said.

"Do you still feel that way? I mean, now that we've been home for a while and things are back to normal."

I didn't know quite what she was getting at—if this were an important question or if she were just being polite . . . or nosey. The truth was that in the months since Faith and Porter had been married, I had yet to fully reclaim my life, but I did not feel particularly put-upon. The process of buying and settling into the townhouses had demanded a lot of time and attention, but it was the type of thing everyone faced. It was not something I blamed on Faith or on her marriage to Porter. As for my private life, I wasn't feeling particularly deprived or lonely. In fact, I welcomed the relative solitude of my nights "alone" and did not miss the distractions that would have come with a relationship of my own— if I had been able to find one. In a way, I was even kind of enjoying my one-sided infatuation with Chase. It was a dynamic I had grown accustomed to through years of hopeless crushes in high school and college.

"I'm okay," I said as noncommittally as possible. "I'm fine."

"Oh, okay. Good."

Several minutes passed again without the sound of a page turning, and I thought Faith might have fallen asleep sitting up.

"Those were strange days, the honeymoon," she said, wistfully, and for a moment it almost seemed as if she were talking to herself. "A bit difficult for me, but you were such a gentleman. You've always been a gentleman about private things. I appreciate that more than you know."

I opened my eyes and turned my head slightly toward her. Porter's nose, out of focus, intervened in my line of sight, but I could see she had lowered the book into her lap, marking her place with the dust-jacket flap, and was looking at me. She leaned forward a bit until our eyes met, and as she did, a curtain of her hair swung down, blocking her view. She pulled it back behind her right ear with her index finger and smiled at me. I sensed a kind of hopeful anticipation in her smile that made me the slightest bit queasy. It was not exactly flirtatious, but it was close.

"It's no problem, Faith. Porter and I have learned how to deal with things like that, to mind our own business and to shut out things that don't pertain to us. I've always thought it must be harder for you to deal with . . . the oddity of it all."

She sighed, and her right hand absently caressed the pastel spine of the book.

"It hasn't been as difficult as I thought it might be," she said. "Or at least not as difficult as my friends and family led me to believe it would be."

"I figured that might be the case—that they might try to dissuade you from getting involved in a situation like this."

I still didn't know where all of this was going, and I was beginning to get sleepy. Porter had been out cold now for at least twenty minutes, and he was slowly pulling me under with him.

"Can I ask you something, Owen?"

"Sure."

"Something personal?"

Uh-oh. Here it came. The big question.

"Shoot," I said.

She paused as if to compose her thoughts.

"You're not seeing anyone, are you? I mean, romantically," she said finally.

"No," I said.

"I didn't think so."

"Why do you ask?" I said. At first I wondered if she might be thinking about fixing me up with someone from work—another nurse. And then it occurred to me that she might be wondering about Porter's role in any romantic—or sexual—relationship I might be having . . . ostensibly with another woman.

"Well, I hope you won't take this the wrong way, but I just wondered if . . . if perhaps this was enough for you?"

" 'This'? 'This' what?"

"This relationship. With Porter and me."

I was dumbstruck. I had to fight the impulse to pull my-self—and Porter—upright, so I could look her in the face to see if she was serious. What the hell was she asking?

"Excuse me?" I said.

"I know it's personal, but . . ."

"It's not that—well, yes, it is personal, I suppose, but I just don't understand the question, Faith. What is it you want to know?"

She sighed and brought both hands up to her forehead to massage her temples. The book slid off her lap into the shallow quilted valley between us.

"Faith?"

"I don't know how to put it any other way, Owen. I guess I had the impression that maybe you didn't need anyone else in your life, that maybe this, what we have—the three of us—was going to be enough for you."

I didn't even know where to begin. At least I had the presence of mind not to say, "Are you fucking crazy?" But after that, what? Clearly, if she thought there was a three-way relationship in which I was invested, there must be one in which she was invested.

"I'm still not sure I understand, Faith. I'm sorry—I'm not trying to be difficult."

There was a long pause during which I'm sure her mind was racing as fast as mine, having realized she had taken a wrong turn somewhere and was now facing a dead end, a blank wall, with no room to maneuver. The best she could do would be to back away slowly, feel her way out, and hope for the best.

"Oh dear," she said. "Oh my."

Although I was befuddled and—let's face it—shocked by her apparent train of thought, I realized with some relief that she was not going to suggest I was gay. In fact, she clearly was thinking the opposite.

"I'm sorry, Owen. I'm so sorry. I misunderstood things. I just, well . . . I just thought you might be feeling something that it's clear you're not."

She started to cry. I tried to remain calm. It was exceedingly strange to be alone with Faith at such an intimate moment. It felt wrong. And I was afraid Porter might wake up to find his wife in tears and blame me for it.

"Faith? Faith, don't cry. Please don't cry."

"I'm sorry, Owen, it's just . . ."

"You don't want Porter to see you like this. We have to re-main calm. *I* have to remain calm."

"I know. I know. It's just that you're . . . you're so sweet, Owen. You've been so nice to me. When, you know, when Porter and I are . . . you're so tender, so caring. I just thought . . . And other times, too. You're so smart and funny. You're different from Porter—in so many ways. You listen to me at times when Porter doesn't hear a word I'm saying. I've gotten used to having you there. I've come to rely on you. I've come to . . ."

"Don't say it, Faith. Please."

She took some time to compose herself, retrieving her book and daubing at her eyes with a couple of pale blue tis-sues from a pop-up box on her night table.

"I'm so embarrassed, Owen," she said. "I feel like such an idiot."

"Well, don't," I said. "I'm flattered you think of me that way. And really, it's only natural, considering the amount of time we spend together and the unusually intimate nature of our relationship—for a brother- and sister-in-law, that is."

But Faith's intimations of a romantic involvement with me were profoundly disturbing. I wondered if she had felt that way from the beginning or if her feelings had evolved as her intimacy with us deepened. To some extent, I felt culpable. Had the small acts of tenderness I had shown her during sex given her the wrong idea? I had simply wanted to make her comfortable, to make the experience feel as complete and natural as possible. In fact, I hoped my actions were making me invisible, relegating me to the background in a way that *lack* of involvement would not, but they had done just the re-verse. While I had merely been supporting her back or neck during intercourse or doing something as simple as trying to maintain my balance, she was interpreting the touch of my hand as a caress, an expression of affection.

I wondered what Porter would think if he knew how Faith

felt about me. Who would he blame—her or me? Even though he knew I was gay, would he resent me because Faith had developed an interest in me? He might wonder who she was thinking of when they were having sex—him or me. Which attributes did she find most seductive in the hours leading up to a romantic encounter? Porter's strength? The feel of his arm around her shoulders? Or my sensitivity? The things I did by way of coaching him—selecting a romantic restaurant, insisting we pick up flowers for her on special occasions? I always let her think those things were Porter's ideas, but I now suspected she knew the truth and had misconstrued my intentions. Had there ever been a time when in the throes of passion Faith had accidentally kissed me instead of him? I didn't think so, but if Porter knew how Faith felt about me, I wouldn't be surprised if he worried about such things. It was not that uncommon for a woman to fall in love with two brothers, especially if they were twins, and under normal circumstances—if Porter and I were not joined— Faith's feelings would verge on the adulterous.

At the same time, it occurred to me that this might be the best opportunity I would ever have to come out to her. She had just more or less confessed to having a crush on me—at the very least—and was feeling foolish and vulnerable, maybe even a little rejected. Perhaps she'd feel better if I let her know not only that I was unavailable but why: that I had not fallen in love with her for the simple reason I was gay. It might be easier to cope with if she understood that I was not merely some shadow of my brother, a stand-in, a spare, and that my life was not merely an echo of his. It was an idea that seemed altruistic, even merciful, while at the same time serving my own needs.

I patted the mattress beside me. "Come sit over here on my side of the bed, so I can see you more easily."

She gave me a puzzled look but placed the book on the night table, got up, and put on her robe. She walked around to my side of the bed and sat down at about knee level.

"I've got something private to tell *you*, too," I said. "Something personal—and potentially just as embarrassing. It might make you feel better."

She relaxed and appeared mildly amused, as if she were expecting whatever I was about to confess to be witty, charming. Her expression seemed to say, "What have you naughty boys been up to, keeping a secret from me?" She may even have held out the hope I was going to own up to having a crush on her, too. Perhaps it was all the romantic tripe she'd been reading.

"I'm gay, Faith," I said, without further preamble. Simple words, but I had rehearsed them silently a hundred times in the past few months, had tried to anticipate the whole range of possible responses.

"Gay?" The look on her face made me think she was having trouble relating to the word, as if I had used an unfamiliar foreign phrase or had begun speaking in tongues. "As in *homosexual* gay?"

"Mmm-hmm." I suppose the crush scenario flew out the window.

"Is that so?" She smiled.

Perhaps she thought I was kidding, that this was a way to defuse the tension—a setup for an elaborate practical joke.

"Yes, Faith, it's so."

"You're gay." Her voice was flat now, deadpan, completely without affect. Neither amusement nor anger was in evidence.

"Yes."

She didn't move. She didn't even blink. Her lips were parted slightly. Her eyes, usually so accessible, were suddenly opaque, as if tiny watertight doors had slid into place. She recoiled ever so slightly, almost as if she had detected the faintest scent of rotten meat. In the silence that followed, I could hear Porter's breathing, regular and undisturbed.

"Is that even possible under the circumstances?" she said,

finally. "I mean, Porter's clearly not gay and you're identical in every way—genetically, I mean."

"It's not necessarily about genetics."

"Well, environment, then. The two of you grew up in the same environment. *Precisely* the same environment."

"Faith, nobody knows for sure why *anyone* is gay." I didn't think now was the right time for a debate on nature *versus* nurture or a discussion of research I had recently read announcing that subtle, natural, chemical modifications in the genes of identical twins may be responsible for differences in personality or variations in susceptibility to diseases as they grow older.

"So what you're saying is that you are actually gay—really and truly?"

"Yes, really and truly."

"And you've . . ."

"Yes, I've . . ."

"Been with another man?"

"Yes, I've been with other men."

"Men? Plural?"

"Men, plural . . . but not at the same time. Only one at a time." I wanted it to sound funnier than I suspect it did.

"Well, that's comforting . . . I suppose."

"I'm sorry about this, Faith," I said. "I'm sorry if you're upset, and I'm sorry I haven't told you earlier, but I didn't want to complicate things. I didn't want to come between you and Porter. I . . . *we* thought it might upset you."

"Yes, I can see how you might have thought that."

She got off the bed and walked to the window, peeking out through the slats of the Levolor blinds, checking to see if the world outside remained intact while the interior landscape had suddenly crumbled around her. She returned her gaze to me and spoke across the distance that separated us.

"Well, I'm not sure what to say, Owen. This is a lot to absorb. I've always known you and Porter were different from one another—surprisingly so. I've gotten into the habit of thinking that you're everything that Porter isn't and vice versa, as if you each got things the other one didn't. Like the sports thing is pretty much Porter, and the . . . I don't know, the movies-with-subtitles thing is exclusively you."

"Yeah, and I got the shopping gene."

This time she laughed, in spite of herself.

"But this—this is *so* different. It's like, for the first time, I see that you're separate, in your heart . . . Oh, dear." A tear rolled down her cheek, and she brushed it away. "I'm sorry," she said.

"It's okay, Faith."

"It's just that, I don't know, it seems so sad. You must be terribly lonely. And I . . . I feel like I'm losing something— something I really love."

Porter stirred, and I was afraid he was going to wake up. I took a couple of deep breaths, trying to calm myself, slow my metabolism. Faith glanced at her husband but continued to pace, maintaining some distance between herself and me.

"You're not losing anything, Faith. You're not losing anybody. I'll always be here. It's just that I need to get on with my own life. And to do that, I have to be honest with you."

"Do you have . . ."

"A boyfriend? No."

"But you do have sexual partners?"

"From time to time."

"Without an emotional commitment?"

"You make that sound pretty awful."

"I've never thought of sex as recreation, Owen."

"Well, *procreation* is not an option for me, so I'm afraid all I have left is recreation."

"But you can have an emotional bond, a commitment."

"Easier said than done, especially for someone like me."

I had meant someone with two heads, but I think she thought I simply meant gay. From the sour, disapproving expression on her face, I could tell she thought I was not trying hard enough.

"I assume you've been tested for HIV and are negative," she said. "I can't imagine you'd do anything that would put me—or the baby—at risk for AIDS or for anything like that. *Anything*," she said. "I couldn't deal with that, not even the slightest risk."

"We've been tested several times—quite regularly, in fact— and we're definitely negative," I said. "We never would have been intimate with you unless we were absolutely certain about that."

Without going into too much detail, I think I managed to convince her that nothing I did would put her at risk.

"Nevertheless, I should get tested—for the sake of the baby."

She sat down on the bed again, but this time on *her* side, her right leg drawn up under her, her left foot still touching the floor, as if she were uncertain about reentering the marital bed after my revelation.

"Does Porter know you were planning on telling me this?" she asked.

"Not exactly."

"Not exactly?"

"We've talked about it, and to be perfectly honest, if it were up to Porter we'd never tell you. I suppose we could wake him up now and tell him, or we can all talk about it together in the morning."

"No, not now. And not in the morning—I've got to be at the hospital early, and I'd like some time to think about it. We can discuss it at dinner."

Dinner. It seemed both too close and impossibly far away.

"Dinner it is," I said.

"Can I ask a favor? About . . . the other thing?" she said. "You won't say anything to Porter, will you? I'm not sure that would be such a good idea."

"Definitely not, Faith. It will be our little secret."

Suddenly, I could barely keep my eyes open. I was exhausted, or more accurately, spent. Having gotten this off my chest was a huge relief, like a psychic orgasm, and I was sure that some sort of endorphins were kicking in.

"I'm afraid I'm going to fall asleep, Faith. It's either that or we're going to have to take steps to keep me awake, and that means waking Porter."

"No, you go ahead. I'll be okay."

I don't know how much sleep Faith got that night. I know that I woke briefly a couple of times, and on at least one occasion, she was not in bed. By the time Porter and I got up, she had gone to work, leaving us a fresh-baked apple crumb cake, which I presume she made during a bout of insomnia. Porter called her at the hospital three times during the day, as he usually did, and their conversations seemed normal to me. Although I tried to hide it from Porter, I was all over the map emotionally—ecstatic one minute, anxious the next. I couldn't concentrate, certainly couldn't write lyrics, and after spending a couple of fruitless hours at the computer trying to finish a song, I finally suggested we call it a day.

"What's up, man?" he asked. "You were so close to getting this song down yesterday, and today—nothing. You haven't written a line, not a single line. It's not like you."

"It's nothing, Porter. I just need a break. Let's go to Home Depot and pick up some paint for the baby's room—get that started."

"You want to paint the baby's room today? You don't even *like* painting. What's with you?"

"It's nothing. The words just aren't coming to me today. That happens sometimes."

By the time Faith got home, we'd draped drop cloths on the furniture in the nursery, masked the trim, and put a first coat on a couple of walls. We'd picked a pale yellow called Lemon Mist, since we didn't yet know whether Faith was going to have a girl or a boy. I liked the color and decided I'd use whatever we had left over to brighten up my kitchen. When she got home from the hospital, Faith was surprised, and I think pleased, with what we had done. I hadn't really given it much thought, but I suppose it was comforting to her to find us working on something for the baby, something for the future, after the unsettling conversation we'd had the night before. She made dinner for us while we cleaned up.

When Faith and I broke the news to Porter, he was more relieved than angry. The fact that Faith had not gone ballistic upon hearing that I was gay had defused the situation for him. Although the hard part appeared to be over, Faith had been giving our conversation a good deal of thought, and she had questions now that she hadn't asked last night. She wanted to know precisely what Porter was feeling when I was having sex, and even more importantly, what he was doing. This involved a more detailed and technical description of the gay sex act than even I was comfortable with. Somehow, when you reduced it to a question of logistics, of plumbing rather than passion, it became somewhat embarrassing.

"What are you thinking about when Owen is having sex?" she asked him.

"Nothing, sweetheart. Nothing at all."

"Nothing?"

"Well, I suppose I think of you."

Wrong answer.

"You think of me while you're having sex with a man? Oh my god, Porter, how could you?"

"Honey, I didn't mean it like that. I just mean, I'm not thinking of *him*. If I'm thinking of anything, I'm pretending it's a woman, and, well, I just naturally assumed you'd want that woman to be you."

I didn't think this answer would go over particularly well. I was reminded of the first night he met Faith, when Porter didn't want to "defile" her by allowing me to jerk him off. He'd come a long way, but things had obviously gotten much more complicated.

"No thank you!" Faith said. "I'd rather you didn't think of me while you were in bed with another man."

"Faith, it's not that way at all," he said.

"I'm sorry, but I'm having trouble with this. I was raised to think that kind of thing was wrong. It's against everything my church teaches. And although I've come to acknowledge, intellectually, anyway, that it's not a sin, I'm still uneasy with it. There's something about it that I just can't accept."

"What can I say that will help you?" I asked. "What will help put your mind at ease?"

"I need to know"—she was clearly struggling with the words, and the concept behind the words—"I need to know that Porter's not *enjoying* it. That he doesn't like it. That he won't . . . *change*."

"Oh my god, honey, there's no way. I'm not going to go over to the other team. Not ever."

I'm not sure she was entirely convinced. Porter reached over and took Faith's hand in his. She allowed him to hold it, but it looked lifeless to me, as if he were holding an empty glove.

Mercifully, that night it was my turn to sleep "alone." I don't think either Faith or I could have dealt with the intimacy of sleeping together just yet. Even the following night, she remained somewhat distant in bed. Perhaps a better word would be "tentative." Over the course of the past forty-eight hours, I think she had realized her mistake. Like so many people, she had failed to acknowledge our individuality. She had come to think of us, however subliminally, as a package deal, as *Porterandowen*. Perhaps it was a defense mechanism, a way for someone as sensitive and modest as her to get around the idea that she was in bed with two men. But that night, she looked at me—at us—in a way I hadn't seen in all the time I had known her. It was as if she were seeing me—really seeing me—for the first time, understanding that I was not merely an appendage to Porter, but that I, too, inhabited this body, a body she had come to think of as her husband's—as her own—and that I had the potential to assert control over it in ways she hadn't imagined. Porter and I slept without a pajama top, and I could almost see Faith drawing a line from our pectoral cleft down to our groin, dividing our body in two, his half and mine, right and left—right and *wrong*?—maybe even imagining something like a miniature version of Hadrian's Wall, manifested as the faint trail of dark blond hair that ran down the center of our stomach, around our navel, to our penis. Perhaps she was thinking that I was laying claim to more real estate than she was willing to cede, that I was something of an interloper, a homesteader on territory she had already claimed and fenced in.

For the next week or so, I felt as if Faith were withholding final judgment. More often than not, she was testy, irritable for no reason. (I tried to reassure Porter by telling him Faith's moods were almost certainly related to hormonal changes due to her pregnancy.) She didn't snub or ignore me, as I feared she might, but instead became excessively polite, as if I were a guest who had overstayed his welcome, someone she wished gone yet did not want to offend. I noticed in conversations that she used our names more frequently—Porter's and mine—as if to delineate those things she said that were meant specifically for Porter, which I should ignore, and those meant for me. I was reminded of the way my mother had attempted to differentiate between me and Porter after I came out to her.

Thereafter, Faith required more time alone but at the same time was acutely interested in where Porter and I had been while we were away. It was almost as if she suspected Porter were having an affair. She frequently could be found on the phone with one of her sisters, and there were times I heard her praying behind closed doors. She seemed happiest when she was dealing with plans for the baby: knitting booties or mulling over names.

As Faith's pregnancy progressed, it took a greater toll on her relationship with Porter than any of us anticipated. She was irritable, cried for no reason, and frequently complained of backaches, nausea, and constipation. She came home from the hospital exhausted, and I could tell she was reconsidering the wisdom of her decision to continue to work. And then her first trimester ultrasound brought some unexpected news that changed everything.

As usual, Porter and I had waited out in the car, lest our appearance send some unfortunate mother into premature labor, and when Faith emerged from the doctor's office, she was pale and trembling.

"Faith, honey, what's wrong?" Porter asked as we helped her into the Volvo station wagon we'd bought in anticipation of having a family. "Are you all right? Is the baby all right?"

She was halfway into the car when a thought hit her. "Backseat, backseat. I need room, space. Backseat," she said as if she had regressed to childhood. She stepped out of the car, lost her footing on the curb, and nearly fell. We each grabbed her under an arm to steady her.

"Faith, what the hell is going on?" I asked.

I could tell she'd been crying. Her eyes were red-rimmed, her makeup smeared. We maneuvered her into the backseat, and Porter pulled us down into a kneeling position at the curb. He held her hand.

"Honey, please, tell me what's wrong. What happened?"

She was crying again and breathing as if she had just narrowly escaped drowning, her left hand alternately flailing and attempting to push Porter and me away, as if we were using up precious oxygen. For an instant, I thought perhaps she had lost the baby right there in the doctor's office—miscarried. The idea occurred to me, fleetingly, that she didn't want this baby and had rejected it, had willed it from her body, inducing a spontaneous abortion on the examination table. But had that happened, surely someone would have been dispatched to the parking lot to get us.

"Twins," she said finally. "Twins. Twins!"

"What about us, honey?"

"No, no, no, not you," she said as if we were children—or fools. "*Twins*. I'm having twins."

"But that's great, honey. That's terrific."

I'll admit at first I didn't understand why she was so upset. So she was having twins—so what? But then it hit me. The nightmare was coming true—at least in theory. Faith was afraid she was going to give birth to a freak, that everything her family had told her behind closed doors was going to come true.

"Honey?" Porter said.

"Porter, come here," I said, trying to pull us up to a standing position.

"What? Wait! Faith . . ."

"Porter, now!"

We stood up, and I eased the car door shut and moved away so Faith couldn't hear me if I spoke softly enough.

"Jesus, what is wrong with you?" Porter said. "Can't you see that Faith . . ."

"Porter, she's upset because she's afraid she's going to have *conjoined* twins, like you and me. She's afraid the baby is going to have two heads!"

"But the odds against that are astronomical!"

"It's not going to happen, but it's probably been in the back of her mind since she found out she was pregnant."

"What can we do about it? What can I say to her?"

"I don't know. There's probably very little we can say at this point. She's just going to have to live with it for a while—get used to the idea. I think maybe it would be a good thing to have her talk to Mom. Maybe she'll know what to say to calm her down."

I'll admit being somewhat concerned myself. What if something *were* wrong with Porter and me, some genetic flaw that predisposed the babies to being somehow defective? I knew the odds were overwhelmingly in favor of normal births, but I couldn't help having morbid fantasies about the possibility of another set of conjoined twins. Perhaps not so dramatically connected as Porter and I, perhaps easily separated, what with all the technological advances in the world of medicine, but troublesome still.

We checked on Faith before getting into the driver's seat. She was still crying, but she was no longer gasping for air. We drove home in silence. When we arrived, I suggested to Porter that we call our mother. It would be good to have Mom talk to Faith beforehand, to calm her down, to reassure her, and to let her know that the Jamison side of the family would be there to support her as well.

"Everything's going to be all right, boys," Mom told us on the phone. "Everything's going to be just fine. Between the doctors who treated you and Faith's contacts at University Hospital, I'll bet we know every neonatologist, pediatrician, and multiple-birth specialist in the Southeast."

The doctors we consulted told Faith that there was an increased likelihood of pre-term labor and delivery with twins, and that she, personally, was at increased risk for hypertension and diabetes. She also would be more prone to mood swings and more likely to experience fatigue, especially in her first and third trimesters—something of which we had already seen evidence. But she could continue to work, should she choose to do so, unless she developed hypertension, and as to the risk that her twins would be conjoined, the odds were a long shot—one in one hundred thousand. As far as anyone could tell from her ultrasound, the twins were normal, but additional procedures would be used to monitor their health and development regularly every four to six weeks.

Faith eventually accepted the fact that she was going to have twins, but it did take a toll on her emotionally and psychologically, as well as physically. As her stomach swelled, her patience shrank. She became more irritable and demanding with each passing day, with each ounce of weight she gained, as if she were being filled not with new life but with some noxious liquid. She required ever more space in bed, not just because she was getting larger but because she was less inclined to be touched by Porter, even briefly, tangentially. He and I were crowded to the right side of our queen-size bed, and I ultimately spent many nights feeling as if I were sleeping at the edge of a precipice, my shoulder hanging over the edge of the mattress. I found myself rejoicing when Porter and I hit the road in February for a ten-day swing through the Pacific Northwest and California—Seattle, Eugene, Portland, San Francisco, Berkeley, Santa Cruz, L.A., and San Diego.

Faith's natural sense of modesty became almost maniacal as she gained weight, and it was exceedingly rare for me to see her naked. But when I did, I was taken aback by how large she had grown and how alien her swollen belly had become. When she was lying down, her stomach was as defiantly protuberant as Ayer's Rock, the monumental Australian sandstone outcropping. Porter took pleasure in rubbing his hand over it—it was the one form of contact Faith tolerated—feeling the babies kick or placing his left ear against it, listening to their heartbeats. But I never touched it, and to this day don't know whether it felt more like a steroidal basketball—firm and sort of reptilian—or something more pliant and pleasurable.

Chapter 22

I awoke to the whispered sound of my name.

"Owen. *Owen!*"

The way Chase said it, it sounded like one syllable: *Own*. He was on one knee beside the bed, leaning in toward me. His mouth was next to my ear and his right hand was on my shoulder, preventing me from making any sudden moves that might disturb Porter.

"Chase?" I said, turning my face toward the sound of his voice. His lips were so close they brushed my cheek as I turned my head. He pulled back. The room was pitch black. It was still the middle of the night.

"Shhh, I don't want to wake Porter," he whispered. His breath smelled of mouthwash and, beneath that, faintly, of beer.

"Is something wrong?" I was self-conscious about my own breath. Had I been asleep long enough for it to go stale? Or was Chase's sense of smell too clouded by his own exhalations for him to notice?

"Shhh, no, nothing's wrong. I just want to talk to you—alone."

"Okay," I said. I breathed deeply, trying to slow my racing heart, which had been startled awake. Within minutes, the increased blood flow would be echoed in the chambers of Porter's heart, speeding up his metabolism, and he, too, would awaken. "What is it?"

"Owen, I've got something to tell you, and I don't want Porter—or Faith—to know. At least not yet."

"What is it?" If he didn't want Porter and Faith to know, it couldn't be an emergency. The house must not be on fire. As fond as I was of Chase, I was put out at being awakened in the middle of the night for something that would not require an evacuation.

"Owen, I'm in love."

That I wasn't expecting, but I was touched by the earnestness of his confession. And I was pleased he trusted me. At last, he was going to come out to me. Perhaps he needed advice about a relationship, although what sort of advice *I'd* be able to give him I didn't know. I wanted to ruffle his hair, to pet him like a puppy that was already adorable but had just done something impossibly cute and endearing: gotten tangled up in Christmas ribbon or batted a bright red balloon around the room.

"How long will it be before Porter, you know, comes to?" he asked.

"Not long. Not long enough for much of a conversation. But we can find a way to do this even if he's awake. We have ways. He can wear headphones."

Try as I might, I could not slow my heart. Holding my breath, which I thought might help, only seemed to make it worse. I could feel the blood pounding in my ears. In a minute or two, Porter would stir.

"Okay, Owen. I guess we can figure something out."

"But you're in love, Chase? That's great."

"Not so great," he said.

"No? Why not?"

For a heartbeat—two, three—he said nothing. Perhaps the moment had passed and he was retreating, thinking that telling me about his boyfriend might not be such a good idea after all, that I might let on to Porter or inadvertently let it slip in front of Faith.

He sighed. "I'm in love . . . with you."

Without another word, he stood up and left the bedroom, the open door briefly admitting the glow of the night-light in the hallway. I was left there, pinned to the bed by shock and my sleeping twin. Was this a dream? No, it was real, all right. I could still smell Chase's warm, sweet breath. Budweiser with a Scope chaser. You don't smell in dreams—not that vividly.

Next to me, Porter turned his head, his overnight growth of beard prickly against my cheek.

"What's going on, O?" he asked. "What time is it?"

"Nothing. It's still early. Go back to sleep."

I knew I had no choice but to go back to sleep as well, lulled by Porter's regular breathing, constrained by the weight of his inert form. For once I was grateful for my circumstances: I couldn't do anything precipitous, adolescent, like follow Chase back to his room and profess my own love for him. So I gave in and tried to match Porter's breathing, to mimic the rhythm of his heart—but my mind was racing. I wondered how long Chase had been in love with me and if he knew that I loved him, too. I wondered what it was that had given him the impetus to wake me on this particular night. Had I tipped my hand somehow? What did he expect me to say—or do? I tried desperately to stay in the moment, to hear his words again, to recapture the scent of hops and peppermint, warm and moist, his mouth, his lips, as close to mine as they had ever been. I discovered that if I thought about the future, my heart began to race again, fearful and insecure, reckless, but if I concentrated on those five words in the present tense—"I'm in love . . . with you"—I could remain curiously calm. Despite the pull of Porter's slumber, I stayed awake until the scent of peppermint was long gone.

In the morning, when Porter and I arrived for breakfast next door, everything seemed normal enough. Faith stood at the stove making pancakes. She had taken to standing sideways while she cooked, to shield the babies from the heat of the stove. Chase had been showering in the downstairs bathroom when we left my place, and he walked in a few minutes later. He didn't exactly ignore me or avert his eyes when I looked at him, but neither did he allow me significant access to whatever it was that was going on behind them. As I ate breakfast, he rarely made eye contact with me, keeping his nose in the technology section of the *New York Times*. When we did connect, his gaze was knowing, like the furtive glances by which gay men expose themselves and identify each other, but remote. We shared a secret, but little additional information was exchanged.

Chase's evasiveness contrasted sharply with the openness and intimacy I observed that morning between brother and sister. Although Faith had grown increasingly distant as her pregnancy had progressed, avoiding or shrugging off Porter's attempts to embrace her even casually, the same apparently did not hold true for her brother. I took note of the number of times she touched Chase fleetingly and the number of times she allowed him to touch her. They had hugged when he first came into the kitchen, her right hand still gripping the spatula, glistening with frothy butter, with which she was flipping the pancakes. With her left hand, she batted awkwardly at his lank blond hair, trying to clean up the irregular part his careless grooming had given him. And after she set his plate down in front of him, laden with pancakes, bacon, and grits (a culinary reminder of their childhood he still relished), she patted him on the shoulder, as if she were encouraging a beloved pet to eat. I yearned for that sort of casual intimacy with him, and I felt a twinge of jealousy. Faith had Porter, whom she had, in a way, stolen from me. Faith had Chase. I had no one—half a body, half a life. In that moment, it was hard not to resent her. I thought back to the night on which she had tried to claim me for herself as well and realized how selfish she could be.

Throughout the meal, I observed Chase as intently as I could without seeming obvious, analyzing every word, every gesture. He spoke mostly to Faith and then only about insignificant things: projects he was working on at Georgia Tech that week, the surprise birthday party they were planning for their mother next month. It was ordinary stuff, almost self-consciously mundane, but I listened to it in a new way, searching for subtle clues as if it were dialogue in a film or play, the kind of patter that seems meaningless to the audience as it washes over them but in which there must be portents of the progress of the narrative—otherwise the screenwriter or playwright wouldn't have wasted precious words. It seemed to me that Chase had to be aware that I was listening to what he was saying, had to be conscious of me as his "audience." What he chose to say and how and to whom was significant. Perhaps he would surreptitiously suggest a rendezvous by outlining his plans for the day, a time and place at which I could meet him to talk. But there were no hints, nothing by which to auger my future.

"So, how's the album coming?" Chase finally asked after washing down a mouthful of pancakes with a couple swallows of milk. I had watched his Adam's apple bob as he chugged it. His tongue flicked at his frothy white mustache. For a moment, he looked about twelve.

"Fine—great," Porter said. "We're getting ready to lay down our ninth track."

"Awesome. Can't wait to hear it." He wiped his mouth with the back of his hand.

"Use a napkin, Chase, for Pete's sake!" Faith said.

"Yes, Mom."

In the face of such a domestic scene, I was stunned to think of the amount of deception going on at that table. I never realized how quickly the complexity of lies grew—whether spoken or unspoken. Last night, Chase had put into play something like an emotional confidence game by revealing himself to me but attempting to keep Porter and Faith in the dark. I did the same by pretending that nothing was different, conspiring to hide our shared secret. Perhaps Chase was attempting to deceive even himself this morning, pretending he had not taken the first step, set loose the first pebble that would become an emotional avalanche.

I had to wonder if Porter and Faith also had secrets, if they actually knew what was going on and were pretending they didn't. Had Porter awakened sooner than he had let on? Had he heard Chase's confession? Did Faith already suspect her brother was gay? Could she possibly imagine that he was in love with me?

Then, too, there was the secret Faith and I had agreed to keep from Porter, which seemed less innocent and more like a betrayal with each passing day.

Infuriatingly, Chase chose not to speak to me about his feelings in the days that followed. In fact, we barely spoke at all. For someone who was living in my home, he was remarkably elusive—up and out of the house long before Porter and I woke up, absent at meals again as he had been last summer, home late at night and occasionally not at all. I had to conclude that it was calculated, that he was consciously avoiding me. It was as if he were insulted by my inability to speak to him at length that first night—or frightened by the implications of the words he had spoken. Obviously, he was not out to his family and probably never would be. Clearly, he'd internalized a lot of pressure. Perhaps it had something to do with him being the only son in the family. The idea, however outmoded, that a son will continue the bloodline in ways a daughter cannot—by carrying on the family name—is deeply rooted in our society. Perhaps that threatens parents, makes them feel vulnerable, as they watch a branch of the family tree, once full of the promise of new life, wither and die before their eyes. Maybe it's something even more deeply ingrained than that. Maybe it's tribal: the need to reproduce in order to survive, to create a family unit that will look after them in old age, when they are too feeble to hunt mastodons themselves.

In the studio, as we tried to wrap up work on the new CD, Porter could tell I was distracted again, as I had been after coming out to Faith.

"Man, where *are* you?" Porter asked when I flubbed a chord for the third or fourth time that day. "You're not here, that's for sure."

"I'm sorry, Porter, you're right. I've got a lot on my mind."

"You have been kind of squirrelly lately—more than just today, although this is the worst it's been in a while."

Because we share a body, Porter and I usually feel exactly the same thing at the same time, at least when it comes to gross physical sensation. It's impossible for me to be hot when he is cold, or for me to be sober when he is drunk. If Porter were to prick his finger, I would not feel the pain, *per se*, but his response to it would echo through our body like the sound of a gunshot in an auditorium. Without any effort on my part, my pulse would quicken, even if imperceptibly, like a seismograph registering an earthquake at some great remove.

But I also pride myself on being able to read Porter's moods, the more subtle gradations of emotion. That's easier to do when the heat of anger or the chill of fear registers in two brains simultaneously, when adrenalin or endorphins flood a common bloodstream, but the process is not foolproof. It requires not only an awareness of the other person's feelings but also an *interest* in them. And that is where Porter and I differ. For whatever reason, Porter seems less interested in my feelings than I am in his. It's difficult to arouse sympathy in him, let alone empathy. And so it surprised me that he noticed how distracted I was in the wake of Chase's announcement. I must have been pretty far gone.

"Is it that obvious?" I asked.

"It's like you're in a fog, bro," he said. "Or quicksand. And sinking fast."

I dared not tell Porter the cause of my malaise. That

would be betraying Chase's confidence. But I appreciated the fact that he had noticed.

"I'm sorry," I said.

"You haven't been yourself since Faith and I tied the knot," he said. "I guess you're feeling pretty left out."

He was right, of course. His wedding day *had* marked the beginning of a metamorphosis for me, but not for the reason he suspected. It was not that I felt left out merely because he had paired off with Faith on that day but that I had fallen in love with Chase. And now, knowing Chase felt the same way but that we were unable to act on our feelings, my sense of frustration had grown exponentially.

"It's not that, exactly."

"What then? You're horny?"

"No, Porter. Well, yes. But that's the least of it."

"You gonna keep me guessing?"

"I can't tell you right now, really. But thanks for asking. I just need some time to myself."

Ultimately, I resorted to sending Chase an e-mail in which, although I hedged my bets, I made it clear that while his announcement had come as a surprise, it had not been unwelcome. But he ignored it. I sent a second one, to which he replied: "I honestly don't see how we can have a discussion about this without letting P in on it, and he will tell F, and I'm just not ready to deal with that yet. I know you said you have ways to ensure our privacy, but what the hell is P going to think we're talking about? I'm sorry I brought this up in the first place."

I suppose I can understand Chase's skepticism about the privacy of our conversation. It's difficult to believe two people can have a conversation so close to a third person without them overhearing at least some of it. And since Porter and I occupy the same body, it's easy to imagine that at the very least, he might be aware of the vibrations of my vocal chords in the same way we fear people around us can hear the nearly silent, involuntary fluttering of our stomachs, the potentially embarrassing, unexpected contractions of our bowels we all think we hear, although the "noise" travels mainly as vibrations through our bodies. I suppose it's also possible to assume that Porter and I are somehow psychically linked, even more so than normal twins. While I cannot read Porter's mind, I can "read" his body, or his half of our body. I know when he is tense or anxious. I don't necessarily know why he is feeling that way, but I can feel its physical manifestations.

But exactly what did Chase think was going to happen if we ever did have our conversation? Just how long did he think we would be able to keep our relationship a secret from Porter? I suppose there would be ways, of course. We could blindfold Porter whenever Chase and I were having sex, but that would be ungainly and I doubted he would stand for it. I railed at the injustice of the situation, the infuriating dead end we faced. It would be difficult enough for Chase and me to become lovers if we were just an ordinary couple of gay men trying to keep a secret from Porter and Faith and the Colquitt family. But there was no way under the circumstances that we could ever keep it a secret from Porter. If Chase could not get past that, there was no hope for a relationship.

In light of all this, I had to ask myself what it was I was feeling for Chase. It was not lust, not in the way I felt lust for nubile young porn stars, with their almost plasticene perfection of face and form and their deliberately provocative poses. Chase was adorable—I was drawn to him from the first moment I saw him—but it was not an attraction that had a hard edge to it. Until now, there had been no urgency about it, no sense that I *had* to have him. Instead, I found myself simply wanting to spend time with him, to get to know him, to enjoy an intimate conversation. I was as comfortable with Chase as I had ever been with anyone, and I felt a definite connection to him, but it was not an overwhelmingly physical thing. In fact, I was surprised the first time I had a sense of missing him, of wanting him to be there when he wasn't. It was an odd sensation, this feeling of needing someone else present in my life. With Porter always around, what I had yearned for most often was solitude.

I suppose you could say that I genuinely *liked* Chase, which meant more to me than loving him. I tend to think of liking people as something real, both more tangible and more immutable than loving them. Love seems to be something over which we have no control, a mixture of magic and chemistry, a kind of alchemy that turns base metal into gold, that transforms people with whom we might not even be friends under most circumstances into people with whom we are intimate, to whom we bare not only our bodies but our souls. The transmuted metal shimmers briefly, then returns to its normal dull state when the magic wears off. What else can explain bitter divorces and marital murders? One day you're sleeping with someone, giving your heart to them, and the next they are cutting your heart *out*—literally.

I wasn't sure I *wanted* to be in love with Chase or wanted him to be in love with me. I would have much preferred to have had him just *like* me. I was more certain of that, less suspicious. But all that had changed when he had uttered those five words. "I'm in love . . . with *you*." The idea that he was offering himself to me, that he did not find me hideous, grotesque, that he wanted me, freed me to feel the same way about him—and damn the consequences.

But what could I do? Unless Chase agreed to talk to me with Porter present, if incommunicado, I had no recourse but to honor his wishes. Blurting something out while the four of us were having dinner one night was not an option. Any unilateral action would inevitably be disastrous.

I was furious. How could he just walk into my room in the middle of the night, announce that he loved me, and then refuse to talk about it? Was it that easy for him to deny his feelings for me? I sent him a final e-mail: "Porter and I have an understanding about our privacy. When one of us asks for time 'alone' with someone, the other one grants it without question. We use headphones and loud music to drown out the conversation, and neither one of us has yet learned to read lips. We couldn't survive if we didn't trust each other. Believe me, Porter is not even remotely interested in anything you are going to have to say to me."

Chapter 23

I am not a particularly religious person. I am rational, scientific in my view of life. I don't believe there is an all-knowing God somewhere who actually thought it would be a good idea to stick two men in one body. Nor do I believe the converse, that there is some sick and twisted all-powerful force out there who thought it might be fun to see two human beings squirm in such close quarters. But there is one small part of me, embarrassingly sentimental, irrationally romantic in the face of all evidence to the contrary, that believes there was something larger at work in the way Faith and Porter met; that they were meant for each other and, through some miracle, they found each other; and that the same holds true for Chase and me. We were *meant* to be together—the four of us. It's the only explanation I have.

I suppose for most of the world, the rules of attraction seem pretty clear. Men are attracted to women and vice versa. But the details of a specific attraction, of a particular man to a particular woman, are far more complex and difficult to discern. It seems to me that if it were possible to map the complexities of the human heart—the romantic heart, not the physical heart—it would take a project as complex and ambitious as that which mapped the human genome. The fact that Porter and I are genetically identical and have been reared in precisely the same environment yet are attracted to people who are so essentially different illustrates

234 / Andrew W.M. Beierle

the complexity of the issue. There must be thousands of pairs of identical twins with diverging sexualities; it's not all genetics, and it's not all nurturing. On the other hand, although Faith and Chase are similar in many respects, they are not genetically identical, and yet they find themselves attracted to, essentially, the same person. Where is the rhyme or reason in *that*? Nonetheless, the mere fact that Chase was in love with me made it somehow easier to understand why Faith was in love with Porter, or at least *that* she was in love with him.

I'm not sure what finally prompted Chase to sit down and talk to me about his feelings. Whatever the reason, he eventually sent me an e-mail indicating he was ready to talk. I told Porter that Chase and I wanted to meet "alone," and he agreed without question, as I knew he would. He was so overwhelmed by impending fatherhood, now doubled, that it never occurred to him to ask me what this was all about. So that night, Porter settled in with his Discman, earphones, and a couple of beers (I limited him to two; more than that and I would begin to feel a bit woozy myself), and Chase and I sat down in my living room to talk. It took some doing to convince him our conversation would remain confidential.

"Go ahead, say something outrageous," I said. "See if it fazes him."

"Like what?"

"I don't know. Say he's a jerk or a wimp or a wife beater," I said, proving by doing so that further tests were unnecessary. Porter remained blissfully unaware, an Evan and Jaron CD cranked up so loud Chase and I could hear its tinny reverberations escaping the padded earphones.

"Okay, I get your point," Chase conceded.

"Now tell me what's on your mind."

"You know what's on my mind, Owen. I've told you already."

"Tell me again."

I wasn't playing games with him. I needed to hear those

words again—to know they were real. He blushed and looked down at his hands, but he complied. Then it was my turn.

"I love you, too, Chase."

"You do?"

"Yes, I do. I've had a crush on you more or less from the minute I laid eyes on you at the wedding-rehearsal dinner."

"You're kidding. Really?"

For a moment he allowed himself to be completely spontaneous. His face lit up, and I swear I saw tears sparkling in the corners of his eyes. Then he remembered Porter was there and that, while Porter couldn't hear what we were saying, he could still see the excitement on Chase's face. He grew self-consciously serious.

"Why didn't you say something?" he whispered. "Why didn't you tell me?"

"I didn't even suspect you were gay until I discovered you'd been reading my gay magazines in the bathroom."

He smiled. "I did that on purpose. You're such a neat freak, I figured you'd notice . . . sooner or later."

"But even when I thought you might be gay, never in a million years did I think you'd be interested in me. I hoped . . . I *fantasized* sometimes. But I never really believed it could be true. And then, just when I was getting up my nerve to say something, you sort of disappeared. You stayed out late, or you didn't come home at all. I figured you must have met somebody and fallen in love."

"I was in love all right—with you—and I didn't know what the hell to do about it. I couldn't stand to be close to you and not touch you. At the movies, at Chastain Park—it drove me crazy, but I was afraid to say anything."

"I wish you had. You drove everybody nuts, not least of all me."

While I was confident Porter could not hear a word we were saying, I nonetheless monitored his half of our body—

posture, heartbeat, alertness—as best I could for any indication he might be attempting to eavesdrop. I was certain he
was not.

"My friends convinced me all I needed to do was to get
laid and I'd forget about you," Chase said. "So I started
hanging out with them, dancing all night at Backstreet and
Metro, and I did meet a lot of guys. But even when I was
with someone else, I was always thinking of you. I finally decided I was going to have to do something, take a stand, and
that's when I started asking around about graduate programs
at Tech. I couldn't bear the idea of not seeing you every day."

"You mean you actively pursued that—it didn't just fall
into your lap? You threw away fellowships at MIT and Stanford for me?"

Chase blushed. "Don't let it go to your head. The program at Tech is great. They're doing some amazing things,
groundbreaking things. It wasn't that much of a sacrifice."

"But you did it without talking to me, without knowing
how I'd react. That was brave."

"Or stupid." He grinned and shrugged his shoulders.
"You be the judge."

I realized the logical thing to do at this moment was to
kiss Chase, to wrap my arm around him and pull him close
to me. But that was impossible without giving us away.

"You do understand that if we pursue this, we won't be
able to keep it from Porter," I said. "I mean, I've thought
about blindfolding him, and that might be doable for a
while. But if anything is going to come of this, we're going to
have to let him in on it, and eventually, Faith. I mean, if we
want to have any sort of honest relationship."

"I know. I understand that. I've thought about it all summer. That's mostly what prevented me from coming to talk to
you. It wasn't that I was figuring out I was gay or anything.
I've known that for years. And it wasn't because I had any
doubts about loving you. To be honest, it was more or less
love at first sight for me at the wedding, too, and it scared the

hell out of me. What kept me from doing anything about it was knowing that if I was ever going to have the kind of relationship I wanted with you, Faith would ultimately have to know I was gay and that I was in love with you. I was afraid she'd feel a moral obligation to tell my folks."

"So what *do* you think she's going to make of all of this?"

"I don't know. I've always thought Faith had figured out I was gay. I mean, no girlfriends—ever. Not in high school, not in college."

"And then there was Kyle."

I thought he was going to choke.

"You know about Kyle? She told you about Kyle? What did she say?"

"Not much, except that he drove a BMW convertible and took you to Bali. She said she thought that was romantic."

"Romantic? She used that word?" He looked stricken.

"She qualified it by saying she meant the romance of the high seas and all that, but I think she may have been backpedaling—you know, sort of covering your tracks."

"Is that all she said?"

"Pretty much. She did say you were always bringing home exotic boys on your way to Florida for spring break. Japanese and Vietnamese guys."

"They were just friends. Fellow geeks. Kyle was the only boyfriend I ever brought to Weathertop. We actually slept together in my room, and the little fucker kept trying to do stuff. He was pretty much a total horndog. I thought I'd cool him down by making us wear some old long johns I fished out of the bottom drawer of my dresser, but he thought that was hot. One pair had a seat that unbuttoned, and you can imagine where we went with that."

"He was adorable, I'd imagine. A Harvard lacrosse player?"

"Yeah, he was cute. A definite hottie. Very Abercrombie and Fitch—with a bad-boy twist. I guess you could say we were totally in love. The trip to Bali *was* very romantic."

"So what happened?"

"Nothing, really. We just sort of drifted apart after a while. He didn't do a very good job of keeping it in his pants. He was a real party-and-play boy and always wanted to fly us to these big circuit parties. I wasn't really into that. He ran with this fast, rich crowd, and I didn't fit in and couldn't keep up. It ended amicably, more or less. I mean, we didn't scream and scratch and bite, the way some of my friends did when they broke up. I saw him around every once in a while, but I didn't love him anymore. I'm not still hurting or anything. It was nice, but now it's over."

"Well, it's his loss."

I wanted to ask Chase why he loved me, how he could possibly want to spend his life with me—if that's what he had in mind—instead of with a normal guy. I figured if he had managed to snag, in his own words, a hot Harvard horndog, he probably had plenty of other boyfriends, or at least dates. Although he wasn't conventionally gorgeous, he was extraordinarily appealing. I'm sure other men saw that in him. But ultimately I couldn't find a way to ask him what I wanted to know.

"In any event, I think Faith will be able to handle the fact that I'm gay, if we break it to her gently. My family won't, but that's okay. I just won't tell them. The big thing is that I'm in love with you . . . and you're in love with me."

"So what do you think we ought to do about this?"

"I think we ought to make love. I've wanted to kiss you for so long, just kiss you, Owen. Let's start there."

"I'm going to have to break the news to Porter before we can even do that much—and ask him not to tell Faith . . . yet."

"Well, then, I guess that's the next step—telling him," he said.

Chase looked happy—no, more than happy. Blissful. I knew at that moment that this was right the right thing to do, even if it were not literally preordained. That night, alone in our bed, I asked Porter what he thought of all this.

"Are you out of your fucking mind? You and Chase? That's what this was all about?"

"Yeah, that's what it was about."

"I don't know, man . . . of all the people in the world to fall in love with, you choose Chase."

"I didn't really choose him. He chose me."

"Yeah, well, whatever. If *I* had a choice in the matter, I sure as hell wouldn't pick Chase for you. But I don't think I have a say in this, so I don't really know that my point of view matters."

"Well, it doesn't, really—in a thumbs-up or -down way. The only reason I'm coming to you at all is because Chase is Faith's brother."

"I like Chase well enough," he said. "But I can't help feeling you're asking for trouble. What is Faith going to think? What's her family going to think?"

"I suspect we're not going to be able to tell them, period. Not ever."

"Now that's interesting. All of a sudden you're the one who wants to keep this from Faith."

"That's not what I meant. I think Faith will have to know. Her family—no. But if Chase and I are going to have a relationship, she's going to have to know."

"Well, *I* think you shouldn't tell her. At least not for now. You don't know what will come of it—of you and Chase, I mean. You don't know if it will last, if it will get serious. Maybe it's just something you both need to get out of your systems. There are plenty of girls I've been with that I didn't want after the first time."

"I don't think that's going to be the case, Porter. It's not like some hookup in a cheap motel room with a fucked-up chick you're never going to see again. It's not like that at all. Chase and I both have feelings for each other. But there are a lot of obstacles to any relationship, and ours would be particularly complicated. I don't want to end up hurting him because we haven't thought this through. And I don't want to damage his relationship with Faith, or your relationship with her."

Ultimately, Porter grudgingly acknowledged my right to make my own choices, in much the same way he had accepted the inevitability of my sexual orientation a decade earlier. He didn't necessarily like it, he didn't agree with it, but somewhere deep inside himself, he knew if we were to survive, he had to let me live my life as I saw fit. Although my initial confidence had been undermined somewhat, I knew I had no choice but to pursue a relationship with Chase.

I arranged a romantic dinner for us at Tiburon Grille, where Porter and Faith had shared so many intimate moments. I was comfortable there, and I think it signaled to Porter that my feelings for Chase were more than merely sexual. Afterward, Porter put on a new pair of wireless, noise-canceling earphones I bought especially for the occasion and disappeared into his music.

It would have been enough simply to have seen Chase naked, to have watched his body emerge from his clothing like some exotic fruit brought back from the New World by Columbus being peeled for the first time in the throne room of Ferdinand and Isabella. But I wanted more, and mercifully Chase gave me more. We made love as delicately and gracefully as we could under the circumstances. He was thoughtful and imaginative, and he did most of the work, presenting various parts of his body to me and exploring my half of my body, first tentatively, then passionately, but always mindful of boundaries, the way a certain type of child takes pains to stay within the lines of his coloring book. He allowed me to inhale him, to taste the sweat that ran down his torso like a salty nectar. Porter stirred only near the end, as we approached climax.

Afterward, Chase lay down beside me, his face at last as

close to mine as Porter's always was. For the first time in my life, I felt my orientation shifting from left to right, from Porter to Chase, from inside to out, and I can truly say that for a moment, if only a heartbeat, I forgot my brother entirely.

Chapter 24

Keeping our relationship a secret from Faith was both easier and more difficult than we imagined it might be. It
seemed perfectly natural for Chase to spend time with Porter,
Faith, and me. After all, he *was* family—and he was living in
my home. If Faith took note of it at all, it was only to say
how nice it was to have him around and how he seemed happier—more settled—than he had been the previous summer,
when he had stayed out late and frequently failed to come
home at all. On the other hand, it was sometimes difficult to
remember to keep our hands to ourselves when she was
around, and on more than one occasion we had to feign a
sort of frat-boy roughhousing when she walked in on an incipient embrace. From time to time, Faith would ask Chase
why he hadn't yet moved into a dorm at Georgia Tech as
planned, but the way she phrased the question always made
it seem as if she were looking out for my interests—as if she
were concerned he was imposing on my hospitality. Chase always managed a plausible response about an unexpectedly
large freshman class and overcrowded dorms.

The notion of maintaining two homes side by side, once
such an obvious and natural choice, now seemed fraught
with potential hazards. The boundaries between Faith and
Porter's "territory" and mine seemed too permeable, too easily breached. When it came to actually having sex, Chase and
I were incredibly discreet. Because my master bedroom

shared a common wall with Porter and Faith's, we moved my bed to the far side of the room to prevent headboard banging. Initially, we even did sound checks while Faith was at work, having Chase lie in my bed and simulate amorous noises while Porter and I positioned ourselves in the master bedroom next door and strained to hear him. But at least in the beginning, Chase often was too nervous to spend the entire night in my bed, because he was afraid Faith might pop in unannounced in the morning. He usually retreated to his own bed as dawn approached, except on those occasions when he was sleeping too soundly to notice that the sun had risen. Porter, Chase, and I once went so far as to discuss the idea of selling my townhouse and moving elsewhere—possibly to midtown Atlanta, some ten miles away—but we decided the idea was ludicrous. Faith would never stand for it. Besides, we ultimately planned to tell Faith about my relationship with Chase, and thereafter we could live openly.

Our deepening intimacy was something of an epiphany for Porter. While he was still somewhat squeamish about certain sexual practices, he had relaxed a bit over time. The boundaries between what he would accommodate and what he would not blurred, became less distinct. He allowed me to engage in until-now unthinkable acts of intimacy, and I was more satisfied sexually than I had ever been with Casey or any of the men who had come after him.

Chase and I debated the merits of coming out to Faith about our relationship and about a timetable for doing so. We knew it was inevitable, but we were enjoying a sort of honeymoon from reality and were reluctant to have it end. Sometimes Porter chimed in with his opinion, which always erred on the side of caution, and that always dampened our enthusiasm for full disclosure.

One Sunday afternoon three months after Chase and I had acknowledged our feelings for one another, Porter and I were at my dining room table preparing our tax records for our accountant when Faith called from next door to say she needed to talk to me. It had taken some doing to get Porter to actually sit down and pay attention to a task we both considered odious, so I was irritated by the interruption. Porter, on the other hand, welcomed the distraction—at least at first.

"I hate doing this shit," he said, pushing away a stack of credit card bills, hotel receipts, and airline tickets. "Remind me again why we have an accountant."

But both of us quickly realized this could mean trouble.

"Chase," I said, under my breath.

"Jesus, O, do you think that's it?" Porter asked.

"I honestly don't know. I thought we'd been careful."

It was difficult to know what to expect. Faith had become somewhat distant toward me since her near-profession of love, and while I wasn't particularly concerned that she still had romantic feelings for me—I was fairly certain my coming out had put an end to that—I still wasn't sure precisely how she felt about me *being* gay. For one thing, our nocturnal chats had come to a somewhat abrupt end, and we no longer talked about truly intimate things. On the nights I slept at Porter's, she usually either retired early and was asleep when we turned in, or she stayed up well into the night reading in the living room, slipping into bed only after both Porter and I were asleep.

When Faith arrived a few minutes later, she sat down in my big leather easy chair, probably the most comfortable piece of furniture in the house. Porter had a matching one next door.

"So, Faith, what's on your mind?" I asked as casually as possible. "And do we need to rig Porter for silent running? You're not planning a surprise party for him, are you?"

"No, it's okay. He should probably hear this, anyway."

"What is it, honey?" he asked so quickly it sounded incriminating.

Faith shifted her considerable bulk in the chair, trying to get comfortable. "Doesn't this thing recline? I could stand to have my feet elevated."

"Here," I said, "let me help you."

We got up and adjusted the chair for her.

"Not back that much. It makes the babies press on my stomach. Just the footrest, maybe. Raise that. Maybe just recline the chair a *little* . . . there. That's good."

Porter and I returned to the love seat. A low travertine-and-glass coffee table separated us from Faith.

"Owen," she began, "this is hard for me to say, but it's been bothering me for quite a while."

"You know you can talk to me about anything, Faith." *Anything but Chase.*

She continued to shift her weight in the chair. Her face bore the expression of one of Cinderella's sisters trying to fit a size-nine foot into a size-five shoe—uncomfortable but determined.

"I understand your need for privacy, and I respect it—I really do," she said, finally. "But I wonder if you've given any thought to the impact it has on me."

"What do you mean?"

"You know, with the birth of the babies and everything that will entail."

"Exactly what is it you're asking?" I said. I relaxed a little. Whatever was on Faith's mind, it did not appear we were in for a round of truth or consequences.

"I'm not sure I'm actually *asking* anything, really. I'm just making an observation. I suppose it's something of a rhetorical question."

"Well, speaking rhetorically, I guess not. I've never really thought about it. I mean, not seriously. Porter and I have always done things this way—split our time down the middle. We've made trade-offs, of course. Switched things around a little. I'm open to that. I've been willing to do that, haven't I, Porter?"

"Oh, yeah, that hasn't been a problem," Porter said.

"Is there something you have in mind? Something specific? A particular day?" I asked.

"Well, not exactly. Not a specific day. But I guess we need to talk about emergencies—special occasions. I mean, what if I deliver on one of your days? Will you . . . ?"

"Of course, Faith. You're not really worried about that, are you? You haven't been thinking I'd . . ."

"No, not really. Of course not. I always assumed you'd be there for me. I mean, Porter would. You've been great about coming to my Lamaze classes. I wouldn't have wanted to miss half of them just because they were on 'your' Wednesdays."

"Well, good. You don't need to worry about those sorts of things—ever. Really."

"It's just that I get lonely when Porter's not with me at night. You know? And it just seems so *pointless* for him to be on the other side of the wall—literally—almost within reach, but not to actually *be* there. I know we talked about this before we got married, and I understood it and agreed to it. But I guess I never imagined what it would be like to be pregnant and to be alone half the time. It's no fun."

"I see." I thought I knew where this was going.

"And my mother's been asking a lot of questions about our arrangement that I can't answer to her satisfaction. She doesn't understand why Porter's not sleeping at home every night. I thought maybe we could work something out, something different, temporary . . . just for now."

"What did you have in mind?"

"I haven't given it that much thought," she said. "Well, that's not exactly true. But I haven't thought of anything concrete yet. I hoped we could work out a new system. An agreement. For the duration of my pregnancy—and after. For the first year, maybe. Something where you could, I don't know, sort of bank the days you give up, save them for when you need them—some time in the future."

A year? She was going to ask me to give up a year of my life?

"I suppose Porter's and my arrangement does seem a bit arbitrary to someone who hasn't lived with it as long as we have," I said. "But it makes perfect sense to us. We've lived like this our entire lives, and it's what has made our situation workable. It's like, you know, a diet or something. If you want it to work, you have to follow it to the letter. No cheating, no midnight snacks, no nibbling between meals. Once you start to do that—sneaking a candy bar here and there, adding butter to your fat-free popcorn—well, you stop losing weight. Pretty soon the whole diet goes to hell, and you just start eating anything you want and you gain back all the weight you lost—and more."

"Owen, this isn't about losing a few extra pounds," she said. "It's about life, about lives—mine and Porter's and soon the babies'. I can't believe you're going to deprive Porter's children of his presence half the time. It's just not fair. I'm going to need help with the babies—and Porter needs to be around them. They need to know him and love him and be comfortable around him. God knows, things are going to be difficult enough as they grow up. But if they barely know their father, if he's around only half the time, things are going to be that much harder—for all of us."

I could see her point, sure, and to be honest, I imagined things would change once the twins were born. I'd probably spend a lot more time over at Porter and Faith's helping with the kids. I was certain Chase would pitch in, too. It would be a family affair. But I bristled at the idea that it was being forced down my throat, that it was expected of me. I was being asked to give up my private life so Faith wouldn't be lonely at night—now, even before the babies were born.

Perhaps it did not occur to her what an incredible invasion of my privacy it was. After all, I had more than a passing interest in Faith and Porter's babies. I definitely was feeling a certain paternal pull, which is a good thing, since I was going to have to share equally in Porter's responsibilities—getting up in the middle of the night to feed the babies or change their diapers, and, in the long term, attending baseball games or ballet recitals. Rather than tuning out Porter and Faith's conversations about the babies, I had been listening to them intently. I even found myself thinking about names and discovering I had preferences that differed from Porter and Faith's. I once read something by one of my Dad's colleagues, a theory that there are biological or chemical changes in parents' brains that help them take care of their children, that give them the patience to tolerate the screaming little shit machines who sometimes send babysitters, single moms' boyfriends, and unlucky airplane seatmates over the edge. It's an evolutionary adaptation that enhances the odds of survival for the infant. Though I have no proof, there's not a doubt in my mind I was going through those changes, too. After all, I was as much a father as Porter was, although no one but me dared think of it like that. So perhaps Faith thought I wouldn't mind giving up a substantial portion of my private life for the benefit of the babies.

What bothered me was the idea that my time was less valuable than Porter's because I was single, "alone"—at least from Faith's perspective—and he was part of a family. It was as if his worth had been multiplied by the number of people who were or soon would be dependent on him, that being married made his life twice as important as mine and having kids would make it exponentially more precious. My own life was expendable; I was expected to sacrifice it for the greater good of Porter and his family.

Whatever concessions I was going to be forced to make, I wasn't going to do so under false pretenses. I was going to have to tell Faith that in fact I wasn't "alone," that I was in love with her brother and he with me. If Porter and I spent every night with Faith, I'd *never* get to sleep with Chase, never have any time alone with him. But I didn't feel I could say anything to her without talking to Chase first. So for now

I tried to reassure her that Porter would always be available, without making any specific concessions or commitments.

"We'll always be there for you and the kids—for their school plays and Little League, and certainly for emergencies," I said. "But you're asking an awful lot of me to just sign away a year of my life. I'll have to think about that."

She seemed surprised I hadn't capitulated outright, as if perhaps I didn't understand the simple moral imperative behind her request.

"I see," she said. "You'll have to *think* about it. Very well. I understand."

With some difficulty she struggled to get out of the chair, but when Porter and I stood up and offered to help, she waved her hand and shook her head.

"Don't go to any trouble," she sniffed.

When I explained my point of view to Porter in private, I found myself once again challenging the limits of his tolerance. He was willing to acknowledge my relationship with Chase but continued to be reluctant to be honest with Faith about it. He was especially concerned about the impact such an announcement would have on his unborn babies. I told him I doubted anything I could say to Faith, no matter how strongly she reacted, was going to stunt the babies' growth or result in missing or deformed appendages, especially at this late date.

"No matter how delicate Faith may seem, no matter how vulnerable, I know she's going to be calmer and more focused now than after the delivery," I told him. "My god . . . all the stress of giving birth, then—boom—having to feed and change and bathe two babies, to worry about them twenty-four hours a day. She's going to be frazzled. We all are."

"I don't know, O. I still think it's a mistake."

But when I explained the situation to Chase, he quickly agreed that telling Faith was the right thing to do, especially if *not* telling her meant we wouldn't be able to sleep together with any regularity for a year or more. Despite his earlier misgivings, he seemed almost eager to get things out in the open, and we resolved to tell her as soon as we had given it some additional thought.

Chapter 25

Perhaps I was being myopic, but the next morning I told Porter and Chase I thought it unlikely Faith would be surprised to discover her brother was gay. She was thoughtful and sensitive, and she had told me more than once that she felt closer to him than to any of her sisters. Gloria, Viv, and Greta were each at least five years older than she and had married and moved out of the house while she was still a teenager; Elizabeth was ten years her junior. Chase had gravitated toward Faith for companionship all his life, especially because his rapid progress through school had repeatedly thrust him into the company of unfamiliar classmates. Surely she must have been attuned to his thoughts and feelings.

"Knowing is one thing—knowing subconsciously," Porter countered. "Acknowledging it is something entirely different. And accepting it—well, who knows?"

I suspect Porter found it somewhat uncomfortable to be double-teamed by Chase and me. He and I had stood together against the world for most of our lives.

"It'll be fine," I said with as much bravado as possible. "I suppose it took her a while to come to terms with me being gay, but things have turned out all right."

"Personally, I still think it would be best not to tell her," Porter said. "You're only going to end up hurting her."

"You know I'd never do anything to hurt Faith," Chase said. "She's my favorite sister, and I love her more than anything in the world. That's all the more reason I've got to tell her this—*we've* got to tell her. Owen and I. I don't want to go on keeping things from her, denying my feelings, pretending to be someone I'm not. I want us to be able to sit down to dinner with you and Faith and look her in the eye and talk about our lives without hiding anything. I want her to know I love Owen as much as she loves you."

"And do you think she'll be able to understand that when you make love to my brother, you're making love to the same penis she does?"

"Christ, Porter, that's disgusting," I said. Chase blushed and looked at the floor.

"You think it's disgusting? How do you think *I* feel?"

"I'm not talking about the act, Porter. I'm talking about the way you put it. Faith doesn't make love to your penis—*our* penis. She makes love to *you*. To your heart, your soul, not to some sexual organ. And the same holds true for Chase and me. We're making love to each other, not to our body parts. I love *him*, Porter, not his penis or his mouth or his ass. Those are just the things we use to communicate our love to each other, like everyone else in the world."

But what if Porter were right? Were Chase and I being naïve? Was it too much to ask of Faith to accept not only that her brother was gay but also that he was in love with me? In light of the risk we were taking, I had to ask myself what I was expecting from my relationship with Chase and exactly why I thought I couldn't live without him. There was, of course, the sex. The very idea that someone would willingly have sex with me—would anticipate it, enjoy it—was still relatively new to me. But Chase loved me. He actually found me sexy, was aroused by me. There were times when I knew he was being deliberately provocative, when Porter and I would return from the bathroom to find he had tossed back the sheets and was lying on his stomach, one leg bent at the knee and drawn up beside him, simultaneously calling attention to and coyly hiding his sweet spot. He was enticing me to have sex with him; he didn't shrink from the idea in horror. That was part of what I would have to give up if I lost him. But there was also the friendship, the companionship, the sense of not being alone when Porter was occupied with Faith. So yes—yes, it was worth it to risk Faith's disapproval, no matter how likely it was, or how strong; to live openly, to be able to have what I wanted even half the time.

I offered to be there with Chase when he told Faith, but he decided he wanted to do it alone.

"I think it will go better if I do it myself," he said. "With the two of us there—or rather the three of us—she'd know right from the start something was up. Anyway, it's really just between Faith and me. It's something I'd have to do sooner or later, whether it was you I had fallen in love with or someone else."

"Fine by me," Porter said. "Personally, I don't want to be within five miles of her when she finds out."

"Thanks for the vote of confidence, Porter," I said. "I'm sure that really makes Chase feel good."

"I'm just saying . . ."

"I know what you're saying. Just shut up."

Chase deliberately chose a Sunday afternoon to break the news. Saturdays were used for errands and chores; Sundays were more relaxed. The mornings were devoted to church, usually followed by brunch and the occasional trip to some place like the Atlanta Botanical Garden if Faith felt up to it. For the past several months, Porter and I had been attending services with Faith every Sunday instead of only alternate weeks, because Faith did not feel comfortable driving. She did not like the idea of having the babies in proximity to the steering wheel, worrying about what might happen if the air bag went off in even a minor accident. So concerned was she about such an incident, even with the passenger-side air bag, that she always sat in the backseat. On this particular Sunday, Chase volunteered to drive her to church and then take her out to brunch while Porter and I stayed home, ostensibly

254 / Andrew W.M. Beierle

to continue working on the babies' room, although little of real substance remained to be done. I suggested for the sake of verisimilitude that Porter and I go to Home Depot and pick up some decorative switch plates. We'd purchased and installed the light switch plates—the selection was limited and tacky: balloons, bluebirds, and clowns (Porter's choice because he thought it was funny that the light switch was where the clown's nose should be)—and we were sitting at the dining room table working on some music when we heard the Volvo pull into the garage next door. It was a full fifteen minutes before Chase arrived to report to us. We moved into the living room, and Chase plopped into the recliner.

"How did it go?" I asked.

"I'm not sure," Chase said.

"What does *that* mean?" Porter asked. "What did she say?"

"Well, Owen, you were right," he said, leaning forward, his elbows on his knees, his chin balanced on his fists. "She wasn't surprised—at all. She seemed relieved, in fact, because she suspected I was gay and had wanted to talk to me about it for a long time. Well, not so much about being gay but about HIV. She got all Florence Nightingale on me and offered to bring me literature from the hospital—you know, safe-sex stuff. I told her I always played safe, and she didn't really ask a lot of questions after that. She did say she'd liked Kyle and was sorry he and I weren't still together, but she didn't ask for a whole lot of details about the current state of my love life."

"So you don't think she had any idea about us?"

"Not a clue. In fact, I think she thought our little talk was over. Then I told her there was someone special I'd been dating for about three months."

"Holy shit, cut to the damn chase!" Porter said.

"Shut up and let him tell the story, Porter."

"No, it's okay, Owen. I understand. He's got as much riding on this as we do."

"If not more," Porter said.

"So anyway, I . . . well, I just *told* her, and I don't really think it sank in. She kind of looked at me with a smile on her face, like she was waiting for something more. You know, *Owen who?* I honestly don't think she even thought about what a coincidence it was that my boyfriend was named Owen. It just didn't register. Finally, I had to just come out and say it: *Our Owen. Owenandporter.* That did it, I guess. She couldn't speak for a minute. Her hand sort of came up to her throat and her eyes got bigger. She looked like maybe she'd swallowed something the wrong way. You know how they say people can't talk when they're choking? I thought I was going to have to do the Heimlich maneuver."

"Oh, Jesus," Porter said.

"So when she finally regained the power of speech, what did she say?" I asked.

Chase fidgeted. His cheeks ballooned, and he pursed his lips and let out a long sigh. His fingers thrummed the leather of the armrests.

"She said we'd have to talk about it. Or more specifically, she said she wanted to talk to *you* about it."

"Me?" Porter asked.

"Owen."

"I see," I said. "Okay. That's okay. I don't mind."

"Did she seem mad?" Porter asked.

"Not mad. What's that word? Betwixt? Bewitched?"

"Bewildered?" I suggested.

"Yeah, bewildered. Kind of confused. Like all of a sudden she didn't know where she was, you know? Like she had just gotten off a plane at some strange airport and was looking for baggage claim. Kinda blank."

I fixed us all some screwdrivers, and we sat down to wait. Porter had put away two drinks and was working on his third when Faith arrived half an hour later. I could tell she had been crying and that she must have spent some time composing herself. Her eyes were red-rimmed, but her makeup seemed fresh and unmarked. Not a hair was out of place. She was cheerful, even perky, given the circumstances. I strongly suspected overcompensation. She did seem a bit distracted and was surprised her brother was still there.

"Chase, honey, didn't you say you had something to do?" she said.

"Uh, yeah. We were just talking. I've got some work I can take care of at the lab."

"Well, come give me a hug before you go," she said, extending her arms in a gesture I saw as a tad passive-aggressive, as if she were simultaneously welcoming him and getting ready to push him out the door.

Chase gave me a quick peck on the cheek—our first official public display of affection—and then walked to the door arm in arm with his sister. He looked back over his shoulder and smiled at me as he left. There was a fragile hope in that smile, as if he were among the lucky few boarding a lifeboat on the *Titanic* but leaving a loved one behind.

Faith stood in the foyer with the door ajar, waving until his car was out of the driveway. Then she eased the door shut, and I heard the deadbolt turn, followed by the clatter of the flimsy security chain, the type that is more reassuring than effective in an actual emergency. In the time it took for her to return to the living room, Porter finished his third screwdriver in a couple of quick swallows. It was hard to tell what was on her mind. Her expression had changed—hardened somehow or become clouded. It was unclear whether she was angry, hurt, or still a bit dazed.

"Can I get you something to drink, Faith? Some iced tea?" I asked.

"You know I can't have any caffeine, Owen—the babies."

"Right. Some water, then?"

"I'm fine."

So much for the niceties. Faith eased herself into the recliner her brother had just abandoned. She looked uncomfortable carrying all that weight, poor thing.

"Honey," Porter began, but she cut him off.

"I really don't know what to say to you, Owen," she said, looking directly at me. Her fingers dug into the armrests like a white-knuckle flyer on takeoff. "You either, Porter. I'm stunned—*stunned*—that you've kept this from me."

"Look, I'm sorry if you're upset about this, Faith. I really am," I said. "But don't take it out on Porter. It's not his fault, really."

"It's his fault to the extent that he kept important information from me. *Lied* to me, if not actively then by default." She looked directly at Porter as she said this, which, combined with the fact she was speaking of him in the third person, seemed peculiarly menacing. "I can't abide dishonesty. Above all, I can't abide that."

Now she turned ever so slightly toward me.

"What you do is your own business, I suppose, Owen. But, oh, I don't know. Maybe it's *not* just your business. I don't know whose business it is. But you, Porter, I really think you owed me the truth about this."

"I'm sorry, honey, I really am," Porter said. "It's just that Owen and I have this understanding . . ."

"I know, I know. Owen's 'right to privacy.' I get that. But we're talking about my brother here. My *brother*."

"Whom I love—and who loves me," I said.

"He's barely twenty-one years old. What does he know about love?" she said. "He's bright, but he's not . . . mature."

"He's legal, if that's what you're saying."

"That's *not* what I'm saying."

"Then what?"

"He's young. He's impressionable. He's vulnerable," Faith said. "Chase didn't have a chance to grow up the way other boys did. He was so focused on his schoolwork, he didn't get socialized the way a normal teenager would have. He didn't date in high school or in college . . ."

"He did date in college, Faith. He dated Kyle. And he dated any number of other guys."

"I meant, he didn't date girls."

"What are you getting at?"

"He hasn't given himself a chance to get to know girls—women—yet. If he did, maybe . . ."

"You think this is a case of arrested development? Something he's going to outgrow? Trust me, that's not what this is about. I knew I was gay when I was fifteen, maybe earlier—maybe much earlier—and I think Chase did, too."

I pointed out that her brother had been a member of the MIT gay student alliance since his freshman year and had come out to everyone except his family two years ago.

"Chase *is* gay," I said. "And I think he's reasonably well-adjusted, despite whatever poisonous doctrine was drilled into him at home and church. Miraculously, he's not plagued by guilt or shame or low self-esteem. He *likes* being gay."

She thought about this for a while. Her grip on the chair relaxed, allowing blood to return to her fingers. One hand moved protectively over her stomach.

"Well, perhaps. And maybe I won't be able to change that. But I think it's wrong for him to get serious about anybody at this point."

"No, you think it's wrong for him to get serious about me."

"Owen, please try to understand. It's not that. Well, not just that. It's . . . Owen, I'm uncomfortable with the relationship."

"I can see that."

"It's not right."

"What's wrong with it?"

"It gives me the creeps."

"It gives you the *creeps*?"

"I can't talk about it."

"You brought up the fucking subject!"

"Watch your mouth!" Porter said.

"Okay, okay, I'm sorry."

"I can't think about it. You and him . . . together," Faith said.

"Having sex."

"Jesus, Owen," Porter said.

"Well, it's what we do. Although I prefer to think of it as making love."

"Oh god," she said.

"Faith, honey, are you okay?" Porter leaned forward, as if he were about to get up and move to her side. I stayed put.

"I think I'm going to be sick," she said.

"Oh, great—my relationship with your brother makes you want to throw up. Now that's an affirmation."

"Jesus Christ, Owen, will you just lay off? Give it a rest."

"Porter, she brought it up. I'm not going to 'give it a rest' until we get to the bottom of this. She's telling me I make her sick."

"That's not what I meant, Owen," Faith said.

"It's what you said."

"You twisted it."

"So let me get this straight. Apparently it's okay for you to have sex with a two-headed freak, but you want to protect your brother from the same fate?"

"That does it, Owen," Porter said. "Shut the fuck up or I swear to god I'll slap you into next month."

"Owen, will you just listen to me for a minute?" Her expression had softened a bit, although she did look a bit green around the gills.

"I'm all ears."

"It's not about . . . It's not about the way you and Porter *are*. It has nothing to do with that."

"Oh, I think it does."

"Well, it does, but not what you're thinking."

"Then what?"

"It's just that . . . Oh god, how do I say this? It's just that it seems . . . it seems sort of . . . incestuous."

"Incestuous? How is it incestuous?"

"Well, I suppose that's not technically correct. But it seems wrong for my brother to be having sex with the same man I do."

"That wouldn't be incest even if it were the case. But he's not having sex with Porter; he's having sex with me."

"But it's the same. It's the same . . . *thing.*"

"You mean the same equipment? The same penis?"

"Oh my god." Porter shook his head, brought his hand up to his forehead. "I can't believe where this conversation is headed."

Faith wasn't looking at me anymore. She was looking past me. Maybe she was making eye contact with Porter; it was hard to say. For my part, I could barely bring myself to look at her, either. She seemed like a stranger to me. I don't want to be cruel, but when I did look at her, I saw her in a different light. The veneer of her expensive education had fallen away. I saw her as what she was: the daughter of hardscrabble farmers from south Georgia. I could almost picture her in a Depression-era Walker Evans photograph, the skin of her face creased from too much sun, her lips sort of curling back in a way that makes poor folks look as if they have no teeth. But I didn't hate her. Not yet, anyway. Not really. I could see she was in a bad position, that she'd probably had to fight for the opportunity to marry Porter, and now there was *this* turn of events, this possibly fatal blow to her relationship with her husband. What would become of her if she left him? There was a good chance she would be shunned by her relatives, and if not her relatives, then at least most of the people in the little town she had come from—the promising young girl who had moved to Atlanta, gone to Druid Hills University, for god's sake, and then married a circus freak. Would she—could she—go back home with her two little babies, who would probably be branded as incipient monsters no matter how normal they appeared?

"Owen, I don't care what you do in bed or who you do it with, as long as it isn't with my brother. I just can't bear the fact that he's being intimate with, you know . . . the same *thing . . .*"

"What, you're jealous? I don't get it."

"Owen, it's disgusting. It disgusts me, okay? I don't want to think about what it is the three of you do."

"The three of us?" Porter said. "Honey, you don't think I'm having sex with your brother, do you?"

"It's hard *not* to think of it that way, Porter."

"Well, I'm not. I guarantee you I'm not. I've got my headphones on the entire time. I'm not paying attention. I don't feel a thing."

"That's not exactly true," I said, though why I chose that line of attack, I don't know. I was only adding fuel to the fire, but for some reason I wanted to be provocative.

"Shut the fuck up, Owen."

"What do you mean?" Faith asked.

"It's not true that Porter doesn't feel anything. He feels the same things I do down there. But when we're with Chase, Porter's heart's not in it. Mine is. It's exactly the same thing that happens when Porter makes love to you. I feel what he feels physically but not emotionally. You can understand that, can't you, Faith? I mean, you're not connecting emotionally with me when Porter and you are having sex, are you?"

"No. No, I'm not."

I didn't quite believe her. I thought back to the conversation in which she came dangerously close to saying she loved me.

"We've learned to separate ourselves from each other when we need to," I said. "It's what we do. It's what we *have* to do to survive. I don't even listen to your conversations most of the time, and I certainly don't listen to what you say to each other in bed. I may hear it, but it doesn't register, it doesn't sink in."

Faith struggled to stand up, then wandered about the room aimlessly. She stood by the front window and absent-mindedly fingered the leaves of the potted ficus.

"I'm sorry, Owen," she said. "What you say makes sense, in a way. I understand that you and Porter are different people. I understand you have your needs, and I think I've been pretty understanding about that. I didn't object when you told me you were gay. But this is different. This is my brother we're talking about. This is . . . it's just plain wrong."

"I don't see anything wrong about it," I said. "We love each other, Chase and I. What could possibly be wrong about that? We're not hurting anyone . . ."

"Not *hurting* anyone? Owen, it would kill my mother— *kill* her—if she were to find out you and Chase were together."

"Then I'd suggest you don't tell her."

Porter made a clucking sound as if he were disgusted with me.

"I certainly don't plan on *telling* her. She doesn't know Chase is gay, and I pray to God she never finds out. But on top of that, finding out he was sleeping with you and Porter . . . If that didn't kill her, I don't know what would. It would certainly end my relationship with her. It would make me look perverted in her eyes, like I had something to do with this sorry mess, like I drew Chase into it somehow by introducing him to you—that I sanctioned it, approved of it."

"Give her some credit, why don't you? I'll bet you thought bringing Porter home would kill her, too."

"Owen, my mother is Christian, a good Christian woman. She's been able to accept Porter—and you—into our lives because of that, because of her loving Christian nature. But she is not able to accept homosexuality, and I doubt she ever will. If she found out you were gay, she'd probably want me to leave Porter. She wouldn't be able to separate your actions from his. She'd force me to make a choice between him and my family. Well, I'll tell you right now, if it comes down to that, I'll choose Porter. I love him and I won't leave him, no matter what anyone says. I'll do my best to make them understand, although I doubt they ever will. And if they cut me off, they cut me off. But this—her own flesh and blood—this would turn her against Chase, unless he renounced it."

"Renounce it?" I said. "Renounce?" *Get thee behind me, Satan!*

"I know I will never—*never*—be able to convince them it's right for my brother to be sleeping with you. They'll think that's sick—perverted—not just because you're a man but because Porter is my husband. If that happens, I honestly don't know what I could do, what I *would* do. I can accept the fact that you're gay. I can even accept the fact that Chase is gay—though I will pray for his soul every day for the rest of my life. But I cannot—will not—accept, now or ever, the fact that you are having sex with him. If that continues, I'll leave Porter. I'll take the twins when they're born and I'll leave him."

Faith stood there for a moment with both hands cradling her belly, as if she were offering to share her unborn children with Porter if he—or rather I—made the right choice, but threatening to withhold them if we chose unwisely. It seemed remarkably similar to the way she had greeted Chase earlier, preparing to embrace him yet simultaneously poised to push him away.

"Oh my god, Faith," Porter said. "You can't! You can't do that."

"I can and I will, and I don't think there is a judge in this state who would stand in my way."

As if to demonstrate the seriousness of her resolve, Faith turned and walked out, leaving Porter and me to contemplate the vacuum she left behind, both immediate and potential. Neither of us said anything for some time. The magnitude of her threat seemed monumental, unassailable, as if we were novice climbers at the base of some emotional Everest who had just been abandoned by our Sherpa guides.

In her fury, Faith seemed unrecognizable to me. I could not believe this was the woman I had attempted to nurture and support in the early days of her relationship with my brother, whose every physical and emotional need I had tried to anticipate and satisfy. Nor could I fathom that this was the same woman who only six months earlier had come very close to confessing that she was in love with me. But perhaps the intensity of her response was, in part, a reaction to those very feelings. I had rejected her in favor of her brother, and she would be damned if she would sit still for that. When I finally was able to collect my thoughts, I felt the need to explain myself to Porter, to defend the choices I had made. But he was in no mood to listen.

"Not now, bro," he said. "Not yet. I really can't even think about this now. Let's just get out of here for a while."

I was all for that. I didn't want to be around Faith, and I sure as hell didn't want to be home when Chase got back. I wasn't ready to face that. I left him a note saying we had gone for a drive, and we got into the Boxster and headed north, driving for nearly two hours, until we were well into the mountains. We sat for an hour or so at a scenic overlook, largely in silence. We didn't really need to speak. I think we could both feel what the other was feeling: the anxiety, the sense of impending loss. When we got home, there were no lights on at either place, and both Faith and Chase were asleep. I decided not to wake him. I had no idea what I would say to him if I did.

Porter and I lay in bed silently, trying to relax. I had never faced anything as difficult as this in my life, never contemplated giving up something I had wanted so much or for so long. Oh, there had been compromises along the way, adjustments I had made, nights that were "mine" that I had given up for Porter, things I had done because he wanted to or not done because he didn't. Most of these concessions were minor, and by and large I had made them without complaint, without even letting Porter know I felt I had sacrificed something, certainly without expecting anything in return—or maybe with the expectation I was building up a reservoir of good karma that ultimately would result in something good happening to me. *Fat chance.*

If I were to pursue my relationship with Chase, Porter

would lose what he had wanted for so long: a wife and family, the normalcy he hoped to achieve in the innocent eyes of his children. Who knows how losing that might affect him? I remembered how badly he took it when Christi Oakes's father forced her to break up with him, how he was too depressed to get out of bed in the morning—or too hungover. Things would be worse now. He had easier access to alcohol and drugs and sex. If Faith left him, we'd be thrust back into the demimonde of Vixana and her pals. I couldn't bear that, couldn't stomach the late nights and booze, the feeling—cheap and dirty—of waking up in a strange woman's bed, not remembering much about what had happened the night before. I'd object, of course, but Porter had ways of making me comply. He was always headstrong, even somewhat of a bully if he had to be, so this was as much an exercise in self-preservation as altruism.

"O, I don't know what to tell you, man," Porter said after about fifteen minutes.

Under the circumstances, I suppose it was the best he could do. He was in the worst position of all of us. I wanted what I wanted; Faith wanted what she wanted. Only one of us would actually *get* what we wanted. But Porter—well, Porter was bound to suffer no matter what happened. How could he possibly choose sides?

I suspected he was leaning toward Faith's point of view, of course. If she felt strongly enough about it, she could leave him; I couldn't. I might be pissed off, but what was I going to do? I wasn't going to disappear. And I couldn't not speak to him for the rest of our lives. On the other hand, he had to feel some sense of responsibility to me, and he had to know how unhappy I would be without Chase. He already had demonstrated his loyalty by not letting Faith know Chase and I were sleeping together—and she had judged him harshly for that.

"Well, I don't see as I have much choice," I said finally.

"Why? What do you mean?"

I sensed panic in his voice.

"Relax, Porter. I suspect the deck is stacked in your favor—or Faith's."

"I'm glad to hear you say that, bro. It would be wrong for this to break up me and Faith, to make me lose my kids. They haven't even been born yet, but I already love them more than I've ever loved anything. I couldn't bear to lose them. I know you love Chase, but I've got so much more invested in this than you do. I'm asking you to do the right thing. I'll make it up to you somehow. I'll never ask for another thing for the rest of our lives. But you've got to give this one to me."

At that point, I resigned myself to ending things with Chase. I simply could not bring myself to destroy everything Porter had. In a way, I suppose I actually was convinced he was right, that he deserved this opportunity for happiness and that my own needs were less valid than his. A small but insistent voice was speaking to me, a voice I didn't want to hear but that carried the authority of the ages, the weight of tradition and orthodoxy: Who was I, really, to deny Porter his wife and children just so I could continue my relationship with Chase—a relationship that would have to remain a secret from my parents and his, that would never be honored and accepted as real or valid in the same way as Porter's marriage?

I knew I would be lonely. I had been desperately lonely before Chase came into my life, however illogical it might seem—if anything, there were too many people in my life. I should crave solitude instead of looking for yet another person to add to my life, another variable in the dynamic of an already complicated set of relationships. But I was lonely when I was with Porter and Faith because I consciously tried to shut them out of my life so they could have as normal a relationship as possible. And I was lonely when we were away from Faith and I had time to fill, choices to make, and no one in my life to share them with—no one but Porter. I had been, in fact, lonely all the time. And then Chase came along, and it seemed like the perfect solution. He was bright, creative, attractive. We wouldn't have to wonder about the impact on the existing relationship because Chase was not an unknown entity. Faith already knew and loved him. I loved him. Porter would love him, as a brother, anyway, once he got to know him. He should have been a stabilizing force, a force for equilibrium. But instead he turned out to be just the opposite.

It was a difficult choice, an ugly choice. Regardless of who won, it would be a Pyrrhic victory. Porter would lose Faith or I would lose Chase. The only question that remained was whether it would be easier to live without Chase or to live with the wreckage of my life if I chose *not* to give him up. And could I really expect Chase to stay with me if it would cost him his sister—his family? Of all the choices, it seemed to me the only reasonable one was for me to leave Chase. I would be unhappy. Chase would be unhappy. But we would both survive. I'd keep my brother; Porter would keep his wife; Chase would keep his sister and his family.

In the morning, I revealed to Porter the decision I had come to: that given our current circumstances, I would end my relationship with Chase. Later in the day, I told Faith somewhat cryptically that in the next couple of weeks I would "take care" of everything we had discussed. So deep was my resentment, I could not bring myself to utter the phrase "break up" to her.

In the interim, Chase remained largely unaware of the turmoil we had wrought. He'd come out to his sister and, at least from where he stood, it looked as if she had accepted not only that he was gay but also that he was in love with me. When we made love, he was almost giddy. Playful, funny, cute. Even Porter commented on his exuberance. After a night of lovemaking, he held my hand under the table at breakfast, tacitly understanding that it might be gauche to be so brazen but assuming that the result of discovery would not be disas-

ter. A frown from Faith perhaps, a pout, but not excommuni-
cation. I suspect Chase sometimes became aroused when he
took my hand; I know I did the first few times. But then my
despair kicked in.

Those days were perhaps the most difficult of my life. I
felt as if I were a condemned man enjoying the last few conjugal visits before his execution, trying to take from them
what pleasure I could, cherishing them but knowing they
were finite in number and rapidly diminishing. Outside, it
was high spring, everything in Atlanta dusted with a thick
layer of chartreuse pollen, but to me it felt like autumn, a
season so gloriously ablaze that no one—at least no one but
me—was thinking about the long months of desolation to
come. I could tell Faith was growing impatient. She was irritable and short-tempered, glaring at me any time Chase
showed me the slightest affection. I knew I could not put
things off for long, and in fact I yearned for some resolution,
but the courage to face that end eluded me.

"When are you going to tell him, bro?" Porter whispered
while Chase was in the bathroom cleaning up after we had
made love, nearly three weeks after he had come out to
Faith. "You haven't changed your mind, have you?"

"No, Porter, I haven't changed my mind," I replied *sotto
voce*.

"Well, you're not doing anybody any favors by putting it
off."

The strip of light at the bottom of the bathroom door vanished.

"All right. Just shut up about it."

Chase emerged wearing just his white briefs, his tighty
whiteys, and slipped into bed next to me. Like his sister, he
tended toward modesty and tried not to be naked around
Porter other than when we were actually in bed together,
covering himself in one way or another even if only for a trip
to the bathroom. Once he was under the covers, he arched
his back, slid his briefs down to his ankles, hooked them

with his right foot, and let them drop off the side of the bed. It was wonderful to feel the warmth of his body next to mine even after just ten minutes without him, to smell his hair damp from the shower, like rain on moss.

"Good night, boys," he said and kissed me.

"Good night," Porter and I said in unison.

Chase folded his slender body over me like a flower closing for the night. He nestled in my arm, his head in the notch of my shoulder, his hand over my heart.

I couldn't bear to put an end to such tender moments.

Chapter 26

I got something of a temporary reprieve when Faith unexpectedly went into labor several weeks before her due date. Although Porter initially was somewhat agitated, Faith remained extraordinarily calm, explaining to him in her most soothing nurse's manner that a somewhat premature delivery was not unusual with twins and that as far as she knew, she was at least thirty-seven weeks into her pregnancy, close enough to term to avoid all but the most unpredictable complications. During the fifteen-minute ride to University Hospital, Porter called Faith's parents and her obstetrician while I drove. At her instruction, he also called her nursing station at the hospital to tell them she was on the way, thus insuring the kind of special attention the hospital staff might be expected to provide only to one of their own.

When we arrived at the hospital, several of Faith's co-workers were waiting for us, and she was taken immediately to the ER's "express service" area. I tracked down Chase on his cell phone and quickly sketched out what had taken place. I also told him Faith had packed an overnight bag in anticipation of her visit to the maternity ward, but in the confusion we had left it behind. He offered to find it, and when he arrived with it half an hour later, he also brought the news that his family was on the road and would arrive in about four hours.

By the time Chase arrived, Faith had been moved to the

birthing suite, and Porter and I soon were reunited with her there. We remained with her during her entire labor and delivery—seven hours—and I was grateful for the instruction we had received in her Lamaze classes. The first twin, Justin, was delivered at 11:55 p.m.; his sister, Christina, at 12:15 a.m. Technically, they had different birthdays, which as a twin myself I thought might be a good thing, a way to help them distinguish themselves from each other. By the time a nurse forced Porter and me out of Faith's room to allow her to sleep, the Colquitt clan was assembled in the hospital waiting room, where they had rendezvoused with my parents. I could only look longingly at Chase as we were swallowed up by his parents and sisters and brother-in-law Peyton, all of whom peppered us with questions about the twins. It was nearly 3:00 a.m. by the time we all made our way to my parents' home for an early breakfast, since it seemed clear no one would be getting any sleep that night.

Given Porter's and my status as rising rock musicians (to say nothing of the fact that we had two heads) there was a flurry of media attention the next day surrounding the birth of the twins, by far the most common adjectives applied to them being "healthy" and "perfectly formed," to underscore their normalcy. Porter and I did a couple of national morning-show interviews from the maternity ward when the babies came home two days later, and a photograph of us—Justin cradled in Porter's arm, Christina in mine—was widely distributed and appeared the next week in the glossy entertainment and gossip magazines found at grocery checkout counters (though not on their covers—America wasn't quite ready for *that*).

Once the twins came home, my mother frequently was there, helping bathe, change, and feed them. She was remarkably attentive and maternal. It was as if she had been given a second chance, an opportunity to be a proud parent without reservation, without holding back any of her emotions, without the fear of having the horrifying secret of her sons' condition revealed when the baby blanket was pulled back. I know she considered this a gift from Porter, a do-over, even an apology of sorts for having been born with two heads. But once again, I remained lacking. I wasn't going to be creating any perfectly beautiful babies for her, and her resentment toward me simmered just below the surface of our relationship. It manifested itself largely as indifference toward me, a sort of benign neglect. While she hung on every word Faith uttered about Justin and Christina, to say nothing of every coo and gurgle of the twins themselves, she frequently failed to acknowledge—let alone respond to—comments I made or questions I asked. I hesitated to mention this to Porter—it sounded a bit self-centered, even somewhat desperate—and when I did, I got the response I anticipated.

"Jesus, O, everything's not about you, especially not now," he said. "Can't you see she's getting off on this whole grandmother thing? Let her have her fun. It's really great to have her around to help Faith with the babies. So just chill."

Just chill. Maybe I should. Things certainly could be worse. There had been no further histrionics in the year since my coming-out announcement had permanently soured my mother's taste for lobster bisque. In fact, my "lifestyle choice" (as she put it) had barely been mentioned. The debutante dinners had ended, of course, and my mother's female graduate students certainly must have breathed a collective sigh of relief, having escaped the fate of permanently filling out a foursome at the dining table of the Jamison *frères*. The subtle barbs had ceased, as well; there were no more emotional kamikaze attacks. Of course, for the most part there had been nothing to discuss. My exceedingly rare trysts on tour had been invisible to my parents (as Porter's pre-Faith dalliances largely had been). It's the nature of the beast that sons don't rub their parents' noses in sexual conquests of any stripe. Had my relationship with Chase not been D.O.A., it might ultimately have become a topic of conversation with Mom and Dad (*We know Faith is close to her brother and we enjoy his company, but . . . ?*). To my great regret, that was no longer an issue. But in a perverse way, maybe I *wanted* a confrontation, some acknowledgment that what I felt, who I was, was somehow significant, worthy of comment. As it was, I once again felt almost invisible.

In fact, that sense of being somehow superfluous manifested itself in other ways, unrelated to the fact that I was gay. Shortly after the twins were born, pictures of Porter and me as infants and toddlers, which I had long thought of as talismans of my parents' pride and courage, began disappearing from their frames at my parents' home, to be replaced with snapshots of the new twins. It was clear Justin and Christina were now the center of our universe and would be for quite some time. Sacrifices would have to be made to insure they grew up in as normal a family as possible, "normal" in this case being somewhat subjective. And soon enough, the question of my relationship with Chase, which had been pushed to the sidelines, became unavoidable. It was the elephant in the room nobody, least of all me, wanted to talk about.

A friend once told me about a former lover who took him out to an especially nice dinner and then broke up with him over coffee and dessert. Although I know the bastard's intentions were probably good—even Christ had a last supper—it ultimately seemed a particularly cruel thing to do. So I didn't make any special plans for the evening on which I planned to tell Chase our relationship was over. I simply told him to reserve the entire evening for us, a rarity these days with all the attention the babies required. My only other preparations were to ask Porter to wear headphones and not to drink. I didn't want alcohol to cloud my judgment or make me overly emotional.

I really didn't know where to begin. How do you explain to a twenty-one-year-old why love isn't enough, what else there is in the world that made it insufficient? My first impulse was to list all the good things about our relationship—all the fun we'd had together, how beautiful I thought he was, how much he meant to me. Would that make it easier for him to bear or more difficult? Wouldn't he know where I was headed from the start? And wouldn't such an inventory provide him with useful ammunition when it came time to respond—reasons for us to defend and preserve what we had? Wouldn't it be better to catch him off guard?

"This isn't going to work," I began, and with those words I felt as if I had stepped onto a frozen lake and heard the ice crack beneath my weight, not a brittle tinkling but a deep, resonant bark, as if the very crust of the earth were splintering.

"What isn't going to work?" Chase said casually, unaware of the gravity of the situation, as if I been muttering under my breath after having failed at some simple but unorthodox task—trying to jimmy a deadbolt with a credit card.

"*This*. Us."

"Of course it's going to work. It *is* working."

"I wish that were true, but it isn't."

I didn't want Chase to doubt my love for him; that would have been unnecessarily cruel. But my first instinct was to try to shield him from the truth: that his favorite sister was at the heart of the problem. I wasn't eager to protect Faith; I gladly would have hung her out to dry. But I thought if I took the fall, at the very least Chase's relationship with her would remain intact—he wouldn't lose both of us at the same time. But I knew I'd never be able to convince Chase I didn't love him. My heart just wasn't in it. I'd have to tell him the truth—the consequences be damned.

"The fact is, Faith disapproves of our relationship," I said.

"She *what*? Disapproves of our relationship?" He looked around the room as if he expected to see Faith hiding in the corner, as if she were in on the joke.

"Yes. She thinks it's wrong."

"She's never said anything like that to me."

"Has she ever told you she was glad we were together?"

"Not in so many words."

"Not in *any* words, Chase. Think about it. Think hard. Has she ever once said to you that she was happy for you, that she was glad we had found each other, that she was sure the four of us would live happily ever after?"

"Nobody lives happily ever after, Owen."

"You know what I mean. Has she?"

I watched Chase disappear into himself, disengage from me, from the present, his analytical mind accessing memories of the past month like a computer scanning a document during a keyword search. What phrases was he hoping to find? *That's terrific, Chase? I'm so happy for you? Owen's a wonderful guy?* What he would discover instead would be blank stares, uncomfortable silences, negative space, the back of Faith's head as she turned away from us when we kissed or hugged or touched in her presence.

"She hasn't, has she?" I said.

"I guess not," he said. "Has she said something to you? I mean, specifically? Has she *told* you she disapproves?"

How honest should I be? How much havoc should I wreak? Should I portray her as merely petty? Jealous? Unwilling to share that portion of her husband's anatomy that was also common to me? Or should I paint a darker portrait, reveal her threats, her emotional blackmail?

"She's more than a little unhappy," I said.

"But why? I mean, it didn't seem to bother her when I told her I was gay."

"Maybe not, Chase, but there's a lot more to it than that. Let's face it, it's a complex and difficult situation we're in—the four of us. This is not just about whether or not she can accept the fact that you're gay—and you should probably know that she's less happy about that than she lets on. But from her point of view, her husband is involved in this, too. Our unique physiology—Porter's and mine—makes him a participant in our lovemaking. Yours and mine. And, understandably, she finds that hard to take. It's like—oh, I don't know—like when she's having sex with Porter, she can imagine you in the exact same circumstances the previous night with me, and apparently it's just too much for her to deal with. She can't live with it."

"She can't *live* with it?"

"Well, she won't *tolerate* it, in any event. It will mean an end to her marriage to Porter. She said if you and I continue to see each other, she'll leave him and take the twins with her."

To some extent, I blamed myself for the fact that Chase was surprised by Faith's response to our relationship. In my own naïve and optimistic way, I had downplayed the potential for catastrophe—to myself and to Chase. I wanted desperately to believe things would work out. I was thinking with my heart, not my head. But in hindsight, the mere fact that we had not been able to be honest with her from the beginning, had not immediately come forward to share the news that we were in love, should have been an unmistakable signal that we both feared her response. But neither of us ever anticipated she would go so far as to hold her children hostage to our capitulation.

"Holy shit, Owen. What are we going to do?"

"There's nothing we can do, Chase, nothing but what she asks."

"I can talk to her. Explain things. She'll understand. She's got to. I love you, Owen. I don't want to lose you."

"You're welcome to try, Chase, but I can tell you right now it's not going to do any good. She's not going to change her mind. You're going to lose one of us. And as hard as it is for me to say, I'd rather it were me, because if you lose her, you're more than likely going to lose your entire family—at the very least your mom and dad—and Porter is going to lose Faith and the twins. I can't be responsible for that. I don't *want* to be responsible for that, and I won't ask you to accept that kind of responsibility either."

Chase stood up and paced the room. This got Porter's attention, and he took off his earphones.

"Not yet, Porter," I said. "We're not through yet."

Chase grew increasingly agitated as the reality of our predicament sank in. I could see him struggling with the idea that his sister disapproved of our relationship, and worse, that she apparently had both the intention and the means to end it. He could see she was holding all the cards: his relationships with her and with his family, Porter's relationship with his children.

"I'm going to talk to her, Owen. I have to hear this from her personally. I know she'll understand when I explain things to her, when I tell her I love you. I can't believe she wouldn't."

"Do your best, Chase. But I don't think it's going to make any difference."

I was not optimistic. For a while, I listened to the raised voices coming from next door as Chase pleaded his case with Faith. Finally, I donned a pair of earphones like Porter and retreated into the music until such time as my fate was determined. The outcome was no surprise.

Chapter 27

Chase wasted no time making himself scarce; he was packed and out of the house within an hour of his conversation with Faith. It was as if he had been ordered to evacuate in advance of an approaching wildfire, taking with him only his most prized possessions and leaving the rest to be consumed by flame. No one expected such a virulent and decisive response. What surprised all of us, not least of all Faith, was that he not only left the house, he left the state. We thought he was simply going to stay with a friend for a few days until things calmed down or he found new living arrangements. It took us two weeks to discover he had moved to San Francisco, where he had hooked up with an old MIT friend at an Internet start-up and begun renegotiating the Stanford aid package he had turned down the year before—information we gleaned inadvertently in a phone call from Faith's sister Greta, from whom Faith tried to hide both her surprise and her immense relief at ascertaining his whereabouts.

"No, no, no, Greta, of course I knew he was in San Francisco," I heard her say. "What I meant was, I didn't know he had reapplied to Stanford."

Faith was fairly seething when she hung up, and I knew the fact that she had heard the news from Greta had wounded her as deeply as Chase's departure itself, perhaps even more so. It was a sign he'd shifted his lifelong allegiance away from his favorite sister to another sibling, although whether he had actually come out to Greta remained unclear. I suspected he had chosen Greta as his new confidante because he thought her marriage to a black man might make her more sympathetic to his own outsider status and would form the basis of an alliance as strong as, if not stronger than, the one he formerly had with Faith.

I doubt Faith had considered this outcome even a remote possibility when she had made her demands. I suspect she thought Chase and I would be contrite, even apologetic; that we would comply unquestioningly, and that a year from now we would not even speak of these unfortunate events. Life would go on—with a few minor adjustments. Who knows? Perhaps she even thought Chase might somehow see the error of his ways and begin dating women.

But the magnitude of her miscalculation became more clear daily—and it was enormous. Her brother was alienated, estranged, incommunicado. And Faith's grief was palpable. When she wasn't actually crying, she appeared to be on the verge of tears, her eyes red-rimmed, her nose runny. I could only assume her distress was so great because in her heart she knew she had broken her brother's heart. He could be here, *would* be here, if only she had found it within herself to accept our relationship. I wish I could say I did not take a perverse satisfaction from this turn of events, but I did. Faith's actions seemed patently willful, self-centered, and inhumane: profoundly deserving of this cosmic retribution.

And yet I sympathized with her to some degree. It's hard to discover your brother is gay when you've been raised in an environment that considers homosexuality an abomination, and I'm sure it was even more difficult to contemplate that her brother was making love to a body that belonged, at least partially, to her husband. *That* might strain anyone's tolerance.

She really had no one other than Porter to turn to for comfort or support, and he was somewhat tainted by his proximity to me. It was impossible to know which of her sisters would be sympathetic to her and which to Chase, and in any event she couldn't fully confide in *any* of them without betraying Chase's secret and precipitating a family crisis. But the fact that she ultimately could not find it in her heart to accept that Chase and I were in love—and that our feelings for each other were valid and honorable—well, that was no one's fault but her own.

Faith's pain manifested itself largely as anger—ostensibly toward me, but also toward Porter because he had failed to disclose my relationship with her brother. She spurned his every attempt to comfort her. For a week after Chase's departure, Faith actually barred Porter—or more specifically, me—from their bed. On the surface, it did not appear to be an overtly aggressive act; she simply told us she thought all of us would sleep better if we slept apart. I agreed with her and said as much. Personally, I was happy to avoid any contact with her that was even remotely intimate. But it seemed obvious she was imposing something of a symbolic quarantine, during which any residual vestige of physical contact with Chase would be removed from my body in the course of normal daily hygiene. Not so much as the faintest scent of her brother could remain on my skin or in my hair when she once again allowed Porter and me into her bed.

I presumed we would make our peace at some point. And why not? I had capitulated to her every demand. But for a long time she remained distant, chilly, if not downright cold. Initially, out of habit, I would put my arm around her when Porter hugged her, but when she continued to break free of our embraces with veiled revulsion, I put an end to that. Thereafter our hugs were lopsided, Porter pulling her close to him, gathering her toward his side of the body. She would turn inward ninety degrees, so her left shoulder bisected our torso and her back was turned toward me.

I was suffering, as well. The pain I felt in the wake of Chase's departure was unlike anything I had ever experienced. Unrequited love, with which I was well acquainted, does not feel like this. That kind of yearning is painful, yes, but it is more like a constant, gnawing ache, the kind one might imagine comes from a chronic inflammation of the joints: uncomfortable and ever present, but easily treated with medication—nothing too strong, perhaps even an over-the-counter analgesic. *This* pain was like having a limb ripped from my body, and it renewed itself each day, like Prometheus's liver, to torment me afresh. I felt hopeless, even though I knew life would continue—of that I was certain. I knew I would not die of grief because Porter would not die of grief—not this grief, *my* grief—and if Porter remained alive, so would I.

For a time, the birth of the twins provided Faith with a host of plausible excuses to avoid intimacy while emotions were at their most raw—she was tired, her body wasn't ready for it, we might wake them. When intercourse ultimately resumed—joyless though it seemed to me—we returned to the reverse missionary position, Porter on the bottom, Faith on top, so she could limit the amount of contact she had with my half of our body. All she had to worry about was her left inner thigh and leg where she straddled us, and I took to discreetly folding a corner of a sheet or blanket over myself to eliminate skin-to-skin contact. It was not a purely altruistic gesture. Although I had once liked Faith and had tried to accommodate her needs in bed, I now found it annoying—even to an extent repulsive—to feel certain parts of her body rubbing against mine. I could tolerate such contact on the one body part I shared with Porter, knowing he was getting pleasure out of it, but from my point of view any other contact was unnecessary and I preferred to avoid it. She took to mounting us lopsided, leaning to her right to minimize contact with me, and from my vantage point she looked like a cowboy on a bucking bronco, flailing wildly and trying to keep her balance.

Outside the bedroom, her disdain evinced itself in other,

more subtle ways. Whenever we were together, she seemed skittish, darting about the room like a hummingbird, allowing herself to hover only when she had reached the point that was furthest from me. It was as if I were a constant irritation—a pebble in her shoe. She blamed me for inserting three thousand miles between herself and her brother and developed the annoying habit of musing aloud about the time difference between Atlanta and San Francisco whenever Chase's name came up in conversation, however tangentially.

"Is it two hours or three?" she'd say innocently, as if she hadn't asked the question a dozen times before. Or, "They're behind us, right? Three hours behind? So it's nine a.m. there now?"

And more than distance and time zones, she blamed me for having plunged Chase into the very fires of hell: San Franfuckingcisco. She was sure he would contract AIDS there and die. And all because I couldn't keep my hand off him.

Sometimes, I looked up from a book or the printout of a song Porter and I were working on and found her staring at me as if she were a telepath trying to pry information from me without my knowledge. When I smiled at her on those occasions, she'd turn away as if we were strangers and I had caught her staring at me in an elevator or a subway car.

One day when Porter and I arrived for breakfast, I noticed only two coffee mugs on the table—hers and Porter's. Without comment, I diverted Porter to the cupboard and got out my usual mug, one half of a "World's Best Twin" set (which a month later mysteriously broke "in the dishwasher"). The next week, my place setting disappeared completely, and again I quietly set about getting breakfast for myself. The pattern repeated itself at dinner a week later. I half expected to begin receiving a grocery bill for the meals I ate at Porter's, even though I regularly anted up at the supermarket. It was difficult to know whether Faith's actions were meant to be vengeful and provocative or if they composed some weird form of denial, a reversal of the macabre practice of reserving a place at the dinner table for a deceased relative: if my dish were not there, I did not exist. If that were the case, I think we were in considerably more trouble than we had bargained for.

I tried not to be angry with her. Perhaps it would be more accurate to say I tried not to let my anger affect my relationship with her—or with Porter—but it was hard not to. I attempted to make the best of it, to think that eventually something positive would come of it. I visualized my pain as a tiny grain of sand inside an oyster shell and around which a pearl would grow—something beautiful coming from something painful. But I knew that was bullshit. Dealing with her became work, and the days I spent with her were like an unending succession of Mondays at a job I hated. By contrast, "my" days, when I could avoid her for the most part, always felt like a weekend to me. It got to the point where even hearing her next door would set me off. The sound of her favorite music on the stereo seeping through the walls (she rarely, if ever, played Janus anymore) or the gurgle of water behind our common wall when she flushed the toilet could send me over the edge.

I spent as much time as possible away from the house, so I wouldn't have to see or hear her. I convinced Porter we should work at the studio, even though I felt I did my best writing at home. We had been well into the process of writing our new CD when Chase and I broke up, and my lyrics turned progressively more gloomy, contrasting with the increasingly upbeat, almost sentimental music Porter had taken to writing since he had learned he was going to become a father. I had a feeling that unless something changed, the CD was going to tank—big time—and I worried about what might happen to Porter and me if we became so estranged from one another that we could no longer successfully collaborate and stopped recording and performing. It would be the most talked-about breakup of a musical duo since Simon & Garfunkel. After our parents died and we ran through whatever money they left us, would we end up like other failed freak-show acts, broke and alone like Daisy and Violet Hilton, dead on the floor of their apartment after a bout with the flu?

It was important not to let this come between us—personally or creatively—but I felt as if I were doing most of the work, shouldering most of the burden. Porter was the one person in the world who truly understood what I had done— what I had sacrificed and what I had saved—and in a way that helped. But I still resented him, since what I had done I had done for him, for the sake of his marriage. And while ultimately he was as sympathetic as I could have possibly hoped for under the circumstances, no amount of sympathy or gratitude was ever going to be enough.

After what I considered a decent interval, I sent Chase a couple of conciliatory e-mails, but I never heard from him. The regret I felt over losing him barely diminished with time, though it increasingly seemed a reckless and foolhardy infatuation that had brought nothing but pain to all involved. It did not help that Faith shared many of his characteristics and mannerisms; sometimes when she laughed, I could close my eyes and imagine him next to me.

It took a while, but life eventually returned to something close to normal. I still felt somewhat isolated—alienated— around Faith, but the intensity of those feelings diminished over time. I'm not sure how any of us would have survived without the twins to both distract and inspire us. They were something of a lifeline for all of us. Porter turned out to be a far better father than I had ever imagined—engaged, loving, responsible. His instincts and expectations had been right on target. Instead of me having to take up the slack, as I had anticipated, I felt almost left out of the process of caring for Justin and Christina. Porter would hold one twin while Faith fed the other, then they would trade. I helped him change the babies' diapers, but he always took the lead, telling me what to do and how to do it. They were beautiful kids—bright, engaging, always happy, or almost always. Porter decided he wanted to write a song about them—not only the music but also the lyrics, something he had never before expressed an interest in doing. He even recorded Christina shaking her rattle and sampled it for use as the percussion line of the song.

I found myself thinking back to the conversation Porter and I had before Faith was even pregnant, when he told me he was looking forward to being the object of his children's adoration, without question or judgment. In a way, I now found myself the unlikely beneficiary of that love, at least tangentially, at a time in my life when otherwise there seemed to be precious little attention or goodwill directed toward me.

I took what I could get.

Chapter 28

Throughout our college career, Porter and I had hit the P.E. center at least three times a week, and after graduation he had insisted on continuing to find time to work out. Even now, with our increasingly rigorous concert schedule and his new domestic lifestyle, he rarely slacked off. In the six years since Porter had stopped playing football, we had lost some bulk—nearly twenty pounds, I'd say—but thanks to circuit training, skiing, and racquetball (we'd developed a way of playing against ourselves, each of us wielding a racquet), we had maintained a body that would have been the envy of almost any man, were it not for our obvious anomaly. As much work as it was sometimes, it was far more constructive than sitting around drinking beer and smoking pot with the roadies, and in the months following Chase's departure, it became for me a welcome respite from being around Faith.

As a type, bodybuilders never have been particularly attractive to me, with their unnaturally dark tans and veiny, rubberized flesh. They look ill at ease in their bodies, uncomfortable, as if they are costumed extras in some sci-fi movie, standing around the set between takes. No matter how large their biceps are, their arms still look somewhat vestigial, resting at a thirty-degree angle against their swollen latissimus dorsi muscles like the stumpy, shriveled wings of chickens bred for their breast meat. I've always been drawn to more classically proportioned men, even to those, like Chase, who might be a little on the undernourished side. I'd take a lacrosse player over a quarterback anytime, and I'd find a lot more of interest in the Atlanta Braves' locker room than the Falcons'. So I didn't expect to be distracted by the denizens of the gym Porter joined after he had gotten married, Hugh Jorgansson's World Class Fitness Center in the old Sears catalog building on Ponce de Leon, a haven for serious bodybuilders and for cops from the adjacent police-precinct headquarters. Jorgansson's was a no-nonsense establishment, redolent of sweat and chalk and the interlocking black rubber mats that covered its bare concrete floor, and it was patronized largely by the type of massive musclemen in whom I had no interest whatsoever, socially or sexually. It was a seemingly humorless crowd, intent mainly on getting a good pump, and Porter and I quickly settled into a fairly rigorous routine. And while most of the guys kept to themselves, we never had trouble getting a spot when we needed one.

Lately, I'd noticed a guy who stood out largely because his gym clothes were always neater and a little more stylish than anyone else's. He was not as big as the other regulars but was quite nicely developed, perfectly proportioned, with a sculpted chest that tapered down to a surprisingly slender waist. His arms and legs were generously flared but not unseemly. He reminded me of one of those gladiators from a campy 1950s Italian film you'd see on American Movie Classics, perhaps considered over-developed for the average man of the time but nothing like the size of today's bodybuilders. And there was something in his eyes, something alive, that made me think there was more between his ears than five pounds of ground round.

Occasionally, I'd see him talking to one or two other lifters, casually and comfortably, with lots of smiles and the occasional friendly backslap or ass-pat passed between them, but more often than not he worked out alone. He went through his workouts quietly and deliberately, with a minimum of huffing and puffing, and rests between sets that appeared precisely timed, seemingly without ever looking at the large, plain, white-faced clock that reminded me of the ones that had hung in my elementary-school classrooms. His body was almost hairless, and I wondered if it were natural or if he shaved. I always found it interesting that bodybuilders, even straight bodybuilders, had no problem shaving their bodies, removing that most masculine of identifiers while at the same time accentuating all of their other manly attributes. Some of them, I noticed in the locker room, even shaved their pubic regions.

I caught him looking in our direction from time to time, but he always turned away without acknowledging us, and it was impossible to tell if he was cruising or just staring. Almost without realizing it, I found myself developing a consciousness about him, an awareness of his presence or absence in the gym, the time at which he usually arrived, the length and pattern of his routine, whom he talked to, the moment he headed for the showers, when he left for the day. Eventually, Porter caught on.

"Okay, who is it?" he asked when he had to rouse me yet again from a soft-core reverie in the middle of our routine.

"Who is what?"

"The one you've got a hard-on for. Who is it?"

"What makes you think . . ."

"Don't bullshit me, O. Your timing's off. You're not pushing yourself. I do twelve biceps curls to your eight. I'll bet you've lost half an inch in your arm."

I knew I was busted. I scanned the room for the object of my desire.

"Him. There. In the red shorts."

Porter turned to look.

"Don't fuckin' stare, Porter, for god's sake."

"Him? Jesus, O, he's like competitive material. Doesn't look gay to me. Although, I don't know. There are more of them in competition than you think."

"Thanks for your enlightened analysis."

"So, you think he's . . . ?"

"I don't know."

"Well, if I were you, I'd be real careful before I said anything to him. He could cream us easy."

I had the feeling the guy knew we were talking about him, even though he was on the other side of the gym, as if the room contained one of those acoustic anomalies that allowed whispers to be heard at great distances.

"In any case," I said, lowering my voice further, "I don't have a hard-on for him, as you so crudely put it."

I hadn't been with anyone in the six months since I'd broken up with Chase, and I still felt his loss keenly every day. The last thing I wanted to do was to make myself vulnerable again, but I'd be lying if I didn't admit I found this man attractive. Of course, I wasn't even sure he was gay. I hadn't noted any characteristics I thought were either particularly gay or especially straight, but if I had to guess, I'd say yes, based purely on the number of times I had caught him looking at me. And I just had a feeling that if he had been straight, something would have tipped me off by now.

We finally spoke one afternoon in the locker room, although it was far from mere serendipity that brought us together. Once I was fairly certain of what time he arrived and how long he worked out, I adjusted our workout schedule so it coincided with his. It took some finesse to do so without tipping my hand to Porter, who I feared might become uncooperative if he caught on, but ultimately we found ourselves in the shower with my Herculean dreamboat.

As Porter and I lathered up two showerheads away from the stranger, I felt both giddy and somewhat abashed at our proximity to him. This close—and naked—he was somewhat intimidating. His body was an unexpected amalgam of animal and machine: his thighs glistened like the freshly curried flanks of a stallion, massive and meaty; his upper body, though, seemed inanimate, his chest like armor plating, his arms like pistons. I had the impression as he washed various parts of himself that he was detached from his body, that he inhabited it but was not part of it, that he was maneuvering it the way a puppeteer manipulates a marionette, his hand dangling lifelessly from his wrist when he raised his arm to scrub the chasm of his armpit.

I became aware that we were being stared at, though once again I could not be sure if he was cruising me or perhaps merely examining the way Porter's and my necks merged into our shoulders, tracing the Y-shaped path of our spines as they joined like two rivers into one three-quarters of the way down our back. But now that I had the opportunity to speak to him, I was speechless with anxiety and self-doubt.

"You're that band . . . Janus, right?" he said, eventually, eliminating the need for me to take the initiative.

"Yeah," Porter answered before I could speak. "Porter Jamison."

I was instantly pissed at Porter. Perhaps unreasonably, I felt the question had been directed at me and that I should have been the one to respond. That's how badly I wanted this man to notice me alone, apart from Porter.

"Griffin Lockhart," he said and leaned toward us, his right hand extended. I leaped at the chance to shake it.

"Griffin," I said, stepping toward him. "I'm Owen."

"Owen, nice to meet you. And . . . Porter?"

"Right."

"Owen and Porter. I'll try to keep that straight."

"Try this," I said. "If you look at the alphabet, O is to the left of P, and if you look at us, Owen, that's me, is to the left of Porter." It was an explanation I'd developed when I was younger to help people remember who was who.

"I'll remember that. O-P, O-P," he said, nodding his head from side to side as he pronounced each letter. He smiled, but I felt like an idiot.

"You guys are good. I like your stuff."

"Thanks, man," Porter said. He put his bar of soap back

in its dish and moved closer to the showerhead to rinse off. I could tell he wasn't exactly thrilled to be chatting with a naked man.

"We'd be glad to comp a ticket for you—a couple of tickets—next time we're playing in town," I said. "Chastain Park, right, Porter?"

"Yeah, I think."

"That's nice of you, but . . ."

"No sweat. I'd love to do it," I said.

"Okay, sure."

"It's coming up soon. A couple of weeks. The end of the month. I'll bring the tickets next time we're in."

Porter was leaning into the spray, rinsing his hair, the last thing he did before turning off the water. When he was done, I followed suit. Griffin continued showering while we stepped onto a rubber mat and dried ourselves off.

"See you around," I said as we headed off to get dressed. Griffin waved and smiled.

"Jesus, O," Porter said later in the car, "you were practically playing footsies with that guy in the shower."

"I was not. I was just being friendly. He spoke first."

"And you fell all over yourself giving him free tickets to our Chastain gig."

"So? So what?"

"You know we promised our comps to Mom and Dad and to Faith's family."

"Christ, Porter, I'll buy the fucking tickets if I have to. Give me a break."

"You've got it bad, O. Real bad. I just hope he doesn't break your heart when he shows up with some babe on his arm."

"I have a feeling that won't be the case, but it will be a great way to find out which one of us is right."

Over the course of the next couple of weeks, I spoke to Griffin with increasing frequency and we occasionally did some sets with him. He was intelligent and quite charming, and after I'd known him for a while, he confided that he'd gotten into bodybuilding to compensate for having been a scrawny kid who frequently was picked on. I gathered he was pretty successful as a real estate agent, based in part on the fact that he had recently sold the old Candler mansion in Inman Park for an amount approaching seven figures.

I may have been imagining it, but I thought Griffin was more attuned to me than to Porter. It was not that he ignored Porter; the two of them frequently talked about weight-lifting technique and such things as diet regimens designed to add bulk without gaining fat. But when he demonstrated a particular exercise, it was always my side of the body he used, tracing the outline of a muscle or moving my arm or leg through a particular motion. And when he stood behind us while we tried out a new exercise he had suggested, it was my ear into which he would count out reps or whisper encouragement, his lips sometimes actually brushing my earlobe. I genuinely thought he was flirting with me, although perhaps he could simply tell I was the one who needed the most motivation.

On the night of our appearance at Chastain Park, Griffin arrived with another bodybuilder, although not someone I recognized from the gym. I suppose I would not have been entirely surprised had he been accompanied by a woman, but the instant I saw him with another guy, all my uncertainty about his sexual preference vanished. I knew they were lovers, and I immediately found myself turning green, although I took some small satisfaction in concluding that they apparently had not been dating long enough to have joined the same gym in lockstep. After the show, while we were mingling with Faith's family and our mom and dad, Griffin stopped by to thank us for the tickets—without his friend. He seemed somewhat surprised when I introduced Faith as Porter's wife.

"I didn't know you guys were married," he said.

"We're not. That is, *I'm* not. Just Porter."

"But . . ."

"I know, I know, it's a *delicate* situation," I said. "But I have my own life apart from Porter. We couldn't be more different in that respect."

"I see," Griffin said.

"So you brought a friend?" I said, largely for Porter's benefit.

"Yeah. He's kind of shy."

"A big guy like him?" Porter said.

"Well . . ."

"It's okay. We understand," I said.

"It's not because . . ."

"Don't worry about it, Griffin," I said. "I hope he had a good time."

"He did, yeah. He likes your stuff. I've bought a couple of your CDs. We play them in the car."

"I look forward to meeting him sometime," I said.

"Sure thing."

After that night, I found myself more troubled and confused about Griffin than ever. I'd gotten the answer to the big question—Is he or isn't he?—and while the result was affirmative, the situation was unsatisfactory. I realized I didn't just want Griffin to be gay; some part of me also wanted him to be available—and interested in me. If he wasn't, it really didn't matter whether he was gay. In fact, I think I would have preferred him to be straight. At least that way I would know that he was forever unavailable.

In the months that followed, Griffin and I spent a good deal of time together. He began joining Porter, Faith, and me for meals—Sunday brunches at first, dinners later. Then he began going to the movies with us. On several occasions, I asked if he would like to bring his friend, but he always declined. I realized I was growing quite fond of him—more than fond, really. Porter became alarmed.

"Dude, what are you thinking? He's got a boyfriend."

"I can't help it, Porter. I'm sure it will pass. It's just an infatuation."

Two months later, I witnessed what I presumed was the end of his relationship in the parking garage adjacent to the gym. It wasn't clear to me whether his partner had come to pick him up or whether he had shown up at the gym to confront him. Porter and I were headed toward our car when we heard raised voices. I looked in their direction and saw Griffin and his buddy. I couldn't make out what they were saying (did I hear the word "freaks"?) but after a brief verbal volley, a car door slammed and Griffin's friend peeled out of the parking lot. I wanted to go over to see if Griffin was all right or if he needed a ride home, but Porter wouldn't let me.

"It's none of our business, O. If he needs a ride, he can call a cab. I'm sympathetic and all that, but he'd probably be embarrassed if he knew we had seen what went down. Better to just leave it alone."

We didn't see Griffin at the gym for a week after that—highly unusual for him—and when he resurfaced he made no reference to his personal situation. But the next time he joined us at the movies, he put his arm on the back of my seat, not quite touching my shoulder but nonetheless a strong indication that our friendship might be evolving into something new.

We began dating officially a couple of weeks after that. Although Griffin was shy about it, I knew things had changed when he asked if we could go out "alone," that is, without Faith. The first time he spent the night was awkward. Porter seemed stunned by the presence in our bed of someone he had come to know at the gym, someone so overtly masculine, so ostensibly straight. I think he was particularly surprised that a man like Griffin could be the passive partner in the sexual act. For several weeks after Griffin and I began sleeping together, Porter felt sheepish and embarrassed at the gym if Griffin were there, and for a while we agreed to work out at different times.

But Griffin eventually integrated himself into our somewhat complicated personal and family dynamic. On alternate nights, he slept with me at my place and joined Faith, Porter, and me the next morning for breakfast or at the very least a cup of coffee. Even on Porter's days, he frequently came over for dinner and spent some time with us in the evening, before Faith, Porter, and I went to bed. Although Faith managed to be cordial to Griffin, she did not exactly embrace him. In fact, there seemed to be a somewhat unusual vibe emanating from her. It was almost as if she thought it unseemly for me to be dating another man so soon after ending my relationship with her brother—a stance I thought odd, considering her role in its dissolution.

"I wouldn't have thought Griffin was your type," she said to me, apropos of nothing, one morning as she was feeding the twins. Griffin had spent the night and had just left for his office. His car was barely down the driveway when she broached the subject.

"Oh?" I said. "Exactly what *is* my type?"

"I don't know. I just thought you'd be attracted to someone more . . . *cerebral*," she said, looking at me, a spoonful of strained peaches poised just out of reach in front of Justin's mouth. The allusion to Chase was unmistakable, but I ignored it. "I mean, he's basically just a salesman, right?"

"He's a real estate agent," I said.

"Which is a cut above a car salesman in my book."

Justin leaned forward and took the spoon into his mouth.

"I don't think you have to have a state license to be a car salesman, Faith, and my understanding is that those licensing exams are pretty tough. You have to know a lot about real estate law and about finance."

"Well, it's not exactly like passing the state bar exam, is it?"

"No, Faith, I suppose it's not like going to law school for three years and then passing the state bar exam."

"Say," Porter said, "Isn't your old boyfriend a car salesman? The one who played football for Alabama?"

"His father *owns* the dealership," Faith replied. "It's the family business."

"Oh, well, that makes all the difference in the world," I said.

She gave me a sour look, her eyes as narrow as an angry cat's, but that was the end of *that* conversation. She turned her attention back to the twins and wiped a bit of drool from Justin's mouth with a yellow terrycloth napkin.

I wasn't exactly sure why Faith was so reluctant to welcome Griffin into our lives. I doubted she had changed her mind about my suitability as a partner for her brother and was planning to engineer a reconciliation, but it seemed to me she would have preferred me to remain perpetually single. Perhaps she would find fault with *anyone* I chose to date. I sometimes wondered if it had to do with a feeling of being outnumbered. The arrival of Griffin in our midst had had an interesting effect on the balance of power within the relationship among Faith, Porter, and me. Faith had always held the swing vote, allying herself with Porter on certain questions and with me on others. That meant she almost always got her way when Porter and I disagreed on things. But our little triangle had now become a rectangle, which in theory should have added stability but instead seemed only to increase the potential for conflict and deadlock.

Ultimately, however, it was Justin and Christina who were the most successful voting bloc when it came to most family decisions, and our daily lives centered almost entirely around their needs. The distinctions between my life and Porter's tended to disappear if one of the twins was having a difficult night and Faith needed help with them. And I'll admit that I gave in more easily than I might have anticipated, especially when Griffin wasn't around. If he was busy attending to the details of a big deal or simply needed a night to himself, I found it difficult to insist upon sleeping "alone" at my place.

In fact, I appreciated the changes that fatherhood had wrought in Porter. He was happier now, more content, than he had been in years. When we were younger, I always thought Porter was remarkably well adjusted to his circumstances—so much so that I sometimes thought he might be in denial. But I've come to see that, although he never spoke about it, Porter apparently often felt that he had to prove himself, whether on the playing fields of Lovett or in the beds of the women he met before Faith. But fatherhood had certainly dampened that impulse, if not negated it outright.

The twins also had an interesting impact on our career. They expanded and intensified the aura of celebrity that had previously surrounded Porter and me because of our musical career. Apparently, all of America wanted to know what it was like for a two-headed father to be raising children. So we quickly became "celebrity dads" and as such were invited to make the rounds of the morning news programs and the female-oriented afternoon talk shows, often accompanied by Faith and sometimes with the twins in tow. (All of us were a little concerned about raising the twins in a freak-show environment, so we agreed to appear with them only on the most reputable programs.)

Faith took to the spotlight better than I would have expected. She was poised and forthcoming during interviews, and her down-to-earth background prevented all the attention from going to her head. We found ourselves in New York and L.A. so often that we began to discuss the possibility of relocating to one place or the other. But even though we'd hired a nanny to help with Justin and Christina, Faith was reluctant to move away from Georgia, where the three of us had family, in the event "something unexpected should happen" that would require the presence of my mom or, more likely, Faith's mother and sisters.

Chapter 29

It was a Sunday morning and the three of us—Griffin, Porter, and I—were sleeping in. We had done a show at the Fox Theater the night before, promoting the launch of our new CD, *Under My Skin,* and afterward Griffin had unexpectedly shown up backstage with roses in honor of our six-month anniversary. I'd remembered the date but was afraid it might be a little sappy to acknowledge it. Griffin apparently did not. We went out for drinks, got home at four a.m., and collapsed into bed.

I was awakened by the touch of Griffin's lips on mine, his breath warm and moist but fresh. He'd obviously been up and brushed his teeth.

"Good morning, handsome," he whispered.

"Morning, Griff," I said.

"You conked out on me last night before I could give you my anniversary gift."

"You bought me something besides the roses?"

"No, I mean this." He kissed me on the mouth, the chin, the throat, and slid down to brush my nipple with his lips and touch his tongue to our navel.

"You'll wake Porter if you're not careful."

"I really don't think he's going to complain, do you?"

He took us into his mouth. Next to me, Porter stirred. Griffin hunched over us as if prostrate in prayer. He shifted his weight forward for leverage and his ass rose in the air. I watched his head bob up and down, his shoulder and neck muscles alternately tensing and relaxing, his torso evenly bronzed except for the ridiculously slender outline of the thong he wore in the tanning bed. By now, Porter was emerging from sleep.

"Hey, buddy, what're you doing down there?" he said groggily, lifting his head to see what was going on.

Griffin laughed—or choked—and kept going.

"Go back to sleep, Porter," I said.

"Feels too good to go back to sleep."

"You're not supposed to be enjoying this."

"Can't help it, O. The man is a genius. You've said so yourself."

As long as Porter was awake, I decided to relax into the moment. I put my leg up on Griffin's shoulder and, surprisingly, Porter did the same. That was a first. Our body had long been divided into three zones, informally labeled "yours," "mine," and "ours." As comfortable as he had been with Chase, Porter still occasionally had shrunk from contact with him in bed, which may have had as much to do with the fact that Chase was Faith's brother as it did with his being a man. Porter would issue a guttural bark, something along the lines of "Yo!" if Chase's hand strayed into territory that was exclusively "his." But in the past couple of months, he apparently had grown more comfortable with the idea of my having sex with Griffin. The two of them had gotten to know each other and enjoyed drinking together and talking sports—so much so that I often felt left out of the conversation. At times, had I been able to do so, I gladly would have left the two of them alone to talk football or baseball or wrestling. Porter genuinely seemed to like Griffin, and because of that, he accepted the fact that I loved him and wanted to show my affection for him. Don't get me wrong. Porter was never going to do anything sexual with Griffin, at least not with any part of our body that was "his" alone, like kissing him or giving him a hand job. But he appeared less averse to allowing me to take pleasure from the things Griffin did or to acknowledging they were simultaneously pleasurable to him.

Griffin's tempo was picking up. I felt an orgasm building. "Oh fuck, Griffin," I shouted. I threw back my head and closed my eyes. Griffin's left hand made its way up to my nipple and pinched it. "Oh yeah."

"Fuckin' A, man," Porter said loudly.

I turned my head in Porter's direction. It was uncharacteristic of him to become *quite* so involved, but I let it go. And then Porter was actually shouting, urging on Griffin the same way he would have encouraged a teammate at a wrestling match. My eyes fluttered open and shut, open and shut, and I glanced down and momentarily saw Porter's hand, a blur on Griffin's head. My eyes snapped shut, and together Porter and I arched our back, exploding into Griffin's mouth.

Afterward, Griffin collapsed next to me on his stomach, his arm thrown across our chest so his fingers brushed Porter's biceps. His face was so close to mine that simply by puckering his lips, he could bridge the gap between us. I could feel his chest expanding and contracting in sync with ours, the three of us breathing as one. I turned my head to kiss him, and my eyes swept down across his glistening body to the rounded hemispheres of his ass.

And then I saw her standing in the doorway: Faith, with this horrified look on her face as if she had seen something so grotesque it defied description. She turned and was gone before I could speak, before I could even call out her name. In that instant, I reflexively replayed the scene in my head as she must have seen it, as if my life were flashing before my eyes at the moment of death: Griffin's face buried in our crotch, his beefy ass in the air, his most private parts directly in her line of sight, Porter and I thrashing in bed, our joint exclamations, his in particular, "Fuckin' A, man," sounding to me now—as it must have to Faith—incredibly gross and obscene.

"Oh my god!" I said. "Oh shit!" I sat bolt upright, yanking Porter up with me. "Oh shit oh shit oh shit oh shit!"

"Owen, what's wrong?" Griffin asked. "You got a cramp or something?"

"Fuck, man. *Faith*. She was here. She saw us. Saw you. Blowing me. Blowing *us*. That's what it looked like to her, I'm sure . . . Porter, you stupid shit! Why the fuck did you choose today of all days to be so animated?"

"What?" Porter said. "Faith? Where?"

"Here! She was at the door, looking in, watching!"

"You sure, O?"

"I *saw* her."

At this point, I heard the front door slam next door—perhaps it would be more accurate to say I *felt* it shudder through the entire house. Porter and I leaped out of bed without a word to each other and pulled on a pair of jeans. By the time we found the previous night's shirt in the pile of discarded clothes on the floor—ours and Griff's commingled—we heard the sound of the Volvo's door slamming and its engine rumbling to life. When we got downstairs and opened the front door, all we could see was a vapor trail from the exhaust pipe hanging in the damp autumn air. We shut the door, and Porter immediately went to the phone and speed-dialed Faith on her cell, but got no answer.

"Damn," he said, after the third or fourth try. "She's not picking up."

"You know she refuses to use the phone when she's in the car—especially when she's got the kids with her."

"No, she's avoiding me."

"Well, that's probably true, too. Give her time, Porter. We all need a little time right now."

We made our way back to the bedroom where Griffin, still in bed, had covered himself with a sheet. He seemed somewhat dazed by the flurry of activity.

"We are *so* busted," I said.

"Why?" Griffin asked. "What do you mean?"

"She saw everything—or just about everything. She certainly saw more of *you* than she ever wanted to." That sounded more accusatory than I wanted, and I immediately regretted it.

"How long do you think she was there?" Porter asked.

"I don't know. She wasn't there when Griffin started, I know that much, but after a while I wasn't really paying attention to much of anything else. I only saw her after we came."

"Maybe she's just embarrassed," Griffin suggested.

"It's more than that. You didn't see her face. She was crying, and I thought she was going to faint."

That didn't even begin to explain what I had seen. Had Faith merely been embarrassed, she would have been blank-faced and blushing; perhaps her hand would have flown up to cover her mouth. Had she simply been shocked, her eyes would have been wide open, her mouth agape. No, she was horrified, really and truly horrified. It would have been one thing if she had inadvertently seen two men having sex— maybe in a video I carelessly had left in the VCR—seeing for the first time the way men were intimate with one another. But I knew this was something of an entirely different magnitude: the realization that her husband was a participant in such a thing, a reluctant participant, an innocent bystander, if you will, with no control over the situation, but *there*, present in the moment.

I did my best to imagine what had gone through Faith's mind while she watched us, however briefly. Seconds must have seemed like hours. At first, it might have been mere curiosity mixed with confusion. It might even have been as simple as wondering what was going on, what the *hell* Griffin was doing. Were we okay? Was he attacking us? Perhaps initially she had been as detached as someone watching two dogs screw in the street or a pair of lions mating on a *National Geographic* special. Or she simply may have been in awe of Griffin's body, a not-uncommon response in both women and men, straight or gay. It is so well developed it seems more animal than human in its power and beauty; it shimmers and ripples as if animated from within. But at what point did curiosity turn into shock and revulsion? When did it become more like watching the aftermath of a car wreck, seeing unnatural bodily configurations resolve themselves into the forms of two—or three—human beings? *Whose leg is that? Whose arm?* There must have been a moment when she realized what she was seeing, a time at which she may even have made a sound—a sigh, a squeal—but we hadn't heard it. Finally, she must have sorted things out, must have understood what Griffin was doing and to whom, must have recognized that one of the legs over Griffin's shoulders was mine and one was Porter's—not, somehow, Griffin's own appendage in some tantric yoga position. There may even have been a moment when she checked herself—left–right, Owen–Porter (as if that hadn't become automatic by now)—to determine whose hand was pressing down on Griffin's head. And then the voices. Griffin wasn't saying much, but she would have been able to discern two distinct voices, mine perhaps differentiated by the fact that it was softer and directed at Griffin while Owen's was louder and more generalized. "Fuckin' A, man."

I suppose if she had ever bothered to imagine Griffin and me having sex, she might have conjured up Porter as somehow asleep, unconscious, perhaps even disembodied, hovering above Griffin and me as if he were having an out-of-body experience, tethered to me by some ethereal umbilical, while his real body, his half of our body, remained inert and sort of ashen even as my half was flushed with blood and sex and excitement. But not this, not the two of us conscious, both of us sweating and shouting. And the hand, Porter's hand, on Griffin's head—that was the final damning evidence.

"God damn it," Porter said. "God damn you, Owen."

"Hold on, Porter," Griffin said. "It's not Owen's fault. It's nobody's fault. We weren't doing anything wrong."

304 / Andrew W.M. Beierle

"That sure as hell isn't what Faith is gonna think," Porter said.

Griffin eased himself off the bed and tiptoed to the bathroom, walking as if he were the survivor of an earthquake in a house made fragile by structural damage. When he returned, he had pulled on a pair of purple nylon running shorts.

"I guess I should go, huh?"

"You don't have to, Griff," I said, trying to convince myself, as well as Griffin and Porter, that this was not so bad. "I'll make us all some coffee. I'll bet in a few minutes we'll all feel better about this."

"I wouldn't be so sure of that," Porter said.

"Where do you think she's gone?" Griffin asked.

"Church, I imagine. It *is* Sunday morning," I said.

"Brooks County," Porter said in an odd voice—deflated, resigned. Ever since Faith had threatened to take the twins and leave him if I did not end my relationship with Chase, his greatest fear had been that he ultimately would lose his children because of me.

"Brooks County?" Griffin said.

"Home," I said. "South Georgia. But she didn't—wouldn't—do that."

In truth, Faith indeed might have thought about going home, but it was a long drive, especially with the twins in the car and no one but her to look after them. The way she doted on them, that would be unthinkable to her. I doubted she'd get much past the perimeter highway before reconsidering, maybe deciding to head over to the home of one of her friends, looking for a shoulder to cry on. I offered this hypothesis to Porter.

"I don't know," he said. "We'll see. But you're probably right. She's not going to drive four hours with the twins alone in the backseat. That's crazy. She wouldn't do that."

Porter and I showered and dressed. Griffin went back to his apartment unshowered, so embarrassed was he by what had happened and so worried about the possibility of Faith returning to confront us. Porter and I debated about where we should be when Faith came home, my place or theirs, and we decided on theirs, so it wouldn't appear as if we felt guilty and were avoiding her. There really wasn't anything to be ashamed about. We were the aggrieved parties, the ones whose privacy had been violated; we were about as culpable as someone who had inadvertently left the door to the bathroom unlocked and was interrupted in the process of doing his business. I was having sex with my lover. Porter was, unavoidably, present. Yes, he did seem a bit more involved than was necessary, but that was to be expected. The man was, after all, having an orgasm. Surely she would understand he couldn't remain entirely passive.

I questioned him about it while we drank coffee and waited for Faith. "You always yell like that? I don't recall hearing anything like that before."

"I don't know. I guess so. I always yell when I come, don't I? Don't I yell with Faith?"

"Not like that. I doubt I've ever heard you say 'Fuckin' A, man,' to Faith."

"Well, I can't help myself. Griffin gives great head. Best I've ever had."

"That's no excuse."

"It wouldn't have made a difference to you if Faith hadn't been watching."

"No, I don't suppose it would have."

"So don't get all preachy and judgmental about it all of a sudden. And don't think I'm turning gay, O. I just enjoy a good blow job, same as the next guy. The next thing I know, you're gonna get jealous of me and Griffin."

"Hey, it's your marriage I'm trying to save, Porter. So don't get on *my* case."

Faith got home two hours later, explaining that she had, in fact, gone to church. She appeared composed, unruffled, but was decidedly distant. She carried Justin and Christina upstairs, put them down for a nap, and after a disconcertingly long interval joined us in the kitchen, outwardly as cheerful and perky as a 1960s sitcom housewife—and about as believable. Try as I might, I could make eye contact with her only fleetingly.

"People asked about you," she said to Porter as she tied on an apron, her eyes directed toward the floor. "I told them it was Owen's Sunday, but that isn't true, is it, Owen? Yesterday was your day, wasn't it? That's why you were sleeping at your place."

"Yes, that's right." I said, ignoring the tinge of sarcasm in her voice.

She began puttering around the kitchen, wiping down the yellow ceramic tile of the countertop repeatedly, even though it was already spotless, occasionally wetting the tip of her finger and rubbing at an imagined blemish. She opened the dishwasher periodically and peered inside to see if anything had materialized within its interior since her last inspection, as if it were a *Star Trek* replicator. Porter and I sat at the breakfast table, mute, gazing wistfully into the bottoms of our empty coffee cups, unwilling to get up and refill them for fear our movement would break the surface tension of Faith's anger and unleash an avalanche of emotion. But when she had taken down each and every bottle from the spice rack, wiped them clean, and tightened their caps, all without further comment, I knew I had to say something.

"Listen, Faith, I'm sorry you had to see that."

"See what?" she said without looking in my direction, continuing to straighten things that didn't need straightening. It reminded me of my mother's response to the news I was gay—pinching dead sprigs of baby's breath off the centerpiece at the Ritz-Carlton.

"Griffin and me. This morning."

"Oh, *that*." She began polishing the chrome sides of the toaster. "That."

"Obviously, we weren't expecting you."

"I've learned my lesson. I won't come into your home unannounced again."

"That's not what I want, Faith. You know you're always welcome."

"I was looking for Porter. For church. It was late. I'd already put the twins in the car. I thought you'd be up and dressed, running a little behind. Maybe you ought to start locking your bedroom door or leaving a little signal for me. A tie on the doorknob—isn't that the standard fraternity-house sign for 'No Entry'?"

"We just overslept."

"It didn't appear to me that much *sleeping* was taking place."

"Honey," Porter said.

"I'm sorry," she said. "That was uncalled for. We've been over this territory before. What you do in the privacy of your own home is your business, Owen."

"But you're upset. Clearly."

She stopped burnishing the toaster and frowned at me as if to indicate I was a master of the obvious. The paper towel she had been using was disintegrating in her hand.

"Look, Faith, I just don't think your relationship with Porter is going to survive unless you accept the facts of our condition, a condition over which none of us has any control."

"Meaning what, exactly?"

"Meaning I am my own person, and I'm entitled to the same rights and privileges Porter has, including the right to love whomever I please."

"I see," she said. "So what you're saying is that my marriage is doomed unless I embrace the depravity of your . . . *lifestyle*."

"Depravity, Faith? That's a new one."

"I'm sorry, Owen. That's how I feel. I've tried to understand and accept your way of life, but I just can't. What I saw today made me physically ill. I had to pull the car over to the side of the road and . . ."

"Oh, honey," Porter said. He tried to stand but I wouldn't let him. I wasn't about to comfort her.

"I know what I saw," she said. "There was no mistaking it: Porter was *touching* Griffin. He had his hand on Griffin's head. He was . . . he was shouting obscenities. You can't say he wasn't engaged. He was *engaged*."

"Faith, it was purely physical. He couldn't help it. At a certain point, our brains stop working and our body takes over."

"That's right, honey," Porter said.

"I know, I know. You've told me a hundred times you both feels things . . . down there."

"And you said that didn't matter, as long as it wasn't with your brother," I said.

"Well, it does. It *does* matter to me."

For a long moment, none of us moved. Faith stood at the counter, the sodden remains of the paper towel limp in her hand until she let it drop into the mirror-bright stainless steel sink. Porter, who had been nervously rotating his empty coffee cup on its bottom edge like a gyroscope, placed his palm flat on top of it. All of us were attempting to come to grips with the implications of Faith's statement. It challenged the very framework on which Porter and I had constructed our lives. Mom and Dad had taught us that Porter and I were two distinct individuals, but Faith was saying that was a fairy tale. If that was the case, we were all in trouble.

"If it were only you, Owen, I could tolerate it. But it's not only you. You've dragged my husband into this . . . this . . ."

"Cesspool?" I offered, acidly.

"Yes, Owen. This 'cesspool' of depravity. Just like you dragged my brother into it."

"Oh Christ, Faith. You're still blaming me for that?"

"I'll always blame you for that. I've lost Chase. He's gone because of you. I'll never forgive you for that."

"That's your choice, Faith, and your responsibility. If you could have found it in your heart to accept Chase for who he is, he'd still be here today, with you—with *me*. So don't blame me for that. I've lost him, too."

"And after today, after what I saw—knowing *exactly* what you and Chase used to . . ."

Visualizing her brother having sex with me—with *us*—seemed to defeat her. The energy she had harnessed to sanitize every surface in the kitchen was depleted, and she slumped into a chair across from us, her elbows on the table, her head in her hands, massaging her temples. She brushed a damp strand of hair away from her forehead with the back of her hand and looked straight at Porter.

"I just don't think I can do this anymore," she said to him.

"Do what, honey?"

"This. Whatever this is . . . this marriage, this relationship—the three of us. It's too complicated, too hard—especially now with the babies. It's too much for me. I don't have the energy."

I could feel Porter's pulse quicken, creating a sudden vacuum in the chambers of his heart that ultimately would draw blood away from mine.

"You don't mean that, Faith. You can't," he said. "We'll figure something out."

"What are you going to figure out, Porter? Is Owen going to stop having sex with men?"

"Listen, Faith," I interjected. "There are two hearts in this chest. *Two*. And they each have to survive in order for both to survive. You said this relationship was too much for you. Well, for me it's not *enough*. I need more. I need someone of my own to love. I hoped that person was Chase, but you couldn't accept that, and believe it or not, I actually can understand your point of view. It *was* asking a lot of you—of all of us. Too much, in the end, I can see that now. But I don't understand why you can't accept Griffin's presence in my life."

"What can I tell you, Owen? It just seems wrong to me. I've tried to understand it, but it isn't easy for someone like me, who was raised in the church. It might be different if you and Porter were separate, but you're not. He's there when you have sex with men, and that horrifies me. It doesn't matter if it's with Chase or Griffin or someone else. I can't abide it. Not in my husband. I didn't want this to come between us, but I honestly can't tell you that it won't."

At that moment, we heard one of the twins crying on the baby monitor, and Faith got up and left the room without another word. We heard her cooing to the baby for a few minutes—and then silence. When she didn't return, I assumed the conversation was over for the time being. I thought I had offered a reasonable analysis of the situation and a compassionate approach to dealing with it, but Faith had shut down emotionally. I figured she needed time to process what I'd had to say.

Porter and I spent the rest of the day at the studio. While he half-heartedly picked out a new melody on the keyboard, I tried to sort out the complexities of our relationships, looking for a solution we all could live with. At some point, it occurred to me that perhaps the situation was *not* entirely black or white. Maybe all of us were living in denial if we didn't acknowledge that Porter and I were not separate individuals but two people sharing one body, indivisible, and that whatever one of us did, the other participated in and had to accept both the rewards and the consequences. Perhaps it was not fair—or even possible—to ask our partners to interact with only one of us, emotionally or sexually; to say that Faith made love to Porter and not, at least in some sense, to me, or that Griffin had sex with me but not with Porter. It made things more complicated, but ultimately it was a reality we all might have to acknowledge. I also realized the time had probably come for me to let Porter in on the little secret Faith and I had been keeping from him. If he knew Faith had once thought she was in love with me, he might be better able to understand why she was afraid he could develop feelings for Griffin.

"There's something you need to know, Porter, something that may help explain Faith's reaction to all of this," I said.

"What's that, O?" He tapped out a few desultory notes on the keyboard. He seemed detached, overwhelmed, as if nothing I said could improve the situation or make it any easier to understand.

"I think Faith's upset about this because she thinks it's possible for you to be attracted to Griffin, maybe even to fall in love with him."

"That's bullshit, Owen." His hand went limp on the keyboard, resulting in an atonal bleat. "I told you I was never gonna turn gay."

"I know that, Porter, but Faith may not. In any event, that's not what I'm getting at."

"Then what?"

"I think Faith may have misinterpreted some things that I've done, may have taken them the wrong way."

"Such as?" His fingers walked silently across the tops of the keys as if climbing a ladder or a set of stairs, barely touching them.

"Maybe you're not aware of it, maybe you've never noticed, but there have been things I've done, little things, that made Faith more comfortable in bed."

"Like fluff her pillows?"

"No, Porter, I mean sexually."

"What the hell?"

"Don't get upset. All I mean is that sometimes I've held her or touched her in bed in ways that mirrored what you were doing. I didn't want her to feel as if she were making love to half a man—lopsided, incomplete. So I may have touched her or shifted our body a little when I thought doing so might make her more . . . satisfied."

"You're not saying you're *attracted* to Faith. That's impossible, right? For a gay guy. Or are you bi?"

"I'm not saying I am *attracted* to her, Porter. I'm saying I've been *attentive* to her when the two of you were having sex. I was aware that she was *there*, that she's a person with feelings, and that I could do things that would make her more comfortable, physically and emotionally. But she . . . well, she may have misinterpreted those things. She thought they meant I had feelings for her and . . . she began to develop feelings for me."

"What the hell? When did this happen?"

"Before I told her I was gay. She said that she . . ."

". . . was *in love* with you? Oh my god!"

"The word love was never used, but she made it clear she felt something more for me than might have been desirable toward her brother-in-law. And that's why she's so concerned about you and Griffin. She's afraid that if she could develop feelings for me, you might somehow be able to develop feelings for Griffin. It doesn't make sense, I know. You're not gay. And maybe I'm wrong about it. But it's something for you to think about."

Porter ran his index finger up and down the keyboard, trilling the notes, then brought his fist down on the table.

"I'll be damned," he said. "Why the hell didn't you say something to me?"

"There was no point, Porter. Nothing *happened*, nothing personal. It's just that she realized she had feelings for me. That's why I came out to her that very night, to let her know I wasn't available. I hoped that would put an end to it. But I think her feelings for me may have made things more difficult when she found out about Chase—in a way, she may have been a little jealous of him. And now I think she's afraid something similar could happen with you and Griffin."

"Like I said, O, that's not going to happen."

"You and I know that. She doesn't"

Over dinner, Faith made no mention of anything that had

taken place earlier in the day, and neither Porter nor I brought it up. But she remained obviously distressed. A troubled look shadowed her face when I inadvertently mentioned Griffin's name, and when it came time to go to bed, she suggested it might be better if Porter and I spent the night at my place, as we had done the night before.

"Have I been kicked out of my house?" Porter asked me when we got next door.

"I wouldn't look at it that way," I said.

"How *would* you look at it?"

"Faith just needs her space right now."

"That's not it, bro, and you know it."

Throughout the evening, we both strained to listen for whatever sounds we could pick up next door. A barely perceptible creak and groan in our common wall indicated Faith had gone upstairs, and we followed her, instinctively, without a word to each other. But there the clues ended. Try as we might, we couldn't even hear her talking to anyone on the phone. We went downstairs, and Porter fixed himself a cocktail. I didn't bother, knowing he'd probably drink enough for both of us.

Faith did not allow Porter back into their bedroom for four days, and when she finally relented, she remained remote. Porter could barely kiss her good night before she turned away from us. In response, he got ansty about me having sex. When Griffin next spent the night, Porter made it clear he wanted nothing to do with him. He was petulant and uncommunicative, and he failed to make even the simplest accommodations to our lovemaking, shrinking from the most casual, glancing touch on his side of our body, throwing his leg as far to the left as possible so Griffin wouldn't accidentally brush it with his own, turning his head away from mine theatrically when Griffin kissed me. I was barely able to achieve an erection and had little success maintaining it, so Griffin and I just cuddled, him lying next to me, careful not to let his hand stray onto Porter's side of our

chest, avoiding the no-man's-land of our lower torso altogether. When Griffin left early the next morning, he seemed
distant, preoccupied. Before Porter and I went next door for
coffee, I confronted him about his behavior.

"What was *that* about?" I asked.

"What?"

"The cold-shoulder routine with Griffin."

"Oh please, Owen."

"'Oh please, Owen,' my ass! You completely ruined our
evening."

"Oh, like you guys haven't ruined my entire life? My marriage is in jeopardy because I let my guard down with you
and Griffin. I'm not going to do *that* again."

"Fine. Control yourself. Stay uninvolved. Personally, I
was not looking forward to a resumption of intimacy with
Faith, either. But there's a difference between remaining detached and acting as if Griffin were some sort of leper, like he
was poisonous or something—*contagious*. You have no right
to behave like that. It's a total violation of everything we've
ever done, of the way we've lived our lives."

"Is that so?"

"Yes, that's so. We have an agreement. We have rules.
We're supposed to be there for each other, and if that means
we have to sacrifice something, then we have to sacrifice it.
You can't get all pissy about something like this and deny me
my time with Griffin. You can't be a factor in our relationship, playing the aggrieved third party in some sort of sick
love triangle. It's *okay* for you to feel something when Griffin
and I are having sex—to enjoy the feelings he gives our body.
It doesn't mean you have the same sort of emotional bond
with Griffin that I have, but the physical aspects of it are undeniable. It doesn't make you gay, and it doesn't mean you're
cheating on Faith, but it does mean you are *there* when I'm
making love to Griffin, just like I'm there when you're making love to Faith. I'm not sure we'll ever be able to explain

that distinction to Faith, but at the very least it's important that *you* understand it."

I can tell when Porter doesn't agree with me, when he rejects outright something I have said. He tenses up. He huffs out a breath as if my words were toxic smoke he inadvertently inhaled. This time he didn't. He didn't acknowledge what I said, but neither did he deny it. He was *contemplating* it (a verb I rarely associate with my brother). I think the fact that he had been "caught" having sex with Griffin—regardless of how innocent or unavoidable his participation had been—had made him realize two things: how inextricably linked he and I were, and how unfair it was for Faith to judge an act of love between Griffin and me. He felt unfairly judged, and so maybe, just maybe, he could see how unfair it was to judge *me*. We didn't talk about it, and I had a feeling that if we had, he might have denied it. But for the first time in a long time, I felt as if Porter actually had some insight into what it was like to be me.

Life in the aftermath of Faith's intrusion into my bedroom became increasingly unpleasant. She rarely spoke to me directly, and she appeared to be withdrawing from Porter as well. She and the twins spent a good deal of time with her family in south Georgia over the course of the next couple of weeks. But while her protracted absences concerned Porter, I saw them as a good sign, an indication she was not prepared to make a snap judgment, that she was being more deliberate, less precipitous, than she had been when dealing with my relationship with Chase. Perhaps she had learned something from the havoc she had wrought then: that simply getting her way was no guarantee she would ultimately live happily ever after. And so while all of us were eager for some resolution, neither Porter nor I was willing to force the issue, fearing if we did so, an ultimatum would be forthcoming.

Chapter 30

One of the silliest and most insensitive questions I have ever been asked is, "Wouldn't you rather have been born with only one head?" The easy answer is, "Well, of course." But I'm not going to fall into that trap. I didn't have that choice, and there's no point in speculating about something I can't change. It's cruel to ask me to do so. Would you ask a black man if he would have preferred to have been born white? Would you ask a woman if she would have preferred to have been born a man? Doesn't the very nature of the question imply they are somehow inferior, that they should *want* to be different? Isn't that the epitome of arrogance?

The fact is, I can't even begin to comprehend what my life might be like if I were not joined to Porter. As much of a pain in the ass as he can be, I can't imagine life without him after all these years of being with him every waking moment, of falling asleep to the sound of his breathing, of catching his colds, of feeling his fevers.

People have always told stories to explain things they didn't understand. Thunder. The changing of the seasons. Death. The metaphor most often used to describe conjoined twins is that we are somehow imprisoned by our condition, joined in a way that is necessarily limiting. When Daisy and Violet Hilton starred in a semi-autobiographical film in 1951, it was titled *Chained for Life*. For me, another movie seems as relevant: *The Defiant Ones*, starring Tony Curtis and Sidney Poitier as two chain-gang convicts who are shackled to each other. They manage to escape, are pursued, and ultimately are captured because Sidney Poitier won't leave an injured Tony Curtis behind, even though the chains that originally bound them have been broken.

The reasoning behind chain gangs, I suppose, is that if you want to control someone, if you want to keep him down, you join him to someone else. It's more than a matter of being physically attached to another person and the natural ungainliness that results: the difficulty running, climbing a wall or a fence, finding a hiding place large enough to accommodate both escapees. It also involves psychological differences, conflicting ideas about where to go, which direction might provide the best escape route, when to rest, when to start up again. The people who organized chain gangs probably gave a great deal of thought to the inherent disadvantages of shackling two men together. They wouldn't assign men to pairs randomly. No, they would identify and capitalize on every conceivable physical and psychological difference. They'd shackle an older convict to a younger one to slow him down, chain a healthy young buck to a con with chronic emphysema, a racist redneck to a black man. They'd join a man with relatives in the north to one whose family lived in the south, so they'd be unable to agree on which direction to head in the event of an escape.

On the other hand, you could look at it as something of an advantage, with each convict providing something the other one didn't have. The smart one could help the idiot. The strong one, faced with a weak partner who slowed him down, might be able to pick him up and carry him. He wouldn't be able to move as quickly as if he were alone, but he'd be able to go faster than if he dragged the poor sucker behind him, and ultimately both would escape.

Most of these films about convicts on the run are actually buddy movies in which the two guys eventually compromise, begin to understand each other, learn to work together, and finally triumph. If Porter and I were ever to star in a remake of *The Defiant Ones*, I'm not sure how it would be cast. In a way, it would make sense for me to portray the Sidney Poitier character, the black man, the outcast. However, it seems just as logical for me to take the Tony Curtis role, the escapee who, because he's been shot, is too weak to climb aboard the freight train that could carry both men to freedom. Ultimately, it's probably impossible to know who has carried whom most often. Porter's popularity in high school made my life more tolerable; my intelligence and discipline helped him earn his college degree. His musical ability and my facility with language combined to give us a successful musical career by which we can earn our keep and maintain our independence. But one thing is clear: both Faith and Griffin have the potential to be spoilers, to upset the delicately balanced life Porter and I have created for our mutual benefit.

Fortunately, we had committed to a three-week West Coast concert tour in support of the new CD, which got us out of the house and away from both of them. Neither Porter nor I would have to have contact with the other's partner, and we'd have plenty of time alone to discuss the situation. When we got to San Francisco, I couriered Chase two tickets for our show at the Great American Music Hall. I wasn't certain he'd show up—or even whether it would be a good thing if he did.

"You really want to see him, don't you?" Porter said as we did our pre-show sound check.

"I thought I'd give it a shot," I said.

"You still love him, don't you?"

"Yeah, I guess I do. He really was my first true love, I suppose, the way Christi Oakes was for you. Of course, at this point I wouldn't leave Griffin for Chase—even if that *were* a possibility, which it isn't—but I do miss the hell out of him. I suppose he resents me for not taking more of a stand against Faith, for not being able to convince her to accept our relationship. But I did what I could and what I thought was best for everyone involved, even if it ultimately hurt him. It was pretty much a no-win situation all around, and I suppose no one was really to blame, at least not to the exclusion of any-one else. I'd just feel better if I knew he understood that. And it might help him deal with things, maybe even reconcile with Faith."

To my great surprise, Chase showed up at the concert and met us backstage after the show. He brought a friend with him—later introduced to us as Brad—a cute if somewhat spindly guy whose style suggested an amalgam of geek and punk I presumed was probably typical of the Internet types Chase found himself among in San Francisco. I didn't know if he was Chase's boyfriend, or really if he was even gay. He seemed . . . not androgynous, but perhaps almost asexual.

The four of us went out for a late dinner, and the presence of Brad—and the ambiguity of his relationship with Chase—initially prevented the conversation from taking too emo-tional a turn, which I suppose was a good thing, if somewhat nerve-racking. There were no apologies but no recrimina-tions either, nothing but polite small talk about the music in-dustry and the dot-com boom. Finally, over dessert, Chase asked about the twins—Porter was more than happy to bring out a wallet full of photos—but he remained determined not to even mention Faith's name.

"So, are you seeing anybody now?" Chase asked as Porter refolded the accordion of baby pictures into his wallet. I ap-parently hesitated long enough to confirm Chase's suspi-cions.

"I take it that would be a yes," he said.

"It would." I blushed and told him about Griffin.

"It's okay, Owen. I'm cool with that," he said. "But what does *she* think of it? She *does* know about him, doesn't she?"

"Yes," I said. "She knows all about him."

"I'll say she does," Porter said.

"What does that mean?" Chase asked.

I told him what had happened on that Sunday several

weeks ago, and he started grinning and shaking his head. Then he put his arm around Brad, as if to finally reveal the nature of their relationship.

"And her head didn't explode when she saw that? Or start spinning around like in *The Exorcist*?"

"Close," Porter said.

"Not even close," I said. "At least not at first."

I explained Faith's restrained if somewhat passive-aggressive response to Griffin and how the issue remained somewhat unresolved.

"Good luck with that," Chase said. "I'm not sure you're going to be able to win this one, either, Owen. It's not that Faith is a hateful person—she's really not. But I just don't think she's really ready to embrace the gay lifestyle yet. It's just too much for her. You know, not everybody was on board with Greta marrying Dooley, either. Oh, nobody said anything. Nobody within the family. We were far too 'enlightened' for that. But I think some of my uncles were none too happy about it, and Mom and Dad lost a couple of good friends over it. But the gay thing is different, even more difficult. And you've got to admit, your particular situation does make things more complicated. It would put a strain on anyone's generosity of spirit."

"So you've forgiven her for . . . for *us*?" I asked.

"Not quite. She's made a couple of overtures to me through Greta. On the QT—you know, very discreet. Greta still doesn't know my story, unless Faith has told her, which I doubt. I haven't responded, and I don't know when I will, though I'm sure it will happen eventually. My advice to you would be to play it cool for as long as possible and see what happens. I know she loves Porter, and now with the babies and all, she's not going to want to tear the family apart. But it's not going to be easy for her to accept this Griffin guy, or God forbid whoever it is you sleep with if this one doesn't work out."

Although Chase appeared to hold out some hope for

eventual reconciliation with Faith, it still seemed unlikely to me that she was going to embrace my relationship with Griffin anytime soon. But I knew if I capitulated, threw in the towel and dumped him, I'd never get another chance. I'd spend the rest of my life sublimating my homosexuality, maybe ordering some rent-boy takeout from time to time in distant cities when Porter and I were on tour. It was not the way I wanted to live.

When we said good night after dinner, Chase gave me a peck on the cheek and said, "Good luck."

Later that night, in bed, I told Porter what was on my mind.

"I'm not going to leave him," I said. "Griffin."

"I didn't figure you would. Not after what happened with Chase."

"You know what that means, don't you?"

"Yeah. It means there's a good chance Faith is going to leave me."

"I hope we can convince her to stay," I said. "But you've had your shot, Porter. Two, really. With Christi and then with Faith. I was there for you both times. I did what I could to make things work with Christi, and I gave up Chase to save your marriage. All that did was make a lot of people unhappy, and I'm not going to make that mistake again. You said yourself at the time that you'd never ask me for another thing as long as we lived. It's time for Faith to make some concessions. If she really loves you, she'll find a way to stay with you, even if some form of denial is the best she can do. If she decides she can't do even that much, then it's her responsibility, not mine, and she'll have to face the consequences. But you and I can't live our lives in a way that completely denies me the chance for happiness."

For a while, Porter didn't say anything. His silence lasted so long, I thought he was stonewalling me, perhaps thinking if he kept his mouth shut, I'd relent. But I wasn't about to concede. And then he did something we hadn't done in years—not since his relationship with Christi Oakes had ended when we were freshmen in college—something we used to do when we were kids, alone in our bed late at night, kept awake by some fear, real or imagined, about what awaited us the next day. Without a word, he lifted his foot slightly, crossed it over my ankle, and interlocked his big toe with mine.

FIRST PERSON PLURAL

Andrew W.M. Beierle

ABOUT THIS GUIDE

The suggested questions are included to enhance your group's reading of Andrew W.M. Beierle's *First Person Plural*.

Discussion Questions

1. The title of this book is *First Person Plural*, yet the story is told in the first person singular voice. Does this narrative belong entirely to Owen? Or is it also Porter's story? How reliable is Owen as a narrator?

2. How might this book have been different had it been told from Porter's point of view or if the author had alternated between Owen's voice and Porter's? Would the story have been more or less powerful? Why?

3. Does Owen seem unusually self-aware for a young man in his early-to-mid twenties? In what way has his awareness of self been shaped by his physical condition? How do congenital deformities or serious childhood illnesses change the way young people view their lives, themselves, and their futures? Do they mature more rapidly? Are they more or less well-adjusted than young people who do not face such difficulties?

4. Is Owen an optimist or a pessimist? Or would you call him more of a realist? Discuss specific things he says or does that support your choice.

5. Why do you think Owen often refers to other pairs of famous conjoined twins, including Chang and Eng Bunker and Daisy and Violet Hilton? What has he learned from the lives they lived and the difficulties they faced? Do you think he considers them role models? Why is Porter not interested in learning more about them?

6. Have you seen or heard of the 1932 film *Freaks* by Tod Browning? How has society's attitude toward disabili-

ties and deformities changed since that movie was made? What happened to the once-common freak shows and circus side shows? How have advances in medical technology and diagnosis affected the number of babies who are born deformed—and their prospects for "normalization" after birth? Are people with deformities or handicaps entitled to minority status in the same way racial and ethnic minorities are? Or are they too diverse a group?

7. Do you consider Owen and Porter one person or two? They were born at the same time and will certainly eventually die within minutes or hours of each other, so they might be said to have just one "life" between them. But at the same time, they have two minds, two spirits, and, as Owen points out, "two very different hearts." What constitutes "a person" or "a life"?

8. At the end of Chapter 3, what does Owen mean when he says, "Sometimes an oddity can provide us with insight into ourselves and our condition—the human condition—in ways something normal cannot. The unexpected illuminates the ordinary." How might so-called "normal" people benefit from understanding Owen's differences or his life experiences? Can you think of other works of fiction in which the main character is significantly different from the rest of the world? (Recommended reading: *Geek Love* by Katherine Dunn; *The Giant's House* by Elizabeth McCracken; and *Mrs. Caliban* by Rachel Ingalls.)

9. What is it about identical twins that is so fascinating? Do non-identical twins, triplets, or other multiple-birth siblings have the same mystique? Why or why not? What insights about twins did you gain while reading *First Person Plural*?

10. Although Owen and Porter could never have been separated successfully, advances in medical technology have made the separation of certain types of conjoined twins more common. Do you believe that conjoined twins should be separated at all costs? Even if it risks the life of one or both twins? Most medical professionals agree that separation surgery should take place as early as possible, generally in infancy, before the affected twins have the ability to understand their situation and give informed consent. Ethically, would it be preferable to wait until the twins reached the age of reason, even if it might complicate the separation process?

11. When conjoined twin Violet Hilton applied for a license to marry Maurice Lambert in 1934, she was turned down in New York, New Jersey, and nineteen other states. Although Faith and Porter ultimately are allowed to marry, they initially encounter some resistance at the marriage license office. Can you think of minority groups who previously were forbidden to marry but now are allowed to do so? When and why were those laws changed? Are there individuals or groups who are still prevented access to the rights and obligations bestowed by the marriage process? Why?

12. Was it morally or ethically wrong for Owen and Porter not to tell Faith that Owen was gay until after she had married Porter? Did she have a right to know? Or should it have been of no concern to her, since she was not marrying Owen? How might things have turned out differently if they had told her sooner?

13. Why does Owen's mother react so strongly when he comes to her? Did the intensity of her response surprise you, considering the difficulties she has faced and the accommodations she has made since the birth of Owen

and Porter? In what way was her husband's response different from hers? Why do you think he reacted the way he did?

14. Near the end of the novel, Owen says it is probably impossible to say who had contributed more to the success of the relationship he has with Porter—or who has sacrificed more. Do you agree with that assessment? Why?

15. How likely is it that Porter's marriage to Faith will last? What about Owen's relationship with Griffin? Which couple faces the greatest obstacles?